John Sandford is the pseudonym of Pulitzer-prize winning journalist John Camp. He is the author of thirteen PREY novels and three KIDD novels. He lives in Minnesota.

ALSO BY JOHN SANDFORD

Chosen Prey

Naked Prey

The Fool's Run

The Empress File

The Devil's Code

Published by Simon and Schuster UK

MORTAL PREY

JOHN SANDFORD

LONDON • SYDNEY • NEW YORK • TOKYO • SINGAPORE • TORONTO

First published in Great Britain by Simon & Schuster UK Ltd, 2002
This edition published by Pocket Books, 2003
An imprint of Simon & Schuster UK Ltd
A Viacom Company

1 3 5 7 9 10 8 6 4 2

Simon & Schuster UK Ltd
Africa House
64–78 Kingsway
London WC2B 6AH

www.simonsays.co.uk

Simon & Schuster Australia
Sydney

A CIP catalogue record for this book
is available from the British Library

ISBN 0–7434–1556–6

Typeset by M Rules
Printed and bound in Great Britain by
Cox & Wyman Ltd, Reading, Berks

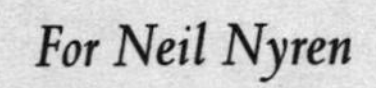

For Neil Nyren

1

THE THOUGHT POPPED INTO HER HEAD AS SHE LAY IN the soft-washed yellowed sheets in the hospital bed. The thought popped in between the gas pains and muscle spasms, through the pungent odor of alcohol swabs, and if she'd read the thought in a book, she might have smiled at it.

She wasn't smiling at anything now.

She stared past the IV drip bag at the whitewashed plaster ceiling and tried not to groan when the pains came, knowing that they would end; tried not to look at the hard-eyed Mexicano at the end of the bed, his hand never far from the pistol that lay under the newspaper on the arm of his chair. Tried not to think about Paulo.

Tried not to think about anything, but sometimes the thoughts popped up: tall, wiry Paulo in his ruffled tuxedo shirt, his jacket on the chair, a glass of red wine in one hand, his other hand, balled in a fist, on his hip, looking at himself in the full-length mirror on the back of his bedroom door, pretending to be a matador. Paulo with the children's book *Father Christmas,* sitting naked at her kitchen table with a glass of milk and a milk mustache, delighted by the grumpy Santa Claus. Paulo asleep next to her, his face pale and trusting in the day's first light, the soft light that came in over the gulf just before sunrise.

But the thought that might have made her smile, if it was in a book, was:

Just like the fuckin' Godfather.

LIKE THIS: AN Italian restaurant called Gino's, with the full Italian-cliché stage setting—sienna orange walls, bottles of Chianti with straw wrappers, red-and-white checked tablecloths, baskets of hot crusty bread as soon as you sat down, the room smelling of sugar and wheat, olives and peppers, and black oily coffee. A few rickety tables outside faced the Plaza de Arboles and the fifties tourist-coordinated stucco church across the way, San Fernando de Something-or-Other. The church belfry contained a loudspeaker that played a full, slow bell version of the Singing Nun's "Dominique," more or less at noon, depending on whose turn it was to drop the needle on the aging vinyl bell-record.

Paulo took her to lunch almost every day, picking her up at the hotel where she worked as a bookkeeper. They'd eat Mexican one day, California or French the next, Italian twice a week. He picked her up about noon, so on most days she could hear, near or far, the recorded bells of San Fernando's.

Gino's was the favored spot. Despite the clichéd Italian stage-setting, there was an actual Gino cooking at Gino's, and the food was terrific. Paulo would pick her up in a black BMW 740iL, his business car, with his smooth-faced business driver. They'd hook up with friends, eat a long Caribbean lunch and laugh and argue and talk politics and cars and boats and sex, and at two o'clock or so, they'd all head back to work.

A pattern: not predictable to the minute, but predictable enough.

ISRAEL COEN SAT up in the choir loft at the back of the church with his rifle, a scoped Remington Model 700 in .30-06. He'd sighted it in along a dirt track west of town, zeroed at exactly sixty yards, the distance he'd be shooting across the Plaza de Arboles. There was no problem making the shot. If all you wanted was that Izzy Coen make a sixty-yard shot with a scoped Remington 700, you could specify which shirt button you wanted the slug to punch through.

Not that everything was perfect. The moron who'd bought the gun apparently thought that bigger was better, so Izzy would be shooting at sixty yards through an eight-power scope, and about all he could see *was* a shirt button. He would have preferred no magnification at all, or an adjustable two- to six-power scope, to give him a little room around the crosshairs. But he didn't have that, and would have to make do.

The problem with the scope was exacerbated by the humidity in the loft. Not only was the temperature somewhere in the 120s, he thought, but the humidity must have been 95 percent. He'd sweated through his shirt at his armpits and across his chest, and the sweat beaded on his cheeks and forehead and arms. When he put the rifle to his cheek, the scope fogged over in a matter of seconds. He had a bottle of springwater with him, and that helped keep his body cool enough to function, but there was nothing he could do about the fogging eyepiece. The shot would have to be a quick one.

No matter. He'd scouted the play for three days, he knew what the conditions would be, and he was ready, up high with a rifle, yellow vinyl kitchen gloves protecting against the inadvertent fingerprint, the jeans and thin long-sleeved shirt meant to guard against DNA traces. Izzy was good.

He'd been in the loft for an hour and ten minutes when he saw the 740iL ease around the corner. He had two identical Motorola walkie-talkies sitting next to his feet. Izzy believed in redundancy. He picked up the first walkie-talkie, pushed the transmit button, and asked, "Hear me?"

"Yes."

"Come now."

"One minute."

TEN OF THEM had been sitting in the back of Gino's, the talk running down, a friend leaving and then another, with his new girlfriend, who'd been brought around for approval. Then Paulo looked at his watch and said to Rinker, "We better get back."

"Just a minute," she said. "Turn this way." She turned his chin in her hand, dipped a napkin into a glass of water, and used the wet cloth to wipe a nearly invisible smear of red sauce from his lower lip.

"I was saving that for later," he protested.

"I couldn't send you back that way," she said. "Your mother would kill me."

"My mother," he said, rolling his black eyes.

THEY WALKED OUT of the Italian restaurant—*Just like the fuckin'* Godfather—and the black BMW stopped beyond the balustrade that separated the restaurant's patio from the Plaza. They walked past an American who sat at a circular table in his Hawaiian shirt and wide-brimmed flat hat, peering into a guidebook—all the details as clear and sharp three days later, in the hospital, as the moment when it happened—and the driver started to get out and Paulo called, "I got it, I got it," and Rinker reached for the door handle, but Paulo beat her to it, stepping in front of her in that last little quarter-second of life. . . .

The shot sounded like a firecracker, but the driver knew it wasn't. The driver was in his pocket as Rinker, suddenly feeling ill—not in pain, yet, but just ill, and for some inexplicable reason, falling—went to the ground, Paulo on top of her. She didn't understand, even as a roaring, ripping sound enveloped her, and she rolled and Paulo looked down at her, but his eyes were already out of control and he opened his mouth and his blood gushed onto her face and into her mouth. She began screaming as the roaring sound resumed.

She rolled and pushed Paulo down on the cobbles and turned his head to keep him from drowning in his own blood, and began screaming at the driver, "Paulo, Paulo, Paulo . . ."

The driver looked at her, everything slow-moving. She saw the boxy black-steel weapon in his hand, a gun like she hadn't seen before. She saw his mouth open as he shouted something, then he looked back over the car and then back down at Paulo. Then he was standing over them, and he lifted Paulo and put him on the backseat, and lifted her, and put her in the passenger seat, and in seconds they were flying across the Plaza, the hospital three minutes away, no more.

She looked over the seat, into Paulo's open eyes; but Paulo wasn't there anymore.

Paulo had gone. She could taste his blood in her mouth, crusting around her teeth, but Paulo had left the building.

IZZY COHEN SAID, "Goddamnit," and he wasn't sure it'd gone right. The scope had blocked too much and he ran the bolt and lifted the rifle for a second shot, the bodies right there, and he saw the driver doing something, and then as Izzy lifted the rifle, the driver opened up and the front of the church powdered around him and Izzy thought, *Jeez . . .*

An Uzi, he thought, or a gun just like it. Izzy rolled away from the window as the glass blew inward, picked up the two walkie-talkies, and scrambled to the far corner of the loft and the steel spiral stair, the bullets flying around him like bees. He dove down the stair and punched through the back door, where a yellow Volkswagen Beetle was waiting with its engine running. Izzy threw the gun in the back, climbed in, and slammed the door. The driver accelerated away from the church's back door and shouted, "What was that? What was that gun?"

"Fuck if I know," Izzy said. He was pulling off the latex gloves, shaking glass out of his hair. Blood on his hand—he dabbed at his cheek: just a nick. "A fuckin' Uzi, maybe."

"Uzi? What is this Uzi?"

"Israeli gun, it's a machine gun . . ."

"I know what IS a fuckin' Uzi," the driver shouted. "*WHY* is this fuckin' Uzi? Why is this?"

"I don't know," Izzy said. "Just get us back to the plane and maybe we can find out."

THE AIRSTRIP WAS a one-lane dirt path cut out of a piece of scraggly jungle twenty kilometers west of the city. On the way, the driver got on his cell phone and made a call, shouting in Spanish over the pounding of the Volkswagen.

"Find out anything?" Izzy asked when he rang off.

"I call now, maybe find out something later," the driver said. He was a little man who wore a plain pink short-sleeved dress shirt with khaki slacks and brown sandals. His English was usually excellent, but deteriorated under stress.

A couple of kilometers east of the airstrip, they stopped and the driver led the way through a copse of trees to a water-filled hole in the ground. Izzy wiped the Remington and threw it in the hole and tossed the box of shells in after it. "Hope it doesn't dry up," he said, looking at the ripples on the black water.

The driver shook his head. "There's no bottom," he said. "The hole goes all the way to hell." The phone rang on the way back to the car and the driver answered it, spoke for a minute, and then clicked off with a nervous sideways glance at Izzy.

"What?"

"Two dead," the driver said. "One bullet?"

"One shot," Izzy said with satisfaction. "What was that machine gun?"

The driver shrugged. "Bodyguard, maybe. Nobody knows."

THE AIRSTRIP TERMINAL was a tin-roofed, concrete block building, surrounded by ragged palmettos, with an incongruous rooster-shaped weather vane perched on top. What might have been a more professional windsock hung limply from a pole beside the building, except that the windsock was shaped like a six-foot-long orange trout, and carried the legend "West Yellowstone, Montana." A Honda generator chugged away in a locked steel box behind the building, putting out the thin stink of burnt gasoline. Finger-sized lizards climbed over walls, poles, and tree trunks, searching for bugs, of which there were many. Everything about the place looked as tired as the windsock. Even the trees. Even the lizards.

From the trip in, Izzy knew the generator ran an ancient air conditioner and an even older dusty-red Coca-Cola cooler inside the building, where the owner sat with a stack of *Playboy* magazines, a radio, and a can of Raid for the biting flies.

"I'll call again," the driver said. "You check on the plane."

When Izzy had gone inside, the driver, now sweating as heavily as the American, dug a revolver out from under the front seat of the Volkswagen, swung the cylinder out and checked it, closed the cylinder, and put the gun under his belt at the small of his back.

Izzy and the driver had known each other for a few years, and there existed the possibility that the driver's name was on a list somewhere; that somebody knew who was driving Israel Coen around Cancún. But the driver doubted it. Nobody would want to know the details of a thing like this, and Izzy wouldn't want anyone to know.

Only two people had seen the driver's face and Izzy's in the same place: Izzy himself, and the airport manager.

The driver walked into the airport building and pulled the door shut. The building had four windows, and they all looked the same way, out at the strip. And it was cool inside. Izzy was talking to the airport manager, who sat with a Coca-Cola at a metal desk, directly in front of the air conditioner.

"Is he coming?" the driver asked.

"He's twenty minutes out," Izzy said, and the airport manager nodded.

The driver yawned. He had twenty minutes. Not much time. "Nice trip," he said to Izzy. He tipped his head at the door, as though he wanted to speak privately. "Hope your business went well."

"Let me get my bag," Izzy said. He stepped toward the door, and the driver pulled it open with his left hand and held it. Izzy stepped out, the driver right behind him, his right hand swinging up with the revolver. When it was an inch behind Izzy's head, he pulled the trigger and Izzy's face exploded in blood and he went down. The driver looked at the body for a moment, not quite believing what he'd done, then stepped back inside. The airport manager was half out of his chair, body cocked, and the driver shook his head at him.

"Too bad," he said, with real regret.

"We've known each other for a long time," the airport manager said.

"I'm sorry."

"Why is . . . Let me say a prayer."

"No time," the driver said. "Today we killed Raul Mejia's baby boy."

He shot the airport manager in the heart, and again in the head to make sure. Back outside, he shot Izzy twice more, the shots sounding distant in his own ears, as if they'd come from over a hill. He dragged the body inside the airport building and dumped it beside the airport manager's. He took Izzy's wallet and all of his cash, a gold ring with a big red stone and the inscription "University of Connecticut, 1986," and every scrap of paper he could find on him. He also found the padlock for the door on the manager's desk, and the key to the generator box in the manager's pocket. He went outside, padlocked the door behind himself, killed the generator. There was a black patch of bloody dirt where Izzy's head had landed. He scuffed more dirt over it, got back in his Volkswagen, and pulled away.

Raul Mejia's baby boy.

The driver would have said a prayer for himself, if he could have remembered any.

RINKER DIDN'T KNOW the names of the players. When she woke up, she was in the hospital's critical care unit, three empty beds with monitoring equipment, and her own bed. Anthony and Dominic, Paulo's brothers, were sitting at the foot of the bed. She couldn't quite make out their faces until Anthony stood up and stepped close. Her mouth was as dry as a saltine cracker: "Paulo?"

Anthony shook his head. Rinker turned her face away, opened her mouth to cry, but nothing came out. Tears began running down her face, and Anthony took her hand.

"He was . . . he was dead when they got here. . . . We, uh, you have been in surgery. We need to know, did you see the man who shot you?"

Rinker wagged her head weakly. "I didn't see anything. I just fell down, I didn't know I was shot. Paulo fell on top of me, I tried to turn his head, he was bleeding . . ."

More tears, and Dominic was turning his straw hat in his hands, pulling the brim through his fingers in a circular motion, like a man measuring yards of cloth.

"We are trying to find out who did this—the police are helping," Anthony said. "We, uh . . . You will be all right. The bullet went through Paulo and fell apart, and the core went into you, in your stomach. They operated for two hours, and you will be all right."

She nodded, but her hand twitched toward her stomach.

"I think I'm, I might have been, I think . . . ," she began, looking at Anthony and then Dominic, who had stepped up beside his brother.

Dominic now shook his head. "You have lost the baby."

"Oh, God."

Dominic reached out and touched her covered leg. He was tough as a ball bearing, but he had tears rolling down his cheeks. He said, "We'll find them. This won't pass."

She turned her head away and drifted. When she came back, they'd gone.

SHE WAS IN the hospital for a week: missed Paulo's funeral, slept through a visit by Paulo's father. On the fourth day, they had her up and walking, but they wouldn't let her go until she had produced a solid bowel movement. After that painful experience, she was wheeled out to one of the family's black BMWs and was driven to the Mejia family compound in Mérida. Paulo's father, rolling his own wheelchair though the dark, tiled hallways, met her with an arm around her shoulder and a kiss on the cheek.

"Do you know what happened?" she asked.

He shook his head. "No. I don't understand it yet. We've been asking everywhere, but there is no word of anything. Some people who might, in theory, have reason to be angry with us from years ago have let it be known that they were not involved, and have offered to help find those who were."

"You can believe them?" she asked.

"Perhaps. We continue to look. . . . There was a strange circumstance the day Paulo was killed." He hesitated, as if puzzling over it, then continued. "Two men were killed at an airstrip not far from here. Shot to death. One was the airstrip manager and the other was an American. There was no indication that they were involved with Paulo's assassination. With that strip, there is always the question of unauthorized landings"—he meant drug smuggling—"but still, it is a strange coincidence. The American was identified through fingerprints. He was not involved in trade, in"—he made a figure eight in the air with his fingers, meaning *drugs*—"but he served time in prison and was believed connected to American organized crime, to the Mafia. A minor person, he was not important. We are asking more questions of our police, and our police are talking with the Americans. We will find out more, sooner or later."

"When you find them," Rinker said through her teeth, her cold eyes only inches from the old man's, "when you find them, kill them."

His eyes held hers for a moment, doing an assessment of the woman he knew as Cassie McLain. They didn't know each other well, but the old man knew that Paulo's involvement with her was more than casual; knew she'd been pregnant with one of his own grandchildren, this tidy blond American with the perfect Spanish. After the moment, he nodded. "Something will be done," he said.

"This dead American at the airstrip," she said, at the end of the audience. "Do you even know where he was from?"

"That we know," he said. He closed his eyes for a minute, parsing the information in his head. He smelled lightly of garlic, and had fuzzy ears, like a gentle Yoda. There was a legend that in his early years he'd had an informer hung upside down by his ankles, and had then lit a fire under his head. According to the legend, the informer stopped screaming only when his skull exploded. Now Mejia opened his eyes and said, "He lived in a town in Missouri, called Normandy Lake. A woman who lived there told the Missouri police that he'd gone to Cancún on vacation. She said she would come for the body, but she didn't come. When the police went back to the house, she had gone. She'd packed all her personal belongings and had gone away."

"That's crazy," Rinker said, shaking her head. But her brain was moving now, cutting through the glue that had held her since the shooting, and she was touched by a cool tongue of fear. After a moment, she said, "I don't want to go home. I'm a little frightened. If it would be all right, I would like to go to the ranch until I can walk. Then I think I will go back to the States."

"You are welcome to stay as long as you wish," the old man said. He smiled at her. "You may stay forever, if you wish. The friend of my baby."

She smiled back. "Thank you, Papa, but Cancún . . ." She made the same figure eight in the air as he had. "Cancún is Paulo. I think it would be better to go away when I am well."

One of the old man's bodyguards wheeled her back out to the BMW, and as the car pulled away, she looked at the driver's shoulders and the back of his head and realized that she now knew more about what happened at Gino's than the old man did.

SHE KNEW THAT the bullet had been aimed not at Paulo, but at her.

If the old man found out that his baby boy had been killed because of Rinker, and that Rinker had never told them of the danger—she hadn't expected it, hadn't believed it could happen—then maybe the old man's anger would be directed at her.

She shivered at the thought, but not too much, because Rinker was as cold as the old man. Instead of worrying, she began planning. She couldn't do anything until she got her strength back, which might take some time. She'd benefited from the report put out by the Mejia family and the Mexican police that she'd been killed along with Paulo—at the time, they'd done it simply to protect her from a possible cleanup attempt if it turned out that she'd seen the shooter.

The story would serve her well enough. The St. Louis goombahs didn't have anything going in Mexico, as far as she knew, and the only information they would have gotten would have come from the newspapers.

On the other hand, with the old man pushing his drug-world contacts, sooner or later the truth would come out. By that time, she had to have made her move.

Before she talked to the old man, she hadn't had anything to do; now she'd be busy. As Cassie McLain, she'd retired, and was living on her investments. As Clara Rinker, she had to move money, retrieve documents, talk to old acquaintances across the border.

She had to be healthy to do it all.

RINKER SPENT A MONTH at the old man's ranch, living in a bedroom in the main house, with an armed watcher to follow her around. The middle brother, Dominic, visited every third day, arriving at noon as regular as clockwork, to bring her up to date on the family's investigation.

All the time at the ranch, she waited for her image of Paulo to fade. It never did. To the very end of her stay, she could smell him, she could taste the salt on his skin, she still expected to see him standing in the kitchen, listening to *futbol* on a cheap radio, his white grin and black tousled hair and his weekend bottle of American-style Corona . . .

BY THE SECOND week on the ranch, bored but still weak, feeling more and more pressure to move while remaining determined not to move until she was solid, she began talking with her watcher. His name was Jaime, a short, hard man with a deeply burned face and brushy mustache. He was good-natured enough, and went everywhere with a pistol in his pocket and an M-16 in the back of his truck.

Rinker said, "Show me about the M-16."

After a little talk, and perfunctory protests by Jaime, he hauled two chairs out to a nearby gully, set up a target range, and showed her how to fire the M-16. She did well with the weapon and he became interested—he was a gunman, deeply involved with the tools of his profession—and brought out other guns. A scoped, bolt-action Weatherby sporting rifle, a pump .22, a lever-action treinta-treinta, and a shotgun.

They spent two or three hours a day shooting: stationary targets, bouncing tires, and, with the .22, they'd shoot at clay pigeons thrown straight away. The clays were almost impossible to hit—at the end, she might hit one or two out of ten, learning to time her shots to the top of the target's arc.

As they shot, Jaime talked about rifle bullets and loads, wind drift and heat mirages, uphill and downhill shooting, do-it-yourself accurizing. He liked working with her because she was serious about it, and attractive. An athlete, he thought, though she didn't really work at it, like some gym queens he knew in Cancún—trim, smart, and pretty in a blond gringo way.

And she knew about men. He might have put a hand on her, himself, if she hadn't been in mourning, and mourning for the son of Raul Mejia. He remained always the professional.

"There is no way that you can carry or keep a long gun for self-protection," he told her. "With a handgun, you have it always by your hand, like the name says. With a rifle, which is very good if you have it in your hand, well, it will be in the bedroom and you will be in the kitchen when they come for you. Or you will be sitting in the latrine with your pants around your ankles and a *Playboy* in your hands—maybe not you, but me, anyway—and the rifle will be leaning against a tree, and that's when they will come. So this gun"—he slapped the side of the M-16—"this gun is fine when you are shooting, but you must learn the handgun for self-protection."

She demurred. She wanted to learn the long guns, she said. Rifles and a shotgun. Not a double-barreled bird gun or anything cute, but a stubby, fat-barreled combat pump. She didn't want to learn how to shoot any fuckin' birds: give her a shotgun and a moving target five yards away . . .

He shook his head and smiled good-naturedly and showed her the long guns, two weeks of first-class tuition, but he kept coming back to the handgun. "Just try it," he'd say. "You are very natural with a gun. The best woman I have ever seen."

"Shooting's not exactly rocket science," she'd said, but the phrase didn't translate well into Spanish; didn't come off with the irony of the English.

IN HER SECOND two weeks on the ranch, she went a half-dozen times into town, to her apartment, and gathered what she needed in order to move. She also wiped the place: There'd be no fingerprints if anyone came looking for her. Then one Wednesday, after she'd been on the ranch for a month, Dominic came out and said, "We've got word about a man who some people say might have been the driver for the shooting. We don't know where he is, but we know where his family is, so we should be able to find him. Then we might learn something."

"When?" she asked.

"By the weekend, I hope," Dominic said. "We have to know where this came from, so we can get back to business. And for Paulo, of course."

THAT WAS ON a Wednesday. She was still not one hundred percent, but she was good enough to run. She'd handled everything she could by phone, she had documents she could get to, she'd moved the money that had to be moved. She would leave on Thursday afternoon.

She'd already worked it out: She had two doctor's appointments each week, on Monday and Thursday. The driver always waited in the lobby of the clinic. When she came out of the doctor's office, if she turned left instead of right, she would be at least momentarily free on the streets of Cancún, and not ten yards from a busy taxi stand.

She should have half an hour before the driver became curious. If she got even two minutes, she'd be gone. She'd done it before.

RINKER AND JAIME went for one last shooting session on Thursday morning, with the shotgun. Jaime had six solid-rubber, fourteen-inch trailer tires that he could haul around in a John Deere utility wagon. They went out to the gully and Jaime rolled the tires, one at a time, down the rocky slope. The tires ricocheted wildly off the rocks, while Rinker tried to anticipate them with the twelve-gauge pump. When she hit them, at ten yards, she'd knock them flat, but on a good day, she struggled to hit half of them with the first shot. She learned that a shotgun, even at close range, wasn't a sure thing.

When she'd emptied the shotgun, they'd pick up the tires and Rinker would drive them to the top of the slope and roll them down while Jaime shot at them. Taking turns. He did no better than she did, though they both pretended that he did. On this day, she made what she thought later was almost a mistake.

Jaime pulled the Beretta from his belt clip and said, "Just one time with the handgun, eh? Make me happy."

"Jaime . . ." With asperity.

"No, no, no . . ." He wagged his finger at her. "I insist. We have time before the doctor, and this you should learn."

"Jaime, goddamnit . . ."

He ignored her. A half-dozen empty Coke cans sat in the back of the John Deere, and he threw three of them down the gully. "You can do this. You will find it much harder than the rifle or the shotgun."

"Give me the gun, Jaime," she said, making the almost-mistake.

He stopped in midsentence, looked at her, and handed her the Beretta. She'd always liked that particular gun when she was shooting nines: It seemed to fit in her hand.

And she liked Jaime and might have wanted to impress him a bit, on this, her last afternoon. She flipped the safety and pulled down on one of the cans and shot it six times in three seconds before it managed to flip its now-raggedy ass behind a rock.

They stood in a hot, dusty, powder-smelling silence for several seconds, then Rinker slipped the safety on and passed the piece back to Jaime.

Jaime looked at the gun, then at her, and said after a while, "I see."

He didn't really. He'd probably find out soon enough.

That afternoon, she ran.

2

LUCAS DAVENPORT PARKED IN THE STREET.

A rusty Dumpster blocked his driveway, which had become a bog of black-and-tan mud anyway, so he parked in the street, climbed out of the Porsche, and looked up at the half-finished house. The place had been framed and closed, and the rock walls had been set, but raw plywood still showed through the second story and parts of the first, although most of it had been covered with a black weather-seal. The lawn between Lucas and the house was a wreck, the result of construction trucks maneuvering over it after an ill-timed summer rain.

Two men in coveralls were sitting on the peak of the roof, drinking what Lucas hoped was Perrier water out of green bottles, and eating a pizza out of a flat white box. Given that they were roofers, and that when they saw him they eased the bottles down behind their legs and out of sight, he suspected that the bottles did not contain water. One of them waved with his free hand and the other lifted a slice of pizza, and Lucas waved back and started across the rutted lawn toward the front porch.

He crossed the ruts and rain puddles gracefully enough. He was a large, athletic man in a dark blue suit and non-tasseled black loafers, with a white dress shirt open at the throat. His face and neck contrasted with the easy elegance of the Italian suit—old scars marked him as a trouble-seeker, one scar in particular slicing down across an eyebrow onto the tanned cheek below. He had kindly ice-blue eyes and dark hair, old French-Canadian genes hanging on for dear life in the American ethnic Mixmaster.

The house was his—or had been his, and would be again. Now it was a mess. An electrician stood on a stepladder on the new front porch working on overhead wiring. A couple of nail guns were banging away inside, sounding like cartoon spit balloons—*pitoo, pitoo*—and as he walked up to the porch, a table saw started whining. He could smell the sawdust, or imagined he could.

Listening to all the commotion, he thought, *All right.* Two guys on the roof, an electrician on the porch, at least two nail guns inside and a table saw. That was a minimum of six guys, and if there were six guys working on the house, then he wouldn't have to scream at the contractor. Seven or eight guys would have been better. Ten would have been perfect. But the house was only a week behind schedule now, so six was acceptable. Barely.

As he climbed the porch steps, he noticed that somebody had pinned a four-by-four beam in the open ceiling, down at the far end. It would, someday soon, support an oak swing big enough for two adults and a kid. The electrician saw him coming, ducked his head to look down at him from the ladder, and said, "Hey, Lucas."

"Jim. How's it going?"

The electrician was screwing canary-yellow splicing nuts onto pairs of bared wires that would feed the porch light. "Okay, I'm getting close. But somebody's got to put in that telephone and cable wiring or we're gonna get hung up on the inspection. The inspector's coming Tuesday, and if we have to reschedule, it could hold things up for a week and they won't be able to close the overheads."

"I'll talk to Jack about it," Lucas said. "He was supposed to get that guy from Epp's."

"I heard the guy fell off a stepladder and broke his foot—that's what I heard," the electrician said, pitching his voice down. "Don't tell Jack I mentioned it."

"I won't. I'll get somebody out here," Lucas said.

Goddamnit. Now he was back in yelling mode again. Much of the problem of building a new house was in the sequencing—sequencing the construction steps and all the required inspections in a smooth flow. One screwup, of even a minor thing like phone and cable-television wiring, which should take no more than a day, could stall progress for a week, and they didn't have a lot of time to spare.

Besides which, living in Weather Karkinnen's house was driving him crazy. He didn't have any of his *stuff*. Everything was in storage. Weather had even lost her TV remote, and never noticed because she watched TV only when presidents were assassinated. For the past two months, he'd had to get up and down every time he wanted to change channels, and he wanted to change channels about forty times a minute. He'd taken to crouching next to the TV to push the channel button. Weather said he was pathetic, and he believed her.

INSIDE THE SHELL of the new house, everything smelled of damp wood and sawdust—smelled pretty good, he thought. Building new houses could become addictive. Everybody was working on the second story, and he made a quick tour of the bottom floor—four new boxes were piled on the back porch; toilet stools—and then took the central stairs to the second floor. One nail-gun guy and the table saw guy were working in the master bedroom, fitting in the tongue-in-groove maple ceiling. The other nail gunner was working in the main bathroom, fitting frames for what would be the linen closet. They all glanced at him, and the guy on the saw said, "Morning," and went back to work.

"Jack around?"

The saw guy shook his head. "Naw. I been working. Harold's been kinda jackin' around, though."

"Rick . . ." No time for carpenter humor. "Is *Jack* around?"

"He was down the basement, last time I saw him."

Lucas did a quick tour of the top floor, stopped to look out a bedroom window at the Mississippi—he was actually high enough to see the water, far down in the steep valley on the other side of the road—and then headed back downstairs. His cell phone rang when he was halfway down, and he pulled it out and poked the power button: "Yeah?"

"Hey." Marcy Sherrill, a detective-sergeant who ran his office and a portion of his life. "That FBI guy, Mallard, is looking for you. He wants you to get back to him soon as you can."

"Did he say what he wanted?"

"No, but he said it was urgent. He wanted your cell phone number, but I told him you kept it turned off. He gave me a number to call back."

"Give it to me." He took a ballpoint out of his jacket pocket and scribbled the number in the palm of his hand as she read it to him.

"You at the house?" she asked.

"Yeah. They're about ready to put in the toilets. We got four of the big high-flow American Standard babies. White."

He could feel her falling asleep, but she said, "Getting close."

"Two months, they say. I dunno. I'll believe it when I see it."

"Call Mallard."

In the basement, Jack Vrbecek was peering up at the ceiling and making notes on a clipboard. "Hey, Lucas. Seven guys today."

"Yeah, that's good. That's good. Looks like things are moving. What're you doing?"

"Checking the schematics on the wiring. You're gonna want to know where every bit of it is, in case you need to get at it."

Lucas bent his head back to peer at the ceiling. "Maybe we ought to put in a Plexiglas ceiling, finish it off—but then we'd be able to see everything."

"Except that the workshop would sound like the inside of the brass-band factory every time you turned on a saw," Vrbecek said. "This will be fine. We'll get you a complete layout, and with the acoustic drop ceiling, your access will be okay and you'll be able to hear yourself think."

Lucas nodded. "Listen, we've got to get somebody to do the cable and telephone stuff, and I heard someplace today, down at City Hall, I think, that the guy from Epp's broke his foot. If we don't get that in, with the inspector coming Tuesday . . ."

"Yeah, yeah. We're moving on it." He made a note on his clipboard.

"And one of the guys up on the roof is drinking what might be Perrier water, but might not be, and if he falls off and breaks his neck, I'm not the one who gets sued."

"Goddamnit. They're supposed to be in a twelve-step program, and if that's a goddamn bottle of beer . . ." They started for the basement stairs. At any other time, Lucas might have felt guilty about ratting out the roofers. But this was the *house*.

TWO MONTHS EARLIER, Lucas had stood on the edge of a hole where his old house had once been, looking into it with a combination of fear and regret. Both he and Weather wanted to remain in the neighborhood, and they were old enough to know exactly what they wanted in a house, and to know they wouldn't get it by buying an older place. Building was the answer: taking down the old house, putting up the new.

Only when he looked into the hole did he realize how committed he'd become, after a long life of essential noncommitment. The old house was gone and Weather Karkinnen was, as she'd announced, With Child. They'd get married when they had time to work out the details, and they'd all live happily ever after in the Big New House.

As he'd stood on the edge of the hole, the low-spreading foundation junipers clutching at his ankles as though pleading for mercy—they'd get damn little, given the practicalities of building a new house—he'd expected to live with the regret for a long time.

He'd bought the place when he was relatively young, a detective sergeant with a reputation for busting cases. He was working all the time, roaming the city at night, building a web of contacts—and working until five in the morning writing role-playing games, hunched over a drawing board and an IBM Selectric.

A couple of the games hit, producing modest gushers of money. After wasting some of it on a retirement plan and throwing even more down the rathole of sober, long-term investments, he'd finally come to his senses and spent the remaining money on a Porsche and a lake cabin in the North Woods. The last few thousand made a nice down payment on the house.

Standing at the edge of the old basement, he'd thought he'd miss the old place.

So far, he hadn't.

THE HOLE HAD been enlarged, the new foundation had gone in, and in short order, the frame for the replacement house had gone up and been enclosed. He found the process fascinating. He'd enjoyed the design stage, working with the architect. Had enjoyed even more the construction process, the careful fitting-together of the plans, and the inevitable arguments about changes and materials. He even enjoyed the arguments. Sort of like writing a strategy game, he thought.

The old house, though comfortable, had problems. Even living in it alone, he'd felt cramped at times. And if he and Weather had kids, the kids would have been living on top of them, in the next bedroom down the hall. The Big New House would have a grand master bedroom suite with a Versailles-sized bathroom and a bathtub large enough for Lucas to float in—Weather, a small woman, should be able to swim laps. The kid—kids?—would be at the other end of the hall, with a bathroom of his own, and there'd be a library and workrooms for both himself and Weather and a nice family room and a spot for Weather's piano. The new house was a place he thought he could happily live and die in. Die when he was ninety-three, he hoped. And with any luck, it should be finished before the kid arrived. . . .

Right now, he didn't want to leave. Not even with the screaming up on the roof. He wanted to hang around and talk with the foreman and the other guys, but he knew he'd just be sucking up their time. He walked around the first floor once more, thinking about color schemes that would fit with the rock he'd picked for the fireplace. Twenty minutes after he arrived, he dragged himself back to the car.

AND REMEMBERED MALLARD. He took the cell phone out of his pocket and leaned against the Porsche and punched in the number written in the palm of his hand. An old lady went by on her bike, a wicker basket between the handlebars. She waved, and he waved back—a neighbor making her daily trip to the supermarket up the hill on Ford Parkway.

"Mallard."

"Is that pronounced like the duck?" Lucas asked.

An instant of silence, then Mallard figured it out. "Davenport. How far are you from the airport?"

"Ten minutes, but I ain't flying anywhere."

"Yeah, you are. You've got a Northwest flight out of there in, mmm, two hours and eight minutes for Houston and from there to Cancún, Mexico. Electronic tickets are already under your name. It's all cleared with your boss, and your federal tax dollars are picking up the tab. I'll meet you at IAH in about six hours, and you can buy some clothes there."

"Whoa, whoa. I hate flying."

"Sometimes a man's gotta do . . ."

"What's going on?"

"Six weeks ago, somebody shot and killed a Mexican guy outside a Cancún restaurant and wounded his girlfriend. The guy who got killed was the youngest son of a Mexican druglord, or a guy who's supposedly a druglord, or maybe an ex-druglord . . . something like that. So the Mexicans started sniffing around, and word leaks out to a DEA guy. The shooter wasn't aiming at the druglord's son. It was a mistake."

"That's really fascinating, Louis, but Cancún is outside the Minneapolis city limits."

"The shooter was going for the girl, see. She was wounded, and the cops put out the word that she was dead, until they could find out what was going on. So after she got out of the hospital, she went out to the druglord's ranch outside of Mérida—that's a city down there—for a month, recovering. Then she disappeared. Like a puff of smoke. Everybody was looking for her, and eventually we get this request from the Mexican National Police about these fingerprints they'd picked up at the ranch. We had one print that matched. Came off a bar of soap."

Lucas finally caught up. "It's her?"

"Clara Rinker," Mallard said.

"What do you want me to do?"

"Get your ass down to Houston, first thing. The DEA has hooked us up with the National Police, and we're gonna talk to some people who knew her down there. You got a better feel for her than anybody. I want you to hear it."

Lucas thought about it for a minute, looking up at the half-completed house. "I can do it for a couple of days," he said. "But I got stuff going on here, Louis—I mean, serious stuff. My fiancée is gonna be pissed. She's in the middle of planning the wedding, she really needs me right now, and I'm running off—"

"Just a couple of days," Mallard said. "I promise. Listen, I gotta go. I'm just coming up to National right now, and I gotta make some more calls before I get out of the car."

"Is Malone coming?"

"Yeah, she's coming, but you're engaged."

"I was just asking, Louis. You got something going with her?"

"No, I don't. But she does. Have something going. I gotta hang up. See you in Houston."

WEATHER WOULD BE UPSET, Lucas thought, looking back at the construction project. The house was only halfway done and needed constant supervision. The wedding planning was completely disorganized, and needed somebody to stay on top of it. Finally, there was a political pie-fight going on at City Hall, as a half-dozen candidates jockeyed for position in the Democratic primary for mayor. The political ramifications of the fight were severe—the chief was already dead meat, her job gone. Lucas, as a political deputy-chief, was on his way out with the chief. But with a little careful maneuvering, they might be able to leave the department in the hands of friends.

He could leave the politics, though—the chief was a lot better at it than he was. The real problem was Weather. Weather was a surgeon, a maxillofacial resident at Hennepin General. She and Lucas had circled each other for years, had had one wedding fall through. Lucas loved her dearly, but worried that the relationship might still be fragile. To leave her now, five months into the pregnancy . . .

Weather's secretary answered at Hennepin General. "Lucas? A patient just went in."

"Grab her, will you? I've got to talk to her right now," Lucas said. "It's pretty serious."

Weather came on a second later, showing a little stress. "Are you all right?"

"Yeah, I'm fine. Why?"

She was exasperated. "Lucas, when you call like this, and you say it's important, and you've got to talk to me right away, tell Carol, 'I'm not hurt, but it's important.' That'll keep me from an early coronary. Okay?"

Lucas sighed. "Yeah, sure."

"So what's going on?" she asked. She was looking at her watch, Lucas thought.

"Mallard called. . . ." He told her the story in thirty seconds, then listened to four seconds of dead silence, and opened his mouth to say, "Well?" or apologize, or something, but didn't quite get there.

"Thank God," she blurted. "You're driving me crazy. You're driving the entire construction company crazy. If you'll just get out of the country for a few days, I could finish the wedding plans and maybe the builders could get some work done."

"Hey . . ." He was offended, but she paid no attention. She said, "Go to Cancún. God bless you. Call me every night. Remember: Flying is the safest way to travel. Have a couple martinis. Or better yet, there's some Valium in my medicine cabinet. Take a couple of those."

"You're sure you don't—"

"I'm sure. Go."

"You're sure."

"Go. *Go.*"

3

THE TRIP TO HOUSTON WAS THE USUAL NIGHTMARE, with Lucas hunched in a business-class seat, ready to brace his feet against the forward bulkhead when the impact came. Not that bracing would save him. In his mind's eye, he could clearly see the razor-sharp aviation aluminum slicing through the cabin, dismembering everybody and everything in its path. Then the fire, trying to crawl, legs missing, toward the exit . . .

He'd talked to a shrink about it. The shrink, an ex–military guy, suggested three martinis or a couple of tranquilizers, or not flying. He added that Lucas had control issues, and when Lucas asked, "Control issues? You mean, like I don't wanna die in an airplane crash?" the shrink—who'd had three martinis himself—said, "I mean, you wanna tell people how to tie their shoes, because you know how to do it better, and that means you don't want somebody else to fly you in an airplane."

"Then how come I'm not scared of helicopters?"

The shrink shrugged. "Because you're nuts."

IN ANY CASE, the Valium hadn't helped. He'd just had time to drive to Weather's place, put some clothes and his shaving kit together, along with a small tube of drugs, and make it back to the airport in the Tahoe. He didn't want to leave the Porsche in the airport ramp because it might get stolen, and even if it didn't, he might not ever find it again. And pound for pound, he'd rather lose the Chevy than the Porsche.

The plane failed to crash either on the way to Houston or on landing—when he really expected it, so tantalizingly close to safety—or even when it was taxiing up to the gate, and a little more than five hours after speaking to Mallard, Lucas led the parade through the gate into the terminal.

Louis Mallard, who pronounced his name "Louie," was a stocky, professorial man who wore gold-rimmed professorial glasses and a dark professorial suit. He had a wrestler's neck and sometimes carried a .40-caliber automatic in a shoulder holster. Waiting with him, in a lighter-blue professorial suit, and carrying a black briefcase, was a lanky gray-haired woman named Malone. The last time Lucas had seen Malone, he'd seen quite a bit more of her.

"Louis," Lucas said, shaking the other man's hand. Malone turned a cheek, and Lucas pecked it and said, "Louis tells me you got one on the line."

She looked at Mallard, who said hastily, "I didn't exactly say *that*."

"Mmmm," Malone said. To Lucas: "It's somewhat true."

"Somebody conservative, well-placed in government," Lucas suggested. "Maybe a little money of his own." Malone was a four-time loser with a taste for artists and muscle workers.

"No," she said. "He's a Sheetrocker."

"A Sheetrocker." He waited for a smile, and when he didn't get one—hc got instead a defensive brow-beetling—he said, "Well, that's good. Always jobs out there for a good Sheetrocker."

Before Lucas sank completely out of sight, Mallard jumped in. "He's also a writer. He's almost done with his novel."

"Okay, well, good," Lucas said.

"You gotta get some clothes?" Mallard asked, trying to keep the anti-Sheetrocker momentum going. "There's a place . . ."

"Nah, I'm okay. I had time to get home." He looked around. "So where're we going? We leave out of here?"

"We catch a ride to another terminal," Mallard said. "The ride's outside."

THEY RODE TO the next terminal in a dark-blue government car, driven by a man whom Mallard never introduced. A junior agent from the Houston office, Lucas thought, who looked a little sour about the chauffeur duties. Malone rode in the front with the agent, while Lucas and Mallard rode in the back.

During the walk to the car and the two-minute ride, Mallard quietly sketched the series of circumstances that had led to the identification of Rinker as the woman who was shot, and to the belief by the Mexican cops that a shooter from St. Louis was involved. The shooter was now dead, probably killed by a Mexican man who was still on the run. "She was pregnant," Malone said. "They killed her lover, and when she was wounded, she lost the baby."

Lucas winced, and Weather's face popped into his head. "You think she's headed back here? Back across the border?"

Mallard shook his head. "We don't know. We've put sketches of her everywhere. Every port of entry. The problem is, she doesn't look all that special. Mid-thirties, middle height, athletic, pretty, that's about it. The other thing is, Rinker just got out of the hospital, so it's possible that she's lost some weight, and might not look like she used to."

Malone turned and said, over the seat, "It's also possible

that she's just running, that she's already in Majorca or someplace. The Mexican police have been tracing the phone calls she made from this ranch where she was recovering—there were six calls up to Missouri and two went out to banks in Mexico. We got on top of the banks right away, but both of the calls went into the general number, so we don't know who she was talking to, or what she did. There aren't any records of large sums of money being moved on the days she called, that can't be accounted for. No big accounts closed or switched that can't be accounted for. With both the Mexican cops and this Mejia guy, this gang guy, taking an interest, we're pretty sure the banks are telling us the truth."

"Maybe safe-deposit boxes," Lucas suggested.

"We're trying to run that down. We thought maybe an off-the-books box. So far, nothing's panned out," Malone said.

"She's good," Lucas said. "But we knew that. How about the Missouri calls?"

"All six guys are connected—all six guys admit that she called and all six say she was asking about John Ross, who we think was her main employer," Mallard said. "All six say they told her nothing, that they didn't have anything to tell her."

"Ross runs things around the river in St. Louis, the port, trucks, some drug connections over in East St. Louis," Malone added. "He has a liquor distributorship. You remember Wooden Head from Wichita?"

"Yeah."

"Wooden Head worked for Ross."

"You believe the six guys? That they didn't have anything to say?"

"She talked to four of them for about five minutes, and the other two for about two minutes. We don't know what was said, but apparently not too much."

"You can say a lot in five minutes," Lucas said. "Does Ross have the six names?"

"Not as far as we know—we haven't talked with him yet," Mallard said.

"Okay. So Clara's boyfriend gets killed and she's wounded and loses the baby, and they think the shooter is from St. Louis and she makes calls to St. Louis asking about this Ross guy, but she doesn't call Ross himself, as far as you know. So. You think Ross sent the shooter? That she's on a revenge trip? A kamikaze deal?"

Mallard shook his head again. "Don't know. We're guessing that's it. Whatever, Rinker's broken out now, she's in the open. I *really* want her. *Really* want her. She's run her score up to maybe thirty-five people: This woman is the devil."

"She's maybe more inflected than that," Malone objected. To Lucas: "We have a good biography on her now. You can read it on the way down to Cancún. She had quite the little backwoods childhood."

THEIR CONNECTION WAS TIGHT: An hour after Lucas's Northwest flight put down at Houston, the Continental flight to Cancún lifted off. Mallard and Malone sat together, with Lucas behind them, next to an elderly woman who plugged her sound-killing Bose headphones into a Sony discman, looked at him once, with something that might have been skepticism, and pulled a sleeping mask over her eyes. When they were off the ground, Malone took a bound report out of her briefcase and handed it back to Lucas. "Rinker," she said.

LUCAS HAD NEVER been able to read on airplanes: The Clara Rinker file was a first. When Malone handed him the file, he'd wondered at its heft, and turned to the last page: page 308. He flipped through and found a dense, single-spaced narrative. Not the usual cop report.

The first page began: "There are only four known photographs of Clara Rinker—three from driver's licenses and one from an identification card issued by Wichita State University. None of the people who knew Rinker were able to immediately pick her photograph from a spread of similar photographs prepared by the Bureau—in each of the four photos, she had obscured her appearance with eyeglasses and elaborate hair arrangements. This is typical of what we know of Clara Rinker: She is obsessively cautious in her contacts with others, and she apparently has, from the beginning of her career, prepared herself to run."

The author of the report—a Lanny Brown, whom Lucas hadn't heard of—had a nice style that would have worked in a true-crime book. Rinker had been killing people for almost fifteen years. The first reports had been of various organized-crime figures, both minor and major, taken off by a killer whose trademark was extreme close-range shootings, many of them with .22-caliber silenced pistols.

Because of the circumstances of the shootings—two of them had taken place in women's rest rooms, although both the victims were men—the Bureau began to suspect that the shooter was a woman who lured the victims into private places with a promise of sex. A friend of one victim, in Shreveport, Louisiana, said that he'd spoken briefly at a bar with a pretty young woman who had a Southern accent, and later had caught a glimpse of the young woman and the victim leaving the club, in the victim's Continental. The car and the man were later found on a lover's lane. The man—who was married—had been shot three times in the head with a .40-caliber Smith.

No fewer than nine people had been executed in stairwells or between cars in parking structures. The Bureau believed that the choices of execution locale indicated that the shooter had carefully scouted the victims, knew where they parked their cars, and favored parking structures because they offered good access and egress, large numbers of strangers interacting with each other—a strange woman wouldn't be noticed—and sudden privacy: Bodies had apparently gone unnoticed for as much as four hours when rolled under a car.

She was also believed to have posed as either a Mormon missionary or a Jehovah's Witness: One quiet evening in suburban Chicago, a "straight-looking" young woman carrying what a neighbor said appeared to be a Bible or a Book of Mormon had knocked on the door of a recently divorced hood in Oak Park, Illinois. Neighbors who'd been sitting in a porch swing in the restored Victorian across the street said she'd spoken to whoever answered the door, then turned away and left.

Three days later, after they'd been unable to get in touch with the bad boy, friends looked in a window and saw him sprawled on the floor by the front door. He'd taken two in the heart and one in the head, and died in a pair of flowered boxer shorts with a tight grip on a can of Coors Light. The time of death was estimated from the fact that he'd apparently just taken off a pair of Greg Norman golf slacks and a midnight-blue and white-hibiscus aloha shirt, which other friends said he'd worn to a golf course three days earlier.

AFTER SUMMARIZING THE executions that Rinker was believed involved in, the Bureau report spent some time with her childhood. She'd grown up on a broken-down farm outside of Tisdale, Missouri, not far from Springfield. Her father had deserted the family when she was seven, and had died, unknown to the family, twelve years later, in a car accident in Raleigh, North Carolina.

Her mother, Cammy Rinker, had divorced Rinker's father four years after he left, and two weeks after the divorce was final, married a man named Carl Paltry. Paltry was an alcoholic and a bully, and had been arrested for beating both Cammy Rinker and Rinker's older brother, Roy. The police had learned of Roy's beating after a gym coach noticed that Roy was peeing blood.

According to Rinker's aunt—her mother's sister—Paltry also had sexually abused his wife Cammy Rinker, Clara, and possibly Clara's younger brother, Gene. The abuse had begun a few weeks after the marriage, when Rinker was eleven, and continued until she ran away from home when she was fourteen. Until she was eleven, she'd had a good record in school, but that went bad after Paltry arrived. The aunt also said that Rinker's older brother, Roy, had sexually abused her.

Paltry and Cammy Rinker had remained married for twelve years, until one day, when Clara would have been nineteen, and already working as a shooter, he'd disappeared. He hadn't run anywhere, the local cops said—he'd gotten drunk and had beaten Cammy so badly that she'd been hospitalized, and Paltry had been arrested. He was out on bail when he disappeared. His car had been found parked, engine running, behind a Dairy Queen in Tisdale. His checkbook and wallet were on the passenger seat. He was never seen again, and the Bureau believed that Clara Rinker may have paid him a visit.

Rinker's mother had almost nothing useful to tell the Bureau. Her memory of Clara seemed uneven; and when she went to get family pictures, she found that all the photos of Clara were gone.

The Bureau had tracked Roy through a series of minor crime reports, and eventually found him in Santa Barbara, California, where he was involved in a lightweight prostitution ring. Roy and a man named Charles Green ran teenaged hookers around to country clubs. The Bureau report quoted one source as saying, "You could get your shoes and your knob polished at the same place and time. It was convenient for everybody."

Roy was two years older than Rinker and had left home two years after she had. He had seen her twice, when she'd stopped in Santa Barbara looking for their younger brother, Gene, who was also someplace in California. Roy didn't know anything about anything, though he said that Rinker appeared to be doing well, and drove nice cars. He had no photographs of her, and denied having sexually abused her. The interviewer thought he was lying.

Rinker's younger brother, Gene, had shown up on three police reports in California, all three for minor drug offenses. He was listed as "homeless" on the police reports and was apparently living on the beaches between Venice and Santa Monica. The Bureau had been unable to find him. Next to this paragraph, a female hand had scrawled, "Lucas: ask me—M."

Lucas reached forward and tapped Malone's arm. "There's a note here to ask you about Gene Rinker."

She turned and said, "Yes. We found him yesterday. He was working for a pool-cleaning company in Pacific Palisades—Los Angeles. We're holding him on a drug charge."

"Good charge?"

"He was in possession of marijuana."

"How much?"

"Maybe a gram."

"A joint? Jesus, is that . . . ?"

"It's more than enough, is what it is. As soon as we get done here, I'm going to L.A. to talk to him. See if he has anything interesting on Clara."

"Okay." Malone turned away, and Lucas sank back into the report.

RINKER HAD WORKED for a bar in St. Louis, then for Ross, who was a liquor distributor. She'd also worked off and on as a bookkeeper-secretary for a mobster named Allen Kent, whose mother's family was closely tied to the old Giancana outfit in Chicago. Eventually, Rinker had put together enough money to buy a bar in Wichita, which had done well until she'd fled after her disastrous involvement in a series of killings in Minneapolis. Where she'd gone immediately after Minneapolis was unknown. She'd eventually popped up in Cancún, where she'd worked illegally as a bookkeeper at a boutique hotel called Passages.

Lucas had danced with her once, not knowing who she was, at her club in Wichita, The Rink. They'd had a good time, for a little time, that night. She'd even chatted with Mallard and Malone. She must've known who they were, although they hadn't known who she was. Later, she'd tried to kill Lucas in his own front yard. She'd missed almost purely by chance . . . as he'd missed her.

READING ABOUT HIS own encounter with Rinker, Lucas was struck with the strangeness of writerly synthesis. He was in the story, but it didn't sound like him, or feel like him. He felt as though he were looking at himself in an old 8-millimeter movie, something that wasn't quite true, but was undeniably accurate . . . and he wondered if the entire report was like that, accurate but not especially true.

Rinker came across as Mallard saw her, as the daughter of the devil. At the same time, almost against the will of the writer, another picture was emerging, a kind of Annie Oakley old-timey story of survival.

AFTER COMPLETING THE detailed review of Rinker's life and activities, the report went on to detail what was known of the business and crime activities of her various bosses: Names were named, connections made, possibilities explored. Much was speculative, but all of it was based on the kind of rumor-fabric that Lucas had lived with most of his working life. Not much could be proven, but much could be understood. . . .

He was two-thirds of the way through the report when he heard the flight attendant saying something, but he paid no attention until the plane's attitude changed with an audible clunk that reverberated through the cabin. He sat upright, looked around, and saw that people were packing up briefcases, putting away computers, sticking stuff back into the overhead. He looked at his watch: They'd been in the air for two hours and were coming into Cancún.

He leaned forward, tapped Malone's arm, and when she turned, passed the report back.

"Finish it?"

"No. Got another hundred pages. And I'll want to read the whole thing over," he said. "Good stuff in there. I can see what you meant when you said . . . *inflected.* Tough life."

"Which is not exactly an excuse for all the people she's killed—especially people like Barbara Allen." Allen had been a rich charity-and-foundation socialite in Minneapolis. Rinker had shot her to death so that her client could get at Allen's husband.

"No. But it was still tough," Lucas said.

"The thing is, you kinda liked her," Malone said. "You

went for that whole perky cheerleader teased-hair bar-owner act."

"What's not to like?" Lucas asked. He said, "Better buckle up," and leaned back out of the conversation.

THE PLANE FAILED to crash in Cancún, but the heat and humidity jumped them as soon as they walked off the plane. They retrieved their luggage and took a taxi from the mainland over to the Island, where Mallard had gotten rooms at the Blue Palms. "Let's get cleaned up and find something to eat," he said. "The hotel restaurant is supposed to be okay."

"How about the Italian place where Rinker was shot?" Lucas asked. "Your report says it's pretty good."

"Saving that for lunch tomorrow," Mallard said.

The hotel room was a blank-faced off-white cubicle with a TV and a minibar, a too-soft double bed, and a bathroom without a tub. The place smelled faintly of bug spray and salt water, and could have been at any seaside anywhere. Lucas hung his clothes in the closet and washed his face, then walked out onto the narrow balcony and looked down at the water.

Rinker had been here, and not long ago. Had worked within a couple of blocks of the Blue Palms, had probably spent time on the beach ten stories down. She might well be in the same kind of place, somewhere else on the globe, looking for a job, trying to settle in.

Or she might have a hidey-hole in St. Louis, ready to go to war on her lover's killers. If she'd simply run, they'd never find her. But if she'd gone to St. Louis, he thought . . .

If she'd gone to St. Louis, they'd get her.

4

THEY HAD DINNER TOGETHER, AND CAUGHT UP WITH their separate lives. Lucas poked at Malone's new relationship with the Sheetrocker, despite Mallard's efforts to warn him away. Malone had almost nothing to say about her friend, except that he had terrific shoulders from lifting the Sheetrock.

Mallard mentioned that his office had been renamed. It was now called the Special Studies Group, and the last big case had involved the destruction of a bank robbery gang operating out of Toronto, Canada.

"They never did a thing in Canada," Mallard said. "They were completely law-abiding truck drivers and auto-parts guys. Then, about once every two months, they'd come down south and hit a bank."

"How'd you bust them?"

"Computers. They always hit the same kinds of banks at the same times of day with the same techniques, which told us that we were working with one gang. So we got all of the robberies with that signature, and plotted them with a geographical information system. The computer took a while, but one of the statistical clusters it turned up was a drive-time thing—all of the robberies were within a couple hours of border crossings. Different border crossings. Anyway, we ran the dates of the robberies against the names of people coming in, which didn't turn up anything, because they kept switching IDs. But then we ran the incoming license plates, and we found them. Two trucks, going through one after the other, the day before each of the robberies. Once we had that, we figured out who they were, and then we watched them move, watched them scout the bank, cleared out the bank a half hour before they were due to come in, and when they came in . . . there we were."

They talked about it for a while, and then Lucas gave them details on a case involving an art professor, on which Mallard's office had provided help. "Marcy Sherrill said your information was so generic that it made her brain hurt," he said.

"Fuck her if she can't take a joke," Mallard said.

"Louis," Lucas said, "the *language.*"

AND THAT WAS THE EVENING.

The next morning, Lucas was a few minutes late getting

down to the lobby: Mallard and Malone were both early risers, and he wasn't. He shaved, stood in the shower for five minutes, lay down on the bed for a few minutes more, dozing, then had to brush his teeth again when Malone called to ask where he was. She was annoyed: "Get going, Lucas—our contact's already here."

When he got down, Mallard and Malone were waiting in the lobby with a Mexican man who wore a gorgeous off-brown suit with a cornflower-blue shirt and buffed mahogany oxfords. Lucas was admiring the Mexican's dress when Mallard said, "Jeez, Davenport, where do you get these clothes?"

Lucas looked down at himself. He was wearing tan slacks with a gray cast, a black silk Hawaiian shirt with red-and-gold cockatoos, a medium-blue tropical-weight wool-knit jacket, and loafers that were the casual variants of the Mexican man's. He thought he looked pretty good. "What's the problem?"

"No problem. . . ."

"You look excellent," the Mexican said, smiling.

His English was lightly accented, and Malone said, "This is Colonel Manuel Martin, Mexican National Police. He arranged the interview with the Mejia family."

Lucas and Martin shook hands. The Mexican clearly had more Indio in his ancestry than Spanish, was six inches shorter than Mallard and a little rounder. His expression was one of weary amusement. Lucas said, "Pleased to meet you," and Martin nodded and said, "I understand you've danced with Clara Rinker."

"She's a good dancer," Lucas said. They were drifting toward the dining room. "What's the story on this Mejia guy?"

Martin's eyebrows arched a bit, and he cocked his head to the side. "I was trying to think how to explain that, and finally I came up with this: He is Mexico's Joseph Kennedy. The father of your President Kennedy? Where the early money came from is not exactly known; it is now legitimate. But because of past associations, the entire Mejia family is very, very careful. And they have excellent connections with the less reputable . . ." He struggled for a word, and finally landed on "element."

"They'll talk to the cops?"

Martin shrugged. "Of course. Joseph Kennedy would speak to the police, would he not? So will Mejia. Especially where our interests are aligned."

THE BREAKFAST WAS AMERICAN—eggs, milk, cereal, sausage, and coffee—though Martin stayed with fruit, bread with cheese, and olives, popping the olives one at a time with his fingertips, as though he were eating pecans. During the breakfast, he gave them a short history of Cancún, drew schematic maps on a paper napkin to explain the lay of the Yucatán, and the cities of Cancún and Mérida, and outlined what was known of Clara Rinker's stay in Mexico.

"She wasn't working for the Mejias before she came here, of that we are certain. They had no idea of who she was. If they had known, it is doubtful that Paul Mejia would have been allowed to continue the relationship. From what we can piece together, he met her at the hotel where she worked—purely accidentally, she was a bookkeeper and he was checking on a business question having to do with automobile parking costs at various beach hotels—and that she did not know about the Mejia family until another woman at the hotel told her, some time after they began seeing each other. She lived quite modestly in a rented apartment."

"Fingerprints?" Lucas asked.

"Nothing. The room had been methodically wiped. There were personal items left behind, but nothing that you could not buy in five minutes in another city. And, of course, nobody ever took a picture of her. There was never an occasion."

"No way to tell where she went?"

"She disappeared after an appointment at the doctor's office," Martin said. "She had recovered from the shooting—the checks. . . . Is that right, the medical checks?"

"Checkups," Malone offered.

"Yes. The medical checkups were routine, and had become more a matter of physical rehabilitation. She had some damage to her stomach muscles, and they needed strengthening. Anyway, there is a large taxi stand not far from the doctor's office, but none of the taxi drivers we've found remembers seeing her or taking her anywhere. That's possibly because they take all kinds of Americans everywhere, and they simply can't remember, or because the Mejia connection had been rumored, and nobody wanted anything to do with her."

"So she takes a taxi and she's gone."

Martin shrugged again and said, "What else can I tell you? We have document checks, of course, for people coming and going, and since that time, we have no Cassandra or Cassie McLain, and of course, no Clara Rinker, entering or leaving Mexico."

MALONE AND MALLARD questioned Martin through the breakfast—they weren't quite rehearsed, Lucas noticed, but they were coordinated. He began watching them more closely, and began to suspect that the coordination was personal, rather than professional. But what about the Sheetrocker, he wondered?

Then, in the government GMC Suburban that Martin himself drove to Mérida, Mallard scrambled into the back with Malone, and Lucas noticed that their shoulders touched during much of the ride, and he thought, *Hmmm.* The two FBI agents pushed the questions even when it was obvious that they were running in circles, as though they were playing a ranking game with each other. . . .

Martin was unfailingly polite through it all. Halfway to

Mérida, the FBI questions ran out, and they rode in silence for a while.

Martin eventually turned to Lucas. "If I might ask . . . where did you get your jacket? It's very nice. Also the shirt, although it's not my style."

"Got it in San Francisco. One of the gay men's boutiques—my fiancée would know the store," Lucas said. He opened the front lapel and read it. "It's a Gianfranco Ferre. I liked the fabric for hot weather, although it does get some pulls in it."

"Hmm." Martin nodded, pursing his lips. "Large people like yourself look authoritative even in casual clothing. I'm afraid my body was made for suits."

"But that's a great suit," Lucas said. "I saw one like it, I think, a friend of mine had one. Ralph Lauren, the Purple Label? Though it was in blue."

"Exactly, this is what it is," Martin said, looking pleased, touching his necktie knot and lapel. "Some people in America think brown suits look bad, but I think, with brown people, they look not-so-bad." And a moment later: "Have you ever looked at a suit by Kiton?"

Lucas said, "I saw some, at a show . . ."

They talked about suits for a while, then about shoes. Martin told Lucas that he'd paid $1,100 for a pair of semi-custom oxblood loafers by an English cobbler named Barkley, only to find that every time he went through an airport metal detector, the steel shanks in the shoes set off the alarm. "So, when I go to the States, my beautiful shoes stay at home. It is the only way I can assure myself of the sanctity of my . . ." He searched again for the word, came up with "rectum," and smiled brilliantly over his shoulder at Malone.

"Don't like those body-cavity searches, eh?" Lucas asked.

"American security is sometimes . . . unusual," Martin said.

When they got out of the truck in Mérida, Malone took Lucas by the elbow and stood on tiptoe, her mouth by his ear, and said, "If you talk for one more fuckin' minute about fashion, I'll fuckin' shoot you."

"Hey . . ."

RAUL MEJIA'S HOUSE was surrounded by an off-white stucco wall, with access through what appeared to be a simple Spanish wrought-iron gate. As they were passing through, Lucas noticed that the bolt was electronic, that the wrought iron was actually steel, and that the black faux wrought-iron leaves at the top of the gate, eight or nine feet up, were essentially knives. If anyone were to scale it, he would need serious protection—like a Kevlar quilt. Without it, a climber's fingers would be lopped off like so many link sausages.

Inside the wall was a small, neatly kept yard, grassy in the North American style, with a stepping-stone walk to the front door of the house. The house itself, from the front, seemed as modest as the outer wall, a high single-story, and was made of the same off-white stucco, pierced by tall dark windows.

Martin led the way through the gate, up the stepping-stone walk, and pushed the doorbell. A moment later, a young man opened it, smiled, and said, "Come in, come in—I'm Dominic Mejia. My father's waiting in the library."

The house was much larger than it appeared from the outside, Lucas realized. From the outside, there was no way to see how far back it extended—but once inside, Dominic led them through a public reception room, across a large interior courtyard, open to the sky, with a small swimming pool, into the back of the house and down another hallway to a library. The library looked as though it might be a hundred years old, all of dark wood with thick shelves set at different heights, to accommodate the books. The bottom two feet of each wall was taken up by cupboards. The books themselves were varied, and included several hundred paperbacks and perhaps three thousand hardcovers. The room smelled faintly of lemon-scented furniture polish and leather soap—it smelled good.

An old man was sitting in a wheelchair at a library table, a book in front of him. He smiled when they entered, pushed back from the table, and said in English, "Colonel Martin, a pleasure, as always. Your friends, as well. Come in. Sit." He gestured at a circle of chairs at the back of the room: two leather reading chairs, and three easy chairs that had apparently been brought in for the guests. Mejia wheeled himself over.

Lucas went along the shelving and said, "This is a good room. I'm building a house now, with a library." He was looking at the books—they all appeared to have been read. Most were on history, culture, and economics, with a selection of Latin American and Spanish novels; all the bindings were modern. Mejia was a reader, rather than a collector.

Mallard was settling into one of the leather chairs, while Malone took the other. Mejia wheeled to get a better look at his shelves, then said, "A library. I envy you the task; the thought. The difficulty is to make the library comfortable and distinguished at once. Much thought and a good architect." He tapped his temple as he said "Much thought." Mejia spoke English well, but not quite as well as his son. He looked at his son: "Dominic—open the folding doors. And find Anthony."

At the far end of the room, two large, four-panel folding doors dominated the center of the wall. Dominic opened them and revealed a built-in desk with a computer console, and an overhead shelf lined with software boxes, then went to find Anthony, whoever that was. "Internet," Raul Mejia was saying. "A wonderful thing, even for an old man. I have this beautiful library where I can sit with my books . . . and a high-speed Internet connection behind harem screens made in Andalusia."

Lucas took one of the fabric chairs as Mallard asked, "Have you ever put 'Clara Rinker' into a search engine?"

"Three thousand references now, on Google, beginning with the investigation in your Kansas and Minnesota," Mejia said. "There is discussion of a movie or perhaps a television show."

"You were surprised to see them all? The references?"

"I was . . ." Dominic came back into the room, trailed by a man who might have been a year or two older, but was obviously his brother. Raul Mejia looked at his sons and said, *"Asombrado?"*

"Astonished. Amazed," Anthony said. His English was as good as his brother's. They sounded Californian.

"More than surprised," Mejia said. He sighed. "I wish she had the baby. This is the real assassination. A baby from my son and a woman like this. This would be a *baby."*

Malone jumped in: "As we understand it, you have had enemies in business, but can find no sign that these enemies made the attack on your son and Rinker. With the St. Louis connection, it seems now that the attack was aimed at Rinker and your son was killed accidentally. Does this change your . . . your . . . *feeling* toward Rinker?"

The old man shrugged. "Of course. But. I can also understand this attachment. Paulo was a good boy, but wild. Crazy, sometimes. This woman, Clara Rinker, there must have been a fire between them. She must also have this craziness somewhere inside. I could feel it myself when

I spoke to her. So. I am angry that she did not tell us, but I understand why she did not. Now . . . what is to be done?"

"You could help us catch her," Mallard said. "You have commercial connections everywhere in Mexico. She needs money and shelter, and she will go places that the police may not see."

"We would also like to know from you . . . this man who was murdered at the airfield—what is his connection with these criminals in St. Louis? He is a Mafia?"

"He has connections with St. Louis organized crime," Mallard said.

"You think some Italians from St. Louis came to Cancún and shot my boy," Mejia said. "By mistake."

"Not so many Italians anymore, but that's basically what we think, yes," Mallard agreed.

"You will tell us their names?"

Now Mallard showed a little nervousness. "We can't do that. But as the investigation progresses, I'm sure you will . . . learn a few of them. We wouldn't want you to take, ummm, any active role in the, ummm, investigation."

"But, perhaps, through my family commercial connections—I have connections with hotels, motels, friends in the States . . . perhaps I could find information for you. If I had the names."

"We really can't bring in civilians."

"He's afraid you would send gunmen to St. Louis to kill the names," Lucas said to Mejia. "He might not mind if they did that, if it would help catch Rinker. But he couldn't tell you the names, because that might turn out to be technically criminal and he would be purged."

"That's not exactly accurate," Mallard said irritably.

"Besides, you don't need him to tell you," Lucas said, still talking to Mejia. "Watch your computer. The FBI leaks like crazy and the names will appear. If Rinker starts shooting, there will be lists in the newspapers. In your search engine, put in 'organized crime,' 'St. Louis,' and the word 'shot.' "

"Goddamnit, Lucas," Mallard said.

Mejia looked at Lucas for a long five seconds, then turned to Mallard. "So, then, from me, you need clues to Clara Rinker."

Mallard nodded. "Yes."

Mejia nodded back. "We will look. If you will give us a telephone number, we will call when we find anything."

Mallard took a card from his pocket, scribbled a number on it, and handed it over. Mejia glanced at it and held it out to Anthony, who, like his brother, was leaning against the library table. "That's my secure cell phone," Mallard said. "I sleep with it. You can call me twenty-four hours a day."

"You're not married," Mejia said.

"Not anymore," Mallard said. "The job was more interesting."

THEY TALKED FOR another ten minutes, but not much came of it. Mejia and his sons gave them impressions of

Rinker. She was a happy woman, they said, and had made Paulo happy. Although she said she was younger than Paulo, they thought she might have been a couple of years older. Would they have married? Perhaps.

Mejia seemed to lack any real information about the crime, which wasn't surprising, since the FBI and the Mexican National Police had the same problem. As they left, Lucas and Mejia talked a few minutes about library shelves, and how to prevent unsightly sagging, and the arrangement of books, which the old man called an enjoyable but impossible task. On the way out of Mérida, Malone said, "Nice old man. For a ganglord."

Martin's eyes flashed up to the rearview mirror to catch hers, and he said, "Maybe not so much *ganglord* talk outside the car. And I do not think many people would agree that he is a nice old man."

"Do you think he'll help us trail Rinker?" Mallard asked.

"If he sees some benefit in it," Martin said. "Benefit for him. He will analyze, analyze, analyze, and if finally he is sure of the benefit, he will help. *Realpolitik.*"

Lucas smiled at the word. "You speak really good English, you know?"

WITH MARTIN AS a guide, they returned to Cancún and toured the restaurant where Paulo Mejia and Rinker had been shot, interviewed the restaurant owner, and climbed into the loft of the church to see the shooting position taken by the assassin.

"Had to have local help to find this," Lucas said, as Martin explained how the shooter had probably fired once, then retreated down the stairs and out the back door to a waiting car.

"There would have to be a driver," Martin said. "You couldn't park a car back there—it would block the entire street and bring attention."

"You know the driver?" Mallard asked.

"We are looking for a man. . . . He is unaccountably absent. Normally, he would go to relatives to be hidden, but they do not know where he is. They knew where he was three days ago, but then he went away."

"Running," Malone suggested. "Maybe he felt you coming."

"He went to a business meeting, his mother says. He didn't come back."

"Mmm."

The loft was hot as a kiln, and smelled like hay, like a midwestern barn loft in summer. A wasp the size of Lucas's little finger bumped along the seam of the ceiling and wall. They looked out on the hot street for another minute, then trooped back to the restaurant for a light lunch. The service was wonderful, which Martin seemed to take for granted. Lucas again noticed the body language between Mallard and Malone, an offering from Mallard, equivocation from Malone. He smiled to himself and went back to the pasta salad.

From the restaurant, they went to the hotel where Rinker had worked as a bookkeeper. She'd worked off the books, illegally, but nobody was being coy about it. With both the Mejia family and the national cops involved, the hotel manager simply opened up and told everybody everything: He'd hired her because she had the bookkeeping skills—she knew Excel backward and forward—and was willing to work whenever she was needed, for as long or as little as she was needed, and there were no benefits or taxes to pay.

"She said she just needed an extra squirt of money to supplement her disability pension," the manager told them. "She was very good. The arrangement was convenient for everybody."

"Is there any possibility that she took the job because she knew she would meet Paulo Mejia?" Lucas asked.

The manager shook his head. "Mr. Mejia never came here—only the once, to look at the parking for an appraisal he was doing. I introduced them when he needed some numbers."

"Purely by chance."

He nodded. "By chance." He explained that he didn't know Mejia was coming that day, and that she'd come in at the last minute to deal with a money problem involving a group of Americans who had asked to extend their vacation stay. "She could not have planned it."

He also characterized her as cheerful and hardworking, and said that her hours were increasing each month. "I would have liked to employ her full-time, if she had not been a foreigner," he said. "She worked very well."

Mallard asked about pictures, and the manager shrugged. "How often do you take pictures of people in your office? We're not tourists—we work here."

ON THE WAY back to the hotel, all four of them were quiet, thinking their own thoughts, until Lucas asked Martin, "Why is it that everybody speaks English? Everybody we've seen. . . ."

Martin sighed. "Gringo imperialism. Cancún business is Americans and Canadians. And English people, and now some Germans. Always Israelis. There's a story—not a story, you would call it a *line*—about Cancún," Martin said. "It's that Cancún is just like Miami—except in Miami, they speak Spanish."

AT THE HOTEL, Martin got out of the truck, shook hands with the three Americans, and asked Lucas to get the name of the San Francisco store where he'd bought the jacket. Lucas said he would find it and call back.

"Not much here," Lucas said, as he watched Martin drive away. Then he, Mallard, and Malone crossed into the cool of the hotel.

"But we got a deal with old man Mejia, which is the

main thing," Mallard said. "If he decides to put a price on her head, Rinker's gonna have a hard time getting any help from the underground. Word'll get around."

"You have more faith than I do," Lucas said. "Most of the fuckin' underground can't read a *TV Guide.*"

"I'm not talking about the assholes on the corner," Mallard said. "I'm talking about the gun dealers and the moneymen and the document people. They'll hear. She'll have trouble moving."

Lucas shook his head; he disagreed. The disagreement was fundamental, and generally divided all cops everywhere: Some believed in underlying social order, in which messages got relayed and people kept an eye out, and bosses reigned and buttonmen were ready to take orders, and a network connected them. And some cops believed in social chaos, in which most events occurred through accident, coincidence, stupidity, cupidity, and luck, both good and bad. Lucas fell into the chaos camp, while Mallard and Malone believed in the underlying order.

WHEN WORKING OUT the trip to Mexico, Mallard had allowed extra time for a certain inefficiency; but Martin had been so ruthlessly efficient that they were done at two o'clock, mission more or less accomplished.

"Swim?" Malone asked.

"Too hot," Lucas said. "I'm gonna get a beer at the bar,

then a couple of papers, and lay up in my room with the air-conditioning on. Maybe swim before dinner?"

"Not bad," Mallard said. "I'm for a beer or two."

"I'll join you," Malone said. "But I gotta run up to my room for a minute."

Lucas and Mallard stopped at the hotel gift shop and bought copies of the *Times* and the *Wall Street Journal,* carried the papers into the cool of the bar, got a booth, and ordered Dos Equis.

"You read the editorials?" Mallard asked.

"Yeah, though I know it's wrong," Lucas said.

"You want the Fascists or the Commies?"

Lucas considered for a moment, then said, "Fascists," and Mallard passed him the *Journal.* They both opened to the editorial pages, looked over the offerings, and then Lucas asked, casually, "How bad you got it for Malone?"

Mallard's newspaper folded down. He looked at Lucas for a long moment, then sighed and said, "Is it that obvious?"

"Yup," Lucas said.

"The goddamn woman drives me crazy. I know you guys . . ." He didn't say it—that Lucas and Malone once spent a happy weekend together. "That's not a big deal. I just . . . *hunger* after her. I thought I was hiding it pretty well."

"I'm a trained investigator," Lucas said. He looked at an editorial headline that said, " 'Sweatshops' Often Build

Sustaining Family Businesses." After a moment of silence from Mallard, he added, "I suspect nobody else knows, except any trained investigators you might have at the FBI. And Malone, of course."

Mallard's eyebrows went up. "You think she knows?"

"Jesus Christ, Louis, she knew before you did," Lucas said. "Women always know that shit first. And she's not backing away. If I were you, I'd set up a *moment* somewhere. Have a few drinks around the pool tonight, tell her a few stories, give her a chance to tell you a few, and you know, going up stairs, put a *hand* on her."

"What about the drywall guy? The Sheetrocker?"

"Fuck the drywall guy. You're not playing tennis."

"Have to be more than a few drinks," Mallard said gloomily. He looked scared to death.

"It's no big deal, Louis," Lucas said. "People do it all the time."

"Not me," Mallard said. "I'm not exactly your romantic hero."

"Yes, you are, Louis. You're a big wheel in the FBI. You're involved in international intrigue. You carry a great big gun. You spend the taxpayers' money like it was water."

"I'm paying for the beer personally."

"Louis, what the fuck are you talking about?"

"Yeah, yeah." The phone in his pocket rang and he slipped it out, answered, listened for a moment, then said, "Oh, boy. When? We'll be out front." He clicked it shut and said, "Martin's coming back. They found that guy who might have been the driver."

"Dead?"

"Not yet. But he's in terrible shape. Martin says he was tortured."

"Where is he?"

"Here. Cancún. He was dumped at a hospital. Martin'll be here in five minutes."

MALONE CAME OUT of the elevator as Mallard was ringing her room. Mallard explained about the phone call on the way to the door. Martin roared in three minutes later, parting the clouds of Volkswagen Beetles like a wolf going through a flock of sheep. "He's at the hospital now," he said, as they scrambled aboard.

"How bad?" Lucas asked.

"He could die before we get there," Martin said. His face had gone grim as a crocodile's, and the easy charm had vanished. They bounced over a curb going out of the parking lot, onto the strip. Lucas had no idea of where they were going. The GMC was rigged with a siren to go with the flasher lights above the bumper, and Martin punched the truck through the traffic.

An unknown person had driven an old Toyota Corolla over a curb at the hospital emergency entrance, Martin said, had left the motor running and the passenger door open, and walked away. When a cop inside the emergency room noticed the car, he'd gone out to order the owner to move it—and found the tortured man sitting in a blood-soaked passenger seat. Nobody saw where the Corolla's driver went. Nobody remembered what he looked like.

Then: "Here it is." Martin did a U-turn and dropped down a slanting concrete ramp to the emergency entrance at the hospital. A cop at the entrance tried to wave them away, but Martin put the truck astride the main door's entrance ramp, hopped out, and showed the cop a card. The cop stepped back, and Mejia said something that Lucas thought might mean, "Park the truck," and they all went inside.

Three doctors were standing in a hallway, smoking. They saw Martin coming, the Americans trailing behind, and the tallest of the three stepped toward them, shaking his head.

"Muerto," he said.

"Shit," Martin said. They spoke for a minute in Spanish, then Martin turned to Mallard, Malone, and Lucas. "He's dead. He died five minutes after they got here. We will do an autopsy, because the doctors aren't quite sure why he died—possibly shock. Possibly a stroke. Possibly something else."

"Like what?"

"They don't know."

"Can we see him?"

"I'm going to. You may if you wish, but you may not want to."

The three Americans all looked at each other, and Malone said, "Let's go."

THE MAN CALLED Octavio Diaz was lying faceup, nude, on a stainless-steel medical cart. His face was covered with blood—his eyes had been poked out—and his arms and legs were black. Lucas took a look and said, "Jesus Christ, what happened to his mouth? And he's black . . ."

"Snipped his tongue off, looks like with a pair of wire cutters," the tall doctor said. "Put his eyes out with a knife, and it appears they did something to burn his ears. . . . So he couldn't see, hear, or speak. He was dying when he arrived. You can't see it so much, but when we tried to get him out of his car . . . Look." He picked up one of Diaz's feet and lifted it above the cart. The leg hung in an almost perfect catenary arch down to his hip. "The bones have been minutely crushed in both legs and both arms. That must have taken a while, and they were very thorough. Picking him up, getting him out of the car, was like trying to pick up an oyster."

Malone made a sour face at the comparison and said, "Why didn't they just dump him out in the jungle?"

"Sending a message," Lucas said.

Martin nodded. "To anyone else who thinks the Mejias have gone soft. They wanted people to see this—to see him alive. The nurses and the doctors. There will be stories everywhere in Cancún in an hour."

"Wonder if they got anything out of him?" Mallard asked, looking down at the body.

"What do you think?" Malone asked. She still had the sour face. "Don't you think you might have answered the questions if they were doing . . . *that?*"

"So if they're looking for Rinker, or the assholes behind the shooting, they've probably got a jump on us," Lucas said. He turned to the doctor. "Can you tell from the wounds when this was all done?"

"The autopsy will give a good approximation."

"How about between, say, eleven o'clock and noon, today?"

The doctor nodded. "From the way the blood is crusted around the eyes, from the extent of the bruising and discoloration . . . I'm no pathologist, but that might be a reasonable guess."

"Nice old man for a ganglord," Lucas said to Malone. To Martin: "He may also have been sending a message to us. With the timing, I mean."

Martin nodded. "Not too much curiosity about this particular killing or the Mejias will be forced to prove their innocence by naming two high FBI officials and an American police officer as their alibis. And perhaps provide some details of what could be portrayed as an exceedingly cynical deal."

"Your English is *really* good," Lucas said.

"They didn't have to do this," Mallard said, moving his hand toward the ruins of Octavio Diaz.

"The killing wasn't done for you," Martin said. "The timing of the killing, possibly—but that would be a minor aspect of it. Perhaps we are even reading too much into that. Mejia needed to send a message to the . . . population. I *knew* that. I knew that Diaz was a walking dead man. But I hoped to find him before he died." He looked at the body again, reluctantly. "I was late."

5

TOM AND MICHELLE LAWTON LIVED IN A STUCCO HOUSE surrounded by rubber trees, with one overhanging tangerine, in Atwater Village off Los Feliz, behind a concrete ditch that everyone in Los Angeles called a river.

Down the river, if there'd been water in it, and you'd been allowed to boat it, and if you'd followed it far enough, you'd come to the Port of Long Beach—which is where the Lawtons berthed their sailboat. They got to the boat in a red '96 Jeep Cherokee with a surfboard rack on top, down I-5 and the 710, rather than down the river.

The Lawtons grew a little weed under lights, kept a couple of red-striped cats, and Michelle read mystery stories and made tangerine marmalade and worked part-time in a chain bookstore, while Tom took meetings on his screenplay. The screenplay involved the shadowy world of flesh smugglers, who ran human cargo into the States against the best efforts of outmanned and outgunned American law-enforcement officers, played by one or both of the Sheen brothers, although Tom'd take Jean-Claude Van Damme and a chick named Heather if he had to.

The few people who'd read the screenplay suggested that it wasn't realistic enough. Not enough violence, they said. Not enough brutality. A mailroom guy from ICM told Tom around a Garden Veggie sandwich in a bagel joint that it could use a little sexual and racial schtick. Maybe the human cargoes should be Chinese sex slaves, and he could try to sell the product to Jackie Chan.

What pissed Tom off was that he and Michelle *were* smugglers of human flesh. Neither one had ever owned a gun or had more than the briefest encounters with officers of the law, for the good reason that they smuggled only one person at a time, never anything but Americans, and those persons always had good documents, which they brought themselves or Tom supplied through a Persian guy from Pasadena who made really good Texas driver's licenses.

The Lawtons weren't overwhelmingly busy as smugglers, but their rates were high and a body a month pretty much covered their nut.

THIS PARTICULAR BODY was a woman, who would come across on Wednesday evening. She had her own ID, and it was good, Tom's man-in-Mexico said.

At Wednesday noon, the Lawtons took their boat, the *Star of Omaha,* out the Long Beach channel. A six- or eight-knot breeze was blowing across the Islands, and they cut the diesel, put up the sails and headed south, taking their time. They weren't going to Mexico. They were going to a *spot* fifteen miles off San Diego. Crossing the border was the job of their Mexican contact, a guy named Juan Duarte.

Duarte owned a twenty-two-foot Boston Whaler Guardian, with a haze-gray hull, just like the American Coast Guard, but without the Coast Guard's bow-mounted fifty-caliber machine gun. The hull color, which was standard, was the closest thing on earth to the Romulans' cloaking device—from twenty feet, on a dark night, it was invisible. Juan put the body in the boat, waited for dark, then idled up the coast to a spot distinguished only by its GPS coordinates. He found the Lawtons with their sails backed, quietly waiting, a couple of cigarette coals glowing in the dark. Though the *Star of Omaha*'s hull was white, they were very nearly as invisible as the Whaler.

"Dude," Duarte called, using the international sailboat hailing sign.

"Juan, how are you?"

Juan tossed a bowline over the sailboat's foredeck and Tom used it to pull the two boats together; the Lawtons had dropped foam fenders over the side to keep them from knocking too hard. The body threw a bag into the sailboat, then clambered up and over the side into the sailboat's cockpit.

"Nice to see you," Tom said, nodding at her in the dark. The body nodded back; she could smell tobacco on him, a pleasant odor. Michelle passed a small package to Juan: "It's an olive-wood rosary from Jerusalem, for your mom. It was blessed in the Church of the Holy Sepulcher, where Mt. Calvary is. Jimmy brought it back," she said.

"Thank him for me," Juan said.

"You good?" Tom called down to Juan.

Juan held up a hand, meaning that he'd been paid, and said, "Cast me off, there." Tom tossed the bowline back in the Whaler, and they drifted apart again. "See you," Juan called. "Maybe got something week after next."

"Call me," Tom said.

That was pretty much all there was to it. The Lawtons gave the body a peanut-butter-and-tangerine-marmalade sandwich, which she'd ordered in advance, through Duarte. They talked in a desultory way, as they loafed through the night. The body had a nice husky whiskey voice, and Tom thought if she kept talking he might get a little wood on the sound alone, though he'd never tell Michelle that. Tom turned on the running lights a few miles north of the rendezvous. They saw boats coming and going; nothing came close.

By morning, they were off Long Beach again, and they took their time going in. There was always a chance that they'd be stopped by the Coasties, but the passenger's documents were good and the boat was clean. Tom had no idea who the body was—his one really salient criminal characteristic was a determined lack of curiosity about his cargoes.

He was not even interested in why an American wanted to be smuggled back into the country. There were any number of people who preferred to come and go without unnecessary time-wasting bureaucratic entanglements, and Tom really didn't blame them. We were the home of the free, were we not?

A few minutes after eight o'clock in the morning, the body walked down the dock, a cheap TWA flight bag on her shoulder. The Lawtons were still on the boat, stowing equipment. The $3,000 that the body left behind was taped to Michelle's butt, just in case. Michelle last saw the other woman walking toward the corner of the ship's store. When she looked back again, a moment later, the body was gone.

RINKER CAUGHT A CAB to LAX, and from LAX, another to Venice, and from Venice, after getting a quick lunch on the beach and walking along some narrow, canal-lined streets for a while, watching her back, she caught another one out to the industrial flats in Downey. The driver didn't much want to go there, but when Rinker showed him a fifty, he took the money and dropped her in front of Jackie

Burke's store. Burke ran a full-time custom hotrod shop on the front side of his warehouse, and a part-time stolen-car chop shop in the back. Rinker had once solved a desperate problem for him.

Burke was a chunky man, strong, dark-complected, balding, tough as a lug nut; his store smelled of spray paint and welding fumes. He was standing beside the cash register, sweating and talking over a hardboard counter to a young Japanese-American kid about putting a nitrox tank in the kid's Honda.

He didn't recognize Rinker for a moment. Women didn't often come into the shop, and he sort of nodded and said, "Be with you in a minute," and went back to the kid and then suddenly looked back. Rinker lifted her sunglasses and smiled. Burke said, "Holy shit," and then to the kid, "Let me put you with one of my guys. I gotta talk to this lady."

He held up a finger, stuck his head through a door in the back, yelled, "Hey Chuck, c'mere." Chuck came, Burke put him with the kid, then led Rinker into the back and to a ten-by-twenty-foot plywood-enclosed office in the back. He shut the door behind them and said, again, "Holy shit. Clara. I hope, uh . . ."

"I need a clean car that'll run good, with good papers. Something dull like a Taurus or some kind of Buick. Sort of in a hurry," she said. "I was hoping you could help me."

His eyes drifted toward the doors, as though they might suddenly splinter. "Are the cops . . . ?"

"No." She smiled again. "No cops. I just got back in the country, and I need a car. Not that you should mention it, if you happen to bump into a cop."

"No problem there," Burke said. He relaxed a couple of degrees. He liked Clara all right, but she was not a woman he would choose to hang out with. "I can get you something off a used-car lot. The guy'll have to file the papers on it, but he can push the date back—for a while, anyway."

"Not forever?"

"No, he'll have to put them through sooner or later, 'cause of bank inventories. If you only needed it for a month or so, he could fake it out that far. Then, if somebody inquired, the papers would show the transfer to the dealer, and he'd show the transfer to you, but there wouldn't be any license or insurance checks or anything. I can guarantee you that it'd be in perfect condition."

"That'd work. I won't need it for more than a month anyway," she said. "Where do I find the used-car guy?"

"I'll drive you over," Burke said. "You paying cash?"

"You think he'd take a check?" she asked.

Burke grinned, not bothering to answer the mildly sarcastic question, and said, "You're looking pretty good."

She smiled back and said, "Thank you. I've been down in Mexico for a while. Got the tan."

"Look like you've been working out. You've lost a little weight since . . . you know."

"Cut off a couple pounds, maybe," she said. "Got a little sick down there."

"Montezuma's revenge."

"More or less," she said; but her eyes were melancholy, and Burke had the feeling that the sickness had been more serious than that. He didn't ask, and after a pause, Rinker asked, "So where's your used-car guy?"

MUCH LATER THAT afternoon, as they were parting, she tossed her new Rand McNally road atlas onto the passenger seat and said, "If anybody from St. Louis calls, you never saw me."

"I never saw you *ever,*" Burke said. "Don't take this the wrong way, but you make me nervous."

"No reason for it," she said. "Not unless you cross me."

Burke looked at her for a long three seconds and said, finally, "Tell you what, honey. If there was enough money in it, I might mess with the guys in St. Louis. But I'm *nowhere* stupid enough to mess with you."

"Good," she said. She stepped closer, stood on her tiptoes, and pecked him on the cheek. "Jackie, I owe you. I will get back to you someday and we will work something out that will make you happy."

She waved, got into the beet-red Olds she'd bought for $13,200, and drove away, carefully, like a little old lady from Iowa, down toward the freeway entrance. Burke went back inside his shop, dug behind a stack of old phone books, got his stash, got his papers, rolled a joint, and walked out back to smoke it. Cool his nerves.

Clara fuckin' Rinker, Burke thought. She was *pissed* about something. God help somebody; and thank God it wasn't him.

RINKER WAS HEADED east to St. Louis—but not that minute. Instead she drove north on I-5, taking her time, watching her speed. She spent a bad night in Coalinga, rolling around in a king-sized bed, thinking about old friends and Paulo and wishing she still smoked. In the morning, tired, her stomach scar aching, she cut west toward the coast and took the 101 into San Francisco.

Jimmy Cricket was a golf pro with a closet-sized downtown shop called Jimmy Cricket's Pro-Line Golf. He was folding Claiborne golf shirts when Rinker walked in, and he smiled and said, "Can I help you?" He was wearing a royal-blue V-necked sweater that nearly matched his eyes, and dark khaki golf slacks that nearly matched his tan. He had the too-friendly attitude of a man who would give you a half-stroke a hole without asking to see your handicap card.

The store was empty, other than Rinker, so she saw no reason to beat around the bush. "I'd like to buy a couple of guns," she said, her voice casual, holding his eyes. "Semiauto nines, if you've got them. Gotta be cold. I'd take a Ruger .22 if you got it."

"Excuse me?" Jimmy's smile vanished. He was taken aback. This was a *golf* shop—there must be some mistake.

"I'm Rose-Anne, Jimmy," Rinker said. "You left me that gun I used to kill Gerald McKinley. You put it in a tree up in Golden Gate Park and picked up two thousand dollars in twenties. You remember that."

"Jesus," Jimmy said. His Adam's apple bobbed. "McKinley." He hadn't known what happened with the gun, what it would be used for. The McKinley killing had been in the papers for weeks, as had the somewhat (but not too) bereaved young wife and the very bereaved older ex-wife.

"It was a sad thing," Rinker said. "A man in his prime, cut down like that."

"Well, jeez, Rose-Anne, I don't know."

"Cut the crap, Jimmy. I'll give you two thousand bucks apiece for either two or three guns."

Jimmy processed this for a minute, and she could see it all trickling down through his brain, like raindrops of thought on a windowpane. Okay, he'd been offered money, in the face of his denials. If she was a cop, it'd be entrapment. And if she was a cop, and knew about the tree in the park, he was probably fucked anyway. *And* if she were Rose-Anne and he didn't sell her the guns, then he might be truly and ultimately fucked. Therefore, he would sell her the guns.

"Uh . . . maybe you should step into the back." The back was behind a green cloth curtain, smelled of bubble wrap and cardboard, and was full of golf-club shipping boxes and club racks. At the far end was a workbench with a vise. Jimmy pushed a couple of boxes aside and pulled out a tan gym bag, unzipped it, and said, "This is what I got."

Rinker, watching his eyes, decided he was okay, took the bag, stepped back, and looked inside. Three revolvers and three semiautos. All three semiautos were military-style 9mm Berettas. She took one out, popped the magazine—the magazine was empty—cycled the action a couple of times, did the same with the other two, and said, "I'll take them." She looked at the revolvers: One was a .22, and she put it with the automatics. "You got any long guns?"

"No. I know where you might be able to pick some up, if you want to run down to Bakersfield."

She shook her head. "Naw. I can get my own. How about ammo?"

"I can give you a couple of boxes of Federal hollowpoint for the nines, but I don't have any .22 on hand."

"Give me the nine," she said. "Silencer?"

"Um, I usually charge two thousand. Good ones are hard to get."

"Can you get it quick?"

"Yes."

"Another two thousand, if it's a good one."

"It's a Coeur d'Alene."

"I'll take it."

He fished around in another box and came up with a purple velvet bag that had once contained a bottle of Scotch. He handed it to her and said, "Quick enough?"

She took the bag, slipped the silencer out. It was a Coeur d'Alene, all right; the absolutely faultless blued finish was the signature. Somewhere, a master machinist was doing artwork. She screwed the silencer onto one of the nines and flipped it out to arm's length, to test the balance. "Good. I'll take the whole bunch."

Jimmy nodded, said, "Okay," moved some more boxes around, picked up a small one, reached inside, and produced two boxes of nine-millimeter ammunition. He handed them to her and asked, "You in town for long?"

Her mouth wasn't grim, but she wasn't exactly radiating warmth. "I was never here," she said.

"Gotcha," said Jimmy Cricket.

RINKER SPENT THE night in a motel outside Sacramento, drawing squares and triangles on a yellow legal pad. Killing wasn't hard: Any asshole could kill somebody. Doing it often, and getting away with it every time, was much harder. What had made her a good killer—besides the lack of revulsion with the job—was her ability to plan. She planned with yellow pads, not in words and paragraphs, but in triangles and spirals, a few with names above them, some with lines connecting them to other symbols. Sometimes she made maps.

Aside from the killing, Rinker hadn't been much different from other young successful businesswomen in Wichita, Kansas, until her facade broke down and she'd had to run. She'd owned a friendly country bar called the Rink, with dancing all the time and live music on weekends. She had a nice apartment that she'd decorated herself, went part-time to Wichita State, and would have liked to have had a pet, but traveled too much to feel good about it. She didn't like fuzzy stuffed animal toys or chocolate hearts, but did tarry at times in front of Victoria's Secret display windows. She had an interest in makeup, read a couple of women's magazines, liked to dance, got a massage once a month, and would drink a beer or a glass of wine.

She liked guns, and the power that grew out of them. Knew enough about semiautos to do her own trigger jobs. Wasn't much interested in cars. Like that.

Lying on the bed in Sacramento, she wrote four names on her legal pad: John Ross, Nanny Dichter, Andy Levy, Paul Dallaglio. All of them knew her face. All of them had the clout to send a gun to kill her. All of them had probably agreed to do it, since they all talked to each other, wouldn't have wanted to go against the others, and because all four must have been worried about her running around loose.

The problem was, Rinker knew *way* too much. She knew where the bodies were buried, and that wasn't a joke, not in the several states where the four men operated, all those good states having opted for capital punishment. If Rinker was taken alive, and if she decided to cut a deal . . .

Rinker lay on the bed and put together an outline. She could fill it in while she drove.

FROM SACRAMENTO TO St. Louis is three solid days, if you're driving a used Oldsmobile, don't want to attract attention, and stay with it. Rinker took four days, passing from one FM station to the next, hard rock to soft jazz to country, through two sets of mountains with a desert between them, then out on the Great Plains, I-80 to Cheyenne, I-25 into Denver, across Kansas and Missouri on I-70, into St. Louis: Red Roof Inn and Best Western, BP and Shell, McDonald's and Burger King and Taco Bell and the Colonel. She stopped at four different shopping centers. She got her hair cut, tight to her head, punky, so that a wig would fit over it. She bought wigs, good ones, in black, red, and blond shoulder-length.

She talked to a woman at a Nordstrom's makeup bar about a Mexican friend of hers who had suffered a facial burn and needed some dark cover-up makeup to conceal the burn, and she got instruction on how to use it. She played with the makeup, trying to make herself look Mexican, but it never quite worked. Instead of brown, she looked orange, and odd. She eventually decided that the black wig looked okay with just a bit of dark eyebrow pencil, as long as she wore long-sleeved blouses.

With a couple of changes of clothes—one from Nordstrom's, one from Kmart—she'd have six distinct looks. Even a good friend of the Nordstrom's perky Light Lady would never recognize the funky Kmart Red. . . .

And she made some calls, cautiously. Had to call three times, starting with the first day in L.A., before she finally got through. Said, "This is me. You remember me?"

"Oh, my God. Where are you at?"

"Out east. Pennsylvania. How's life?"

"I've run out of time. Like we talked about."

"What are you going to do?"

"You know . . ."

"I've got an idea, but I haven't worked it out yet. I'll call you back. When's good?"

"Three o'clock is good. Like now."

"This line?"

"Yeah . . . this is as good as any. You never know, though." Never know what might be monitored.

"I'll get you a clean phone," Rinker said. "I'll call again. Three o'clock."

WHEN SHE'D BEEN pushed out of her life, forced to go on the run, Rinker had been killing people for a long time—felt like a long time, anyway. She was not deliberately cruel in her paid assassinations. She did the shooting and went on her way, a businesswoman taking care of business. She had once been necessarily cruel to a man in Minnesota who'd betrayed her, but that had been a matter of survival. She still thought about him from time to time. She wasn't morbidly fascinated or neurotically fixated, but the image of his body tied to the bed sometimes popped into her mind's eye as she drifted off to sleep.

The fear he'd shown. She thought about the fear as she drove—and the other fears she inspired.

The people who'd directed her, who'd used her as a weapon, had no reason to fear her guns, because Rinker was entirely loyal to friends. These were people who'd helped her out of a life that had been headed straight for a white-trash ghetto. She appreciated that. If the cops had taken her, she would have gone to the gas chamber, or the death gurney, or whatever it was, without saying a word.

These former friends didn't know that. Or decided they couldn't be sure. If they'd simply tried to kill her and had failed, she might have let it go, on the rational grounds that if she hit back at them, she was putting herself at risk.

They hadn't just failed. They'd killed her lover, they'd killed her baby, and they were most likely still looking for her now, not just from fear of the consequences if she was caught, but fear of her guns. No matter where she went, there was always the possibility that some asshole from St. Louis would pick her out of a crowd, and another gun would be sent.

There was no question that her survival in Cancún had been a matter of luck. As Rinker had once told another woman who'd been interested in her business, *anyone* can be killed, if the assassin is patient enough and the victim is not aware of a particular threat. She didn't exempt herself from that truism. She'd never felt a thing in Cancún. She hadn't known she'd been spotted, hadn't known she'd been stalked. The only guarantee of survival was the elimination of the threat.

AND THERE WAS the revenge factor.

She'd had few friends as a child. She'd taken care of her younger brother, who was somehow wrong in the head: not stupid, but constantly preoccupied, even as a baby, but he was not really a friend. He was too much younger, and too psychologically distant.

There were two or three girls from school that she could recall, but only one that was close—the one she hoped was still living in St. Louis. Her stepfather and older brother had thoroughly abused her, and the sense of abuse had kept people away. In that part of the country, nobody would say much, but people would know, and stay clear. Watching Rinker grow up was like watching a slow-motion car wreck.

Her life in St. Louis hadn't been much different. The people she knew well, with three or four exceptions, mostly feared her. Then she'd been in Wichita, and in Wichita, there'd been two or three people that she might have become close to, but she hadn't quite gotten there, when the cops had broken her out.

Then she'd had to run, and almost magically, everything had changed. She'd found a friend in Mexico, in Paulo. Both a lover and a friend. The beginnings of several friendships, really, and the beginning of a family—she loved Paulo, and she also liked and laughed with and felt safe with his brothers and his parents. They seemed to like her back. She'd started taking birth control pills when things got serious with Paulo, but after a few months, when she needed to refill the prescription, she simply hadn't. Kept thinking, *Gotta do it,* but didn't.

The missed period could have been natural, a change in the way she lived . . . but she knew better than that. Felt nothing stirring yet, but felt heavier, more serious.

A child.

Then the gun. And Paulo was gone, and the child, and the family . . .

DRIVING ACROSS THE high plains, late at night, she had what she later thought was a vision, or wide-awake dream: She saw her child, a girl, a dark-haired kid playing on a tree swing in what must have been the Yucatán. Paulo was there, wearing a pair of white pleated shorts, bare-chested and barefoot, pushing her. Water in the background, so it must have been near the coast; and then the little girl screamed with laughter and Paulo stopped pushing her and walked around the path of the swing and Rinker could see a hand, her hand, with a Popsicle reaching toward

Paulo. Their hands touched, and there was a spark, and he was gone, with the vision.

She snapped back to the present, and far away, saw the lights of a truck approaching down the interstate. How long she'd been on mental cruise control she didn't know, but she felt that she'd been there, in a different future. She could see the little girl now—her little girl—in her mind's eye, and Paulo five years older, and her own life, and she began to weep, holding tight to the steering wheel, weaving down the highway.

IF THE PEOPLE in St. Louis feared her guns, they had good reason.

RINKER GOT OFF the interstate highway system at Kansas City, made a phone call from a mall. A man answered with an abrupt "What?"

Rinker, leaning on a trashy south-Missouri accent, asked, "Is this Arveeda?"

"Sound like fuckin' Arveeda?" The phone crashed down on the hook, and she smiled: T. J. Baker was still in residence and, from the sound of it, still an asshole. Out of Kansas City, she turned south on local highways, headed for the town of Tisdale, fifteen miles east of Springfield. The biggest industry in Tisdale was the poultry-processing factory, which killed and plucked six thousand chickens a day, and left the entire town smelling like wet chickenshit and burned feathers. Hell of a thing, she thought, when the thing you remembered most about your hometown was the bad smell.

At midafternoon she stopped again, made another call. A man answered: "Sgt, McCallum, ordnance."

She smiled and hung up. She dialed again, a different number, and a different man answered.

"Yes?"

The voice was a slap in the face, and her lingering smile vanished. The last time she'd heard the voice, she'd been threatening its owner with death. She almost hung up, but hesitated.

"Yes? Hello?"

Rinker said, "You killed my baby. I wanted you to know that. I was pregnant, and a piece of slug hit me in the stomach and I lost the baby."

He was as startled as she'd been a moment earlier. He got it together and said, "Clara, I heard something about this, but I . . ."

"Don't lie to me. I'm coming to kill you, and I wanted to give you time to think about it, instead of just popping up and shooting you in the head. I want you to think about what you're losing: all the rest of your life."

After a moment of silence, the man chuckled and said, "Ah, shit, what can I tell you? Bring it on, Clara. You know where to find me. I'll tell you what, though, don't let me catch you. I'd have to make an example out of you. Now, you got anything else?"

"That's about it. You'll be hearing from me."

The man laughed and said, "Yeah, well—take it easy, honey."

"You, too."

T. J. BAKER LIVED in a weathered white house next to a creek outside the west city limit of Tisdale; the house was surrounded by a chain-link fence. Two pit bulls roamed the yard, only marginally restrained by their long chains. Baker was rough with the dogs, whipping them regularly with a wide leather belt until they screamed with anger. They'd be killing rough on anyone who crossed into the yard while they were out—though that was not likely to happen.

The fence was spotted with signs that said "Beware of Dog," and if an illiterate trespasser happened along, one look at the dogs themselves would be warning enough.

Rinker called Baker twice from Springfield, once at six o'clock and once after dinner, at seven, and got no answer. Baker had always preferred the second shift at the chicken factory, because it gave him daylight with the dogs, or to hunt. Or kill, anyway. His greatest joy was sniping rats at the landfill.

WHEN THE SECOND call got no answer, she called the chicken factory, asked for Baker by name, and finally was put through to a man who said, "Hang on, I gotta find him. He was here a minute ago."

"Ah, that's okay. If he's not right there, I'll call back."

"Whatever."

She got in the Olds and drove out of Springfield; thought about driving past the place she'd grown up, where her mother still lived, but decided against it. There was really nothing she wanted to see, nobody she wanted to talk to. She went instead to Tisdale, through town, past the Dairy Queen and Haber's Drive-In Root Beer, which was closed, boarded up, past the bank and the pharmacy and the bakery and out the west side.

Baker's house was on a county road, his nearest neighbor a half-mile away. His driveway ended at a ramshackle garage that looked as though it had been too long blown upon by the northwest wind; it leaned toward the house, shingles peeling off, paint shedding into the pastel-pink hollyhocks that surrounded the brick foundation.

Rinker pulled nose-in to the gate. The dogs had been sitting near their stake, in the middle of the yard, in a dirt circle worn free of grass. When she pulled up, they stood, silently, watching. When she lifted the latch on the gate, they moved, like black-and-tan leopards, toward her, still silent, disciplined like soldiers, dragging their long chains. She walked the gate open, careful to stay out of range of the dogs, got back in her car, and drove up to the garage.

Now she was in killing range, and the dogs moved up to the driver's side of the car. They were snuffling, a sound that was almost a growl but not quite: The throaty slavering was actually more threatening than a growl. They sounded like they wanted to *eat.*

Rinker reached under the seat and took out the .22. She'd bought a box of standard-velocity hollowpoints at a Wal-Mart in Kansas City. She checked it, almost unconsciously, then ran the window down. The bigger of the two dogs stood on its hind feet, its front feet lightly on the door. It was peering directly at her, and she remembered reading in a book somewhere about a killing dog that had eyes like coal. This was *that dog:* The black eyes peered at her, hungered after her. This dog *wanted* her.

No romantic when it came to dogs, she pointed the pistol at the animal's head and shot it between the coal-black eyes. No romantic itself, it dropped dead. The other dog took a step back, looking at its dead companion. Before it could do anything else, Rinker killed it.

The two shots sounded like nothing else but shots. If anyone was at the house a half mile away, the shots might have sounded like popcorn popping. Two light pops in the evening breeze, coming from Baker's house. She doubted that anyone would be curious.

On the other hand, there was no point in taking chances. She dragged the dead dogs back to the stake in the middle of the yard and rolled them upright, as though they were sleeping on duty.

Baker's back door had another sign: "Forget the Dog, Beware of Owner." Rinker ignored it, and used the butt of the pistol to knock a hole in the window. She reached through, flipped the bolt, and let herself in.

Baker had two gun cabinets that she knew of, both of them bolted into the concrete floor in the basement. Neither was really a safe, in the strictest sense, but they wouldn't be easy to get into, either. Rinker intended to use an ax on the doors, and if that didn't work . . . well, bad luck for Baker. She'd wait for him to come home.

Now she called out: "Anybody home?"

Nothing but silence. She went to the basement door, turned on the light, and went down the stairs. The two gun safes sat at the far end of the basement; one of them was open an inch. Empty? Unlikely. More likely that Baker just started feeling safe, all these years gone by with no burglaries, the dogs in the yard, his reputation . . .

Fuckin' Baker, she thought. Leaving the door like that was purely laziness. She reached out to pull it open, but with her hand just an inch away, she stopped. Boy, that was convenient, the way the door just hung there. Rinker didn't believe that life was easy. Something was wrong. She stepped away, looked around, spotted a length of two-by-two propped in a corner. She got it, stood back away from the safe, and eased the door open.

The shotgun blast nearly killed her—not from the steel shot, but from the shock of it. The gun was behind her, under the stairs. The blast had gone right past her into the gun safe. She staggered back away from it, her legs stinging, her hands at her ears. She was deaf, her head aching, her eyes watering. Her legs hurt. She looked down; her jeans looked okay, but when she lifted the pant legs, she found little stripes of blood trickling down into her socks.

She left the gun safe and went back upstairs and peeled off the pants in the light of the kitchen. She'd been hit by three pellets, all ricochets, all buried just beneath her skin. She popped them out with her fingertips, found some Band-Aids and a bottle of peroxide in the bathroom, wiped the wounds and bandaged them.

Fuckin' Baker. As she worked, the ringing in her ears faded, and she could again hear her feet moving around on the bathroom floor.

When she was done, she went back downstairs and looked at the now-empty double-barreled shotgun. It had been rigged with a simple wire on a pulley. The wire ran from the safe door, through a hole in the back of the safe to a pulley on the wall, up to the ceiling joists, across another pulley to the stairs, down to the trigger on the shotgun. The trigger itself had the lightest pull she'd ever experienced in a weapon. She was tempted to rig it backward, pointing up the stairs, but hell—it was *his* house.

She went back up the stairs, out to the garage, got Baker's ax, carried it into the basement, and went after the second gun safe. She worked at it methodically, and it took her five minutes, cutting through the front, then using the ax handle to pry a gap in the metal. There were nine rifles in the safe, all with scopes: four bolt-action varmint rifles, two in .22-250 and two in .223; three bolt-actions in larger calibers, a Remington 7mm Magnum, a Steyr .308 and a Winchester .243; plus two semiautos, a Ruger Ranch Rifle in .223 and a military-style AR-15, also in .223. Three gun cases were stacked beside the safes; each could handle two rifles. She packed the three larger calibers, plus the AR-15 and the two .223 bolt-actions, and carried them up to the car. She threw the other three rifles on top of the packed guns, and around them she stacked seventeen boxes of ammunition, two shooters' sandbags, two packs of paper targets, and a sawhorse with a clamp on the bottom, which was used to hold the targets.

She didn't need all the stuff, but couldn't afford to be selective. Gun thieves wouldn't be, and she'd prefer that nobody got the idea that Clara Rinker had long guns. As she was leaving, she thought again about the shotgun, and thought about burning the house down. Decided against it, looking at the lumps of dead dog in the front yard. Pretty even, she thought, though her ears were still ringing.

She left Tisdale an hour after dark, headed northeast, toward St. Louis. In the dark she crossed a river, stopped, and threw the three loose rifles into the dark water. She spent the night halfway up the state, in a cash motel in the town of Diffley. There was an abandoned quarry outside Diffley, where the locals sighted-in their guns. Not many people went, and in her gunning days, she'd often driven down from St. Louis to work with new pistols.

The next morning she got an egg-and-sausage McMuffin at McDonald's, then drove out to the quarry. She was alone, and spent an hour sighting the rifles, leaving the AR-15 for last. The AR-15 looked a lot like Jaime's M-16, and even had a selector switch. She fired off a couple of single rounds, landing them just where she'd expected. Then she flipped the selector switch, aimed it, and squeezed off a burst.

Whoa. It *was* full-auto. She looked around, a little self-consciously—if anyone had heard *that,* she could be in trouble.

All the guns were right on, as she expected. After the burst of automatic fire, she decided she'd better get out of town. She quickly but carefully repacked the guns, got out of the quarry, and drove the familiar, homey roads into St. Louis.

SHE'D ALWAYS LIKED the place. Neat town, lots of things to do. Good bars, and she was a student of good bars. Rolled down along Forest Park, stopped in Central West End and got a sandwich, picked up a book, and walked around in the afternoon, getting back into the feel of the place. She did a little shopping, and then, at four o'clock, went down to the southeast corner of the city, to Soulard, along the Mississippi. She sat in the car and drew more triangles and squares on her yellow legal pad as she watched the people come and go on the sidewalk. She thought about the vision she'd had of the dark-haired girl, closed her eyes, and let the feeling come back. But now all she had was a memory. The vision was gone.

Outside the car, a woman walked by, carrying a string bag with what looked like a green glass lamp inside. She was a large woman, and Rinker sat up when she saw her coming. Then she thought, after a minute, *Too old.*

The woman she was looking for was three years older than Rinker. Her name—now—was Dorothy Pollock.

6

BEFORE THEY LEFT CANCÚN, LUCAS ASKED MALONE IF she could either lend him a copy of the Rinker file he'd scanned in the plane coming down, or make a copy and send it to him in Minneapolis. She shook her head: "A lot of that stuff is speculation. We're not even supposed to show it to you the first time."

"You mean it's classified or something?"

"Like that."

"Like if it got out, Rinker could sue you?"

"Like if it got out, there are about a hundred people who could sue us. They wouldn't, but they'd be calling up their friends in Congress, who'd be pissing and moaning about violations of privacy and human rights and the way we spend our budget."

"If I can't copy it, could I read it overnight? Spend some time with it?"

"Sure." She said it without thinking, because she didn't actually know him very well. "Give it back to me in the morning."

THE BLUE PALMS didn't have a business center, but the Hilton did.

In the evening, after dinner, Lucas told Mallard he felt like a walk. The heavy food and all. He strolled six blocks down to the Hilton and talked to the concierge about the business center. He was a writer from Los Angeles, he said, and he needed access to a xerox machine very late in the evening, as soon as he finished compiling his research. Would it be possible to rent one of the Hilton's machines for a couple of hours?

That courtesy was not usually extended outside the hotel, the concierge said. He would have to think about it—and after thinking about it, he decided that it would be a generous thing to do, and would help the Hilton's image with traveling businessmen. At one in the morning, Lucas walked back with the file, met the concierge, and took care of the rental and courtesy fees. By two-thirty, he'd finished copying the file, and by three o'clock, was safely back in bed, the copy snugged away with his shirts.

The next morning, they gathered in the lobby to check out, and Lucas gave Mallard a look. Mallard turned away.

There'd been no *moment* with Malone, Lucas thought. He muttered "Chicken," and Malone asked, "What?"

"Nothing."

Lucas held on to Malone's copy of the Rinker file until they got to Houston, where they split up. "If there's anything I can do, call me," Lucas said. He handed the file back to her. "Sorry I wasn't more help in Cancún. If I think of anything from the file, I'll call."

"You helped," Mallard said. "Between us, we gave old man Mejia, ummm, a *clearer* view of the situation. There are things that Malone and I just can't say."

Lucas nodded. "Whatever. I'll be watching you guys. When are you going to St. Louis?"

"We're already moving our setup crew in. Malone and I will be there as soon as there's any hint that she's there," Mallard said. "Given her whole psychology, the way she was abused from the time she was a kid, then her true love getting shot, and losing the baby . . . can you think of any more likely place than St. Louis to pull her in?"

Lucas shook his head. "Nope. If I were her, I'd be there."

Malone smiled at him, her nasty lawyer's smile. "That's another reason we asked you. You two think alike."

LUCAS WAS BACK in Minneapolis by midafternoon, having unexpectedly survived both flights. He stopped first at the new house, counted six guys working on it, talked to the foreman, and was told that the cable and telephone wiring was going in the next day. He collected a sample pad of parquet blocks that the designer was proposing for the library floor, and headed downtown.

MARCY SHERRILL WAS sitting at her desk, staring at a computer screen, when Lucas walked in. "How's Cancún?" she asked, looking up.

"Hot and humid. Full of foreigners," Lucas said. He yawned: already a long day. "Anything new?"

"Ummm . . . Bob Cline croaked yesterday—did you know him?"

"Yeah, vaguely." Cline was an aging radio talk show host known for his unwavering support of the police department, no matter who had done what. "How'd he die?"

"Heart attack, I guess. He was at a Saints game and he was on his way home when he pulled over to the side of the road and died. Called 911 on the car phone but never said a word."

"Not a bad way to go. . . . Anything else?"

"Rose Marie wants you to come by. She called twice. The homicide guys—Sloan, basically—got the name of a kid in that bus-stop drive-by on Thirty-third. They say he's the one, but they can't find him. His family says he went to New York, which probably means we oughta look in L.A."

"That's it?"

"That's it."

"All right. I'll go talk to Rose Marie." He yawned again. "What're you doing?"

She yawned back, picking it up from him. "Vacation and comp time report."

"Okay." He opened his briefcase, took out the copy of the FBI report, which he'd transferred from his suitcase, and handed it to her. "I sneaked a copy—this is illegal. Read it and tell me what you think."

"How was Malone?" She asked the question with a *tone.*

"Be nice," Lucas said. "She's dating a paperhanger or something."

"You mean like Hitler?"

"What?" She'd lost him.

"Hitler was supposed to be a wallpaper guy, or something. Before he became a dictator."

"Oh. Well, he's not exactly like Hitler, I don't think. I'll ask her next time I see her. . . . Read the file. Mallard's in love with her. With Malone."

Marcy perked up. "Which one told you that? Or did you just *perceive* it?"

"Mallard told me. I told him to grab her ass, but he didn't."

"Jesus, Lucas, grab her *ass*?" She was appalled.

"You know what I mean. Make a *move.*"

"Grab her ass," Sherrill said, shaking her head. "He told him to grab her ass."

"Not exactly that . . ." Then he had to explain, but it was too late. As soon as the word *ass* had come out of his mouth, he'd fulfilled all female expectations of insensitivity, and nothing more was necessary. He finally gave up trying to explain and went to see Rose Marie Roux, the chief of police.

LUCAS SOMETIMES SUSPECTED that the chief was a self-switching manic-depressive, willing herself into periods of gloom or frenzy as an antidote to the emotional control required of her chiefdom. When he walked into her office, and found her smoking one cigarette while another one burned in an ashtray on the windowsill, he realized that she'd pushed herself into the manic.

"You're gonna get busted someday on the cigarettes," he grunted, waving a hand through the layered smoke. Her office smelled like a seventies bowling alley, and indoor smoking was prohibited in Minneapolis.

"I'm down fifteen pounds since I started smoking again," she said. "When I get down twenty, I'll go on a program to maintain the weight, and then quit again. I just didn't quit the right way, last time."

"That's the stupidest thing you've ever said," Lucas said, irritably. "In the meantime, you've got two cigarettes going."

"Yeah, yeah." She snuffed out both butts, dug through a pile of paper on her desk, and said, "Sherrill got the top score."

Lucas smiled, dropped into her guest chair. "Excellent. I thought she might."

"Which means that if we can get Pellegrino to retire, I can slip her into that slot as a temporary replacement. She'd have to wear a uniform for a month or so, but then Leman will go in September, and I can move her into his slot, and she'd be set. It's a regular lieutenant's job."

"She'll be good at it," Lucas said.

"Not only that, she'll owe us," Rose Marie said.

"So what about Pellegrino?"

"I'm talking to him. He's at the max percentage for his retirement, so his only reason to stay here is to pick up any pay raises that come along. But if he moves over to the state, he's in a whole different retirement plan, so he gets a double dip. There's a slot in the public information office that's empty, and he'd be perfect for it."

"Is he gonna take it?" Lucas asked.

"Yes. His wife's nervous, but she's coming around."

"What about the governor? Unless he commits to you publicly . . ."

"He's making the announcement Friday. I'll take over as of November 1. I'll leave here October 15, and you can leave anytime you want. You probably wouldn't actually get pushed until the new guy comes in, and that might not be until the first of the year."

"I'm gonna go when you go," Lucas said. "But Jesus, two and a half months. If we're gonna swap Marcy for Pellegrino, we gotta get him out of here quick."

"He'll put in his papers next week."

They talked about the personnel maneuvers for another ten minutes. The mayor was not running for reelection, and none of the leading candidates would reappoint Rose Marie as chief: She'd made too many bureaucratic enemies during her tenure. So she was out.

But as a former longtime state senator, she had solid political connections and loyalties. When the governor, Elmer Henderson, had gone looking for a new director for the department of public safety, a group of her political pals had had a quiet word with him, and she'd been anointed.

As soon as the deal was done, she'd begun shuffling members of her city management team into protected job slots—Marcy Sherrill would be the new head of Intelligence—and slipping old departmental enemies into jobs where they would be lethally exposed. The new mayor might not be willing to appoint Rose Marie to a third term as chief, but he was going to get her team whether he liked it or not.

With a few exceptions.

Lucas was a pure political appointee, with no civil-service protection at all, and his job would expire with hers. Rather than try to find a protected slot, he'd agreed to follow her to the state, where he would head a new special investigations team with the state Bureau of Criminal Apprehension.

Del Capslock would leave Minneapolis at the same time, to join Lucas's team. Lucas had also quietly offered a job to his old friend Sloan, but Sloan had decided to stay with the city: He was nonpolitical, liked what he was doing, didn't need the double dip, and suspected that the state job would take him out of town too much.

When they finished the personnel talk, Rose Marie leaned back in her chair, lit a cigarette with a blue plastic Bic, and asked, "Was it Rinker?"

"Yes. They think she's headed up to St. Louis. Gonna kill a few assholes."

Rose Marie shrugged and said, "Part of the overhead."

Lucas agreed. If you went into organized crime, sooner or later you'd get the bill. "Yeah. For Rinker, too. They're gonna try to trap her. They're already papering the motels and hotels and bars with the old photographs and the composites. They're moving a big special team in, all hush-hush. They've mostly cut out the St. Louis cops."

"Are you going back down?"

"If they ask, I guess," Lucas said. "It's an interesting situation—a top killer turning on her own people, with all her special knowledge. With her record of successful hits, the knuckleheads gotta be pretty freaked out."

"And no matter what happens, the FBI wins," Rose Marie said, peering at the ceiling. "If she kills a few people, they can squeeze the rest of the assholes with protection deals. If they catch her, they can squeeze her with the death penalty."

"Yeah—and she's out for revenge, too, so if the feebs get their hands on her, they've got that going. Another reason for her to talk. Not much downside."

Rose Marie puffed on the cigarette, exhaled, smiled, and said, "The governor liked that shit we did with Qatar." Qatar was a recently deceased serial killer. "If we could squeeze a little more good PR out of St. Louis, it'd be worth doing. Elmer got elected on his family money, and everybody considered him a pencil-necked geek. He likes the idea of having his own goon squad. Makes his testicles swell up."

"I thought it was idealism," Lucas said.

Rose Marie snorted. "Let me know when anything happens."

ON THE WAY OUT of the building, an old-timer cop sidled toward him and Lucas said, "Ah, Jesus, Hempsted, go away."

"I just got a business tip for you," the cop protested. "You heard about the big Pillsbury merger, right?"

"Something about it," Lucas admitted.

"Well, after everything was said and done, Pillsbury wound up owing the Trojan company."

"What?"

"Yeah. They're coming up with a self-rising condom."

"Get away from me, dickweed."

"You're laughing to yourself, Davenport," Hempsted called after him. "I can always tell."

WEATHER KARKINNEN WAS sitting at her desk in her office at Hennepin General, peering into a computer monitor.

Lucas caught her unaware, and leaned in the doorway, watching her face. She'd put on weight with the pregnancy, had gone rounder and softer. She'd always been a sailor, the girl on the foredeck hauling on the spinnaker, wide shoulders and crooked nose, the sun-bleached hair and windburned cheekbones. The softness and weight was so different—he'd seen her, just out of bed in the morning, standing naked in front of a door-mounted mirror, measuring the changes in herself.

She moaned about the weight, about the changes in her figure. But it all sounded to Lucas like the war stories he'd heard from other women who'd gone through childbirth, stories akin to male basic-training tales, but female, a bunch of women sitting around talking about water weight and stretch marks and ultrasounds and episiotomies.

"YOU LOOK TERRIFIC," he said, and she jumped.

"God, don't do that," she said, smiling, blue eyes crinkling at the corners. She stood up, stretched, and came around the desk, put her arms around his waist, and stood on tiptoe to kiss him.

"I mean it," he said. He had her hands on her waist, his thumbs near her navel, the growing part of her. "You make my heart feel funny when I look at you."

"That kind of talk could get you somewhere," she said. "When did you get back?"

"Just a few minutes ago," Lucas said. "Talked to Rose Marie—the conspiracy is flourishing. She'll quit Minneapolis in the middle of October and move over to the state on November first."

"That'll be the busy season, with the baby coming."

Lucas nodded. "I don't have to be there the exact minute she is. I'm thinking, I could quit Minneapolis when she does, but not move over to the state until December or January. Have a couple of months off to get the house together and you and the kid set up."

She tapped him on the chest. "That's the best idea you've had in weeks."

"So we'll do that," he said.

"How about Rinker? Was it her? Are you going to be involved?"

"Maybe. The feebs think she's headed for St. Louis. As soon as something happens, they'll let me know what they want to do."

BUT NOTHING HAPPENED. A week went by. Lucas and Weather spent one Sunday sailing in a regatta on Lake Minnetonka, and Lucas took two days to work on his Wisconsin cabin, never far from the cell phone.

Finally, he called Mallard. "What's up?"

"Malone's been out in L.A., squeezing the brother. Not getting much."

"He probably doesn't know much, if that file was right."

"It's a little more than that. . . . He's borderline mentally impaired. Not dumb, exactly, but not quite right. The public defender is giving us a hard time about holding him, but we're gonna hang on anyway. We figure we can keep him for a couple of months before we have to go to trial."

"How about Clara?"

"Nothing. She's gone," Mallard said.

"You still think . . . ?"

"Doesn't matter what I think. St. Louis is what I've got, and that's what I'm sticking with."

7

DOROTHY POLLOCK WAS A HEAVYSET, HARD-FACED WOMAN, pale from a life under fluorescent lights, a duck waddler with bad feet from standing on concrete floors, a victim of Ballard-McClain Avionics, where she worked at a drill-press station.

Her job came to this: She would take a nickel-sized aluminum disk from a Tupperware pan full of disks, and an extruded aluminum shaft, about the length and thickness of a pencil, from a pan full of shafts.

Each disk had a collar at the center, with a hole through the collar, so it looked like a small wheel. Pollock would fit the end of a shaft through the hole, make a ⅓₂-inch freshly drilled hole through the collar and shaft, and then tap an aluminum rivet into the hole. Finally, she'd use a pair of hand pinchers to crush the ends of the rivet, fixing the disk to the shaft. She'd drop the finished shaft, which would become a tuning knob on a radio, into another plastic bin. Then she'd make another one.

Every hour or so the foreman would come by and take away the finished shafts. Pollock was expected to finish a hundred shafts every shift. She got two fifteen-minute breaks, one in the morning and one in the afternoon, and a half hour for lunch, which she could stretch to forty minutes if she didn't do it too often. She made $9.48 an hour, and the year before had gotten a 28-cent-an-hour raise, which worked out to a little more than three percent, or $11.20 a week.

She'd taken the raise, but hadn't been doing any handsprings about it. If she saved all the extra money for a month, she'd have just enough, after deductions for Social Security, state and federal income taxes, and union dues, to pay for a bad haircut. She wasn't all that unhappy when Clara Rinker came along and offered to pay her a thousand dollars a week for her spare room.

Not that she had much choice, if she'd thought about it. Twelve years earlier, in Memphis, Pollock had killed her husband, Roger, in his sleep, by hitting him six times on the head with a hammer. While she was hiding out in Alabama, she'd read a smart-ass newspaper column in the *Commercial-Appeal* that quoted a prosecutor as saying the first four whacks could have been emotional, but the last two indicated intent: They were looking for her on a first-degree murder warrant.

The cops never caught up with her. Rinker had, in fact, taken her in, had hidden her, had used her special skills to get Pollock a new name, an apartment and a job.

POLLOCK HAD BEEN walking home from work, sweating from the humid evening heat, through the bread-smelling yeasty air outside the Anheuser-Busch brewery, carrying a plastic grocery sack containing a loaf of white bread, a vacuum-sealed variety pack of sliced salami, and a six-pack of low-cal custard puddings, when she saw Rinker cutting across the street toward her.

She hadn't seen Rinker for three years, except in the newspapers. She stopped and said, delighted, smiling, "Clara! My Lord! Where you been, girl?"

"Been a while, Patsy," Clara said, smiling back, and calling Pollock by her real name.

"My Lord, you look *good,*" Pollock said. And thought: *She does.* She and Rinker went back to childhood, growing up in similar trashy small towns. Both had changed, Pollock for the worse, Rinker for the better.

Pollock had always been too tall, too skinny, with hands and feet too big for her bones. Over the years, she'd put on sixty pounds, and limped with the weight and weariness, like a woman fifteen years older. Rinker, on the other hand, was wearing jeans and a white blouse that looked fitted to her, with a haircut that cost a hell of a lot more than thirty dollars; and she held herself as rich ladies did, straight up, easy-walking, casual-eyed. Small hoop earrings that looked like gold.

"You still drink beer?" Clara asked.

" 'Course I do. You got some?"

"A sackful of Corona and a couple of lemons. I gotta talk to you about something."

Rinker got a grocery bag out of her car and she and Pollock walked side by side down the slanting sidewalk. Pollock had a two-bedroom apartment in a red brick house that had been painted white and looked as though Mark Twain might have walked past it. An elm tree had once stood in the patch of front yard, but had died years back of Dutch elm disease. The stump was still there, along with what her neighbors called a sucker maple, a clump of foliage that was a cross between a tree and a bush.

Pollock's apartment was two-bedroom only technically—the second bedroom might have been more useful as a closet. Pollock called it her shit room, because that's where she put all the shit she didn't use much. The place smelled of twelve years of baked potatoes and cheddar cheese and nicotine and human dirt. A small dry aquarium sat in a corner, the goldfish long gone. A photograph of Jesus hung over the TV, his hands pressed together in prayer, his eyes turned heavenward, his sacred heart glowing through his robe.

Rinker followed Pollock through the door and looked around. She didn't say, "Nice place," because Pollock was too old a friend, and they both knew exactly what kind of place it was: the kind of place that you could still rent for two hundred and fifty dollars a month, utilities included.

Pollock dropped her grocery sack on the kitchen table and said, "You want some ice in that beer?"

"Wouldn't mind," Rinker said. They'd drunk iced beer when they were kids. She put her bag on the table next to Pollock's, fished out a couple of bottles, and twisted the tops off. Pollock found glasses and filled them with ice, put a slice of lemon in each and a dash of salt. They went out to the front room, and Pollock dropped on her couch. Rinker took the La-Z-Boy, poured a little of the Corona over the ice, and held her glass up. "Big City," she said.

Pollock held hers up: "Big City." They both took a sip, and then Pollock said, "What's going on?"

"I'm running from the cops," Rinker said. "I need a place to stay for a couple of weeks."

"You got one," Pollock said promptly.

"More complicated than that, Patsy," Rinker said. "This is heavy shit. Everybody in the world is gonna be looking for me. The FBI, the St. Louis cops. If they find me here, and take you in, and fingerprint you, you're toast."

Pollock shook her head. "Makes no never-mind to me. You got a place. When I was running, you kept me for three months. Besides, they put me in jail, couldn't be no fuckin' worse than this place and my job."

"I got a load of money," Rinker said. "It won't cover the risk, but I'll give you a thousand a week plus whatever I got left over at the end." Pollock opened her mouth to object, but Rinker held up an imperious finger. "Don't want to hear about it. I'm leavin' the money, and you take it and spend it on something stupid."

"I can do that, no doubt about it," Pollock said. "Maybe buy a stair-climber, or something." She sucked up an ice cube, ran it a couple of times around her mouth, and then spit it back into the beer. "So tell me what you're up to."

POLLOCK THREW MOST of the shit out of the shit room, and Rinker put down an inflatable guest mattress she'd bought at a Target store, with a sheet and an acrylic blanket. Her clothes stayed in her suitcase. Pollock's landlady had an extra space in the garage next door, and Pollock walked around the house and rented it, thirty dollars a month, so that Rinker would have a place to put the California car. That night, Rinker left Pollock in front of her television and began to scout the men she'd come to kill.

NANNY DICHTER WAS the richest of the bunch, with a home in Frontenac; he had a fountain on the front lawn. The fountain, in the figure of a small girl with a water jug on her back, was carved out of golden marble imported from Austria. Dichter sold drugs, and had for most of his adult life. He'd been one of the first to make cocaine imports into a business, instead of an adventure. He was married, had two sons and four daughters, and three or four live-in servants. He owned the majority interest in a chain of midwestern mall-based import stores that sold native art to the aesthetically impaired, and provided a convenient network for his bulk cocaine sales.

Paul Dallaglio worked with Dichter, taking care of competitive issues, which was how he'd met Rinker. He'd used her nine times and paid her a little more than a half million dollars. He lived not far from Dichter in a home on a heavily wooded lot in Creve Coeur. He was executive vice president and part owner of the import chain.

Andy Levy was a banker, and worked a straight job as vice president of development with First Heartland National of St. Louis; he handled most of the mob money in St. Louis, including Rinker's, before she moved to Wichita. He lived in a huge old redbrick cube in Central West End, and was a patron of the performing arts—he dated dancers, and sometimes actresses. Rinker had killed Levy's wife and her lawyer when the marriage went on the rocks, and the lawyer was foolish enough to threaten Levy with the exposure of his money operation. Levy liked to walk in Forest Park. He'd once been banned from the zoo for throwing center-cut pork chops to the lions.

Finally there was John Ross, who'd originally recruited Rinker and taught her the gun trade. Ross ran an overworld liquor distributorship, and had interests in vending machine and trucking businesses. He had parallel shadow businesses in cocaine, sports betting, and loan-sharking.

He was retail, to Nanny Dichter's wholesale. He'd also acted as Rinker's agent, selling her guns for cash, and taking his cut in clout rather than money. Ross lived off a semiprivate street in Ladue in the center of six acres of lawn. He'd been Rinker's friend and protector, though when she'd been broken out by the cops, he'd tried to have her killed. She gave him that one, because of their history, but had warned him at the time that if there was another unsuccessful attempt, she'd be coming for him.

Dichter and Ross were smart and personally violent. Dallaglio was essentially a criminal executive who worked by remote control. He'd never gotten his hands bloody, but he did know how to protect himself. Levy barely thought of himself as criminal—he was just a guy who knew some guys, and like a bunch of Rotarians, they all threw business at each other.

Every one of the four men knew too much about each of the others, and more than enough about Rinker. While any one of the four could have authored the assassination in Cancún, it was unlikely that any one of them would have done it on his own hook. They walked carefully around each other, and none of them would want to be blamed if something had gone wrong, as it had. They'd have talked.

RINKER SLEPT IN Pollock's room for three more days, going out at night, getting a handle on the town. She knew it well from her days as a dancer, and with Ross at the liquor warehouse, but there were always changes, and she'd never really surveyed it from the perspective of an assassin.

She needed to know what was open, and when. Where she could ditch, if she ran into trouble. Where she could pick up a car in a hurry. Where the targets did their business. As she wandered around town, she refined her ideas about her approaches to the targets.

One night, she dropped Pollock at a country joint with twenty dollars and a hand-sized Sony tape recorder, and told her to sit as close to the jukebox as she could, have a couple of beers, and tape-record the bar. Pollock did all of that, and Rinker listened to the tape on the way back home. The tape sounded fine, and reminded her of the Rink.

SHE MADE THE first open move on a Monday night, with a stop at the BluesNote Cafe at LaClede's Landing on the river. The BluesNote was owned by John Sellos. The club had never done well, and without a variety of minor criminal activities—the barkeeps ran a sports-betting business, and a back room became an informal office for a fence and a branch office for one of Ross's loan sharks—the place would have closed fifteen years earlier. As it was, it struggled, and Sellos worried incessantly.

Rinker wore black jeans for the job, a black blazer, and

black Nike running shoes. She carried one of the nine-millimeter pistols in her jacket pocket. She parked a block from the club and sat in the car for a while, gathering herself, watching the street.

She knew she frightened people, but she knew that was only an edge. Physically, she was in good shape, but a large man was still a large man. Even an out-of-shape cigarette freak like Jackie Burke in L.A., or Jimmy Cricket in San Francisco, could pull her arms off if he was pissed, or desperate, and forgot about her reputation for a minute.

That meant that when she wanted to talk to a man, she had to get on top of him immediately. She didn't have to flash the gun, but it had to be there, in his mind's eye, right from the start. She had to be the cold-eyed killer right inside his shirt.

A blond couple, the woman a little wobbly, and a single man in cowboy boots went into the BluesNote as she watched, and one man left. The man who left stopped just outside the door and looked up and down the street: looking for action, which meant that not much was going on inside the club. When Rinker had run her bar in Wichita, she'd hated the sight of a man looking both ways on the sidewalk outside. The Rink hadn't come through for him.

After watching for ten minutes, she got out of the car, hung a purse on her shoulder, and walked down to the club. The door was surrounded with predistressed wood that was now genuinely distressed; the doorknob rattled under her hand. She stepped inside the door, paused, let her eyes adjust to the gloom. A longhaired young man sat on a dais at the end of the main room, a guitar on one knee. He was saying, ". . . learned this song from an old Indian guy up in Dakota. I was working the wheat harvest, this was back in '99 . . ."

Rinker thought, *Jesus.*

When she could see, Rinker walked along the left wall straight back to the kitchen doors, through the doors and up the stairs. She knew the place from her years at the liquor warehouse: Nothing had changed. The door at the upper landing was closed, but there was light coming through the crack at the bottom. She put a hand on the pistol in her pocket and pushed through the door.

Sellos was sitting behind his desk. When Rinker pushed through the door, without knocking, he jumped, saw her face, and settled back into his chair.

"You scared me," he said, smiling hopefully.

"Good," she said. She kept her hand in her pocket, noticed that Sellos was watching that hand, and said, "Yeah. I got a gun."

"You gonna shoot me? I haven't done anything to you." He was a thin man, with a big nose and a yellowish tint to his skin. He looked as though somebody large had blown nicotine and tar on him; he looked like he should be wearing a brown fedora.

"I didn't come here to shoot you," Rinker said. "I need about four of your cell phones, and I need you to make a call for me."

"Whatever's good," he said.

"If you mess with me, I'll shoot you right in the heart," Rinker said. She eased her hand out of her pocket, letting him see the gun with the fat snout. "I got no patience for being messed around."

His Adam's apple bobbed once, and he said, "I don't have the phones here. I gotta make a call."

"Call." She waggled the pistol at the phone.

He picked up the telephone, punched in four numbers, and said without preface, "Have Carl bring me up four phones. And you know that poster we got under the bar? Give him that, too, I want to show it to a guy."

"Who's Carl?" Rinker asked when he hung up.

"Old guy. Works for me. Could you put the gun away?"

"You got folk music downstairs, John," Rinker said. An accusation, and it made Sellos uncomfortable. She slipped the pistol back into her jacket pocket. They listened for a minute, and heard, faintly, through the floor, the singer's scratchy voice: . . . *the Sioux and Arikara are gone, driven by the white man's trains, across those treasured free-wind plains, where the wheat waves like dollar bills, and overflows some banker's tills . . .*

"Gotta pay the mortgage, Clara," he said. "The guy costs me nothin'."

"How're you gonna grow your bar traffic, John, with some asshole singing about freight trains and wheat? Folk music is *worse* than nothing. Hiring folksingers does nothing but encourage them. It's like letting cockroaches into your house."

"I gotta have *something,* and I can't hire country," Sellos said defensively. "Country people won't come down here. And blues are dead, except with the corduroy university crowd, and they can make a whole night out of a beer and a dish of free peanuts." They heard footsteps in the hallway, and both turned their heads: then a knock. Sellos got up, opened the door, took the phones and a piece of paper, said, "Thanks, Carl," and shut the door again. He stepped back behind his desk, looked at the back of the telephones for a few seconds, then put them where Rinker could reach them.

"How much?" Rinker asked.

"You don't have to pay," Sellos said. "Just take the fuckin' things."

"How long are they good for?"

"Couple of weeks, anyway. Two of them are arranged, the other two are on vacation." Arranged phones were phones that the owner arranged to have stolen, for a fee. Vacation phones were lifted in burglaries of people who were out of town.

"All right. You know the numbers for these phones?" Rinker asked.

"They're on the tape on the back."

She looked at the back of one of the phones, found a piece of white adhesive tape, with a number in blue ballpoint. "Write this down," she said. She read the number off, and Sellos wrote it on his desk pad. "Soon as I leave here, I want you to call Nanny Dichter on his private line and tell him to call me at this number. I don't talk when I'm driving, so I won't turn the phone on until I'm somewhere safe. But you tell him to call me, okay?"

"Are you and Nanny, uh . . . are you *lookin'* for each other?"

"You don't want to know about this, John. You call Nanny, tell him I want to talk about John Ross. Eleven o'clock, right around there."

"Nanny'll be pissed at *me.*" He shook his head sadly, thinking about it.

"No, he won't. Just get in touch with him when I leave, and tell him I was pointing a gun at your head. I'll tell him the same thing."

"You gotta promise me," Sellos said. "To tell him that."

"Cross my heart," Rinker said. "Now. I need a home phone number for Andy Levy."

Sellos was puzzled. "Andy who?"

"Levy. The bank guy."

Sellos shook his head "I don't know him."

"John . . ."

"Honest to God, Clara, I never heard of him. He's a Jew

or something? I don't know hardly any Jews. Honest to God."

Rinker looked at him for a moment, her best *look,* and decided that Sellos was nervous but was probably telling the truth.

"All right. I'll find it somewhere else."

"I'd do anything, Clara. . . ."

Rinker stood up. "The best thing for you to do, John, is to give me a few minutes before you call Nanny. Or anybody else. If the cops come screaming down the street, I'll come back and kill you first."

"No problem, I won't call the cops. You ought to see this." He pushed the piece of paper across the desk. It looked like a wanted poster and had Rinker's face on it.

"Where'd you get it?"

"It's in every goddamn bar and motel in St. Louis," Sellos said. "The picture's not very good—it could be anybody. But if you know you, it looks like you."

"Why're you telling me?" Rinker asked.

He shrugged. "I always sorta liked you . . . when you were working out of the warehouse. I didn't know about the gun stuff until it was in the papers."

She nodded—he *had* liked her, she thought. She remembered that. "All right. Give me a couple minutes." She stood up and stepped away, to the office door, and then said, "Listen, John, you gotta get rid of that fuckin' folk music, okay? Promise me?" She let out a thin smile. "I mean, I'm not gonna shoot you if you don't, but just do it for . . . American civilization?"

NANNY DICHTER LIVED on Chirac Road, a semiprivate dead-end lane in Frontenac. All the houses sat well back from the lane, and any car turning into it could be seen—watched—from any of the houses along it. On the other hand, any car coming out of the lane could be seen up and down Nouvelle Road, the main street. At ten minutes past ten o'clock, Rinker parked on Nouvelle Road, three blocks from Chirac. Ten or fifteen cars lined the street; a party. She parked at the end of the line closest to Chirac, turned off the lights, and slumped behind the steering wheel, watching Chirac in the rearview mirror.

Bunches of kids were still arriving at the party, and a couple left. From her spot in the street, Rinker could hear their music and see flickering multicolored lights. Some kind of techno shit, she thought. Better than folk music, anyway. A little after ten-thirty, a kid wandered out of the party, stood on the front lawn of the party house, and began vomiting. He continued for a minute, then walked on to his car, got in, got back out, vomited again, then got back in the car and drove away.

Happy trails, Rinker thought.

At ten-thirty-five, she began to wonder if Dichter was going to call her, or if he'd been home when Sellos called him—what if he'd been at his office, working late? She'd be sitting here and never know. There was no chance that he'd call from either his house or his business, though. The feds probably had him so tapped that they knew every time he opened the refrigerator.

At ten-forty, a Mercedes rolled out of Chirac Road, sat for a minute, then turned right, away from her, and headed down the street, slowly. Dichter always drove a Mercedes. Rinker reached for the key, then stopped. The Benz was a little obvious, don't you think, Clara? Rolling up and stopping like that, so anybody could get a look?

She sat still as the Mercedes disappeared at a corner three blocks away. *Maybe a mistake?* Maybe he'd be calling in two minutes, and she'd have no idea where he was?

Then another car rolled out of Chirac, a station wagon—a Volkswagen, she thought—and turned left, toward her. This car did not hesitate at the street entrance. When it passed her, she saw two men inside; one had a hand to his head, as thought he were talking on a cell phone—probably to the driver of the Benz, Rinker thought. She let the car get two blocks down Nouvelle, over a hump and out of sight, before she followed.

She didn't think Dichter would go far. Any phone would do, as long as it wasn't his. She started to tighten up now. Started to feel the adrenaline, the hunting hormone, flowing into her bloodstream. She'd always liked the feel of it, the stress.

And she thought about Paulo, dead on the ground in

Cancún, his blood all over her, his blue eyes vacant. Thought about her baby, the way things were going to be forever. The adrenaline was a familiar thing, but now something else flowed in, a coldness that she'd felt only once before, about her stepfather.

Hate. And it was liquid and cold, like mercury flowing through her veins. Nanny Dichter, two blocks away, still breathing, while Paulo lay rotting in his grave . . .

SHE KNEW ENOUGH not to try to get close to the Volkswagen. She stayed way back, turned off her lights once, followed the Volkswagen around a corner west onto Clayton Road, worried that she'd lose him. Clayton Road had more traffic than the side streets, and she closed up just a bit. The Volkswagen continued on, turned north off Clayton, then west again, and finally cut into a Lincoln Inn.

She continued past the hotel, down the block, to a second entrance. Kept looking back and saw the Volkswagen pull up to the reception bay, and a man who looked very like Nanny Dichter get out and go inside.

She parked as close to a side door as she could, picked up the Sony tape recorder, and turned it on. The Dixie Chicks were singing something inoffensive. She got out of the car and walked toward the hotel's side door. The door was locked. She took a step away, looking toward the front, thinking about the second man in the Volkswagen—and saw a young guy coming down the hallway toward the side door, carrying a sleepy, red-eyed kid. The guy pushed through, and Rinker held the door, smiled, and was inside.

The telephone rang. She punched it on, held the tape recorder close to her face as she walked along the hallway, and answered. "Hello?"

"This is me," Dichter said. "What do you want?"

"I want to know whose idea it was to go to Cancún," she said. "Was that John? Or was that the whole goddamn bunch of you?"

"I didn't know anything about it until the feds told me," Dichter said. "I got with John . . ."

"Hold on," Rinker said. "I'm gonna go outside. I can barely hear you."

"Where are you?"

"In a bar," she said tersely. She pulled the tape recorder away from the phone, as though she were walking away from the jukebox, and clicked it off. Then: "Wait a minute, a guy's coming. . . . Let me get over here."

A guy *was* coming. A hotel guy, with a chest tag that said "Chad." She put her hand over the phone's mouthpiece and asked, "Could you tell me where your pay phones are?"

"Down the hall, into the lobby, turn right, then around the corner and they're right there."

"Thanks." She continued down the hallway, into the lobby, phone to her ear. Slipped the safety on the nine-millimeter. Into the lobby, not looking at the few faces passing through it.

Glanced to the left, her vision sharp as a broken mirror, picking up everything as tiny fragments of motion—the Indian woman behind the desk, the guy with the suitcase talking to her, another guy in the tiny gift shop, a sign that said, "Elevators," and she was saying into the phone, all the time, "That fuckhead killed my guy and killed my baby, and I'm gonna take him out." The righteous anger was surging in her voice, and was real and convincing. "You can get in or get out, whatever you want, but if you're with John, I'll take you right along with him."

"Listen, listen, listen . . . ," Dichter was saying, his voice rising.

And she turned the corner and heard the last "listen" both through the phone and in person: Dichter was there, his back to her, talking into the pay phone. He felt the movement behind him and turned, his face going slack when he saw her face and the gun leveled at his forehead. He had just time to say, "No," and Rinker shot him.

The first shot went in between his eyes. The second and third went into the side of his head as he slumped down the wall, leaving blood lines down the yellow wallpaper.

The shots, even with the silencer, were loud, enough to attract attention. Rinker shoved the gun into her jacket pocket, screamed, and ran into the lobby. "Man's got a gun," she screamed. "Man's got a gun . . ."

She was looking over her shoulder at the hallway, and somebody else screamed and the man with the suitcase ducked but didn't run. He was looking at the hallway where Dichter had fallen. She turned down the hall where she'd come in, out of sight from the lobby, now running, banged through the side exit, heard shouting behind her, forced herself to a walk, went to her car, was in, was rolling . . .

Was gone.

8

THERE WAS NO EASY WAY TO DRIVE TO ST. LOUIS FROM the Twin Cities. The easiest was to head east into Wisconsin, then south through Illinois on the interstate highways. The interstates were full of Highway Patrol cops, though, so Lucas took the Porsche straight south through Iowa, along secondary highways and country roads, spending a couple of extra hours at it but having a much better time. He eventually cut I-70 west of St. Louis and took it into town, arriving just after sunset on a gorgeous, warm August evening.

Dichter had been shot the night before, and Malone had called at midnight. As they spoke, Mallard was on his way to St. Louis with his Special Studies Group, with Malone to follow in the morning.

"No question it was her," Malone said. A late-night caffeinated excitement was riding in her voice. "Two people got a pretty good look at her, but nobody knew who she was. They thought the shooting was coming from somewhere else—she must have used a silencer—and they were all running around like chickens with their heads cut off. She got out of the place clean. Nobody saw her car or where she went."

"How'd she know Dichter was in the hotel?"

"She's got a stolen cell phone. Dichter was killed on a pay phone, and we traced the number he'd called to a phone owned by a guy from Clayton—that's just outside of St. Louis, to the west. The Clayton cops went to the guy's apartment and talked to the manager, who said the guy was in Europe. So they checked the apartment and found the place had been broken into, ransacked. We called the guy in Europe and asked about the cell phone, and he said it should have been home on the dresser in the bed room. No phone. It'd been taken."

"How'd Rinker know Dichter'd be calling from that pay phone? Did she know him that well? Or was she watching him?"

"We don't know."

"If she's watching her targets, you could set up a surveillance net around anybody else she might go after. See if she comes in on them," Lucas said.

"We've talked about doing that. Take a lot of guys—maybe twenty at a time, three shifts. Sixty guys. That's a lot."

"How bad do you want her?"

"That bad," Malone admitted. "But we have to get the budget."

"St. Louis must have a few stolen-phone dealers. The cops should have some lines on who might be selling them."

"You don't think Rinker stole it?"

Lucas said, "Jesus Christ, no. She's not a burglar. She just knew about the guy who deals them, that's all. Probably a bar guy—she was a dancer, remember?—or a barbershop in the barrio, if they've got a barrio. Get somebody to look in the Latino community, or the African community—I'll bet there's a dealer who wholesales them to a couple of guys who retail them out to people who want to call Colombia or Somalia, like that. That's pretty common. A couple of dozen overseas calls will pay for a pretty expensive phone. Ask the St. Louis cops."

"I'll do that. Can you get down?"

"I'll drive down tomorrow," Lucas said.

"No problem with Weather?"

"Nope. She's pretty interested in the whole project, and she's far enough out on the pregnancy that she doesn't really need me here."

"See you then. I'm flying the first thing in the morning."

THE FBI CONTINGENT was housed in a block of rooms at the Embassy Suites Hotel, a couple of blocks off the waterfront. There was no garage, but Lucas found a spot within direct eyeshot of the front door, parked, and carried his bag inside to the reception desk.

"FBI?" asked the woman behind the desk, looking him over.

"No," Lucas said. So everybody knew the feds were in town. He pushed his American Express card at her. "I'd really appreciate something comfortable."

"That's not a problem," she said pleasantly. Her accent came from farther down the river. She was looking at a computer screen as they talked, and said, "I see you have a message."

She stepped to the left, looked through a file, produced an envelope, and passed it to him.

"Are there a lot of FBI people in the hotel?" Lucas asked.

"Mmm," she said. Then: "They think that lady killer is here—Clara Rinker."

"Here in the hotel?" She was nice-looking, a fair-skinned black woman, and Lucas thought a little moonshine couldn't hurt, especially with a southerner.

She picked up on it and smiled at him. "Not in the *hotel,* silly. In St. Louis."

"I'll look out for her."

They chatted as she checked him in, the kind of light southern flirting that established a mutual pleasure in the present company, with no implications whatever. The room was decent: The space was okay, with a small sitting room, the bed was solid, and if he pressed his forehead to the window, he could see the towboats working up the river. One was working up the river the first time he looked, maybe one of the same tows he'd see from his place in St. Paul. Not bad.

He dumped his bag on the bed, powdered his nose, splashed water on his face, and opened the envelope. The note said, "We're at the local FBI office. Easy to get to, too far to walk. Ask at the desk."

Though it was warm, he got a jacket, a crinkled cotton summer-weight, before he headed out. Downstairs, the southerner was working the desk and he asked, "Can you tell me where the FBI office is?"

She looked at him, a little warily—was he hustling her, trying to extend the FBI comment?—and he said, "Really. I have a meeting."

"Big fibber," she said. "You said you weren't—"

"No, no, I'm not FBI. I just have a meeting."

"Well . . . if you're really not fibbing . . ."

"Really."

"Okay. If you were, it's only ninety-nine dollars federal rate for your room. You save fifty dollars."

She paused, but he shook his head. "Okay, the FBI building. It's about, ummm, twenty blocks from here. You want to go out this way to Market. . . ." She pointed him out the door. He retrieved the Porsche, found Market, took a right, and five minutes later was easing into a parking space outside the FBI building. He'd expected a high-rise office with security. He got a low, flat fifties-look two- or three-story building that must have covered a couple of acres, with big green windows, a well-trimmed lawn, and a steel security fence on the perimeter. Lights were burning all through the building.

Inside the front door, a guard checked him off a list. Lucas declared no weapon, and the guard said, "We have a weapon pass for you, Mr. Davenport."

Lucas shrugged. "I thought it'd be better to leave it for now."

"Fine. I'll show you the conference room. Mr. Mallard is there now with the rest of the Special Studies Group." He handed Lucas a plastic card with a metal clip. "Put this on."

The guard led him to an elevator, while another guard took the desk. The first guy was older, mid-fifties, Lucas thought, with a mildly unfashionable haircut and a nose that might have been broken twice. "You ever a cop?" Lucas asked, as they got in the elevator.

The guard glanced at him. "Twenty-two years, City of St. Louis."

"You let these FBI weenies get on top of you?"

The guard smiled pleasantly, showing his eyeteeth. "That doesn't happen. You a cop, or a consultant, or what?"

"Deputy chief from Minneapolis. I've bumped into Rinker a couple of times, and Mallard thinks I can help."

"Can you?"

"I don't know," Lucas said. "She's a problem. You think these guys'll get her?"

The guard considered for a minute, and the elevator bumped to a stop one floor up. "Ah, these guys . . . aren't bad, for what they do," the guard said, as the door opened. They took a left down the hall. "We used to think, downtown, that they were all a bunch of yuppie assholes, but I seen some pretty good busts come out of here. What they do usually has a lot of intelligence, lot of surveillance. Patience, is what they got. They might have trouble with a street chick. . . . Here's your room."

The conference room was unmarked. Lucas stopped and said, "You ever have a beer when you get off? Bite to eat?"

"Usually," the guard said. "There's a late-night place up on the Hill—get together with some of my old pals."

"I don't know St. Louis."

"If you're out of here by eleven, stop at the desk. I'll give you a map. You driving?"

"Yeah."

"No problem, then."

"What's your name?" Lucas asked.

"Dan Loftus."

"Lucas Davenport." They shook hands. "See you later."

THE GUARD HEADED back to his station, and Lucas knocked once on the conference room door and stepped inside. A dozen people—seven or eight men in ties and long-sleeved shirts with the sleeves rolled up, and four or five women in slacks and jackets—were sitting around two long tables, with Mallard at the front. A white board covered the front wall, and somebody had drawn a flow chart on it with three colors of ink. Five or six laptop computers were scattered down the conference table. Malone sat in a corner, wearing a skirted suit: She lifted a hand.

"Lucas," Mallard said. He stepped over to shake hands and pointed Lucas at a chair. "This is Chief Davenport," Mallard said to the group. "Treat him well." A few of the agents nodded. Most looked him over, then turned back to Mallard.

Like that, Lucas thought. Not a member of the tribe. On the other hand, he had his own tribe. He thought of the guard and leaned back in the chair to listen.

MALLARD HAD SIX names on the whiteboard: six local crime figures who might have been tied into Rinker. They included Nanny Dichter, now dead; Paul Dallaglio, a business partner of Dichter's in the import and dope businesses; Gene Giancati, involved in sex and loan-sharking; Donny O'Brien, improbably a trustee of a half-dozen different union pension funds; Randall Ferignetti, who ran the biggest local sports books; and John Ross, who ran a liquor-distribution business, a trucking company, several lines of vending machines, and an ATM-servicing company.

"We think Rinker's most likely target is Dallaglio," Mallard was saying, tapping the white board. "He and Dichter were like Peter and Paul—the salesman and the organizer. If Dichter was involved enough with Rinker that she killed him, then Dallaglio's got to know her."

"Can we talk to him?" a blue-shirted agent asked.

"I called him this morning, but he wouldn't talk," Mallard said. "He said he'd have an attorney get back to me, but we haven't heard anything. We suspect there's some pretty heavy conferencing going on right now."

"We could put a net around him without asking," the agent said.

Malone chipped in: "We could, if we could keep it light enough that he didn't know. The problem is, he's hired private protection—Emerson Security out of Chicago. We don't know who yet, but Emerson has a whole bunch of ex–Bureau guys. If they put up their own security net, they'd spot us."

"So what?" another agent asked.

"So we want him scared," Mallard answered. "Officially, we're reluctant to get involved in this, unless we get something back. If we do it right, we might do a lot of damage to these guys."

"Maybe he'll just hire Emerson forever."

"No. Good protection from Emerson's gonna cost him between three and five thousand a *day*. He's got money, but he's not a rock star," Mallard said. "We're gonna let both him and Emerson know that we're watching his banking activity—that the IRS will want to know where the money's coming from, and where it's going to. Probably most of his money is offshore, and getting it back here, in big amounts, won't be easy, especially to pay off a legit company like Emerson. They won't take cash under the table, not in their business, not when they know we're watching."

"Maybe we'll eventually put a net around him," Malone said. She and Mallard were double-teaming the briefing. They were good at it, practiced, coordinated without awkwardness or deference. "Right now, though, we want to put some light tags on the other people. Keep track of them. Maybe somebody will run, and we'll want to know that."

"Do we have anybody on the street?" asked a woman in a square-shouldered, khaki-colored dress that made her look like a tomboy or an archaeologist. "She's not in any hotel within two hundred miles, she's not staying with anybody we've got in our history, her face is all over the place on TV and in the newspapers, but nobody sees her. Where is she? If we can figure that out . . . What do people do when they come to St. Louis but the cops are looking for them? They still got boardinghouses or something?"

They all thought about that for a few moments, then started making noises like a bunch of ducks quacking, Lucas thought—no reflection on Mallard.

"Lucas . . . what do you think?" Malone asked finally.

Lucas shrugged. "You guys are always putting up

rewards like a million dollars for some Arab terrorist. If she's ditched underground with an old crooked friend . . . why not offer a hundred thousand and see if you get a phone call?"

"Rewards cause all kinds of subsidiary problems," a gray-shirted agent said. "You get multiple claims . . ."

"You guys got lawyers coming out of your ears, to be polite," Lucas said. "Fuck a bunch of multiple claims. Bust her first, litigate later. Once you have her chained in the basement, you can work out the small stuff."

"It's an idea," Malone said, without much enthusiasm. "We'd have to get the budget."

A guy in a white shirt said, "We know every place she ever worked here in St. Louis. What if we ran the Social Security records on every place she worked, and got a list of all her coworkers, and cross-matched them."

That idea turned their crank. Mallard made notes, and Lucas looked at his watch. When they sorted it out, one of the agents asked, "Is Gene Rinker going to be a genuine resource?"

Mallard looked at Malone, who said, "Two possibilities on that. First, we use him to talk her in. He's resisting. The second is, at some critical point, we throw him out there as a chip. Come in, we guarantee no death sentence, and your brother walks on the dope charge."

Lucas was twiddling a pencil, anxious to get going, but asked, "Where is he? Gene?"

"We're moving him here."

"How're you going to face him off to Clara? How is she even going to find out about him?"

Malone shrugged. "The press. They've been all over the Dichter thing. This is a large story here. There'll be a story on tonight's news that we're bringing Gene here to assist with the investigation, and we've let it be known that we've got him by the short hairs. Rinker'll hear about it. Unless she's in Greenland or Borneo."

Lucas blinked, and twiddled, and Malone finally asked, "What?"

"I like blackmail as much as the next guy, when you're dealing with small-timers," Lucas said. "Clara isn't. I don't see her turning herself in. If you hang her kid brother out to dry—he's the only person we've been able to find who she cares about—she could do something unpredictable."

"Like what?"

"I don't know. If I did, it wouldn't be unpredictable."

"Well, God, Lucas, what do you want us to do?"

"He's a resource," said another guy. "We don't *have* to use him."

"I think we'd be remiss if we didn't keep him available," said a third. A woman chipped in, "He's a violator. I say to heck with him."

THE MEETING BROKE up a little after nine. When Lucas went by the guard desk, Loftus, the guard he'd talked to, wasn't there. The guard who *was* there said, "You've got a note from Dan. He's hung up for a while," and passed Lucas a piece of typing paper. Outside the door, Lucas opened the paper and found a map drawn with a ballpoint, and next to that, the words "11 o'clock."

Lucas went back to the hotel, got a corned-beef sandwich from room service, unpacked his suitcase, talked to Weather for fifteen minutes, watched the news, and headed out the door a few minutes after eleven o'clock. St. Louis was easy enough to get around, and Lucas found the place on the first try: a corner tavern with Budweiser and Busch signs in the window, and a flickering-orange "Andy's" sign hung over the front door. A half-block up the street, a couple of guys were working on what looked like an eighties Camaro, using shop lights on orange extension cords that led across the sidewalk to the car at the curb. He could hear traffic, at some distance, and a nearly full moon was high and squarely aligned with the street. Felt kinda good.

Inside Andy's, a long bar led away from the door into the interior. A half-dozen guys and one woman seated at the bar turned their heads to see who was coming in, and gave him a good look when they didn't recognize him. He could smell microwave pizza, popcorn, and beer; a jar of pickled pig's feet sat at the end of the bar, beside a jar of pickled eggs. A bartender was wiping glasses, and as Lucas ambled past, he asked, "You looking for Dan?"

"Yeah. Is he here?"

"In the back on the right. Their pitcher is probably pretty down by now."

"So give me another one and a glass," Lucas said. He gave the bartender a twenty, got his change, and carried the pitcher down the bar. Loftus and two other guys, who both looked like ex-cops, were sitting in Andy's biggest booth, big enough for six or eight.

When Lucas came up, Loftus lifted a hand, and Lucas slid into the booth with the beer. Loftus pointed at the other two men. "Dick Bender, Micky Andreno. Dick was homicide, Micky was a patrol lieutenant when he retired."

Lucas said hello, and they all poured beer and Bender said, "I called a guy up in Minneapolis and he said you weren't the worst guy in the world. Said you got shot a lot, and that you like to fight. Said you got shot by a little girl."

"Right in the throat," Lucas said. "That was a good fuckin' day."

So he told the story, and they told a few, about car chases and assholes they'd known, one story about a cop who'd been killed when he'd run through a stream of water from a fire hose and got his neck broken, and then Lucas had to tell the story of the Minneapolis guy who'd fired a blank at his own head as a joke, and blown his brains out, and Andreno told about the three women—a grandmother, a mother, and a daughter—who had all been beaten to death by the men in their lives, the daughter when she was only seventeen: "She already had a kid of her own, a daughter, she's growing up somewhere. How'd you like to have that curse on you?"

After the dog-sniffing, they got another pitcher and Loftus asked, "How was the meeting?"

"I'll tell you, guys, they might get her, but if they do, it's gonna be by accident," Lucas said. "They're gonna run computer programs all night, trying to nail down every single person she ever worked with. They figure she's got to be staying with somebody she knows."

"Probably is," Bender said.

"I know, but Jesus, she worked for a big liquor company and a couple of bars here in town, with all those contacts, and she went to two different colleges that we know of—maybe they'll get lucky, but that's a hell of a lot of people," Lucas said.

"So what's the choice here?" Andreno asked. "I don't see that you've got an edge."

Before Lucas could answer, a fourth guy showed up, a former patrol sergeant named Bob Carter. He slid into the booth and was introduced, and said, "Pour me one of them beers. . . . Some asshole parked a Porsche outside."

"That'd be me," Lucas said.

"Really? A fuckin' C4?" Carter was not embarrassed. "They must have good bennies in Minneapolis."

Then they had to dog-sniff some more until Lucas finally got back to Andreno's question. "She bought a hot cell phone here in St. Louis—so she's already gone to somebody. That guy might know where she's at, he might know who she's calling. How many guys you got selling hot cell phones here?"

" 'Bout a hundred," Loftus said.

"Wholesaling them? Well enough established that she could come back after a few years away and go straight to him?"

"Don't know that she did that," Andreno said. "She might have called a friend, who got them for her."

"That's right, but she must've called somebody connected, because Dichter called *her,* on her cell phone. And the feds have Dichter's phone calls, both business and home from every phone we think he had, and she's not on the list. Her phone isn't. She never called him. She can't have been here for more than a few days. Somehow, she got to Dichter through an intermediary. And she bought a phone at the same time."

"If Dichter was calling her at night, at eleven o'clock, I bet he didn't have her number for long," Bender said. "Why would you sit around all day looking at the cell phone number and then go out at eleven o'clock to call her?"

The St. Louis cops sat and looked at him for a moment, waiting for Lucas to absorb the point. Lucas had absorbed it, and after a moment said, "That's one thing the feds didn't come up with," and then, "Anybody who can't keep their mouth shut, raise his hand."

Nobody raised a hand. Carter said, "Whataya got?"

"I'll tell you, if this shit gets out, Dan could be guarding a parking ramp," Lucas said.

Loftus didn't bother to look around the table. "They won't talk. Whataya got?"

Lucas took a paper out of his pocket. He'd pulled it out of the information packet that Mallard had passed around. All the packets were supposed to remain in the building. "List of phone numbers that called Dichter," Lucas said. He put it on the table, and the St. Louis cops huddled over it. Andreno finally said, "Pay phone at Tucker's, down at LaClede's Landing."

Carter said, "Yeah?"

"Tucker's is right next to the BluesNote. John Sellos."

Loftus leaned back and said to Lucas, "There you are. Sellos is connected, he knows Dichter and all the rest of them, and he'll sell you a phone if you ask him right."

"Tell you what else," Carter said. "Sellos used to work for John Ross, driving a truck. This was years and years ago."

"Maybe I oughta go see him," Lucas said.

Andreno looked at his watch. "Got time for a couple more beers—but if you're going, I'd like to ride along. I know Sellos from way back."

"Don't go hittin' anyone. You don't have a badge anymore," Loftus said to Andreno. To Lucas: "Micky sorta liked to fight, himself."

Andreno shook his head. "Those days are gone. Now all I do is hit golf balls and wonder what the fuck happened."

They had a couple of more beers, and talked about what the four cops were doing in retirement. None of them was sixty, and all were looking at twenty years of idleness before they died. "If the goddamn pickled pig's feet don't get to me first," Carter grumbled.

A few minutes later, Loftus asked Lucas, "Did you meet Richard Lewis, the AIC?"

"Yeah, he was in the meeting for a while. Dark suit, one of those blue shirts with a white collar?"

"That's him. I'll tell you what, he don't like this Mallard guy coming in and taking over. He's running a little hip-pocket operation of his own, looking for Rinker. He's got his intelligence guys doing it." Loftus said it in a way that suggested a further step into treason—all in the way of the brotherhood of cops.

"Got any names?" Lucas asked.

"Striker, Allenby, Lane, and Jones," Loftus said.

"Let me . . ." Lucas took a pen out of his pocket and jotted the names in the palm of his hand. "Striker, Allenby, Lane, and Jones."

"Don't tell anybody where you got that." Lucas looked at him, and Loftus said, "Yeah, yeah."

AT ONE O'CLOCK, Andreno tipped up his beer glass, finished it, and said to Lucas, "Let's go."

As they stood up, Loftus looked at Lucas and said, "Might be best if we don't spend too much time talking at the office—but I'll be sitting here tomorrow night."

"We're gonna kick some ass," Lucas said. He burped. "Fuckin' Budweiser."

"Jesus Christ, watch your mouth," Loftus said, and he crossed himself.

ANDRENO WAS A slick, hard, neighborhood boy: capped teeth, probably paid for by the city after they got broken out; forehead scars; too-sharp jackets, hands in his pockets; and the attitude of a housewife-slaying, mean fuckin' vacuum cleaner salesman. Even if he hadn't had an Italian name, Lucas would have bet that he'd gone to a tough Catholic high school somewhere, probably run by the Psycho Brothers for Christ.

Andreno liked the Porsche and cross-examined Lucas on how he could afford it. As they rolled along through the night, top down, the moon in the rearview mirror, Lucas told him a little about the role-playing games he'd written in the seventies and eighties, how he hired a kid from the University of Minnesota to translate them into early computer games, how that drifted into simulations for police 911 systems . . .

"Holy shit, you're rich," Andreno said.

"Comfortable," Lucas said.

"Bullshit, you're rich," Andreno said happily. "Why

don't you give me this car when you leave? I'd look great in it—clubs in the passenger seat, kind of casual-like, driving along with my sunglasses and the Rolex."

"Couldn't do that. You have to have a certain level of sexual magnetism before you're allowed to drive a Porsche," Lucas said.

"And I'd have to get a Rolex," Andreno said. He pointed at a slot near the curb, a half-block from the BluesNote. "Put it there. Then it'll be close if we have to run for it."

"Run . . . ?"

"Pulling your weenie," Andreno said. "John's actually an okay guy, if you like crooked barkeeps who suffer from clinical depression and progressive hair loss."

"Think he'll be there?"

"He always is. He's got nowhere else to go."

THE BLUESNOTE WAS only a couple of blocks from Lucas's hotel, one of a collection of nineteenth-century brick buildings called LaClede's Landing. Bars, mostly, a couple of music spots, all kinds of restaurants, tourist junk shops selling St. Louis souvenirs. Cobblestone streets. Like that; what you got in any older city when the city engineers decided to do something hip. At the door to the BluesNote, Andreno said, "Stay close behind me. Place is kinda dim."

They went in fast, straight to the back, though the kitchen doors and up a flight of stairs that had a "Private" sign above the first step, and at the top of the stairs. Andreno went straight on, across the landing, and pushed open the door at the top. "John . . . ," he said.

John Sellos was a thin man, tired-looking, worn down, sitting behind a wooden desk in the screen glow of a cheap laptop computer. He looked at Andreno, and Lucas behind him, and said, "Ah, shit." He said it in a quiet way, as though Andreno, or somebody like him, had been expected. Then: "What're you doing? You're not on the force anymore."

"I'm showing my friend around," Andreno said. "This is Lucas Davenport—he's a deputy chief from Minneapolis and is working now with an FBI task force on Clara Rinker. You heard of her?"

"I heard of her," Sellos said uncomfortably. He leaned back and crossed his legs. "What do you want?"

Andreno glanced at Lucas, who looked at the two chairs in front of Sellos' desk, carefully brushed off the seat of one of them, and sat down. "John . . . Can I call you John?"

"You can."

"John," Lucas said. "You helped set up Nanny Dichter to be murdered by Clara Rinker. We know that and you know that. And you know what the penalty is for felony murder in Missouri." Lucas made a delicate slashing gesture across his throat. When Sellos didn't immediately answer, Lucas knew that they were on the right track. So did Andreno.

He moved off to lean against a wall, and nodded at Lucas, his chin dipping a quarter-inch. "We've got Nanny's phone records, John," Lucas continued. "We know you called him—we've got a witness who can put you on the phone. We've got Clara's phone number, though she isn't answering it. We know where the phone came from, and pretty soon we're gonna know who stole it, and that person is gonna get on the witness stand and he is gonna put you on death row."

"I better get a lawyer," Sellos said. His voice lacked enthusiasm, and he didn't reach for a phone.

"The question is, do you need a lawyer?" Andreno said, pushing away from the wall. "You don't for me, because I'm not a cop anymore. Lucas, here, isn't exactly official. We're just a couple of street guys trying to come up with some information."

"So?" They were projecting rays of light, and all Sellos saw was bullshit and lies.

"So we talk," Lucas said, shrugging. "No need for everybody to get excited about a telephone. I mean, if the feds find you later, that's their problem and your problem. But we're not gonna talk to them about it. We got our own thing going."

Sellos turned skeptical. "You're not going to tell them?"

Andreno shook his head. "Nope. If you'll help us out, I'll give you my beeper number, and if Clara calls, you beep us. That'll be it."

"But you've gotta tell us the rest of it now," Lucas said. "Otherwise . . . you're gonna need a lawyer—a really good lawyer—and you're gonna need him really bad."

"I didn't help set Nanny up," Sellos said. He didn't bother to deny any of it. "I had no idea what Clara was going to do. I thought she was going to try to talk to him and needed a safe way to call him. She came in, she put a gun on me—a big fuckin' automatic. You know how many people have looked down Clara's guns and walked away? Not many. Anyway, she got the phones—four phones—and she told me if I talk to you guys, she'll kill me. And she will, if she hears about this. Not ten years from now on death row, she'll kill me this *week*."

"When was she here?"

Sellos told them the story. At the end of it, he stood up, went to a half-sized refrigerator, got a Heineken, popped the top off, took a sip. He didn't offer one to Lucas or Andreno. "She wanted Nanny to call, and she wanted this Andy Levy guy's phone number, the banker, so she could call him. That's it, other than that she'd kill me if I talked to anyone."

Lucas asked, "You've never heard of this Andy Levy?"

"No. When she mentioned him, that was the first I ever heard of him."

Lucas looked at Andreno and cocked an eyebrow. Andreno shook his head. "Never heard of the guy."

Back to Sellos. "You think he's here in the city?"

"That's the impression I got."

They ran him through the story again, but Sellos had nothing more to say, except that Rinker had not disguised herself at all. "She looked just like she did when she was working at the warehouse, except richer. She looked pretty well-tended."

"Well-tended," Andreno repeated, as though he liked the phrase.

"Very well," Sellos said.

They left him behind the desk, worrying. Lucas said, "*We* won't talk to anyone, and you better not. I mean, we're a couple of friendly guys. I don't think Clara would be all that friendly."

Andreno left his beeper number with Sellos. Sellos said he'd call the minute Rinker got in touch with him, if she did. "You aren't gonna run, are you, John?" Andreno asked.

"No, no. Somebody would find me. Either you or Clara. I got nowhere to run to."

OUT ON THE STREET, Andreno stretched and yawned and looked down the quiet streets and up at the sky, and said, "What a great fuckin' night. This was more fun than I had in five years."

"Operating," Lucas said.

"That's exactly what it is," Andreno said, poking a finger at Lucas. "I'm operating again." After a moment: "Is there anything else I can do? Any other way I can cut into this?"

"Let me think about it," Lucas said. "I'll see what the feebs say tomorrow, when I drop Andy Levy on them. If Andy Levy isn't dead tonight."

9

LUCAS GOT UP EARLY, FOR HIM, A LITTLE AFTER EIGHT o'clock. He pulled on jeans and a T-shirt, went to the lobby and got a *Post-Dispatch* and a couple of Diet Cokes, returned to his room, lay in bed and drank the Coke and read the paper. Gene Rinker, in orange prison coveralls and chains, was on the front page, being taken into a jail somewhere, behind a row of shotgun-armed marshals.

A show. A movie. The FBI was making a movie about being tough, about kicking a little Rinker ass. The *Post-Dispatch* quoted Malone on Gene Rinker's arrest, and described her as a tough, flinty FBI agent, a veteran of the mob wars. A small photograph at the bottom of the story showed Malone talking to a marshal, looking flinty.

"Maybe she is," Lucas thought, and he extracted the comics and read them while room service put together some pancakes and bacon. During the leisurely breakfast, he started calling local banks, and got lucky with the fifth one.

LUCAS GOT TO the FBI building at nine-thirty. Loftus wasn't yet on duty; another man gave him his neck card and escorted him to the meeting room. When he stepped inside, the collected agents turned to look, and Mallard said, "We started at seven."

"Had a late night," Lucas said. "Out drinking."

"Oh, good," one of the male agents muttered.

"Let's try to keep ourselves together, folks," Mallard said, but he was exasperated. Behind him, on the white board, was an expanded list of names, heavy on the Italian.

"Rinker's probably going after a guy named Andy Levy. A banker," Lucas said, as he found a chair. He pulled it back from the table so he could stretch his legs. "She had a list of at least two guys when she came into town: Nanny Dichter and Andy Levy. There's an Andy Levy who's a vice president at First Heartland National Bank here in St. Louis. I don't know he's the one, but he's a possibility."

They all turned to look at him again. Malone, who'd been sitting in the corner poking at a laptop, asked, "Where'd you get this?"

"On the street," Lucas said. "While I was out drinking."

"Drinking with any specific guy?" asked the tomboy agent, who the day before had been wearing khaki. Now she was wearing an olive-drab blouse, with epaulets. Lucas liked the look, sort of square-shouldered Italian Army.

"Nobody specific," he said. "Just a bunch of guys."

"Maybe nothing to take seriously," said another one of the agents.

"Gotta take it seriously," Lucas said. "You don't take it seriously and Andy Levy gets hit, and the papers hear about it, then you're a laughing stock. That's not the FBI way. Or maybe it is, but it's not something you'd want to talk about."

"Who'd tell the papers?"

Lucas shrugged. "I might. I always liked newspaper guys."

Mallard said, "Ah, man—Lucas, let's step out in the hallway for a minute, huh? We gotta talk."

MALLARD PUSHED THE door shut, stood with his back to it, and asked, "Who's your source?"

"A guy I ran into last night," Lucas said. "If you wind up desperately needing him—and I can't see how that would happen—then I'll tell you who he is. Until then, the information's got to be enough."

"Is it good information?"

"It's good. It comes right out of Rinker's mouth. But I'm not sure the guy at Heartland is the right guy. Rinker's the one who called him a banker, and my source doesn't know if she meant a mob banker or a legit banker or what. If Levy's legit, maybe Rinker's got some money with him."

"That'd be good—that'd be *really* good. Anything else I ought to know?"

"Yeah. The AIC here is running another Rinker group out of his back pocket. Four guys named Striker, Allenby, Lane, and Jones, out of Intelligence. He doesn't like you being here. What that means is, there are about six groups of cops looking for the same woman and not finding her. But pretty soon, they're gonna start finding each other."

"Boy—you *do* keep your ear to the ground. Where'd you hear this? On the street?"

Lucas grinned. "Everybody knows about it. You're the last."

Mallard sighed and said, "Listen, I'm going over to talk to John Ross. That's really why I was a little anxious about your not being here. I want you to come along, and we're leaving in fifteen minutes."

"Could have called."

"Never occurred to me that you might be sleeping in," Mallard said. "I figured you were up to something . . . and I was right. And listen, take it easy in here, okay? I know they're a little chilly with outsiders."

"A little chilly, my ass. I almost froze to death last night," Lucas said. "I'm sure your guys are good at what they do, but that's not what I do. I think I'd be more valuable doing what I'm doing—hooking up with the locals, seeing who is doing what."

Mallard shrugged. "That's fine with me, as long as you stay in touch. I sort of value your input."

"I'll be around."

"Andy Levy, a banker," Mallard said.

"That's right."

"Let's go back in."

BACK INSIDE, Mallard looked at one of the agents and said, "I want you and four more guys on this Andy Levy, and I want a list of all the Andy Levys in the metropolitan area. As soon as we've got the right guy, I want a team on him around the clock. Start now—find him. Take whoever you want, except Sally."

The woman named Sally, in the epaulets, sat up and tapped the eraser end of a pencil on her yellow pad. Why not her? Mallard answered the question without being asked.

"Sally, Lucas is going to be running around town. I want you to run around with him as our liaison."

She shook her head, looked at Lucas, unhappy.

"I can't do that," Lucas said.

"Don't be a princess, Lucas," Malone snapped from the corner. "Take Sally. Her old man is a cop, her brother's a cop, she understands."

"I don't care if her father's the fuckin' Pope of Cleveland, I ain't taking her," Lucas said. "The people I talk to aren't going to talk to me if she's around."

"Don't tell them that she's with the Bureau."

Lucas looked at Mallard. "Think about the second piece of information I gave you. That'll give you a clue about where some of my sources are, and why I can't take Sally along."

"Are you . . . ah, man." He got it in one second. At least some of Lucas's sources were with the FBI. "All right. Sally, you work here with Malone, but Lucas, Sally's your contact with us. She'll get you what you need, from our side. Call her anytime day or night. Feed her everything you collect, all right? And try to get to the morning report on time. Seven o'clock, okay?

"Okay," Lucas said, with no sincerity whatever.

MALLARD WENT THROUGH the list of the day's assignments, then said to Malone, "I'm outta here. I doubt that we'll be with Ross for an hour, and I'll be on the phone the whole time."

"Good luck," she said.

SALLY FOLLOWED THEM out into the hall. "Give me two minutes with Chief Davenport," she said to Mallard. Mallard said, "I'm going to hit the john," and walked away. To Lucas, she said, "What was the second piece of information?"

Lucas shook his head. "You'd have to get that from Louis."

"I surmise that one of your informants is with the Bureau."

He shook his head again, kept his face straight. "You'd have to get that from Louis."

"It's really good to build up this level of trust with the guy you're coordinating with," she said.

"I don't need my balls busted by the FBI," Lucas said. "I'm getting tired of leading you guys around by the hand."

"I don't think that's the case," she said.

"Bullshit. You guys couldn't find your own elbows with two agents and a pair of binoculars."

Her lip twitched, and Lucas thought she might smile. "My old man would've said, 'You couldn't find your asshole with both hands and a flashlight.' "

"That was my thought," Lucas admitted. "I edited it because of your tender years."

"I'm not that tender," she said. "What are we doing?"

"I'll get your number and give you mine. It's always on, except at night."

"Good." They finished the arrangements in two minutes, and she asked, "That Andy Levy stuff isn't just a rumor, is it?"

"No. But I don't know anything about him."

She nibbled at the inside of her lip. "We'll have a formal profile in an hour. We're very good at that."

Lucas started down the hall. "Then do it. When you find anything out, call me," he said over his shoulder. "And hey—I like the epaulets."

THEY TOOK A dark government car, a Dodge, Mallard in the back, a younger agent driving, Lucas riding shotgun. On the way over, Mallard browsed through a file on Ross, reading out occasional anecdotes.

The anecdotes covered Ross's youth (he'd taken piano lessons for four years as a child, but didn't like them; he had allegedly pushed the piano out of his parent's fourth-floor apartment and down the stairs, it had rocketed through the side of the apartment house and into the street); his love life (he was on his fourth wife; his third had died tragically in an unsolved hit-and-run shortly after the divorce, while Ross had been vacationing in alibi heaven); and his legitimate interests (his long-distance trucking company was "Mother Trucker of the Year" for '98, and was listed in *Missouri* magazine as one of the top 100 Missouri companies to work for).

ROSS LIVED ON a semiprivate street in the town of Ladue, in the middle of a broad, rolling lawn of faultless green, dappled here and there with flower beds. The house, a rambling redbrick mansion with white trim, was set at the crest of a low hillock, and was surrounded by mature, artfully spaced trees. If Ross had any kind of security system,

Rinker would need a rocket launcher to get at him, Lucas thought.

The driver stayed with the car, while Lucas and Mallard went to the door. Ross's wife answered the doorbell. She was a striking woman in her mid-thirties, with strawberry-blond hair, a smooth oval face, and jade-green eyes—way too much for her Missouri accent. She was wearing tennis whites and carrying a bottle of orange Gatorade. She led them across polished wooden floors, past colorful, intricate framed prints, back to a home office, and called, "John—they're here," and then said to Mallard, "Well, I'm off to play tennis," as though she found the idea amazing.

"Good luck," he said. She turned away as John Ross came up to the office door.

"Come in," Ross said, looking after his wife. Mallard and Lucas followed him back into the office.

Ross looked like what he was: a hood. The smart, hard kind of hoodlum, the borderline psychopath, the kind who might have run the docks in New York in another era. He weighed maybe two-twenty, Lucas thought, and had wide sloping shoulders. He was square, with heavy lids over dark eyes, a dark, saturnine face, and fingers like fat stubby cigars.

The office around them was attractive, just as old man Mejia's library had been: all good wood and well-coordinated, the furniture sitting on a blue-and-beige oriental carpet that glowed at them from the floor. Two orchids sat on his desk, and another on a side table. One of the orchid blooms was the exact color of green that Lucas remembered from a huge Luna moth that had once visited his Wisconsin cabin.

"Beautiful flowers," Mallard said, as they settled around Ross's desk.

"My principal hobby," Ross said. "I have two thousand of them."

"You take care of them yourself?"

Ross nodded. "Mostly." He wasn't interested in talking about his flowers. "What can I do for you folks?"

"You've probably got a pretty good idea," Mallard said. "You once employed Clara Rinker. She just killed Nanny Dichter, and we think she is probably going after you. She blames you for the killing of Paulo Mejia."

Ross made a hand gesture, a *what can you do* gesture, and said, "I never had anything but the best relationship with her. I was amazed when I found out that she'd been killing people. But her career started way before I met her—at least, if what the papers say is correct."

"Look, you know as well as I do that the Bureau has a major file on you," Mallard said. "I think that some of the . . . surmises . . . made in those files are correct. But I don't care about that. I don't care if you're a big-time mobster, because my job right now is to find and stop Clara Rinker. What I want from you is any ideas you may have of where she's staying, who she may be working with. Old friends, people she could force to take her in—anything like that."

Ross was shaking his head. "I'd have no idea. I will go around and ask, though. When she worked for me, she mostly worked in the warehouse, and there must be twenty or thirty people out there who knew her. I'll have one of my guys talk to everyone."

"How about if we talk to them?"

"I've got no problem with that," Ross said. He leaned forward, opened a small drawer, and took out a sheet of paper and a yellow pencil. He scribbled on it and pushed it at Mallard. "This is the manager's name and phone number. I'll call him as soon as you leave, and tell him to expect a call from you."

Mallard nodded. "Thank you. . . . You personally have no idea. . . ."

Ross shook his head again. "None. I'll tell you, I'm really not sure that she's coming after me. I'm not sure exactly why she went after Nanny Dichter—I mean, you hear these rumors that Nanny played by his own rules, sometimes, but I didn't know they had any prior . . . relationship. Maybe that'll be the end of it. Nanny."

"That's a possibility, but she has at least one more man on her list for sure—not you. And we know that she made a series of phone calls from Mexico, to Missouri, after the shooting, and that you were the main topic of conversation. So we think there are at least two more people on the list, and you are one of them."

"Who's the other guy?" Ross's dark eyebrows went up.

"Sorry," Mallard said. "I can't . . ."

"Paul Dellaglio?"

Mallard shook his head. ". . . really give you that information. Why would you think Dellaglio?"

"Because anything Nanny Dichter did, Paul was part and parcel of. Unless the Rinker thing involves sex."

"Don't think so."

"Neither do I. Nanny didn't get around so much. So I would guess that Paul's the other guy on your list."

Mallard shook his head and said, "I'll have a couple of our agents around to your warehouse this afternoon."

"Anything I can do," Ross said.

THAT WAS THE INTERVIEW. After a few more unpleasantries, Ross took them out. On the way, they stopped in a room whose leaded-glass wall overlooked the back lawn. To the left, a greenhouse stood facing the south. A resort-sized rectangular swimming pool was straight ahead, and with its black-painted bottom, acted as a reflecting pond. To the right was a tennis court, where Ross's wife was batting tennis balls around with a white-haired man.

"Tennis lessons," Ross said ruefully. "That guy costs me fifty bucks an hour."

"Your wife's got a nice swing," Lucas said.

Ross looked at him with a tiny spark in his eye, the first sign Lucas had seen of humor. "Yes, she does. Always has had," Ross said.

Ross stood in the doorway and watched them go. When they were in the car, he pushed the door shut and walked to the opposite end of the house, moving silently on the thick carpet. Two men were in the billiards room, one of them looking out the window, while the other, a fiftyish man with a bald, pink scalp and a long Swedish face, was flipping playing cards down the length of a billiards table, at a tweed hat.

Ross watched him for a moment. Johnson's dour face reminded him of someone, but he couldn't think who. Ross did not like Honus Johnson—nobody did—but he was sometimes afraid that he'd let that attitude leak through, and that Honus had picked it up.

Honus was a throwback, a genuine sadist who'd found his perfect place in life as an interrogator, a punisher, with Ross's organization. Some of the others used him from time to time, with Ross's approval, but he was Ross's creature . . . and like most people who owned creatures, Ross sometimes wondered if the beast would ever turn on him.

Johnson, with his playthings, his hammers and saws and pliers and wire, would give a man a hard way to go.

He stepped into the room, and both men turned to him. "They're gone," Ross said. "They have no idea where she is. But they pretty much said what I told you—she has to be staying with somebody she knew from before. I want you guys to get out there and start talking to people."

"If we find her?" asked the man from the window.

"If you find her—if you literally find her, like walk in on her—you won't have to worry, because she'll kill you. But if you *hear* where she is, get back to me. We'll get some guys to pick her up."

"I don't know if I can be of much use," Honus Johnson said. "I'm not a scout."

"I want you to go along with Troy, here, and stand in the background," Ross said. "People have some ideas about you. That might convince them to be more forthcoming. And I have something else for you."

"Hmmm?" Johnson didn't quite look eager.

Ross looked at Troy. "You remember that woman Nancy Leighton? Used to work in fulfillment? Black hair, little mustache . . . Quit maybe three years ago?"

"Drove a Camaro," Troy said.

"That's the one. She used to be a good friend of Rinker's. I think she's got an apartment down on the south side somewhere. Get in her apartment, take her apart."

Johnson's eyebrows went up. "Take her apart? Completely?"

"Completely. Be careful—no prints, no DNA, but we want it to be noticed. We want it in the newspapers. Front page. Make it ugly."

"An example," Johnson said with relish. He rubbed the

edge of one hand through the palm of the other, back and forth, like a saw. Then: "Do I get Clara if we pick her up?"

"I'd have to think about that," Ross said. "I do like the girl—but she's a very bad example, hitting Nanny like she did."

"I'd like to have her for a while," Johnson said. His flat tongue flickered out to his thin lips, his flat pale eyes catching Ross's. "It wouldn't have to be long."

At that moment, when he caught Ross's eyes, Ross realized who Johnson looked like: the old man in the Grant Wood painting *American Gothic,* the somber old man with the pitchfork standing next to his equally somber wife. "Old rivals, huh?" Ross said, and smiled at the thought. The two of them had been a powerful combination.

Too bad about Clara.

AT THE FBI BUILDING, Lucas said goodbye to Mallard and got into his car. "Gonna roll around town for a while," he said. He dug up Micky Andreno's phone number and dialed it. Andreno was out in the yard and snatched up the phone on the fifth ring, as Lucas was about to hang up. "Washing the car," he said.

"Know anybody at Heartland National?"

"No, but one of Bender's kids works there. Want me to call him?"

"I think that Andy Levy's a vice president. I did some calling around."

"Oh, shit. . . . Oh, *shit.*"

"What?"

"I'm so fuckin' stupid. How could I be this fuckin' stupid?" Andreno sounded shocked.

"What?"

"Nine, ten years back, there was a double murder—a woman and her divorce attorney were found together in bed, shot to death. Actually, the guy was in bed and the woman was on the floor right beside the bed, and the way it was reconstructed, they'd been screwing. Right in the act. This was at her house. Somebody walked in and shot the attorney twice in the back of the head with a small-caliber weapon. The woman apparently tried to slide out from under and get out, but she was shot in the forehead and then twice in the temple. There was a hideout in the bottom of her dresser, and a bunch of jewelry was taken . . . worth maybe ten grand? Something like that. The husband was a guy named Levy—I think it was *Aaron* Levy—but I'll tell you what: Nobody knew it at the time, but looking back, it sounds exactly like Rinker. Like one of her hits."

"Aaron Levy, Andy Levy . . . could be the same. Or maybe Sellos got it wrong," Lucas said. "No arrests on the two killings?"

"Never a smell of one. Levy, this guy—a young guy—was like at some big Jewish convention somewhere, with several thousand witnesses. His wife's name, I think, was

Lucille. Lucy. That's what I remember. Bender could probably get a file. He's still tight with the guys in homicide."

"See if he can. Ask him if his kid will talk to us," Lucas said. "Call me back when you know."

"Pick me up," Andreno said.

"Sure. Call Bender."

Lucas dialed the number Sally had given him. She answered with "Yes?"

"I just talked to a guy who said there was an Aaron Levy, a case nine or ten years ago, whose wife Lucille and her divorce attorney were shot to death in her bed. Execution-style, Rinker-style, small-caliber weapon, close range, head shots. No arrests."

"Hang on a minute."

He heard her repeating what he'd said, and then Malone came on. "Interesting," Malone said. "Louis just walked in. . . . I'm on-line. . . . Let me get this . . . Aaron Levy and Lucille? Conventional spellings?"

"That's the names I got."

He could hear her typing, and then she said, "Here it is. Case still open. Nothing here . . . let me search." She hit a few more keys, then said, "Nothing here on Rinker, so nobody attributed it to her. All I get is Aaron—no Andy, no bank job. No job reported here."

A male voice in the background said, "That's him, though. We've got a newspaper file from the *Post-Dispatch* website, a speech for the Chamber of Commerce. He's listed as Aaron parenthesis Andy parenthesis Levy, vice president at Heartland National Bank. This is five years ago."

Then another male voice: "Where is Davenport *getting* this shit?"

Malone said, "I'm speeding everything up. We're putting a screen around Levy right now. We've got to talk some tactics here, but I'm going to suggest to Louis that we might go see him. Go see Levy."

"Let me know," Lucas said. They talked for another minute, then he rang off. Five seconds later, before he could put the phone away, another call came in. Andreno.

"Bender's going downtown to see if he can get the Levy file. He doesn't think it'll be a problem to look at it, but he'll have to slide around a little to Xerox it. He'll try to get it."

"What about the kid?"

"He's calling the kid."

"Outstanding."

"If it works out. Let me tell you how to get where I am. . . ."

ANDRENO LIVED IN an aging brick house in a narrow street of older brick houses, all shoulder-to-shoulder, with tiny yards and high porches, and pairs of bedroom windows looking out over the porch roofs toward the street; working-class, 1920, maybe, Lucas thought. A movie set for an Italian neighborhood.

Lucas pulled up in front, and Andreno banged out through the door a few seconds later. Lucas climbed out of the Porsche and said, "Want to run it?"

"Sure."

Lucas tossed him the keys, got in the passenger side, and located the instruments for the other man. Andreno eased away from the curb. "Now we got to drive around in front of all my ex-girlfriends' houses. That's gonna take a while."

"Never got married?"

"Got married twice, loved both of them to death, but they didn't like me much, I guess," Andreno said. "I can be an asshole."

"Any kids?"

"Two. One with each. *They* seem to like me all right."

"Got one myself, with another one in the oven," Lucas said.

"Gotta have kids," Andreno said. "Otherwise, what's the point?"

THEY WERE HALFWAY downtown, the old courthouse on the horizon with the Gateway Arch behind it, when Bender called. Andreno answered, then handed the phone to Lucas: "I can't talk and shift."

Lucas took the phone. "What's up?"

"My daughter's name is Jill. She's got a friend in the computer systems department over at Heartland, and he can get you a list of Levy's private clients. Take about twenty minutes."

"Can he do it without anybody knowing that he's the one who printed it? We don't want Levy pissed at anybody, in case . . . you know, in case Rinker's a friend of his."

"We talked about that: He can get it without anybody knowing. Turns out he pipes stuff out to a business guy at the *Post-Dispatch,* so he's done it before. Jill's gonna get it, she'll meet you at Tony's Coffee."

Lucas looked at Andreno. "Tony's Coffee?"

"Sure. Right downtown. Ten minutes."

"We'll be at Tony's," Lucas told Bender.

"How're we doing?"

Lucas laughed. "Everything that's broken on the case was broken by us. We're rolling."

"Hang around Tony's. I'll see you there myself in a half hour," Bender said.

JILL BENDER WAS a thin redhead with a big nose and wide smile. She found them two-thirds of the way back in Tony's, huddled over cups of coffee. She slid in beside Andreno and asked, "Where've you been keeping yourself?"

"Playing golf," Andreno said. He introduced Lucas and then asked her, "How's your mom?"

"She still hurts. They say they replace both knees at the same time, because if you only do one, you'll never do the other, because of the pain."

"Better than being crippled," Andreno said. To Lucas: "Arthritis."

"I heard that about the knee thing," Lucas said. "My fiancée's a surgeon."

Bender was digging in her purse, and came up with a plain white business envelope. "You never heard of me," she said.

"If they really busted their asses, could they figure out how it got to us?" Lucas asked.

She shook her head. "I don't see how. Nobody knows about me and Dave, and even if they did, it'd be a long train. And dad sounded excited about the whole thing . . . so take it."

Lucas took the envelope and put it in his pocket. "I'd like to buy you something: a cup of coffee or a diamond necklace or something—but it'd probably be better if you got out of here."

She bobbed her head. "Yup. You guys be careful. Make Dad be careful."

They said they would, and she patted Andreno on the thigh in a niece-like way and left. Lucas took the envelope out of his pocket and spread the four sheets of paper on the table. On the left side of the paper was a list of names and addresses, and on the right, a bank balance and account number. He scanned them, but nothing in particular caught his eye. As he finished each page, he pushed it across the table to Andreno. When Andreno had read the last page, Lucas asked, "See anything?"

"I know a couple of the companies, the names," Andreno said. "Nothing out of line. But did you see the balances? Nothing under four mil. Bronze Industries at thirty-two million? What the hell is Bronze Industries?"

"I don't know. Some kind of metal deal? I never heard of it."

"Only four individuals, never heard of any of them. I don't know what to tell you."

"I gotta get this back to the feds," Lucas said. "This is what they're good at."

"There's a copy place down the street—they probably got a fax."

ANDRENO WAITED AT Tony's for Bender, while Lucas walked down the street. On the way, he punched Sally's number into the cell phone, got her, and asked for a fax number. She came back with it, and he scribbled it on the palm of his hand.

"What is it?"

"Andy Levy's private client list, with addresses, account numbers, and current balances. You need to look at them and see what they lead back to. Most of them are companies."

"Where'd you get it? This might not be legal."

He heard somebody else in the room ask, "What?"

Lucas said, "Look, I'm gonna fax these things to you. If you don't want them, shred them. As far as *legal* is concerned, I'm not a lawyer. I just got them from a guy."

He punched off and, five minutes later, started dropping the sheets into the fax machine; the machine on the other end was running, and accepted them.

BENDER AND ANDRENO were drinking coffee when Lucas got back. As Lucas sat down, Bender pushed a neat stack of paper across the table. Lucas thumbed through them: xeroxes of a police file.

"I read some of the crime-scene reports while I was xeroxing them," Bender said. He was pleased with himself. "Rinker killed them. Look at the pages I marked with the red pen."

Lucas started pulling out paper: reports from a crime-scene team, from a pathologist, from a cop who ran the case. The killer got in without breaking anything, and there were no signs of tools used around the door—the killer almost certainly had a key, which didn't mean much. There were ways to get keys.

The killer also knew where to find a jewelry hideout box—a concealed vertical slat on the side of a dresser in the master bedroom. The investigating cop described it as "built-in and invisible. In my opinion, the perpetrator must have had prior knowledge of its location."

Further along was a note that Levy had receipts and appraisals for the missing jewelry, setting its value at about sixty thousand dollars.

"Sixty thousand on the jewelry," Lucas told Andreno.

"My memory's getting bad . . . or maybe it's just the inflation."

Some of the jewelry Levy had purchased for his wife, but most she'd inherited from her grandmother and a great-aunt. The Levys' insurance covered only a small fraction of the valuation, no more than five thousand dollars, because they'd neglected to get a jewelry rider on their home insurance policy. There was also a later note, by a second investigator, made when the active investigation was suspended, that much of the value of the inherited jewelry was not in the stones but in the maker's mark—early Tiffany gold and diamonds—and that value would be lost if the pieces were melted down or broken up. Though a knowledgeable thief might try to sell them intact, nothing had been recovered.

"Typical Mafia greed-head would have been insured up to the nuts," Bender said.

"Maybe he thought that'd be too much of a tip-off," Lucas said. "Like pulling the family pictures out of the house before you torch it."

Andreno said, "Might even consider it a nice touch—losing the jewelry."

The victims had been sexually engaged when they were killed. The man was shot in the back of the head. There were no exit wounds, and according to the pathologist, the .22 hollowpoints had made mush out of his brains. Because there were no exit wounds, there were no spatter marks to indicate his exact position when shot. The woman had tried to push him away, but was shot herself before she could get entirely from beneath him; she was draped over the bed onto the floor, with one leg under the man's body.

Lucas tapped the papers back together into a neat stack. "Somebody comes in after a lot of research, gets very close, kills with a .22 that none of the neighbors hear—maybe a silencer—provides Levy with a *nice touch* on the jewelry, and is long gone before the bodies are found. Very efficient."

"Rinker," said Bender, finishing his coffee.

BENDER OFFERED TO drop Andreno. Lucas took the Porsche back to the FBI building, went through the identification rigamarole, and found Malone sitting in the conference room by herself. She looked up from her laptop, blinked a few times to refocus, and said, "Lucas."

"Where is everybody?"

"Most of them are working Levy. Louis is down talking to the AIC, and the two computer guys went to lunch. Got anything new?"

"You get the faxes?"

"We're running them now. Davy Mathews, the organized-crime guy—we introduced you, the guy with the blue suit and white shirt?—thinks he remembers three of the names from references back in Washington. If he can remember three off the top of his head, then there are probably more. Levy could be a serious matter." Her eyes drifted back to the laptop.

"Okay. When is Mallard getting back?" Lucas pulled out a chair and sat down, dug a legal pad out of his briefcase.

"A few minutes. He's just trying to get straight on who's doing what."

"You want to see the St. Louis file on the Levy murder?"

Now she turned to him, one eyebrow raised. Lucas had heard that the one-eyebrow ability was genetic, like the ability to curl your tongue. "You have access?"

"I got the file," Lucas said. "Not the original, but a complete xerox." He took it out and pushed it across the table, and Malone walked her office chair over and thumbed quickly through it. "I'll have somebody check it and cross-reference the names. Thanks."

"Sure."

"What are you going to do now?"

"Sit back, close my eyes, and think," he said. He put his feet and calves on the table, tilted the chair back and closed his eyes.

After a minute, she asked, "You're just going to sit there?"

"For a while."

Malone watched him for a few more seconds, then shrugged and went back to the laptop. After a minute or two, his eyes still closed, he asked, "Louis make a move on you yet?"

Heavy silence, then: "No."

"Is he going to?"

"I don't know. He's certainly taking his time."

"He wants to. But he's too shy. I tried to get him to grab you in Mexico, and he got in a heavy sweat. He's sorta that way. You may have to help him along."

"Ah, jeez," she said. And after a while: "I'm not one hundred percent sure I want to. He's not the most . . . I don't know."

"Not a paperhanger?"

"Sheetrocker. The Sheetrocker is like a fantasy. Big arms, big legs, little butt. Dumb as a bowl of mice. He'll never finish his novel. He only has a novel because he's just barely smart enough to understand that women aren't impressed by Sheetrocking. I doubt that he's faithful; jeez, I *know* he's not. I mean, I haven't caught him running around or anything, but it just isn't his *nature*."

Lucas cracked his eyelids and looked at her. She was sitting in her chair facing him, shoulders hunched, hands in her lap. She looked *lonely*. "You guys . . . Look, try him out. Mallard. Really. Take him out for a cup of coffee, and just . . . take a meeting, for Christ's sake. You both know how to do *that*."

"Thank you for your concern, Chief Davenport."

"Fuck it. I'm going back to sleep."

AFTER A WHILE, he dropped the chair back down, scratched his head, and asked, "I guess you're monitoring Clara's cell phone, in case she calls anyone?"

"Yeah."

"Did you think about asking her brother to call her on that number?"

"Why'd you have to mention Louis?" Malone asked.

"I thought somebody ought to. Put the poor bastard out of his misery, if nothing else." She sniffed, and Lucas said, "No, no no . . . you know the rule: no crying."

She wiped her eyes with the heel of her hand, and he went back to his question. "Anyway, did you think about having her brother call Rinker? Like, early in the morning? If he did, and she answered, and he kept her on for a few minutes, maybe we could zero in on the neighborhood where she's staying. She's gotta be ditched with a friend."

"We're talking about that," Malone said. "We don't have the street contacts here, but we've got the brains. We've talked through most of the possibilities, based on what we've got."

"You gonna do it?"

"Probably—if she doesn't move on Levy. Or one of the others. We're doing a full-court press."

"You got the budget?"

"Yes, we did. . . ." She sniffed again and said, "You know, I always thought I was going to grow up and be pretty glamorous, an FBI agent, high up, with a gun and a computer and fly in jets. And all I wind up doing is marrying stupid guys and I get to be a joke. I'm too tall and I'm too thin and I always dress too conservatively. I'm *flinty*. This isn't the way it was supposed to *be*."

"Jesus, Malone, *you* married them. I can't tell you about that."

"It always seemed like such a good idea at the time. You know, one of the guys, the actor, we got married at the courthouse by a judge and we went outside and he asked me if I had enough money for a cab, and I thought, *This isn't going to work.* We'd been married exactly seven minutes."

"Talk to Louis, for Christ's sake. . . . I'm going back to sleep."

LUCAS LEANED BACK again. He could hear an occasional flurry of keystrokes from the laptop, as Malone pushed through a file somewhere out in electronic FBI-land.

His basic personal asset in the investigation was a bunch of guys who knew the town—but that didn't mean much at the moment, because there was no way to leverage that into more information. If they had even a rough idea of where she was, then some of the FBI data, combined with street information, might get them close. Until then . . . He'd read in an informational brochure at the hotel that there were more than two and a half million people in the St. Louis metro area.

Too many.

Another thought popped up. "Say, did you check Levy's

past account records, to see if Clara's in there? If we could tell where she's moved her money, that'd be good. Or maybe Levy would know."

"Workin' on it," Malone said. "If we can figure out these other accounts, we may have something to squeeze him with."

"Huh."

TWO MINUTES OF silence, then another thought: "She probably crossed the border illegally. I mean, you know, wetbacked it across. She can't know the level of surveillance at the border, she wouldn't want to take a chance of a random check on faked or stolen documents."

"So?"

"So, if she crossed the border illegally, that means she probably crossed in Texas, New Mexico, Arizona, or California."

"Yeah?"

"I drove out to California last year, and there aren't that many ways to get from those places to the Midwest, in a hurry. She could fly, but she never flew much when you guys were tracking her before, because there's always a record and they want ID to get on the planes. . . . I bet she crossed out of Mexico and bought a car. She'd need one when she got here. And I think she'd stick to interstate highways, because there's more volume of traffic and she'd be less conspicuous. And she'd probably pay cash for everything. . . ."

"Where's this going?"

"You'd only have to backtrack down a couple of interstates . . . Seventy, Forty-four."

"Maybe Fifty-five," Malone said, getting interested now.

"Ever since gas theft became a deal, most of the interstate stations have surveillance cameras snapping photos of the cars as they gas up. What if you gave the ID photos to all the local sheriff's departments and had them paper the gas stations along the interstates? If somebody recognizes her . . ."

"If we could even find out what *day* or even *week* that she was at a particular place, we could run *all* of the plates and check the anomalies."

"Long shot," Lucas said.

"But it's a shot," she said.

THEY WERE STILL talking about it when Mallard arrived, looking harassed. Lucas's eyes met Malone's across the table, and she gave a tiny negative shake of her head: not now. Lucas turned to Mallard and asked, "You all meetinged out yet?"

"Meetings are the water we swim in," Mallard said. He fussed with some paper. "But now we all agree who's running this particular investigation." He paused. "Me."

"What about the net on Levy?"

"We're all over him. He's in his office, and if he walks down the hall to the rest room, we'll know." He looked at

Malone. "When I was listening to all that bullshit from Lewis, I was thinking about Levy. I want to contact him now. This afternoon. Get everything we can on him, go over there, tell him he's on Rinker's list, and ask him why. Find out if he knows her, or knows where her money is. At least get him cooperating with the net."

"What if he runs?" Malone asked.

"What if she kills him?" Mallard said.

They all thought about that for a moment, then Malone asked, "If you make the call, I can put it together in an hour."

Mallard looked at Lucas. "What do you think?"

Lucas shrugged. "If he decides to run, can you stop him? Running would be the safest thing for him—and he wouldn't even have to talk to you. If you have something—anything—that would keep him from leaving, I'd put it on him. Because if he has money ditched offshore somewhere, and he splits, it could be a long time before any of us see him again."

Mallard nodded. "We'll find something. You can't live in this country for two days without breaking some law, somewhere."

"You want me to put it together?" Malone asked.

Mallard nodded. "Yes. Do it."

10

RINKER HAD SPENT THE EARLY MORNING WATCHING the outside of Andy Levy's mansion—*mansion* was the only word she had for the place. She was parked a block and a half away, across a busy street, waiting for any kind of movement. She needed to know that he was home, and not hiding out somewhere else. She'd been waiting for an hour when the front door opened, and Levy, in a robe and slippers, stepped out on the stoop and picked up the newspaper, opening and turning it in his hands as he stepped back inside. He was reading the follow-up on the Dichter killing, she thought. If the story was anything like what she'd been watching on television, it should spook him even further. Before he closed the door, he looked carefully up and down the street. Even from a block away, he looked worried.

She grinned as she tossed the glasses on the passenger seat and put the car in gear. She needed him worried. She needed him eager to make a deal, eager to explain, eager to talk.

WHEN SHE GOT back to Pollock's, she found a copy of the *Post-Dispatch* on the kitchen table with a piece of typing paper on it; Dorothy had scrawled, "READ THIS." Rinker picked up the paper, didn't take in the headline at all, but saw the man in the orange suit and the chains, and there was a click of recognition but she couldn't place him, and then she thought, *No, no . . .*

They had Gene, and they were dragging him.

RINKER READ THE story through. An FBI agent, a woman named Malone—Rinker recognized the name from Minneapolis—was dragging Gene. Gene, she said, might provide clues to Clara Rinker's whereabouts, and was inclined to be cooperative because he'd been arrested for possession of drugs. This was his fourth arrest on drug charges, and this time, Malone said, he could be going away for a long time.

Rinker put the paper down, sprawled on the couch, and stared at the ceiling and thought about it. She thought for ten minutes, then rolled off the couch, still uncertain, walked out to the car, climbed inside. She needed someplace reasonably far away, like in Illinois. . . .

She drove north, crossed the river, drove across East St. Louis without looking down, and on the outskirts found a truck stop with a half-dozen pay-phone booths designed for truckers. She got five dollars in quarters, checked the phone book, called 612 information, got the number, and called the Minneapolis police department and asked for Lucas Davenport.

The phone rang once, and a woman answered: "Marcy Sherrill."

"Is this Chief Davenport's office?" she asked.

"Yes, it is, how can I help you?"

"Can I speak to Chief Davenport, please?"

"I'm afraid he's not here right now. . . . I'm not exactly sure when he'll be back. Could I help you, or have him call you?"

Rinker thought again, then frowned and asked, "Is he still in St. Louis?"

"Yes, I think so. Who is this, please?"

"Um . . . Charlotte. Could you tell him Charlotte called?"

Now the woman on the other end of the line sounded pissed. "Charlotte? Charlotte who?"

"Just . . . Charlotte. Thanks a lot." She hung up, then grinned to herself. Sounded like she had gotten Davenport in trouble.

She thought about crossing back to St. Louis, since Davenport was there. But the pile of quarters was right in front of her, with a couple of phone books, so she turned to the yellow pages, found "Hotels," and started calling those with the biggest advertisements. She found him on the fifth call. Nobody in his room. Thought another minute, looked around, found a white pages for St. Louis, looked up the FBI.

What was the name of the woman in Minneapolis? Marcy? Or Cheryl? Marcy, she thought.

She got a central switchboard at the FBI office and said, "My name is Marcy, and I'm with the Minneapolis Police Department. I work for Chief Lucas Davenport. Chief Davenport is there in St. Louis, working with Special Agent Malone. I really need to talk to him—it's an emergency with a case he's on."

"Please hold."

AND THEN, after a minute and a half on hold, like magic, after a click or two, Davenport was on the line. "Marcy?"

"Lucas?"

"Yeah . . . Is this Marcy?"

"No, actually it's not, Lucas."

A long silence, then, his voice gone suddenly deeper: "How've you been?"

"Not so good—but you should know about that." She could imagine the ferocious gesturing and waving on the other end of the line.

"Yeah, I heard you were hit pretty bad." He sounded

calm enough. "I'm really sorry about the baby. My fiancée is pregnant. . . . I'm doing that whole trip myself. Gonna get married in the fall."

"Your fiancée—anybody I'd know?"

"No. She's a doctor. Pretty tough girl. You'd probably like her."

"Maybe . . . but to cut the b.s., I just wanted to call you and to tell you to keep Gene out of this. I knew the federales were going to get involved, I wasn't surprised when I saw that woman Malone in the paper, but we all know that Gene isn't quite right. Putting him in jail won't help anything. I'm not going to come in—you can't blackmail me. But you can tell whoever's running that show over there that I take Gene real personally, and if they mess him up, if they put him in prison, or hurt him, or do any of that, then they better look to their families. I won't try to blow up the president. I'll start killing agents' husbands and wives, and you know I'll do it."

"I'll try to get him cut loose. But I'm not a fed." In the background, faint but clear, she heard a man's voice say, "She's not on her cell."

"You'd lie to me anyway," she said.

"Hey, Clara—I'd put your butt *under* the jail if I got my hands on you, but I'm not fuckin' with Gene. I think Gene is a bad idea, and I'll try to get him cut loose. I'm just not sure how much clout I've got."

"Okay." She looked at her watch. They'd been talking

for exactly one minute. "I gotta go now. They're probably pretty close to busting this line. Give me your cell phone number."

"I don't have—"

"Goodbye."

"Wait, wait, wait . . . I was just trying to stall you." He read off the number, and Rinker jotted it down. Without saying goodbye again, she hung up, moved quickly out to her car, and put it on the highway back to St. Louis. Six miles out, an Illinois Highway Patrol car went by in a hurry, going east, all lights and no siren.

Maybe a train wreck, she thought.

SHE WAS RESTLESS, and though she wasn't inclined to move around in the daylight, she headed back downtown. Maybe, she thought, another little probe on Andy Levy. Maybe she should call Levy, to sweat him a little, to get him used to the idea of talking. And she thought about *that:* Davenport was in town.

She'd been told that he was not only ruthless but lucky, which really frightened her. Ruthless she could deal with. Lucky was a problem. When she'd been stalking people, she'd always been so careful, but always so aware that at any moment, luck could turn and strike at her like a rattlesnake. In her disastrous visit to Minneapolis, she and her client had twisted and turned and worked and struggled and never had been able to pull the last piece of sticky-tape bad luck off their backs. Luck had beaten them, not intelligence, skill, or bad planning.

But maybe she'd had a piece of luck this time. She'd heard that man's voice talking about a cell phone. They must have the number of the cell phone that Dichter had called: They would have traced the number he was calling when he was shot, and when it came up with a stolen phone, must have known it was her. What if they'd traced it to John Sellos? She'd asked Sellos about both Dichter and Levy.

BEFORE SHE WENT to look at Levy again, she might as well ask Sellos about it. She saw a sign for a BP station coming up, took the off-ramp, rolled in to a drive-up phone, found Sellos's number in her phone book, and punched it in. Sellos answered—Sellos, who was always home. Rinker said, "If you tell me why you talked to them, if you tell me honestly, I won't hurt you."

"What?"

"I won't hurt you."

After a pause, and then in what was almost a groan, Sellos said, "They knew all about it. I didn't have a choice. They said if I didn't talk to them, they'd bust me on the Dichter murder, as an accessory, and send me to death row. They said they could trace the guy who stole the phone. I didn't know what to do."

"You gave them Levy's name."

"Clara, what could I do? I figured I could either tell them to screw themselves, and maybe wind up on death row, or maybe sneak it past you."

He was honest enough, anyway. "Goddamnit, John. Was Davenport there? A guy from Minneapolis? Big, dark hair, good-looking guy?"

"Yeah. Guy from Minneapolis. Tough guy. He came in with a local ex-cop, another tough guy. I don't know how they found me, exactly."

"All right."

"You gonna kill me?"

"No. But I'll tell you, John, the feds are cutting a wide swath with this one. If they really think you're involved, you could be in deep shit."

"Ah, you don't know half of it. . . ."

"What?"

"Clara, you know that guy Troy who works for Ross? Muscle guy with a flattop who always puts that tanning stuff all over himself?"

"No. He must've been after me."

"Well, he's a real mean asshole, and he's going around to everybody, asking if they've seen you, or heard where you might be. Guess who he's traveling with?"

"I don't know, John. Why don't you tell me?"

"Honus Johnson." Again, it came out almost as a groan. "I *know* you know Honus."

"I know Honus."

"Honus said that if they find out I'm lying about you, that he'd spend some time with me. He said it in that real queer way, and he touched me on the cheek. I've been washing my cheek every five minutes."

"But you lied."

"Well, I like you, Clara. But I'm really scared now. Between the cops and you and Honus."

"I'm sorry about this," Rinker said. "If I were you, John, I'd go away for a while. It really would be for the best. For you. In six weeks, it'll all be over."

"What if *you're* over. Honus Johnson—"

"Before I leave, I'll take care of Honus Johnson," Rinker said. "So: Go away, John."

"I got the *club,* Clara."

"Yes, I know. But you can't add value to the club if you're dead. Be very calm, make arrangements with your accountant and the bartenders, and then go."

"Oh, man . . ."

"That's my last word, John. Good luck to you. Goodbye." She hung up, and thought, *That answers that.* The feds had Levy's name, and that meant they were probably crawling all over him by now. More to think about. And she had to consider Honus Johnson and his toys. Honus once told her that in his work for Ross, he preferred Craftsman tools from Sears, because of the *guarantee.* It hadn't made her laugh, because Honus had been serious.

Then it occurred to her that luck *had* been with her this

time; Sellos had provided a lot of critical information. And then she thought, *As long as the cops weren't monitoring Sellos's phone.* She looked around for a cop car, a finger of fear touching her heart, then peeled out of the BP lot, and didn't start breathing again until she was back on the interstate.

AT POLLOCK'S, she turned on the television, looking for the local news. When you don't need it, you can't find anything else. When you do need it, you can never find it. She spent an hour clicking around the local channels, then clicked over to CNN Headline News and, after a twenty-minute wait, saw a short piece of tape of federal marshals taking Gene into what was either a courthouse or a jail. She saw Malone again, apparently supervising. The tape made her so angry that she jumped off the couch and walked around the house, back and forth, punching at the air, talking to herself, "Fucking hurt him, you fuckin' *hurt* him," imagining what she'd do if they fuckin' hurt him.

In the tape, Gene had looked utterly forlorn. He couldn't take much jail time. He was claustrophobic, along with everything else. If Davenport didn't get him out of there, she'd have to do something. Move on the FBI? That would kill her.

Maybe she should simply leave. She thought about *that.* Her money was well hidden, and she had a place to go, a warm place with beaches—if it weren't for Gene, she could just give it up, make a call to Ross to warn him off again, let Dichter stand as a warning. She could *leave.* Now she couldn't, not until Gene was taken care of.

POLLOCK USUALLY GOT home around three o'clock. When she was going out, Rinker liked to go with Pollock, because then Pollock became part of the disguise. By two o'clock, she'd been thinking about Gene for so long, and had looked at the *Post-Dispatch* article so many times, that she finally said the hell with it and went back out, looking for another phone. In the morning, she'd gone east, so this time she turned west, out I-64. She eventually stopped at an upscale shopping center called Plaza Frontenac to make the call.

She called the *Post-Dispatch,* but it wasn't easy. The *Post-Dispatch* operator switched her to the reporter who'd written that morning's story about Gene, but the reporter wasn't in, and his voice mail handed her to a woman on the city desk. The woman sent her back to the same reporter before Rinker could object, and the voice mail sent her back to the city desk again. This time, she told the desk woman that "I just need to talk to somebody who covers this Clara Rinker thing. I used to know her."

The woman on the other end was unimpressed with the information, and said, in as close to a monotone as anyone could manage, "I could switch you to either Fabian

Broeder, who's our organized-crime reporter, or to Sandy White, the metro columnist."

"Well, which one do you think? Who's the most important?"

"Sandy's the best known. He's working on a Rinker column for tomorrow."

"Let me talk to him."

She was on hold for another three seconds, then the phone rang once and a man's voice said, "White."

"Are you reporting on the Rinker case?"

"I'm writing a column," White said. "Who is this?"

"Clara Rinker."

A moment of silence. Then: "Bullshit."

"Bullshit your own self," Rinker said. "You got something to take notes with?"

"Yeah. But I still don't think this is Rinker."

"That's what I'm gonna prove to you, dumbhead. Just listen. There's a cop from Minneapolis working with the FBI on this case. His name is Lucas Davenport"—she spelled it for him—"and he's a deputy chief from Minneapolis. I had a run-in with him up there, and he chased me out of my bar in Wichita. Now he's down here helping the federales. You got that much?"

"Yeah." He was typing like crazy, the computer keys rattling in the phone.

"Okay. Here's how I prove who I am. I called him this morning about ten o'clock from East St. Louis and talked to him about the case. He told me that his fiancée is pregnant. I called him at the FBI building."

"Pregnant. Jesus. Are you kidding? Is this really Rinker?" His voice was rising; he was starting to believe.

"Yeah. This is Rinker. If you call Davenport and ask him about his fiancée, he'll confirm that I called him and that nobody else could know about it. About that part of the discussion. Now, I have a statement, okay?"

"Go."

"What?"

"Go with the statement," White said.

"Oh. Okay. Um, the FBI arrested my brother Gene in California on some made-up drug charge. Gene isn't right in the head. He never has been. He's not stupid, but he's just not in this world, you got that? And he's claustrophobic. They are torturing him by putting him in jail. He's an innocent kid, and they're torturing him because they think that will make me surrender. But I won't. I will tell you and everybody else this: If anything happens to Gene—he's just like a helpless kid—if anything happens to him, the blood is on their hands and I will wash it off them, one at a time. One at a time, off them and off their families. Off the FBI people who've done this."

"Go ahead."

"That's all I've got."

"You say the drug charges are bullshit?"

"You sure swear a lot, for the telephone," Rinker said.

"Sorry. I'm kind of excited."

"Okay. Ask them, the FBI, about the charge on Gene. Gene never had more than a single doobie in his whole poor life. He never had more than ten dollars. When was the last time you saw somebody dragged from California to St. Louis in orange prison overalls and chains because he had a doobie?"

"Okay."

"Oh, and something else. The FBI are all over a guy named Andy Levy from First Heartland, because they think I'm going to kill him next. But I'm not going to. Andy used to handle money for me, but he hasn't for a long time. I just wanted to talk to him."

"First Heartland?"

"Yes. Andy's a vice president at First Heartland, and he does the banking for the Mafia here in St. Louis. The FBI knows that, and they've got him protected because they hope they can catch me. But they're wasting their time. I've got no interest in Andy."

"Holy shit. First Heartland."

"There you go again."

"Sorry, but listen. . . . Who *are* you going to kill next? I'd like to send a photographer."

Rinker laughed—almost like a quick cough. The guy had some balls. "I gotta go."

"Let me read this back."

"I don't have time. But you talk to Davenport."

"I don't . . . What, uh . . . why in the hell is a guy from Minneapolis down here?"

"The FBI brought him down because they think he's the most likely guy to catch me."

"Are they right?"

"Maybe. But he hasn't caught me yet, and he's had his chances."

RINKER ARRIVED BACK at Pollock's in time to see Pollock climb the porch steps and then disappear inside. She pulled her car in a tight U-turn, took it down the dirt driveway to the garage, hopped out, lifted the door, and parked. When she let herself into the house, Pollock was in the kitchen. Pollock leaned into her line of sight and called, "You okay?"

"I'm good," Rinker said.

"Got a hornet's nest going," Pollock said.

Rinker looked at her for a minute, then said, "If you think I should go . . ."

"I just think you should lay low for a few days," Pollock said. She came out of the kitchen, wiping her hands on a dishcloth. "I heard on the radio about you calling the FBI. There are cops all over that truck stop, if that was really you."

"It's on TV?"

"It's everywhere on TV," Pollock said. "They're taking fingerprints, they're talking to witnesses. They're making a sketch of you from witnesses."

"All right," Rinker said. "Soon as it gets dark, I'm gonna take off for a while. I'll be gone two or three days, outa here."

"I don't want to know where you're going."

But she did; and Rinker said, "Anniston, Alabama, the garden spot of the Deep South."

"I been there. I don't remember no garden," Pollock said.

"That's okay, because I'm not going after carrots," Rinker said. "I'm going to see an old Army buddy."

11

THE DAY WAS DRAGGING ON.

Malone had put together an approach to Levy, and one of the feds was doing a PowerPoint presentation on Levy's connections in the overground banking world and his possible ties with underground money-laundering activities. Levy's private-client list had turned up a vein of investment by people tied to organized crime. A three-man team had put together a half-hour-long briefing after six hours of financial research.

The team was taking questions when a silent strobe began flashing on a phone on a corner table. Malone was irritated by the interruption, but she was closest. She leaned back and picked up the receiver, listened for a second, and then looked at Lucas. "Marcy wants to talk to you. Problem at your office," she said in a quiet voice.

She'd met Marcy during the Rinker investigation in Minneapolis.

"Sorry. She should have called me on the cell." Lucas walked around the table and took the call, half-turned his back to the guy making the presentation, pushed the hold button, and said, quietly, "Marcy?"

"Lucas?" Didn't sound like Marcy, unless she'd developed a cold.

"Yeah . . . Is this Marcy?"

"No, actually it's not, Lucas."

It took him just a second. In that second, he remembered what she smelled like, the nice smell of perfume and a little beer, the time they danced in her Wichita saloon. "How've you been?"

Lucas started waving frantically at Mallard, who looked puzzled for a second, then caught on. He said, silently, miming the name with his lips, "Rinker?"

Lucas nodded, but missed part of what Rinker had said. He caught, ". . . you should know about that."

Around him, the feds were scrambling for phones and one man dashed out the door, a yellow legal pad spinning to the floor behind him.

"Yeah, I heard you were hit pretty bad," Lucas said. His heart was pounding, but he thought, *Cool down, cool down. She's too smart to give herself away.* He groped for something that would make a human connection and keep her talking. "I'm really sorry about the baby," he said. "My fiancée is pregnant. . . . I'm doing that whole trip myself. Gonna get married in the fall."

One of the feds looked up at that and gave him the thumb-and-forefinger *attaboy* circle-sign. He could hear Malone mumbling into a phone: "Need an immediate trace on the call . . ."

Rinker said, "Your fiancée—anybody I'd know?"

"No. She's a doctor. Pretty tough girl. You'd probably like her."

"Maybe . . . but to cut the b.s., I just wanted to call you and to tell you to keep Gene out of this. I knew the federales were going to get involved, I wasn't surprised when I saw that woman Malone in the paper, but we all know that Gene isn't quite right. Putting him in jail won't help anything. I'm not going to come in—you can't blackmail me. But you can tell whoever's running that show over there that I take Gene real personally, and if they mess him up, if they put him in prison, or hurt him, or do any of that, then they better look to their families. I won't try to blow up the president. I'll start killing agents' husbands and wives, and you know I'll do it."

"I'll try to get him cut loose. But I'm not a fed," Lucas said. One of the feds behind him said, "She's not on her cell," and Lucas thought, *Ah, shit.*

"You'd lie to me anyway," Rinker said.

"Hey, Clara—I'd put your butt *under* the jail if I got my hands on you, but I'm not fuckin' with Gene. I think Gene is a bad idea, and I'll try to get him cut loose. I'm just not sure how much clout I've got."

"Okay. I gotta go now. They're probably pretty close to busting this line. Give me your cell phone number."

"I don't have—"

"Goodbye."

"Wait, wait, wait—I was just trying to stall you." He recited the number. There was a pause, and he added, "You can call that anytime."

But she was gone. "Holy shit," Lucas said. He turned to the room. "She's gone. We got the line?"

Malone was on the phone, waving him off. Then the man who'd dashed out of the room hurried back in and said, "We're jacked directly into the highway patrol. When we get the line—"

"We got the line," Malone blurted. "It's in Illinois."

"Damnit," said the man who'd contacted the highway patrol. "We've got Missouri Highway Patrol on line one. They must have a quick way to get to the Illinois cops."

Malone punched up line 1 and, after identifying herself, told the Missouri cop that "she was calling from Illinois. How quick can you get to them? How long? Go, then. Here's the location. . . ."

A truck stop. Lucas said, "When the cops get there, don't let anybody leave the truck stop. Isolate the phone she was on. We need to see if we can get more prints, see if we can get some people who saw her who can tell us what she looks like now."

Malone nodded, and started repeating what Lucas said. Mallard said, "I've got a car. Let's go."

"If it's just you, let's take my Porsche. I'll get us there in a hurry."

Mallard said to Malone, "I'll be on the cell phone. Call me in two minutes and vector us in on the truck stop."

"It's right off I-64. Get on I-64 and go east, and I'll call you and get you there."

"I've got a flasher for my car," Lucas said over his shoulder, as he and Mallard headed for the door. "Tell the patrol that we're coming through."

THE DISTANCE WAS a little better than thirty miles. Once on the interstate, they flew, with Mallard hunched over his cell phone, listening to directions and updates from Malone, talking over the rush of the wind, sheltering the face of the phone away from the red flasher behind the windshield. Between calls, Lucas filled him in on what Rinker had said: the warnings about her brother.

"We've dealt with people a hell of a lot more dangerous than she is," Mallard said.

"Maybe not—maybe not as personally dangerous," Lucas said. "Most assholes aren't focused on a particular group of agents. That makes them easier to nail down. She's not nuts. Not in that way."

"The warning just tells us that the brother ploy is effective—it's working on her," Mallard said.

"Hope it doesn't bite you in the ass," Lucas said.

Mallard went back to the phone and filled in Malone on the warning from Rinker. When he got off, he said, "Malone's routing out a crime-scene guy to print the phone and another guy with a laptop ID kit. She talked to the manager of the truck stop and told him to keep people off the phones. If we can find one guy who got a good look at her, it'll be worth the trip."

Lucas looked out the window. "You know, if Rinker's staying here in town, and if she went out there just to make the call, the chances are we're driving right past her. Over in the other lane."

Mallard looked over into the westbound lane and said, "So close."

THE TRUCK STOP looked like all truck stops—a yellow steel building with blackout windows in the middle of an oversized, oil-stained concrete fuel pad with a double line of gas pumps and a couple of diesel sheds. Inside, a convenience store was hip-joined to a macaroni-and-cheese restaurant, with a set of rest rooms in the middle and a locked suite of drivers-only showers. A half-dozen cop cars were parked around the place when Lucas gunned the Porsche up the ramp and into a narrow slot between two highway patrol cruisers.

An Illinois highway patrolman had just stepped up to the door, going in, when Lucas pulled up, and he shook his head and then stepped toward them when Lucas killed the engine. Mallard was out first with his ID. "FBI," he said.

The cop looked at Mallard, then at Lucas, then at the Porsche, and said to Mallard, "You guys're getting pretty fat rides these days."

"Hey, the income taxes are pouring in—you can't believe it," Lucas said. "We figure, might as well enjoy life."

Mallard said, "He owns it personally. He's rich, he's an asshole, he works for the city of Minneapolis. The federal government drives low-end Chrysler products that would make your mother cry with shame." And: "Who's running things?"

"I don't know, I just got here myself," the cop said.

THE FIRST COP on the scene had been a highway patrol sergeant named Eakins who hadn't known exactly what was required, and as an old hand, adept at covering his ass, had done exactly the right thing: He'd frozen the scene. Nobody out until the feds said so, nobody near a phone.

"Don't make much difference anyhow—everybody's got a cell phone," he said.

"Anybody see her?"

"Two guys think they might have—they're in the restaurant eating pie," Eakins said.

"All right," Mallard said. "Just keep doing what you're doing."

"Can we let people out?"

"Yeah. If you're pretty sure they're okay. But get IDs, truck tag numbers, just in case. Check the trucks, make sure nobody's hiding behind the seats. Anybody coming in, we should warn off—if they can move along, let them go. If they've got to stop here for some reason, tell them there could be a delay before they can leave."

"We can do that," Eakins said. "Let me show you the pie guys and then I'll get organized outside."

THE PIE GUYS looked remarkably alike, big square-faced over-the-road drivers in checked shirts with guts hanging over their tooled-leather belts. The woman they saw was probably Rinker. They'd both had a chance to look her over: nice-looking blonde, they said, trim, short hair. Classy, but looked like a pretty good time. "She was in a hurry," Blueberry Pie said. "I was kind of watchin' her out of the corner of my eye. She made a couple of calls, but she was real quick with them—like a businesswoman. That's what I figured she was. A real-estate lady, checking on calls or something."

Apple Pie added that she had a nice ass and thought she might have been heading toward a Ford Explorer when she went out the door. "I didn't see her get in it, but there weren't a hell of a lot of cars down there, and when the cops come running in the door, I noticed that the Explorer was gone."

"What color?"

"Umm, dark red. Liver-colored, sorta."

"You didn't . . . ?"

"Naw. Never looked at the plates. I was too busy looking at her ass."

Both pies agreed that Rinker had used the second phone from the end in a bank of phones on the back wall of the convenience store.

As Lucas and Mallard finished the interview, a black Tahoe pulled up and a half-dozen feds climbed out. Then another Tahoe, and more of them, all in suits. "Looks like a podiatry convention," Lucas said to Mallard.

They looked at the phones, which looked like a lot of other phones, and talked to other people who hadn't seen Rinker, and to people who hadn't seen her car, and to one guy who was fairly sure that he'd seen "a black feller" getting into the maroon Explorer.

"That's good," Lucas said to Mallard. "Now we're not sure about the Explorer."

Malone arrived, with another batch of feds. They all went to look at the phones again, and a fingerprint technician said, "I'm pretty sure those pie guys were right about the phone. This was the phone she used."

"How's that?" Mallard asked.

"I don't think any of the other phones will be this

thoroughly wiped," he said. "Looks like she sprayed it with Windex."

AN HOUR AFTER they arrived, now convinced that they were wasting their time, Lucas bought a purple-flavored Popsicle, took Malone aside, recited the Rinker conversation as close to word-for-word as he could, through the crumbling bits of faux-grape ice, and said, "I want to talk to Gene. Maybe Clara's got some other reason for trying to push us away from him."

"We've got some pretty good guys talking to him," Malone said.

"I know, I know. I just want to chat with him. See what he has to say. Look him over."

"Can I come?"

"You can listen if you want, but I'd rather you not be inside with me. I'm looking for a nonfederal vibe."

She thought about it for a second, then said, "Okay."

"I want to bring another guy to listen. Old-cop type."

"Your friend Del?" She'd met Del in Minneapolis.

"No. A guy from down here. Old buddy, he's got a good ear. Maybe he could pick up something local, if Gene knows anything local. A hint, a little . . . *anything.*" He looked around, finished with the Popsicle. "Where do I throw the sticks?"

She said, "No. Not the floor." Then: "I'll set it up for this afternoon. It's getting late, so it'll have to be soon. The Gene thing."

"What about Levy? You were all set to walk in on him."

"We're still go on that," she said. "We'll take him home, and when he gets there, we'll knock on the door."

THEY TOOK AN HOUR to get organized, get in touch with Andreno, and make it to Clayton, where Gene Rinker was being held in a rented cell at the county lockup. "I thought it was better from a security point of view, given Clara's style, to hold him here," Malone said, as they went up in the elevator. "We're not moving him in and out of an obvious spot when we want to talk to him."

Andreno, who'd been waiting for them in the parking lot, said, "So, you guys been working day and night on this thing? Round the clock?"

Malone glanced at him. Andreno had changed to a lush gray double-breasted chalk-striped suit that he'd apparently bought from Mafia Tailors. "Pretty much," she said. "We have more than fifty agents in the field right now."

"Got some great Italian restaurants in this town," he said.

Lucas shook his head. "She already has romantic entanglements," he said.

Andreno worked his eyebrows. "Yet another reason she might want to try the local rigatoni."

Malone looked troubled, and turned to Lucas: "He's not even a very good Sheetrocker. I realized that last night."

Andreno was puzzled: "A Sheetrocker?"

"The bottom line is, her heart belongs to another," Lucas said. "We're just trying to identify him."

Andreno shook his head. "If . . ."

"Ask me later," Lucas said to Andreno. "We'll get a cup of coffee and talk about feelings."

"Fuck you," Malone said, but she didn't say it in a mean way.

The elevator bell dinged, the doors opened, and they got out.

GENE RINKER WAS already in the interview room. Malone hung back, while a jailer let Lucas and Andreno into the room. The jailer gave Rinker the *be good* look, and shut the door.

Rinker sat wordlessly as Lucas and Andreno settled in. Rinker was an inch short of six feet, and slender, but not thin: unhealthy, as though he ate bad food, his face so weathered that it actually seemed to be pitted with grains of sand. His hands were rough, as weathered as his face, slack in his lap; the roughness made them dark, but the first two fingers of his right hand were nicotine-stained. His hair was limp, dishwater blond, and fell lifelessly to his slumping shoulders. He wore a gray T-shirt and jeans a size too big, with white gym shoes—the clothing appeared to have been given to him by somebody who'd guessed at sizes. He didn't look straight at either Lucas or Andreno.

If Lucas had seen him on the street, he would have

thought, *Loser, a throwaway kid, a street kid, probably did a little dope, probably stole a little, probably too unsure of himself to go violent.* As Lucas and Andreno sat down, he rubbed one finger between his eyes, nervous, then dropped his hands back to his lap.

"We're not feds," Lucas started. "I'm a cop from Minneapolis, this other guy's a cop from St. Louis. . . . I've actually talked to your sister a couple of times. Talked to her yesterday."

Rinker was skeptical, but too scared to say anything. Lucas grinned at him. "You would've liked it. She called me in the FBI building, right in the middle of a meeting, and told me to get the feds off of you. There were FBI agents running around like chickens. We figured out where she called from, but by the time we got there, she was gone."

Rinker nodded, cleared his throat. "Good," he ventured.

"Listen, son, the feds only got one handle on Clara, and you're it, and they're pissed," Andreno said. "They're gonna stuff you in a drawer someplace if we don't catch her pretty soon, and you're not gonna like it. They got some tough goddamn prisons in the federal system." He was using his sincere voice, and it came off. He sounded absolutely paternal, Lucas thought.

"Catching Clara would be the best thing for everybody," Lucas said. "I know you don't want to hurt your sister."

"Not gonna hurt her," Rinker said.

"That's good, that's family feeling. I'm Italian, and we got that feeling," Andreno said. "The problem is, Clara's gonna get hurt. There's no way around it. The feds are gonna hunt her down, and they're probably gonna kill her. If we could get her off the street . . . I mean, hell, she has to have a trial and everything."

A spark of intelligence showed in Rinker's eyes: "They're gonna put her to sleep anyway, no matter what you say," he said. "One way she's free, and maybe she'll get away. If you get her in jail, they're just gonna put her to sleep. Better to get shot than that, having to wait around in a place like this"—he flipped one hand at the sterile room—"and then have somebody tie you to a table and put a thing in your arm."

"Maybe, but maybe not," Lucas said. "But I'll tell you this: She's not only hurting herself, and you, she's hurting her friends. She's crashing someplace around here, with one of her friends, and whoever that is . . . she's just as guilty now as Clara is. She's taking her friends down with her. Does that sound right?" He put a little authority into it, and watched Rinker's wavering intelligence crawl back in a hole.

Rinker mumbled, "I guess not," and he looked at his hands.

"Do you know her friends here?" Andreno asked.

Rinker said nothing at all, didn't seem to have heard

the question. His eyes flattened, he seemed even slacker in the shoulders, as though his mind had slipped away.

Andreno repeated himself: "Do you know her friends?"

Rinker stayed away for another few seconds, then his eyes focused and he pulled himself out of wherever he'd gone. He shook his head. "She never said nothing about friends around here. I didn't know anything about St. Louis. I took off for Los Angeles as soon as I was old enough." He stopped, catching himself.

Lucas pushed: "Then where *were* her friends? She must have had friends back home somewhere."

"Maybe," Rinker conceded. He licked his lips. "I wouldn't know nothin' about that. She was older'n me."

They worked on him for another fifteen minutes, but nothing came out of it. He was not only a thrown-away kid, Lucas realized; he *did* have some mental deficit, or otherness. He slipped away when they pressed him, and only reluctantly came back.

When they ran out of questions, Lucas and Andreno sighed simultaneously, and Lucas said, "Well, hell," and Andreno said, "Wish we could help you, son. These goddamn feds . . . they can be real assholes."

"I gotta get out of here," Rinker said, struggling to come alive. "I got all my stuff back in L.A. If I don't get back, Larry or Jane is gonna find it and they'll just flat sell it. They'll sell it first chance they get. Got some good stuff, there. Got a suit. Got a radio."

"I wish—" Andreno began.

"I gotta get out of here," Rinker said, cutting him off. His eyes were big, and going oily, and he looked around the room, looked for a window or a crack or anything that might let in some air. "I mean I just . . . I just . . . I gotta get out of here. I can't breathe, I got dreams . . ."

"About Clara?" Lucas asked.

"About me. I'm like this big moth, like the moths that come at night when you've got flowers, they're like hummingbirds, but they're moths, and I'm one of them, and these guys catch me and I'm flapping my wings and they keep pulling at me like they're gonna pull my wings off, and my feelers. I got these big feelers like feathers and they're gonna pull them off. And they were all laughing and when I sat up on the bunk last night I thought I was there, that they were pulling my wings off, and I couldn't breathe, I just kept flapping my wings. . . ."

LUCAS CALLED THE jailer, then told Rinker, "We'll try to do something. Gotta be a little patient, though."

Andreno chipped in: "Hold on, son."

When the jailer took him away, Rinker looked back at them and said, "I really gotta get back. All my stuff is in L.A. They're gonna sell it if I don't get back."

MALONE HAD A TAPE. "If you want to listen to it again, it's all there," she said, as they took the elevator down.

"I only saw one thing," Lucas said, looking at Andreno. "Clara had a friend or maybe a couple of friends back home. He didn't want to say it."

"Shouldn't be hard to find, if they're still there," Andreno said. "Town's about two blocks long."

"We've had agents out there," Malone said. "Interviewed everybody—nothing. Her mother's a vegetable, barely remembers Clara. We've gone over the whole house, from top to bottom, looked at every scrap of paper."

"Find any friends?"

"Nobody. Not many people even remembered her. The family was sorta . . . isolated."

"Huh." Lucas thought about it, then asked Andreno, "What do you think?"

"What else have we got?"

"Maybe our friend the phone guy," Lucas suggested.

"We could try him again. If we don't get anything, it's about three hours down to Tisdale. We can go down late tonight, after we talk to Levy, poke around tomorrow morning, stop at the Bass Pro Shops store, and still get back by early afternoon."

"Gotta think about it," Lucas said. To Malone: "And you gotta think about cutting Gene loose. There's nothing there. He could use some . . . help."

"This whole thing will resolve itself in the next week or so," Malone said. "We've got so many people looking that we'll either turn Rinker up, or she'll leave. When it's resolved . . . yeah, we'll probably cut him loose. If we don't catch her here, we'll let him go and keep an eye on him for a few months, see if he has any visitors."

THEY DEFLECTED MALONE'S curiosity about the phone guy. She made a call, talked to Mallard for a few minutes, lifted her face away from the receiver to tell Lucas that they'd rendezvous in Central West End at seven o'clock, and go from there to Levy's. Levy, according to his watchers, usually worked late at his office and got home sometime after six o'clock. "Louis wants to find a place to eat before we go in." She looked at Andreno.

Andreno thought about it for a second, then brightened. "Perfect spot. Tell him there's a place called the Black Lantern, five-minute walk from Levy's place. Steak joint. Good salads. Good martinis. We've got just enough time to eat comfortable."

Malone relayed the information, listened for a moment, then said goodbye and hung up. She told Lucas, "He says you're supposed to call Marcy at your office. She says it's semi-urgent."

When they got out on the sidewalk, Lucas used his cell phone to dial the office in Mineapolis. Black picked up, then switched him over to Marcy. "What's up?" Lucas asked.

"A columnist for the St. Louis *Post-Dispatch* called here, trying to get you. He says that Rinker called him this afternoon and gave you as a reference for some stuff she told him. He says he's pretty sure it's Rinker who called."

"Gave me as a reference?"

"Yeah. Whoever this is, she told him that she talked to you," Marcy said.

"She did. She said she was you."

"*What?* Tell me . . ." And in the background, Lucas could hear her say to Black, "She called him. She said she was me." She sounded thrilled to have been touched by a celebrity.

"I'll talk to you later," Lucas said. "What's this news guy's name and number?"

"His name's Sandy White. . . ."

Lucas jotted the name and number in the palm of his hand, rang off, and told Malone and Andreno what had happened.

"Jesus," Andreno said. "Who's running this operation, the FBI or Rinker?"

"There seems to be some disagreement about that," Malone said.

"So do I talk to White?" Lucas asked. "You make the call."

"We'll have somebody else talk to him. I'll call Louis on the way down to Central West End," Malone said. "That way, White can't push you, because our guy can deny knowing too much about it. And we find out what she said."

THE BLACK LANTERN was an old-style steak house, set a few steps below street level and smelling of sizzling beef fat and beer. Mallard had already taken a table, and was reading a menu the size of a wall calendar.

Lucas introduced him to Andreno, and Mallard asked, "Does anybody read this guy Sandy White?"

"Probably not more than half the people in St. Louis," Andreno said. "He's got a job as a TV editorial guy, too, so he'll have that going, along with the column."

"Goddamnit," Mallard grumbled. "I talked to him. Rinker called him, all right. He's running a piece tomorrow, warning us off her brother. White talked to a cop somewhere and got Gene Rinker's arrest record, and they know we're holding him on simple possession."

"One good thing about it," Lucas said, as he studied the menu.

"Tell me, please."

"If somebody gets screwed for this, it's gonna be you, not me," Lucas said.

Andreno nodded and said, "Got that straight."

They ordered wine, and Malone told Mallard about the interview with Gene Rinker, and then Mallard and Malone ordered salads and Lucas and Andreno ordered steaks, and Andreno said, "Gene Rinker is a troubled young man. I don't think it was dope—looked like he was fucked from the git-go."

"And you got nothing from him," Mallard predicted.

"Eh," Lucas said. "Probably nothing. We might run down to Tisdale and poke around."

"Tomorrow?"

"Tonight, if nothing comes up. Get a bed in Springfield."

Mallard shrugged. "We talked to everybody she knew—but hell, if you want to, it's fine with me. Maybe you'll turn something up."

"She didn't make good friends. She was too messed up," Lucas said. "We think she might have had some friends when she was a kid. We keep thinking, she's gotta be staying somewhere. She's not sleeping in her car."

"Whatever . . ."

The steaks came a few minutes later and they talked about the case a bit, and Lucas thought about the friend that Rinker must be staying with, and said, gesturing with a neatly forked square of rib eye, "You know, if you really don't care how you get her—I mean, dead or alive—you ought to talk to all the local assholes and tell them that she's staying with a friend. *Somebody* in that whole grapevine would know who her friends were. She worked for them, and *somebody* would know. Especially if there was some money on the table."

Malone nodded. "There would have been no reason for her to keep her friendships secret back then."

Mallard said, "Except that she's smart. We know she's smart, and this whole thing with this White guy makes me think she's a little smarter than I realized. I mean, she's messing with us. She's gonna have a bunch of civil rights attorneys on our asses in the morning. All that makes me think—she'd know that her old pals might sell her out. She'd be ready for that."

LEVY LIVED ON a semiprivate street four blocks from the Black Lantern, a huge black-brick pile with a marble entrance and a carriage house visible in the back. One end of the street was open, but with warning signs against nonresident parking; the other end was closed with a wrought-iron fence.

They'd decided to go in cold. The supervisor in the group covering Levy called Mallard toward the end of the meal to say that Levy had arrived home. "He's scared. He's got a guy traveling with him, apparently a bodyguard. He took his car straight into the carriage house, and the bodyguard *ran* between the carriage house and the main house. Somebody met him, and then Levy ran up to the house while the bodyguard waited at the door."

"Must be pretty sure that nobody's in the carriage house, then," Lucas said.

"Our guys said both the house and the carriage house are wired up tight."

"Well, at least we know he'll be there. Doesn't sound like he expects to go barhopping," Andreno said.

They took their time walking over, looking at the houses along the side streets. There were lights everywhere, people moving around. If Rinker was in one of the houses on Levy's street, or behind Levy's street, she'd have a tough time getting out, Lucas thought. "As soon as we talk to him, you oughta have the net guys start going door to door, making sure that Rinker's not holding somebody in one of these places," Lucas said.

"We'll do that," Mallard said. At the entrance to Levy's street, they passed though a wrought-iron gate, closed it behind themselves. A man in a suit climbed out of a car and walked toward them. He was carrying a pale straw hat, and said, "Louis."

"David. Everybody, this is David Homburg," Mallard said to Lucas and Andreno. To Homburg: "We're going in—you and me and Malone, and Lucas. And, uh, Mr. Andreno, I guess."

"Hate to miss it," Andreno said.

Mallard told Homburg to leave two watchers on the front and back of Levy's, and to have the rest of the net begin knocking on doors, two men at a time. Homburg stepped back to his car and spoke on a radio for a few moments, then rejoined them. "Done."

"So let's go," Mallard said.

LEVY WAS NOT what Lucas expected—he'd expected one of the tough-faced finance guys, and instead got a round-faced beach boy, middle forties, with bleached tips on his light brown hair, a carefully revised nose, dark brown golf shirt under a soft leather lounging jacket with fawn slacks, and leather moccasins without socks.

The bodyguard was another case altogether. He was a

muscular size 48, with a buzz cut; he looked like he was made from leather that the cobbler had thrown away before making Levy's shoes. He'd come to the door carefully, checking them from a side window, then through the security-glass window on the door.

Mallard and Malone held up IDs so he could read them, and when he opened the door, he still had a hand on his back hip pocket, where, Lucas thought, he had a gun.

"Federal Bureau of Investigation," Mallard told him. "We're here to talk to Mr. Levy."

"I'll see if he's in," the tough guy said.

"We know he's in, because we've had a net around him all day, watching him. We just watched you take him from the carriage house to the back door, running. When you see if he's in, you might suggest to him that Clara Rinker is unlikely to show up with a committee."

"Wait here." The tough guy left them standing on the porch, one minute, two, looking at their shoes and the trees, listening to the cicadas fiddling down at them.

"Nice night," Mallard said eventually.

"Fuckin' guy," Andreno said.

Then the tough guy came back, looked them over again, and said, "Come in."

LEVY, BLEACHED-TIP HAIR and sockless mocs, stood with his hands in the pocket of his jackets, in the doorway of a library.

"Mr. Mallard? Could I see your ID again?"

Mallard handed him his ID. Malone and Homburg held theirs up so he could scan them as he read down Mallard's. Then he looked at Lucas and Andreno, a petulant frown creasing his forehead. "What about these gentlemen?"

"They're essentially hired thugs," Mallard said. "They don't have ID. In any case, we really don't want to spend any more time sorting through the personnel, Mr. Levy. Clara Rinker is here to kill you. We know that for sure. We're trying to catch her. You might be able to help."

"How do you know it for sure?"

"Because one of our agents talked to a gentleman who she interrogated, and your name was prominent in the discussion. We think you know all of this—we've been watching you for a couple of days, and we've noted the precautions you're now taking . . . like the man with the gun."

Levy stared at Mallard for a moment—Mallard looked placidly back—then said, "Why don't we sit down?"

They filed into the library. The library was a stage setting, Lucas thought, filled with decorator book sets, bought by the running foot, an oversized mahogany desk with an inset leather top, an expensive-looking oriental carpet, and a globe the size of a weather balloon. Levy settled into a chair behind the desk; Mallard and Malone took guest chairs facing the desk, Homburg found a seat on a faux Louis XIV, and Lucas and Andreno picked out places to lean. Andreno seemed fascinated by the globe, and began turning it under one hand as Mallard and Levy talked.

Levy said, "How do you know she's looking for me?"

"She blames you and several other people for the attempt on her life in Mexico. You managed to kill her fiancé. She was also pregnant, and when she was wounded, she lost the child. She has now clearly gone over the edge. She's insane. We frankly think you have one small chance to stay alive: cooperate with us."

"What if I decide to take care of myself?"

"Then you'll die," Mallard said. "Nanny Dichter was as well protected as you are, and she picked him like a bad apple."

Levy said, "I really don't know anything about what happened in Mexico, and my involvement with her was only peripheral. One of my other clients once asked me to help her set up a retirement account, which I thought was entirely legitimate."

"You can cut the shit," Malone said. "We've known about your private-client accounts for quite a while. We let you run them because we were learning so much about the crime club around here. But just leave out the bullshit, okay? It'll make this conversation a lot shorter."

Lucas suppressed a smile. The Mallard and Malone good-cop/bad-cop act was back in town, and Malone made an excellent bad cop. The vulgarities slipping from her notably prim mouth made her that much more effective.

Levy leaned back. "I do not know—"

Mallard interrupted. "What we would like to do is slip a few people in here, as soon as we're sure that she isn't watching. Then we'll pull back our covering net, and let her walk into the trap. That's what we want."

"What if you don't have enough guys?"

"This isn't a TV movie. She's not invincible, she's not Wonder Woman. Once we see her, we'll take her," Mallard said. "We'll have two or three guys who could take her by themselves, and we'll have two or three guys to back them up, and then we'll have a couple more guys to back *them* up. We'll have a net to take you downtown, and another trap at the bank. You'll be safer than the President."

"So all I have to do is agree?"

"I'll be blunt, Mr. Levy. We think we could build a hell of a money-laundering case against you," Malone said. "We think we could see you into Leavenworth for twenty years, and there'd be no parole. You might want to get a lawyer and see what you can negotiate. If you had any kind of information for us, we'd be happy to take that into account. Otherwise, do what you want—but it's in both of our interests to take out Clara Rinker."

Levy made a steeple of his fingers, resting them on his chest. Then: "I'm gonna want to talk to my guy, my counsel. My attorney. I'll get him over here tonight. Until then, keep her off me."

"If she sees us, we'll be wasting our time," Mallard said. "You've got to decide tonight so we can get our people out of sight."

"I'll decide," Levy said. "Let me call my guy."

They all sat for a moment, with nothing more to say, until Andreno said, "This is a hell of a globe. Where do you get a globe like this?"

LEVY LEFT THEM talking in the library while he called his attorney. Seeing no point in waiting, Lucas collected Andreno and told Mallard that they were going out—"Have a couple of beers, talk to people. Maybe head to Springfield."

"Back tomorrow?"

"Late afternoon, unless something comes up. You've got my cell phone."

ON THE WALK back to Lucas's car, Andreno asked, "You think she'll walk into it?"

"Mmm. No."

"Could happen."

"It *could* happen, but I doubt it. She ain't gonna walk up and ring the doorbell. It'll be something trickier. I just don't know what."

"Let's find Sellos. Maybe she's come back to him."

They headed downtown, but when they got to the BluesNote, they found that Sellos had disappeared. The bartender said, "He went to golf school."

"What?"

"Yeah. A short-game school." He polished a glass and held it up to a light, looking for smears. "You know, from a hundred yards in. Don't know where, exactly."

Andreno looked at Lucas and said, "Now what?"

Lucas leaned close to the bartender and said, "Give me four bottles of Dos Equis. Just crack the caps."

OUTSIDE AGAIN, with the four bottles of beer in a paper bag, Lucas said, "Where do you think he went?"

"If he's alive, maybe . . . Michigan? They've got good golf courses."

"Mmm. I guess Palm Springs would be a little hot this time of year. . . ." A warm breeze scuffled down the street. Lucas looked up at the moon. "Nice night for a road trip."

"Unless the highway patrol catches us with open beer."

"Like they could catch us," Lucas said.

12

THE PAIN PUSHED THROUGH THE SLEEP LIKE AN ARROW, and he rose to the surface and tried to sit up and stretch his right leg, but the cramp held on and got deeper, and Lucas groaned, "Man, man, man-o-man-o-man," and tried to knead it out, but the cramp held on for fifteen seconds, twenty, then began to slacken. When it was nearly gone, he climbed gingerly out of bed and took a turn around the hotel room.

His calf still ached, as though with a muscle pull. He sniffed, and looked around, getting oriented: He was on the eighth floor of a Holiday Inn outside of Springfield, Missouri. Like most Holiday Inns, it was nice enough, neat and clean, but still . . . smelled a little funny. Nothing he could quite pin down.

Years before, in college, he'd ridden buses down to

Madison to see a particular University of Wisconsin coed, and had noticed that there was always the faint snap of urine in the air, and assumed that it was . . . urine. Then one day on a longer trip, on an express bus, they'd all been asked to get off in Memphis so the bus could be cleaned. When he got back on, one of the cleaners was still at work, and the urine smell was not only fresh, but intense and close by—and he realized that the ever-present urine smell was nothing more than the cleaning agent, whatever it was, and not the end product of somebody pissing down the seats. He hadn't ridden those buses in years, but he could still summon up the memory of the odor.

As he limped around the hotel room, it occurred to him that the funny smell in Holiday Inns—something you could never quite put a label on—might be built-in. If it was, he thought, they should build in something else.

He stopped the circular march long enough to click on the TV, hoping to pick up the weather. He got CNN by default, and as he was about to click around for the Weather Channel, the blond newsreader turned expectantly to her left, and the shimmering image of a St. Louis reporter came up, and under his ruddy round face, the label "Sandy White, St. Louis Post-Dispatch."

". . . sounded distraught, and while people may certainly have no sympathy at all for Miz Rinker, I personally find the plight of her brother, Gene, to be intensely painful. He was arrested and charged on a crime that usually produces something on the order of a traffic ticket in California, and here he is being dragged across the nation and exhibited to television cameras as if he were a criminal mastermind. In fact, Betty, there is good evidence that Gene Rinker is mentally impaired, and may not even understand why he is locked up in a special high-security cell in one of the hardest jails in Missouri. . . ."

"Ah, Jesus," Lucas said to the TV, as the two heads continued to talk. He watched the rest of the segment, which produced nothing more of intelligence, then clicked around until he found the Weather Channel. He sat on the bed rubbing out his calf until the local segment came up, and headed for the bathroom happy with a prediction of late-afternoon thunderstorms. That was okay. They'd be out of Springfield before the storms arrived.

He shaved, brushed the sour taste of overnight beer from his teeth and tongue, and was in the shower for two minutes when Andreno called. They agreed to meet in the breakfast bar in fifteen minutes, and Lucas finished cleaning up. He'd brought one change of clothes in a plastic laundry bag stolen from the St. Louis hotel. He changed into jeans, golf shirt, and a light woven-silk sport coat, stuffed the dirty clothes back in the plastic bag, and headed out.

"You get a chance to look at CNN this morning?" Andreno asked.

"The Gene Rinker thing, with that Sandy guy? Yeah. Assholes."

"Of course, he's right. Sandy White is."

"Fuck him, anyway." Lucas snarled silently across the breakfast room at a pretty young waitress, who hurried over. "Two waffles, maple syrup, two cups of coffee for me." He looked across the table at Andreno. "And what do you want?"

Andreno ordered, and when the waitress had gone, Lucas said, "Malone and Mallard are smart people. They'll figure out Gene. I'll call them."

"Yeah."

"Fuckin' CNN."

"Jesus, you sound like you got up on the wrong side of the bed."

"I'll cheer up," Lucas said, thinking of the leg cramp. "I don't usually get up at seven o'clock. Christ, I'm amazed that they already let the air outside."

When the pretty waitress came back with the food, he smiled at her and tried to make small talk; but she'd already written him off, because of the silent snarl, and he finished breakfast feeling like a jerk.

"I feel like a jerk," he told Andreno, as they left. He'd overtipped, and that hadn't helped.

"Not me," Andreno said. "I think she sorta took a shine

to me. Before you got there, I told her if she could get off for a few minutes, I'd run her around town in my Porsche."

"What'd she say?"

"She said she couldn't get off."

Lucas started to laugh, and a little of the gloom lifted.

Tisdale was the second-largest town in Mellan County, after Hopewell, the county seat. They drove through on the way to Hopewell, where the sheriff could meet them at 8:30.

"What is that *smell?*" Andreno asked, as they bumped across a set of railroad tracks into the town.

"I don't know," Lucas said. "It ain't rosebushes."

A minute later, they passed what looked like four of the biggest yellow-steel pole barns in the Midwest. Painted neatly on the side of each building was "Logan Poultry Processing," and under that, in small letters, "Really Pluckin' Good."

"The smell," Andreno said. "Like a combination of scorched feathers and wet chicken shit."

"Which it probably is," Lucas said. "You know, if you breathe through your mouth . . . you can still smell it."

There was nothing in Tisdale. They drove past Rinker's mother's house, a mile out in the country, and saw nothing moving. The house was short, a story and a half, with peeled-paint clapboard siding and drawn curtains. A neglected driveway projected into a single-car garage. The door was open and the garage was empty. A small brown-and-white dog sat under the rusted rural mailbox at the end of the drive, and looked lost and thirsty. In the back, an ancient Ford tractor sat abandoned and rusting in a crappy, brush-choked woodlot.

"What if we busted in with our guns out, and Clara was sitting at the kitchen table eating oatmeal?" Andreno asked.

"She'd probably shoot us both and throw our bodies in the septic tank," Lucas said.

"So, let's go see the sheriff."

MELLAN COUNTY SHERIFF Errol Lamp was not an impulsive man, and when Lucas and Andreno showed up at the county courthouse in Hopewell, he questioned their credentials and had a deputy check with the feds in St. Louis. Eventually, he got to Mallard, who told him exactly where his bread was buttered, and who buttered it. As they were talking, a woman stuck her head in the office and said, "Errol, you know that Porsche out by the Rinkers'? It's these guys."

The sheriff looked at them with his slow eyes and said, "You went by the Rinkers', huh?"

"Yeah. How'd you know?"

"Neighborhood crime watch," the sheriff said. "They report anything suspicious. Like a Porsche. Lot of drug runners drive Porsches."

Seconds before Lucas would have lost both his patience and his temper, Lamp assigned a deputy to take them around the county and, Lucas thought, to fill him in later.

"BEEN TEN FEDERAL people here to see Rinker's mother, and none of them went in believing what we said, but they all came out believing," said the deputy, whose name was Tony McCoy. McCoy was a heavy, sweating man in khakis, with a straw Stetson, a rodeo belt-buckle, and deep-blue cowboy boots. They were in his Jeep Grand Cherokee.

"What's that?" Andreno asked.

"That's she's crazier'n a goddamn cuckoo clock. She won't have no idea what you're talking about."

"So let's not go there," Lucas said. "Let's go to the school."

"The school?"

"Yeah, you know—brick building full of kids."

McCoy gave him a hard look, and Lucas smiled into it. Lucas had kindly blue eyes, but his smile often came off as a threat, and McCoy flinched away. "Wanna go to the school, the school it is," he muttered.

The Mellan Consolidated School was larger than Lucas expected, with two academic wings built around a gymnasium. The principal was a thin, youngish woman with carefully colored hair, a single eyebrow that extended straight across her brow ridge, and glasses that sat a quarter-inch too far down her narrow nose. She had the habit of pushing them back up with her middle finger, and as Andreno said later, "Every time I looked at her, she was flippin' me off."

"We have cooperated with a number of FBI requests and interviews, and frankly, we just don't have much," she said. "There was an agent here named Josh Franklin. If you were to talk to him . . ."

"We're looking for different angles," Lucas said. "If you know anybody who knew Clara Rinker, or any of the Rinkers—"

"I'm sorry, but I'm about the same age as Clara, so when she left here, I was in ninth or tenth grade in Weston, Oklahoma," she said. "We only have two teachers here who remember her, and so far, nobody's found them helpful."

"If we could just get a couple of minutes with them. . . ."

"Of course. We're happy to cooperate," she said unhappily.

The two teachers, both women, both in their late fifties or early sixties, remembered only one new thing. The older of the two said, "It might not mean anything at all, but one thing I do remember about Clara, and never told anybody else because it hadn't happened yet—and it's not exactly about Clara—is that Ted Baker got all his guns stolen last month and his guard dogs were shot. This was before Clara showed up in St. Louis. Ted was only two or three years older than Clara. And he used to run with Clara's older brother, Roy."

"Huh," Lucas said. "All his guns?"

He looked at the deputy, who scratched his head and said, "That's right. We handled the break-in. I figured it was one of those gun nuts that Baker hangs out with, if he didn't do it himself, for the insurance. I didn't know that he knew Clara."

"He did," the teacher said. "Don't tell anybody I said so."

McCoy said he knew where they could find Baker. "If he's not at the landfill, shootin' rats, or out pluckin' chickens, he's usually around his house. He's got some new dogs, and he's training them."

MCCOY DROVE THEM from Hopewell back to Tisdale. They stopped at a Dairy Queen and got chocolate-dipped cones, agreeing that they must be low-cal because they were ice milk, not ice cream, and then rode out the west side of town on the county road. Baker's house was a close cousin to the Rinker homestead, a beat-up, seventy-year-old frame house with a tired garage off to the side. The house was surrounded by a waist-high chain-link fence, and two young German shepherds were staked out behind it.

McCoy ran down the driveway as far as the gate, then leaned on his horn. Baker, a rawboned man with shaggy brown hair and a two-week beard, stepped out onto the porch. He had a can of Budweiser in his hand, squinted at them, pointed a finger at the dogs, who dropped back to their stomachs, and walked up the driveway.

They talked over the fence.

"Never occurred to me that it could have been Clara, though it sounds stupid to say it," he told them when Lucas explained why they were there. "I didn't even hear about her coming back to St. Louis until a couple weeks after I was hit. I never put it together."

"You think it was her?" McCoy asked. "You got some crazy friends running around out there."

Baker grinned at them through light-green teeth and said, "Shit, McCoy, there's nothing wrong with those boys."

"Yeah, like Harvey?"

"Well, Harv . . ." Baker considered the name reluctantly.

"Harv's a couple cans short of a six-pack, is what he is," McCoy said.

"Well, Harvey . . . tell you the truth, it crossed my mind that it might be one of them, except I can't think who'd shoot the dogs. Takes a cold man to shoot the dogs. Even Harvey wouldn't."

"You think Clara could do it?" Lucas asked.

"I'll tell you what," Baker said. "The last time I seen Clara was five or six years ago—she came through to see her mama, and I bumped into her down to the root-beer stand. She asked me what I was doing, and I said, 'Shootin', and working at Logan's,' and that's about the end of it. We wasn't, like, good friends, not that I wouldn't have liked to fuck her, if you know what I mean."

"Know what you mean," McCoy said, hitching up his khakis.

"She had these nice little hard tits like cupcakes," Baker continued. "And you got the feeling she'd probably fuck back at you."

"The dogs?" Lucas repeated.

"I don't know. If she can shoot all those people she's supposed to, I guess she could shoot the dogs. Somebody did," Baker said. "Right in the head, bam bam."

"Anybody figure out what kind of gun it was?"

"It were a .22," Baker said. "I couldn't bring myself to dig out the slugs, but I looked at the holes and I'd say it was a standard-velocity .22. Good tight entry wounds, no sign of bullet breakup, no exit wound. Good shootin', too. They never knew what hit them."

"And you haven't seen her for all that time."

"Nope. Kinda like to, though, if you catch her. I might go see her in jail. She was a nude dancer before she was a killer. I bet she's got some stories to tell."

"Bet she does," McCoy said, nodding. His tongue flickered over his lips. Tasty stories.

"Did she know about your guns?" Lucas asked.

"Oh, sure. Pretty much everybody around here knows I got an interest," Baker said. "I used to hang with her brother, and she was over here a time or two when we were gunnin'. I'm the one who taught her brother how to reload."

"So you *were* friends," Andreno said.

"Nah. Not with Clara. She was around, because Roy took her around—I personally think Roy may have been knocking a little off her, you know what I mean?—but she was standoffish, even when she was little. She'd just *look* at you. I didn't have much to do with her."

"Did you know any of her friends?" Lucas asked.

"I don't think—" Then he stopped and looked from Lucas to Andreno. "You know about Patsy Hill, right?"

Lucas and Andreno shook their heads, and Lucas said, "Haven't seen the name."

"Jeezus." Baker looked at McCoy. "You know about Patsy Hill?"

McCoy shook his head.

Baker said, "Great fuckin' police work, huh? All you runnin' around like maniacs and you haven't heard of Patsy Hill?"

"Well, who is she?" Lucas asked.

"Patsy lived over by Clendenon, over toward Springfield. That's where Carl Paltry came from."

Andreno said, *"Who?"*

Lucas remembered the FBI report. "Rinker's stepfather."

Baker nodded. "That's right. I think he was fuckin' her, too. Clara. Anyway, he come from over there, and I think maybe they even lived there for a little while, or off and on, if you know what I mean. That's where Rinker met Patsy Hill."

"So who in the fuck is Patsy Hill?" McCoy asked.

"Another goddamned killer," Baker said, with a wide green smile. "I always thought it was amazin'. Two small-town girls, get to be best friends, and they both grow up to be killers. Cops was all over the place here, about ten years ago, must be, maybe longer, because Patsy was living down in Memphis with her husband, and she killed him with an ax or something like that. Maybe it was a hammer. Whacked the shit out of him. Then she ran, and they never caught her."

"Never?" Lucas asked.

"Not as far as I know, and I think I'd probably hear about it. I know some people who growed up over there. It ain't that far."

"Cross the county line, near to Springfield," McCoy said. He was plainly relieved: not his jurisdiction.

"Clara and Patsy didn't go to the same school?" Lucas asked.

"Not here," Baker said. "I don't know where Patsy went to school, maybe Springfield. But there was a time when Patsy and Clara was like this." He crossed two fingers. "They both grew up to be killers."

"She got any family around? Patsy?" Lucas asked.

"Yeah, over in Clendenon. Right there on Tree Street."

THEY TALKED A while longer, got a list of the stolen guns, and headed back into Hopewell. Lucas thanked McCoy for his help, then he and Andreno drove back toward the interstate in the Porsche.

"We going to Clendenon?" Andreno asked.

"We might be onto something," Lucas said. "The feds don't know about this—I read the whole file. If this Patsy Hill killed somebody years ago, and ran, and Rinker hid her, and if she's somehow living and working around St. Louis . . ."

"Then Hill could be paying Rinker back. Letting her stay over."

"And Hill couldn't turn Rinker in, no matter how big the reward was. Even more, I'll bet none of Clara's Mafia friends knew about Hill. Why would Clara tell them? One of them might have been tempted to use Hill as a get-out-of-jail card," Lucas said. He looked over at Andreno. "I'll tell you what. I'll bet five United States dollars right now that Rinker is staying with Hill. I don't know where Hill is, but if we can find her, we'll find Rinker."

Andreno thought about it for two minutes, then said, "No bet." He said it with a *tone:* Like Lucas, he could smell the trail.

A little farther down the road, Lucas said, "Let's not forget about that list of guns, huh? She's always been a pistol queen, but now she's got a carload of rifles. We gotta let Mallard know. We need to spread the net around Levy."

ON THE WAY to Clendenon, Lucas got the address for a Hill family on Tree Street, Chuck and Diane, and the phone number. He tried to call ahead, but there was no answer and no answering machine. "We could be here for a while," he said to Andreno.

Clendenon was a small town, not quite a suburb of Springfield, with a block-long downtown and a BP station at the end of that block. They asked the gas station attendant about Tree Street, and got detailed instructions. "You might want to keep your speed down in that Porsche," the attendant said, as they turned to go. "The town cop figures out speeds based on his best estimate, and your car looks like it's going forty when it's sitting at the gas pump."

"Thanks," Lucas said.

"No problem. You'll find the cop just about a block down that way . . . sitting behind that blue house. Take 'er easy."

They crept by the blue house at twenty miles an hour, and if there was a cop in the black Mustang parked at the curb behind the house, he made no move to come after them. They took a left two blocks farther on, and found Tree Street two more blocks down. Lucas took a left, found the house numbers going the wrong way, made a U-turn, drove two blocks down, and parked in front of the Hill place.

As with the Rinker and Baker houses, the Hills' was an older place, small, with a detached garage; but all of it was neatly kept, with a front window-box full of yellow- and wine-colored pansies and a strip of variegated marigolds along the driveway. When they got out of the car, Lucas could smell freshly cut grass. They knocked, got no answer, tried the neighbors. A woman in a housecoat told them that Chuck Hill worked at the grain elevator and Diane went grocery shopping in the morning and should be back at any moment: "Saw her leave an hour ago, so she oughta be . . . Here she comes."

DIANE HILL ARRIVED in an aging Taurus station wagon, bumped up the drive, and got out with a plastic grocery sack. She saw them coming, and waited in the driveway. Lucas identified them, and she said sullenly, "What do you want?"

"When your daughter disappeared, she had to go somewhere. We think she might have gone to Clara Rinker, and we think Clara might be with her now."

A transient look of—What? Pleasure? Lucas thought so—crossed Hill's face and then vanished as quickly as it had come.

"We don't have any idea where Patricia might be. We just hope to God that everything is all right with her, after the hell that her husband put her through."

"She never got in touch, just to tell you that she's all right?"

"Yes, she's called from time to time, and I told the police that. She calls sometimes, and she cries because she can't come home and she can't tell us where she is, because she's afraid that somebody will find out and the police will come get *us.* She's protecting us by not telling."

Andreno tried: "Mrs. Hill, honest to God, we don't care about Patsy—Patricia—she's somebody else's problem. But Clara is killing people—"

"Mafia hoodlums," Hill snapped.

"She's killed a lot of innocent people," Lucas put in. "She's going to kill more."

"That's not my problem," Hill said, clutching at her groceries. "All I know is, she was kind to my daughter when my daughter needed some kindness, and couldn't come here to get it. And I know what happened to poor Clara when she was just a girl, and it doesn't seem strange to me at all that she's grown up to kill people. Where were the police when her stepdaddy was working his perversions on her, and her not even fourteen? Where were they when Patricia's husband was burning her back with a clothes iron?"

"Mrs. Hill . . ."

"You tell me where the police were then."

"Mrs. Hill . . ."

"And if I were you, I wouldn't go talking to Chuck—that's my husband—because he's gonna be a damn sight less cordial than I've been. We don't approve of any kind of criminality, but if the police really took care of crime, there wouldn't be any Clara Rinker and our Patsy would still be with us. Excuse me." She marched up the driveway and into the house, and slammed the door.

After a moment, Andreno said, "I think we handled that pretty well."

"We oughta get a warrant and tear the house down."

"Really?"

Lucas shook his head. "No. Shit."

"Want to try Chuck?"

"I'll drop you off, if you want to."

"No, thanks. Back to St. Louis, then?"

Lucas sighed, looked up at the Hill house. "I guess."

TEN MILES OUT of town he said, "The Hills didn't mention any other children."

Andreno shook his head. "No. I sorta got the impression that Patsy might be the only one."

"Huh. How many long-distance phone calls you think come pouring into the Hills' house?"

"Mmm."

"I bet she calls on Christmas," Lucas said. "Or New Year's, or right around then."

"I bet the feds can get a warrant for their phone records."

"Bet they can, too." He picked up his cell phone.

"Gonna tell them?"

"About the rifles, so they can spread the net around Levy. I want to tell them in person about the Hill idea—I don't want them pissing on it when I can't defend it. They've sat around that conference table and pissed on every idea I've had, even when they paid off."

"They're feds. That's what they do."

13

THERE'S NO GOOD WAY TO GET FROM ST. LOUIS TO ANNISTON, Alabama, in a hurry, any more than there's a good way to get from Minneapolis to St. Louis. Rinker couldn't hurry anyway, because she couldn't risk a traffic stop. She took I-64 east to I-24, and I-24 down to Nashville, where she picked up I-65, and I-65 all the way to Birmingham, and then I-20 east to Anniston.

She started late in the afternoon and was still driving at dawn. She listened to a St. Louis Cardinals game heading down to Nashville, thinking about those times in the liquor warehouse, about a million years earlier, when the Cards games always ran in the background, and she, no baseball fan, knew every man on the roster.

She lost the Cardinals outside of Nashville, and poked around the radio looking for some decent country, but that was hard to come by. She finally found a local station along the Alabama line, playing a long string of LeAnn Rimes, including "Blue," one of Rinker's favorites. When that station faded, she spent the rest of the night dialing around the radio for more good places to listen.

At 6 A.M., a little beat-up, but pleasantly so—she always liked road trips—she checked into a cheap motel called Tapley's, and when asked how many there'd be, she said, "Well, my husband's probably coming over during the day, he's a sergeant in the Army, but I'm not sure if he'll be staying the night."

The lady clerk looked at her with a touch of warmth in her eyes and said, "We'll put you down for one, and if that changes, honey, just let me know."

"I'll do that, and thanks," Rinker said. "I'd give you a credit card, but I don't know if it'd work. He's probably put a bass boat on it. I'll just give you cash, if that's okay."

"That'd be fine."

SHE CALLED WAYNE MCCALLUM at eight o'clock, and got him on the first ring: "Sergeant McCallum, ordnance."

"Wayne George McCallum. How are you?" She used her best whiskey Rinker voice.

There was a pause, then: "Oh, shit."

"I need to talk."

"I wouldn't doubt it, but things are pretty hectic right now." His voice was casual, with an underlying layer of stress.

"Did you take that twelve-step I heard about, or are you still running down to Biloxi on the weekends?"

"I sure as shit ain't took no twelve-step," he said. McCallum had a fondness for craps.

"So come on. I got something you need, and you got something I need."

"I can't talk right now. Could you call me at my other number, in about five minutes?" He gave her a number.

"I'll call," she said. She waited while he ran out to a pay phone, gave him an extra minute, and dialed. He picked up on the first ring. "I can get you two good ones, equipped. Three thousand."

"I don't need them. I need something special."

"Special."

"Real special."

"We better talk. See you at the usual?"

"The usual."

SHE GOT FOUR hours of sleep, and a little after noon, got cleaned up, changed into jeans, running shoes, and a short-sleeved shirt, and clipped one of her pistols into a pull-down fanny pack. Behind the pistol she stuffed a brick of fifty-dollar bills, wrapped with rubber bands.

When she was ready, and feeling a little adrenaline, she headed south to Talladega, then east into the mountains of the Talladega National Forest. She stopped at a wayside park, where a hiking trail started off into the woods. She sat in her car for a moment, watching, then retrieved the fanny pack from under the front seat and strapped it on, with the pack in front. She also dug out one of her cell phones, checked to make sure it was the right one, and carried it with her.

FOR YEARS, Wayne McCallum had been her main source of silenced nine-millimeter pistols, and she'd dealt with him twenty times. They'd once had a long talk about meeting places, places to talk, places to exchange equipment for money. They had agreed that cleverness was its own enemy. If you met in a crowded public place, which was one theory on how you do it—the crowd bought you protection from the person you were meeting—and if somebody was onto you, you'd never see them coming. If you could just see them coming, there was always a chance. A lonely spot, but still technically public, where you wouldn't seem suspicious just for being there, was the best solution.

A hiking trail was perfect, as long as she had her best friend along . . . with a full magazine and a spare.

She climbed out of the wayside park, up the hiking trail, then looped up a secondary track to a scenic overlook. When she got to the top, she found it empty. She had, in fact, met McCallum a half-dozen times at the overlook, and, except for McCallum, had never encountered another soul. The overlook was nothing more than a circle of rocks around a patch of beaten earth, on the edge of a steep hill. There was a good view back toward Talledega, and no sign of recent use: nothing but old cigarette filters scattered around the rocks, and a couple of weather-rotted clumps of toilet paper back in the bushes. She expected the filters would last until the next ice age—longer than the rocks, anyway.

McCallum arrived precisely at one o'clock, driving an older Cadillac. He'd always driven a Caddy, because that's what men like him drove, and there'd always be a set of good golf clubs in the trunk. He climbed out, smiled up at where he thought she was, and came puffing up the trail, a fat, red-faced man in civilian clothes, way out of shape. *Welcome to today's Army,* Rinker thought.

"We gotta find some goddamn place flat," he said, as he wheezed into the overlook. He was close enough that she could smell his breath, and it smelled like Sen-Sen. She wondered if they still made it.

"Or you gotta take off some weight," Rinker said. She smiled. "How are you?"

"A hell of a lot better than you," McCallum said. He looked her over, then said, "After all that shit up in Minnesota, I figured the next time I saw you, we'd both be in hell."

"Not there yet," she said.

"If you don't stay the fuck away from St. Louis, you will be," he said.

"Got a couple more things to do before I take off." She pulled the top off her fanny pack, let the pistol unfold, then dug behind it for the brick of fifties. She tossed it to him, and he caught it, glanced at the denomination on the top bill, and said, "This is a lot."

She held up the cell phone. "Remember you told me about that Israeli thing?"

He laughed, and said, "You're shitting me." He ran two hands through his short hair, then scrubbed at his scalp like one of the Three Stooges—Rinker could never remember their names, but it was the fat one. "You're not shitting me."

"I'm not. Can you really do it?" she asked.

"Hell, yes. I've been itching to." *Jeez,* Rinker thought, *his eyes are bright.* "Banged off a couple myself," he said, "up here in the hills, just to make sure it works. It works. It works beautiful."

"How about the plastic? Can they get back to you?"

"It's all civilian. They could never bring it back here. Back to me."

"How long to do it?"

"Couple hours. I could have it tonight," he said. He was getting excited. Aroused. "I mean, it's real easy. 'Bout everything you need is already built into the phone. You need one chip and the plastic."

"It'd be a favor, Wayne," Rinker said. She gave him her number-three smile. "The quicker the better."

SHE DROVE BACK to Anniston, leaving after he did, taking a different route, checking her back trail. At the motel, she slept the rest of the afternoon, and spent the early evening watching television. At eight o'clock, she drove out to an interstate gas station and a telephone. McCallum picked up on the first ring.

"We going out, or what?" she asked.

"I'm ready, honey-bun. Tell me where."

"How about Boots?" Boots was an Army bar. She'd been there once before, in the parking lot.

"See you there."

Again, she was there before he was. That was part of the deal. Though she had little faith in the idea that she could spot cops, she was virtually certain that McCallum wouldn't turn her in. He'd helped her too many times, and Alabama had primitive ideas about the proper punishment for murder.

When the Caddy rolled in, she watched for five minutes, then decided she'd buy it; she'd seen nothing that worried her. She rolled down the hill into the parking lot, up close to the Cadillac, and dropped the passenger-side window. Neon lightning rolled off the Caddy's hood, reflecting the on-and-off "Boots" sign overhead. McCallum saw her, got out of his car, stepped over, climbed into the passenger seat, and fumbled the cell phone out of his jacket pocket.

"Here's the phone," he said. He sounded eager to get rid of it, or to please her—like a child giving a gift to a teacher. "If you was to take it apart, and knew a lot about phones, you might find the plastic. If you didn't, and if you just looked into it, you'd never see it."

"What happens if I call out?"

"Nothing. It's still a perfectly good phone. But I'll tell you what, you don't want to call out to 6-6-6. 'Cause if you do, the beast'll blow your ass off."

"You're sure."

"I'm sure." He nodded in the dark. "Same thing when you're calling into it. You call, you make sure you got your guy, and you punch 666. Then you won't have your guy anymore."

"How powerful is it?" Rinker asked. "I mean, would it blow up this car?"

"Oh, hell no." McCallum shook his head. "I got a chunk of plastic in there not much bigger'n a .22 slug. No, the damage would all be to the head, but it'll flat knock a hole in that. If you were to put it in the backseat, and it went off, you probably wouldn't *hear* much for a few days, and there'd be a hell of a hole in the upholstery, but it wouldn't kill you. It's 'bout like a charge in a, say, a .338 mag."

Rinker looked at the phone, then back up at the soldier. "Wayne, if you'd gone into this business fifteen years ago, I wouldn't have had a job."

"Weren't no cell phones fifteen years ago," McCallum said. "And you know what? Puttin' this thing together made me kind of horny. I'd like to see it go. I mean, I could *do* this."

"You're a freak, Wayne," Rinker said.

"Of course I am, sweetheart." McCallum beamed at her, his fat sweaty jowls trembling with excitement. " 'Course I am."

SHE CHECKED OUT that night; told the woman working behind the counter that things just hadn't worked out. Going past the 'Bama border, she looked for the country station that had featured LeAnn Rimes, but it was an AM station and she lost it in the static of the thunderstorms closing in from the west.

She caught the rain at Nashville, lightning bolts pounding through the inky dark night, radio stations coming and going, the jocks talking of tornado warnings and multiple touchdowns near Clarksville. She came out the other side of the squall line before dawn, and rolled on into St. Louis on dry pavement.

Kept thinking about the telephone.

This wasn't like her. Should work—and could flush a couple of more quail.

14

ANDRENO WAS A LITTLE BASHFUL ABOUT ACCEPTING THE neck-tag ID, but Lucas shooed him through the FBI's entrance check, and a guard led them to a new room—"They outgrew the old one," the guard told them on the way. "They call it the command center now."

The command center had twice the space of the old conference room, and windows. A dozen men and three women were sitting around the main table, the men in shirtsleeves, coats draped over their chairs, a litter of paper spread across the tables and between the laptops, the phones, and the PowerPoint projector. Mallard had his place at the far end of the table, with Malone at his side. Malone was listening at a telephone when they walked in.

Mallard was still in a suit, harried but happy. He called, "Rifles?"

"Bet on it," Lucas said. He'd talked to Sally, with the epaulets, from the car, and told her about Baker and the rifles.

"That's not good news," Mallard said now, about the rifle theft. "We've got a team on the way to completely debrief Mr. Baker."

"So what else is happening?" Lucas asked. Behind him, Andreno popped a piece of Dentyne and snapped it a couple of times with his teeth. He looked like a schnauzer in a pen full of greyhounds.

"Working Levy," Mallard said. "Nothing moving at this point. Waiting her out . . ."

"We may know who she's staying with," Lucas said.

There was a pause in the work around them, and Malone said, "Hang on a minute" and took the phone down. Mallard frowned and said, "Staying with? Who?"

"A woman named Patricia Hill," Lucas said. "But there's a teeny problem."

Mallard said, "What?"

"Patricia Hill killed her husband ten years ago and disappeared. We think she came here. She'd be living under an assumed name."

"How did you . . ."

Lucas explained it, with Andreno chipping in on parts of the argument. "The good news is," Andreno said, and he snapped the gum for emphasis, "we think she might call her mom. If you could check the Hills' phone records, you might find a few calls from St. Louis and then we'd know where she's at, and we'd get a twofer: two killers for the price of Rinker."

Malone shrugged. "The records are a piece of cake—the rest of it sounds like moonshine, though."

"We gotta check," Mallard said. "I kinda like it."

THE RECORDS *WERE* a piece of cake. The Memphis cops pulled the Patricia Hill file, scanned it, and shipped it in an hour. Patsy Hill, ten years earlier, had been a tall, thin blonde with a large nose and bony shoulders. A high-res color version of the digital photo was sent to an ink-jet printer somewhere else in the building, and fifteen minutes later came back as a finished paper photograph.

"Doesn't look like anybody in particular," Andreno said, as the photo went up on the bulletin board.

"Better than what we've got on Rinker," Lucas said.

Malone said, "Her husband was sent to jail twice for abusing her."

"So what?" Andreno asked.

"So maybe there's a little more here than a simple murder," Malone snapped.

"So what?" Andreno asked again.

Malone put her hands on her hips. "What's this 'so what' attitude?"

"Do you give a shit about Hill?" Andreno asked. Malone opened her mouth to reply, but Andreno kept going. "*I* don't give a shit about Hill. I'm chasing Rinker. If Hill gets in the way, I'd pick her up and send her back to Memphis to stand trial, but otherwise, I wouldn't drive around the block to find her."

Malone looked at Lucas, who shrugged: "I'm with him."

TWO AGENTS WERE assigned to dig up the phone records. They made calls to technicians, talked to lawyers for both the phone company and the FBI, and two hours after Lucas and Andreno walked in the door, a list of phone calls had been downloaded to the task-force computers in Washington and bounced out to the St. Louis laptops.

With the lists running simultaneously on four different screens, they determined that the Hills did not get a lot of incoming long-distance phone calls—but that at least two and usually three times a year, they'd get a long-distance call from the St. Louis metro area. One call always came Christmas morning. Another always came August 14. After checking with the Missouri driver's license division, they determined that August 14 was Diane Hill's birthday.

"Are we good, or what? Patsy's calling Mom," Andreno said to Lucas.

One of the agents nailed down the addresses of the telephone numbers and found that all but one came from convenience stores or gas stations—the odd one, from the first year that Patsy Hill was on the run, came from a

Greyhound station. The agent put the addresses on a computer map, each one represented with a red dot, and projected it with PowerPoint.

"Goddamn," Mallard said, peering at the map. "What is that?"

"It's called Soulard," Andreno said. He circled an area of southeast St. Louis with a finger. "It's not that big a place. I mean, hell, a few thousand people, maybe, as residents. But the brewery's down there, and a whole bunch of factories and truck places, so she could be working there, and living somewhere else."

Mallard looked at Malone. "What do you think?"

"We'd have to coordinate if we want to sweep the area—we don't have the manpower to do it on our own, if we want to keep Levy and everybody else covered."

"You get a bunch of flatfeet pounding on doors, they'll either get out ahead of the sweep, or, if we manage to surprise them, you'll have a couple of dead cops," Lucas said.

Mallard spread his arms and said, "Well?"

"Well, we were once looking for a black kid, this gang-banger, hiding out in Minneapolis, and figured if we went door to door with a bunch of white cops, everybody would see them coming. So we got our black guys and they went around and talked to friends, who hooked them up with other friends and asked everybody about who was where. We covered the whole goddamn area in four days, with four guys, we knew who was where in every single house—we got six leads, and one of them paid off."

"We could do that," Andreno said to Lucas. "Just, you know—our guys. I must know five or six people down there myself."

Lucas looked at Mallard. "We're not doing much anyway."

Mallard: "Sounds good to me. Especially if it works."

"And it's cheap. It's cost-effective," Malone said. "Heck, it's almost free."

"THINK SHE'LL STAY PUT?" Andreno asked Lucas, as they headed down the hall.

Lucas said, "No reason for her to run, not until she's done here."

"Want to go cruise Soulard?"

"Sure, if we can do it in your car. She's seen mine."

ANDRENO DROVE A two-year-old silver Camry, the perfect spy car, comfortable and inconspicuous and foreign and underpowered, unlike cop cars. He took them on a tour of Soulard, which was much like the fading neighborhoods near the St. Paul breweries, not far from where Lucas lived—lots of redbrick apartments, grimy with age, old houses, some of them in good repair, some of them on the edge of collapse with sagging roof-ridges, scaling shingles, flaking paint. Some had been substantial residences. Some, built after the neighborhood began its decline, had been poor from the start. Here and there, like good teeth, were fully restored buildings, all tuck-pointed and painted. Lucas picked up on the place in ten minutes, bumping over the narrow, swaybacked streets: "Lots of illegal apartments, rented rooms being lived in—if she lives down here at all."

"Now you sound like you don't believe."

"Oh, I believe," Lucas said, peering out the passenger window at two old ladies hobbling along the crazy-quilt sidewalk. "This is one place where you might wind up if you were on the run."

"Let's see if we can get the guys down here—Loftus can't do it, but if we could get Bender and Carter, along with us two . . . we could cover some ground."

"I'll call them tonight. Get going tomorrow," Andreno said.

"Seven? Eight?"

"Jesus, no. Not *that* early. I got a date."

"Heavy date?"

"I do have plans involving sex. Then I'll probably have to talk to her for a while and probably won't be outa there until three o'clock or so."

"You sensitive types are going out of style," Lucas said. "Women are going back to the more macho, tough-talking guys."

"What I got is what I got," Andreno said, and he eased the car away from the curb.

NOT MUCH MORE to do this night.

Lucas got a sandwich, then walked to a downtown mall, bought a pile of magazines and a couple of newspapers, and carried them back to the hotel. He thought about Andreno going out, and felt a little sad. In the past, out of town, he'd always been happy enough to make the rounds at night, seeing who was doing what to whom—and who might be available for a tightly scheduled romance, a meaningful overnight relationship.

No more, he thought. But hell: He was wearing pajamas most of the time now. The bottoms, anyway. And reading *Barron's,* in hotel rooms, at eight o'clock at night. Getting older; and life goes on.

For some people, anyway.

Lucas had a good night, the kind of night you have after a good day, when you traveled, learned a few things, felt like you were making progress. But the phone rang way too early. An agent named Forest said he was calling on Mallard's behalf to tell him that Gene Rinker had committed suicide in the jail out in Clayton.

"WHAT THE FUCK are you talking about?" Lucas asked. Or shouted. "I thought he was on suicide watch."

"He was. But he knew what he was doing."

"Well, what the fuck did he do? What time is it, anyway?"

"Five-forty-five. He cut his wrists with the punch-out thing, the hole, from a can of soda. He had a can of soda at dinner, and he must've palmed it."

"Jesus, they didn't find him? Where in the hell were the—"

"He had one blanket—this is what I'm told, I haven't been there myself—he had one blanket and he got down under it, and after one of the checks, cut himself. They say he knew what he was doing. The cuts are real deep, vertical, right down both wrists. There's a second set of scars going the wrong way, across the wrists, so he had some experience. He messed it up the first time he tried, and this time, he knew better. After he'd cut himself, he curled up under the blanket and bled to death. They were watching him in the camera—they thought he was sleeping until the blood started to drip on the floor and they saw the puddle. . . ."

"Ah, man."

"Emptied him out. Mr. Mallard's over there, Malone's on the way. They thought . . . you might want to run out."

LUCAS TOOK TIME to clean up. An extra ten minutes wouldn't make any difference to Gene Rinker now, and Lucas had taken enough unexpected calls to know how crappy he'd feel later in the morning if he didn't clean up now. In the shower, he thought about Rinker. He thought about what she might do. Could they turn this to their advantage? And he thought about Sandy White and the St. Louis *Post-Dispatch.*

And before he left the room, he dialed Andreno, smiling grimly as he did it. At least this piece of misery would have a little company.

Andreno picked up the phone and groaned, “What?”

“Gene Rinker cut his wrists. He’s dead.”

Silence for a beat, a couple of beats. “Awww . . . shit.”

15

THE CELL HAD THE BLOODY-STEAK SMELL OF SUDDEN death, riding over the usual odors of floor wax, paint, and disinfectant. The medical examiner's assistants had rolled Gene Rinker's body, but not moved it off the bunk.

Rinker's ferretlike face was paper-white but finally peaceful, almost happy in death, except for the dry salty tear paths that ran sideways across his nose and cheeks. He'd been crying as he went down, Lucas thought. There were no marks on his body of the kind that usually accompany violent death, except that his lower arms and legs were coated with dried blood, and there was a stripe of blood in his hair where he apparently had pushed back his long bangs after cutting himself. The blood puddle had soaked into the mattress.

When Lucas and Andreno stepped inside the cell to

look, the ME's assistant moved back to improve the view, and said, "He's got old transverse scars—he tried before."

"Got it right this time," Lucas said.

"Gives me the goddamn willies," Andreno said. "I'm afraid of flu shots. But cutting yourself, man . . ." He shuddered at the thought.

After cutting his wrists, and probably wiping the hair out of his eyes, the ME's assistant said, Rinker had rolled onto his side, into a fetal position, and clasped his hands between his thighs. There were three new cuts on one wrist, two practice marks in addition to the killing cut, but only one on the other. The cuts ran vertically beside the ligaments that ran down to the hand.

"NOW I WISH I hadn't brought him," Malone said from behind them. Standing just outside the cell, she was gray-faced, tired, on the edge of anger. "These people . . ." She looked around. "How could they let this happen?"

Andreno opened his mouth to say something, then closed his mouth, shrugged, and went past her toward the exit, past the line of locked cell doors.

"What's with him?" Malone asked.

"I think he, uh, was kinda depressed by the whole thing," Lucas said. "Where's Mallard?"

"He went down to talk to the people who were on duty last night. Not that there's going to be much—they followed procedure, but the procedure was bad."

"Probably don't have that many people cutting their wrists with Coke-can holes," Lucas said.

"Just goddamn incompetence," Malone said bitterly. "And some of the mud's gonna stick to me. What a disaster."

"I gotta find Mallard. Are you coming?"

"I'm going to wait until they move the body. I don't want anything else screwed up," Malone said. She looked past his shoulder and said, "Here's Louis."

Mallard came up, blocky, thick-necked, face sour, as angry as Malone. He was wearing a suit jacket over what might have been a silk pajama top. He looked at Lucas and shook his head. "Bad business. Gonna be hell to pay for this."

"Especially after White's column yesterday."

"I don't blame people for being mad—this is unbelievable," Mallard said. "These people . . ." He looked around and shook his head.

"Louis . . . Rinker's gonna call me when she finds out," Lucas said. "We gotta be ready. I think we should move all your people and whatever kind of detection equipment you can find down to Soulard. She'll use the cell phone, but I bet she doesn't drive a hundred miles to do it. I bet she calls from wherever she's hiding, or maybe goes out a few blocks. But she'll be pissed, and I bet she'll call."

"You think?"

"I'd bet you a hundred dollars."

"So then maybe we want it on TV," Malone said. "This Gene Rinker thing is bad enough, but if we can snag Clara, then maybe some good'll come of it."

"She's gonna call," Lucas said. "She's gonna freak out. I'm gonna head down to Soulard myself, and wait. There's nothing else to do."

"I'll get everybody going. I'm gonna try to get some choppers in. We've got a couple in Chicago that are equipped to spot cell-phone calls. And we gotta keep the net on Levy—but every other guy I got, and the technicians, I'll have them down there."

ANDRENO WASN'T IN the building. Lucas looked around for him, then stepped outside and spotted him leaning against his car's fender in a handicapped zone. He saw Lucas and pushed away from the car, and came up the sidewalk to meet him. "Those assholes," he said.

"Who?" Lucas asked, but he knew.

"The fuckin' feds. Malone and Mallard," Andreno said. He was fuming. "For Christ's sakes, they're the ones who did this, not some poor broke-down jailer. But guess who's gonna take it in the ass?"

"Friends of yours?"

"Not exactly. But—they're *our* guys. They're not some big-shot assholes piped in from Washington to run the world."

"If the jail people have any sense, they'll announce an

investigation and all, but then they'll go out the back door and talk to press and blame the feds . . . and nothing'll happen to anybody."

"Maybe," Andreno said, squinting at Lucas.

"That's what would happen in Minneapolis," Lucas said. "I'd take care of it myself."

"If you were gonna take care of it yourself, would you call White directly, or go through a friend, or what?"

"Everything," Lucas said. "I'd know White would bite, because he's a hometown boy and he's inclined to piss on the feds. He's already started. Then, if I had any media friends, I'd fill them in, get them on my side. That's if I was in Minneapolis."

Andreno nodded, and then said, "And that's just taking care of yourself. Nothing to do about that poor fuckin' Rinker kid." Lucas shook his head, and Andreno continued: "I grew up in a shithole, and half the kids I went to school with wound up in jail, or dead some bad way. I feel like I'm about one inch from Gene Rinker. If it hadn't been for my mom . . . Why'n the hell did they have to drag him out here? Wasn't right, Davenport."

"No, it wasn't. But I've done something like it, a few times, myself."

Andreno thought about it for a minute, then nodded quickly, a head jerk: He'd done it, too. "So'd I, but I always knew what was going on. I always knew the guy I was fuckin' with. I wouldn't have done it with Rinker, if I'd known him. You could see this coming. Both of us could."

"Didn't do much about it," Lucas said.

"Yeah . . ." Andreno shook his head again, in disgust. "What're you gonna do now?

Lucas told him: He'd head for Soulard, wait for the news of Gene Rinker's death to be released, and then wait for the call from Clara.

"Drive around in the Porsche?"

"I guess," Lucas said.

"I got a couple errands to run," Andreno said. "When I get done, I'll call you. We can hook up, cruise in my car."

"See you then," Lucas said. "Good luck with the errands."

Andreno looked up at the jail. "Yeah, well, fuck those fuckers."

LUCAS WENT BACK to the hotel, had breakfast, went up to his room, checked his cell phone to make sure it could receive calls inside the room, and then sprawled across the bed and read the paper. A second Sandy White column was stripped across the top of the front page, this one from inside the St. Louis police—some of the cops apparently thought his Rinker column was a little too pro-outlaw, so now it was kiss-and-make-up time. The favored cops agreed that if Rinker was caught, she'd be caught by a cop on the street, probably during a traffic stop.

Lucas yawned through the column. The next day's story

would be better, he thought, when the paper found out that Gene Rinker was dead. White was about to become a prophet, which, over the long term, was unfortunate, Lucas thought. In his experience, few newspaper columnists could resist prophet status, and after assuming the robes, became tedious and eventually stupid.

When would Clara Rinker hear about Gene? And how? On television, probably. Maybe on the radio. Word was probably leaking already—certainly was if Andreno had carried out his preemptive strike on the feds. Could be any time. He went into the bathroom to take a leak, and thought, halfway through, that maybe he shouldn't be in the bathroom—maybe the phone wouldn't work in there, with all the tile. . . .

He was back on the bed, with the paper, when the room phone rang. He frowned at it: Could Rinker have his room phone? They hadn't thought of that. He picked it up. "Hello?"

"Instead of sitting around pulling our weenies, I got Bender and Carter meeting us down in Soulard in half an hour. Bender got a big map from the assessment guys, shows everything," Andreno said. "So you gonna sit on your ass or what?"

"See you there," Lucas said.

RINKER NEVER THOUGHT about the television or the radio. She unpacked the guns and the booby-trapped telephone, and tucked them into a handbag, got undressed except for her underpants and a man's T-shirt that she used as a nightie, then hit the bed and fell into a shallow, restless sleep. The dreams came in little shattered fragments of her life with Paulo, shards of the bar in Wichita, little wicked pieces of jobs she'd done for John Ross.

Her eyes popped open when she heard the key in the door. She felt stunned, her mouth tasted bad, but she was coming back in a hurry, rolling across the mattress. Something wrong. She hadn't been asleep long enough. She looked at the clock: just after noon. Pollock wasn't due back until three o'clock. She pulled one of the nines from the handbag and crouched behind the bed, watching the door as the intruder clumped across the floor and it sounded like . . .

"Clara?"

Pollock. Rinker exhaled, slipped the pistol back into the bag, and stood up. "Yeah." She stepped over to the door and pulled it open.

"Hey," she said. She was smiling. "What're you doing home?"

Pollock's face was congealed gloom. "Been watching TV?"

"No."

"Oh, God, Clara . . ." Tears started down Pollock's face. "Gene is . . . Gene died."

"What?" The smile stuck on Rinker's face for a few

seconds, as though she were waiting for a punch line. There was no punch line.

"I heard it on TV in the lunchroom," Pollock said.

"He died?"

"That's what they say on TV."

"I can't . . ." Rinker forgot what she was about to say, and brushed past Pollock to the television and fumbled the remote and finally managed to click it on, her hand shaking as though she were being electrocuted. "I don't think . . ." and she couldn't remember what she didn't think; words weren't making connections for the moment.

They could find nothing at all on television. They looked at all the local channels and clicked around to all the cable channels and found nothing at all.

"Clara, I promise you, I heard it. I went over to watch—they said he was found dead in his cell."

"Ah, God . . ." Rinker headed back to her room and began pulling on yesterday's clothes.

"Where are you going?"

"I gotta make a phone call," she said. She got her bag with the guns and the booby-trapped phone from the bedroom. "I'll be back. . . . Can I borrow your car? I just . . ."

"I'll drive," Pollock said. "You're not in shape to drive."

"Thanks."

LUCAS, ANDRENO, BENDER, and Carter worked down a list of names that the three St. Louis ex-cops cobbled together as they sat around in a deli drinking cream sodas. The names included personal friends and known community activists and local politicians. "It's been a while, and people move around down here," Carter said. "Some of them won't be there—but most of them will."

"The idea is, we spread out geographically," Lucas told them. "We ask all these people about their friends and neighbors, who we know are safe, and then about people who fit Patsy Hill's profile. Tall woman, late thirties. Probably living alone. If she'd remarried or had a family, Rinker probably wouldn't stay with her. We make a list of both kinds of people, and check off their houses."

"Take forever," Bender said.

"Three or four days at the most," Lucas said. "We could get lucky and hit her on the first day. We go to the politicians and the community people first. They'll be able to rule out a heck of a lot of people. Then we extend the contacts to other people they know."

"If we think we've found her, then what?"

"Then we bring in the feds. We *don't* go in ourselves. I think she could be on a suicide run, especially after this Gene thing, and if we just jump her, she's gonna shoot until she's dead. And she's good."

Bender nodded. "Okay. Let's go."

LUCAS STUCK WITH Andreno for the first few interviews, because he didn't know the people they were looking for.

They talked to an elderly Democratic Party voter registration woman at her home, crossed off twenty houses, and got eight more names for interviews. A woman who was a member of a city zoning advisory board eliminated a dozen more, and gave them a half-dozen more names for interviews. A real-estate agent spotted houses that he thought were unregistered apartments, and gave them even more names. A mail carrier they encountered on the street crossed off forty houses, suggested two more mail carriers that they should talk to, and also gave them two Patsy Hill candidates. Lucas ran the Patsy Hill possibilities through Sally, at the FBI war room, and she came back with negatives on both: "They've both got long histories, and one has a low-level arrest record for disorderly conduct. Not her."

AT TWENTY AFTER twelve, they were sitting in Andreno's Camry, at Benton Park, eating egg-salad sandwiches. Andreno was looking at the map, and was saying, "Shit, we got ten percent of the thing done, all by ourselves. . . ." when Lucas's cell phone rang.

They both froze for a second, then Lucas fumbled the phone out of his pocket. "That's her."

"Could be anybody with a quarter."

Lucas hooked his head, thumbed the talk button, said "Hello," and Rinker was there.

"Is it true about Gene?"

"I'm afraid it is," Lucas said, nodding at Andreno. "We

had him on a suicide watch. They were checking him every fifteen minutes and watching him in a camera, but he . . . man, he did it."

"You assholes." She was screaming. "I told you what would happen if you killed him, I told you . . ."

Lucas said, "Clara, listen, goddamnit, Clara, listen. Listen. You wanna know what happened?" But she was crying, and Lucas thought she hadn't heard, and he said again, "Clara, do you want to know—"

"I heard you," she said. "I *know* what happened."

"You know that he tried to do it before? He's got scars on both wrists where he'd cut himself before. The kid . . . goddamnit, Clara, this is awful, but the kid had tried before. This time he did it."

"He cut his wrists?"

"Yeah."

"With what? In a holding cell? What'd he cut them with? Somebody loan him a jackknife?"

"Somebody tried to be a nice guy at lunch and gave him a can of Coke. He stole the hole punch-out thing, you know, the hole, and hid it, and that's what he used. He covered himself up with a blanket, and by the time they figured things weren't right . . . he was gone."

"Okay. Okay, I got a message for you for the feds. . . ."

"Clara, Clara, wait a minute. Listen. Get out of here. Pick up your shit and go to Spain or South America or somewhere, but stop this. You might want to get these guys, but you don't have to get them right now. Right this minute. Stop now, come back some other time."

"You're giving me friendly advice?"

"It's gotta stop." Lucas was looking at Andreno, who gave him the *keep-rolling* sign.

"All right, you're holding me on the phone. Well, good luck with that," she said. Her voice had gone cold as ice. "Here's the message: *I meant what I said.* You got that? *I meant what I said.*"

"Clara . . ." But he was talking to himself. He looked at the phone, shook his head, said, "Gone," and punched it off.

"We had her for a while," Andreno said. He was on his own phone; when it was answered, he said, "Andreno and Davenport—you got her? Yeah. We're rolling."

"Where?" Lucas asked when Andreno had hung up.

"Right up on I-44. She switched cells going west. Close."

"So she does live around here—it's not that Patsy works for Anheuser. She wouldn't drive to where Patsy works to make a call. And she was pissed. She called me as soon as she thought she was okay."

"Sounds good to me. What do you wanna do? Run around Soulard? Doesn't seem like much point of going out on the highway."

"Yeah—let's just wander. Who knows?"

FIVE MINUTES LATER, Lucas said, "I'll tell you something—it's one thing to cover the streets, but this is fucking ridiculous. Every single street's got a car with two guys in it, driving at ten miles an hour. It looks like a goddamn Shrine parade."

Andreno snorted. "So Mallard talked to our guys, who probably talked to everybody else. . . . We probably got five agencies and fifty cars down here, all looking for Clara."

"If they find her, I hope to hell they can shoot. I don't think she's gonna go easy," Lucas said.

"She sounded pissed?"

"She sounded psychotic."

POLLOCK AND RINKER turned onto Tucker Avenue, and two blocks ahead, Rinker saw two large American cars stopped in the street, the occupants apparently talking to each other. "Take the next right," she said to Pollock.

"But . . . you think those are police?"

"Maybe. Take a right."

They went right at the corner, up a block, and turned left, back toward Pollock's place. Another block, and Pollock, looking in the rearview mirror, said, "Another car turned in behind us, end of the block. Going really slow."

"Keep going." Rinker slipped down in the foot well, the handbag in her lap.

"Got another car, up at the corner, ahead. There's a stop sign—I'm going to slow down and stop and let him go."

She slowed down and stopped. A few seconds passed, and then she accelerated away. "Two guys, and they really looked me over," Pollock said. "I think they were police."

"Any more cars?"

"The one behind us just stopped at the corner. They might be talking to the other guys. . . . Now they're coming again."

"How far from the house?"

"A block."

"Pull into the driveway, then get out—get something out of the trunk, let them see you. They'll know you're not me."

"Dear God," Pollock said.

But she did it. Bumped up into the driveway, got out, fished around in the trunk, then dropped the trunk lid with a bang. A minute later, she said, "Nobody coming. You can move now, but I'd hurry."

In ten seconds, they were inside, watching through a crack in the curtains. Another cop car went by every minute or two. "They're all over the place," Rinker said. "They can't be doing this everywhere—they must know we're here."

"How?"

Rinker shook her head. "I don't know. We've got to think about that."

16

LUCAS AND ANDRENO HOOKED UP WITH BENDER AND Carter, and they compared maps, and Lucas told the others about the call from Rinker.

"Scary," Bender said.

"Gotta find her quick," Lucas said. "She's outa control."

They put the maps together and Lucas, comparing the crossed-off houses and eliminating duplicates, said, "Terrific. We don't have half, but we've got a third or more. If she's down here . . ."

"I'm worried that she's over on the flats, working for one of those companies or the brewery," Carter said.

"I don't think so," Lucas said. "Because Clara isn't working, and I think Clara was close by when she found out about Gene. I think she came right out of here, somewhere. Could be west a little more, but not as far over as the Hill."

"Why?"

"Because Clara was freaked when she called." He explained what he thought that meant, and they all nodded and went back to looking at the maps. "We oughta get those other letter carriers tonight," Carter said. "Me'n Bender could look them up."

"Do that," Lucas said. "I think Andreno and I better get back with the feds. We don't want to leave them alone too long, with nobody but themselves to talk to."

WHEN THEY GOT off the elevator at the FBI building, they could see the door to the operations center was standing open, and they could hear the feds snarling at each other. Starting to think about *blame,* Lucas thought.

". . . all a goddamn theory," an agent named Brown was saying when Lucas and Andreno came through the door. Everyone around the table glanced their way, and the discussion died.

"The authors of the theory," Malone said dryly. She was sitting at the end of the table, legs crossed, looking beat.

"What's the problem?" Lucas asked.

"The problem is, the whole Soulard search and Patsy Hill and cell-phone idea is a stretch, and we've got too much pinned on it," Brown said.

"It's the only goddamned theory we've got, and it paid off," Lucas said. "She called from the right area."

"She was on the interstate. Everybody's on the interstate. There's a million cars on the interstate."

"She was going west. Which meant that she had to get on it somewhere east of where you had her, right?" Lucas asked. "And that means, from where you had her, she either got on in Illinois or she got on in Soulard, or on the edge of it, anyway."

"So what're we gonna do, sit around and wait for her to call you?" Brown rapped. "Next time, she'll be up in Florissant."

"So what're you suggesting?" Andreno asked. "I mean, we really need *something,* and if you got, don't be shy."

"Big reward," Brown said. "A million bucks. We can get it. We put a million bucks on her—we'll have her in twenty-four hours."

"I thought, uh, that was a problem," Lucas said. "If you can get the money, I'm all for it—though I don't think Patsy Hill would turn her in. She really can't."

"The Hill thing is just a *theory,"* Brown said, twiddling a yellow pencil between his fingers so fast that it looked blurred, like a propeller.

"Well, Jesus, you gotta work on something," Lucas said. "You can't sit around a fuckin' mahogany table and pull on your weenies."

"There's Levy and Ross," Mallard objected. "We got that going."

Lucas jumped in: "I'll tell you something else that's not a theory."

Brown: "That'd be a goddamned relief."

"Clara Rinker is gonna come after our ass," Lucas said. "I promise you. She was nuts this afternoon."

"What's she gonna do?" Mallard asked. He sounded curious, rather than skeptical.

"She's gonna kill somebody, or try to," Lucas said. To Mallard, he said, "If you've got any family that she can figure out, or if Malone has any . . . She mentioned Malone the first time I talked to her, so she remembers her from Minneapolis."

Mallard and Malone were both shaking their heads. "Not really," Malone said. "I've got my folks, of course, but I don't know how she could figure them out. She'd have to pull my file at the Bureau, and all that stuff is pretty locked up. We've had some pretty tough hackers make a run at it."

"She's gonna do *something,*" Lucas insisted. "If she figures out that we've got a net around Levy and Ross, she might try to hit one of the guys on the net. They've gotta be warned, and we've got to set up some kind of reaction procedure in case that happens. So we're not just running around in a circle waving our arms."

"We'll talk to everybody right now," Malone said. "I think that's a good point."

Even Brown nodded, but he added: "We're not being proactive. We gotta be more proactive. We gotta find something. . . ."

Andreno said, "Hey . . . we're listening."

Malone: "Washington's gonna come up with some ideas if we don't. They're getting anxious."

Snarling, Lucas thought, like a pack of yellow dogs.

RINKER AND POLLOCK had watched the street when they got home, had seen the big cars trolling by, way too many of them, and talked about Pollock's life. "So nobody knows where you're at," Rinker said.

"Not exactly where I'm at," Pollock said. "My folks know I'm around somewhere. I think they know it's St. Louis. I call them every once in a while."

Rinker looked around, felt the house closing in on her, a rat trap. "You call them? From *here?*"

"No, of course not," Pollock said. "I go out."

"How far?"

Pollock thought for a minute, then said, "Up to the gas station, the minimart, you know."

"Close by."

Pollock thought again, and finally said, "Shoot. That's it, isn't it? They looked up all the phone calls to my mama, and they figured out that they all came from down here."

They thought about the implications of that, and then

Rinker said, "Ah, jeez, Patsy, I'm sorry. They never would have come looking if it weren't for me."

"We don't know . . ."

"It's Davenport. I'm gonna wax his ass one of these days. I swear to God."

"The guy you danced with."

"Yeah. He's *lucky.*" Then she said, sadly, "You're gonna have to run again. They'll be going house to house."

But Pollock shook her head and said, wryly, "Naw. I ain't gonna run. I'm gonna turn myself in."

"Sounds like a plan," Rinker said, her eyebrows up.

"I can't stand this shit anymore," Pollock said, sinking into a couch. "I can't stand my job, I can't stand this place—I'd just as soon be in prison and get it over with."

"You never been in prison, you don't know what you're talking about."

"I've read about it, all kinds of things, at the library," Pollock said. "I been thinking about it for three or four years now. I talked to my folks about it, and they're for it. Did I ever show you my back?"

"Your back?"

"I kinda hide it. . . . I'm not a swimsuit girl." Pollock stood up, turned around, and pulled her blouse up. Rinker didn't know exactly what she was looking for, then noticed what seemed to be a large, paler birthmark on Pollock's pale back.

"What the heck is that?"

"What does it look like?"

"It looks like . . . an iron," Rinker said.

"Rick held me down on the bed one day and ironed me. And I got scars from a few more cuts and burns. Cigars, mostly. I think, after all these years, if I turned myself in . . . I kinda think I'd either get off, or they wouldn't put me away too long. And I want to go home, Clara. I know you don't like it down there, Springfield, and I don't blame you, but I want to go home someday and see my folks and be able to walk down the street without worrying."

RINKER TOOK A quick turn around the living room, intent now. "You know what? If you're gonna do this, if you really want to, you gotta do it now, right away, and you've gotta turn me in."

"What?"

"Yeah. That'll alibi you. You tell them I showed up and insisted on staying, and you got scared and ran for it, and decided to turn yourself in. You could use that in a trial, good faith and all that. Do you know an attorney?"

Pollock nodded. "I got a name from the Memphis magazine—she's a criminal attorney and she's a big feminist deal down there. She's got a reputation for defending women who were beat up, and did something about it."

"Is she good?"

"The magazine says she is. She was like a winner in their mover-and-shaker issue."

"Okay, then. This could work. This could work. But you've got to think about it harder. I've got money, we could get you out of here. Seattle, or somewhere really out of it."

"Nah . . ." Pollock looked around. "I hate this place. Everything's gray, nothing's mine. I never felt like I could hang a picture, because Old Lady McCombs would get pissed about me hammering a nail in the wall. If I go somewhere else, it'd be the same thing all over again."

Rinker looked at her for a long moment and then said, "Let's think about it."

"You think . . . ?"

"I think it's reasonable," Rinker said. "Tell me about this attorney."

THEY TALKED THE rest of the afternoon, and then Pollock went out and brought groceries and a bottle of wine, and they had fish and white wine and a nice spinach salad. Halfway through, Pollock started to sob, and Rinker said, "You're gonna be scared for a while."

"Ah, jeez."

"And it's a risk. The papers say first-degree murder."

"It's no risk. I'm dying right here, one inch at a time."

"Then let's run with it." Clara grinned at her, the first smile since she heard about Gene. "But not until tomorrow. I got a couple of things to do tonight. You could call the lawyer tomorrow morning and head down to Memphis in your car."

"I'd like to talk to Mama first."

"I shouldn't go out until after dark—things'll be safer on the street then," Rinker said. "We can make the call from the gas station."

THEY WENT OUT after dark, both wearing skirts and dark blouses, hoping to look like old women. They went downtown first, to the Heartland National Plaza. Rinker found a Federal Express station and took an envelope. She called a cab from a pay phone, then put the booby-trapped cell phone in the envelope with a note she'd written that afternoon, and walked out to the sidewalk and waited.

The cab showed in five minutes, and she gave the driver the envelope and twenty dollars, and took his card. As soon as the cab was out of sight, she waved Pollock over, and they wandered farther west, found a gas station with an outside phone, and Pollock called her mother and told her what she was planning.

Rinker watched the rearview mirror for fast-moving cars, and after two minutes, gave Pollock the *hang up* sign. Pollock talked for another thirty seconds, then hung up, and they pulled out.

"Davenport," Pollock said.

"What?"

"Davenport was at my folks' home. Mama put a bug in his ear, sounds like." She smiled, and suddenly looked almost happy, Rinker thought. "She remembered his name because she always called a couch a couch, and Dad always called it a davenport."

"Really," Rinker said.

"So we're going back to my place? I oughta pack a few things and maybe put some stuff in a box and send to Mama tomorrow. I could go to the post office before I leave for Memphis."

"I could mail it for you. . . . Tell you what—let's get out of town someplace, someplace over in Illinois, and get us an ice cream. One big last calorie blast before you take off."

Pollock started crying again, and Rinker let her go. A minute later, Pollock wiped her nose on the shoulder of her blouse and said, "That sounds really good, Clara."

LUCAS WAS AT the hotel, reading an *Esquire* about fall fashion, and what anyone not a savage would be wearing in October, when Mallard called: "Showtime," he said.

"She's coming in?"

"No. She sent Levy a cell phone in a cab, in a FedEx envelope. He didn't know what it was. He thought it was from his office, so he opened it, and there was a cell phone and a note. She says she wants to talk about money, and about some other things. Said she was afraid to call him at his office and his home phone was unlisted, and that the feds are probably watching him. She said not to tell anybody about the phone. He might not have, if he'd had a choice."

"Does the note say when she's gonna call?"

"Yeah. She said she'd call at ten—twenty minutes from now. The guys already tried out the cell phone, and it's the one she's been using to call you, so she'll either be calling from a new cell phone, or she'll be calling from the ground. We're ready to go either way. We've got choppers to look for the cell phone, and we've got guys all the way along the major interstates—we should be able to get to any ground station in two minutes. We're all over Soulard. So you've got a choice. You've got enough time to get to Levy's, barely, or you could head down to Soulard."

"Okay. Ah . . . are we gonna be able to set it up so we can all hear what she's got to say?"

"We're trying, but I don't think there's time. We can tap it, but we won't be able to hear it live. Listen, I gotta get going."

"Wait, wait, one second. How many guys are down in Soulard?"

"Five teams."

"Too many already. I'll see you at Levy's."

LUCAS PARKED A BLOCK from Levy's at eight minutes to ten, and hurried along. As he passed through the wrought-iron fence at the blocked end of the street, he looked to his left, into the dark, and said aloud, "Davenport."

"Go."

He went to Levy's front door, knocked, and another agent let him in. Mallard was in the library with Levy,

Malone, two more agents, including Sally with the epaulets, and a technician.

"Three minutes," Mallard said. He was excited, rolling.

"Are we looking around the neighborhood? This could be an excuse to pull you or Malone into range."

"We got guys with night-vision glasses all up and down the streets, for two blocks around. We're covered."

"Two minutes," the tech said. He had a Sony tape recorder, and it ran to a pickup fastened to the cell phone. Levy sat staring at it, as though willing it to ring. To Malone, Levy said, "So I answer her questions and then I ask her about John, if she's seen him. And ask if she knows what he's done with his security. I say I was out at his place and he's got some guys outside with night-vision glasses. . . ."

"Just like the ones you saw here—describe them, like you were impressed," Malone prompted.

"Yeah, I say that—"

"You gotta keep coming back to the idea that you didn't know what was happening in Mexico, and you didn't know about her brother. Ask about her other brother, Roy. That'll keep her going. We need two minutes, minimum, and every second after that increases the chances of getting her."

"Ah, Lord," Levy said. "What'd I do to deserve this?"

"Joined the fuckin' Mafia," Lucas said.

"Does this guy have to be here?" Levy asked, looking at Lucas but talking to Mallard.

"Yeah, pretty much."

"Then maybe you oughta tell him that I got nothing to do with any Mafia, for Christ's sake. That's like some kind of fairy tale. What do you know from Mafia up in Minneapolis? What, you got one Italian guy in the whole freezin' fuckin' place?"

"Keep talking, I'll pull your fuckin' nose for you," Lucas said, and smiled.

"Shut up, everybody," Mallard said. "We got one minute."

Three minutes later, they were still waiting.

"GOTTA MAKE ONE CALL, then we better get back," Rinker told Pollock.

"Okay." They'd gotten cherry cones at a Breyer's store in a strip shopping center.

Rinker went to the pay phones, dialed the number of her old cell phone, and got a "Please deposit one dollar" recording. She dropped four quarters and the phone rang at the other end.

"THERE SHE IS," Levy said. He licked his lips once, picked up the phone, and pushed the talk button.

"Clara? . . . Yeah, this is me. . . . Okay, let me see. One time, I was at the warehouse with John, we were doing some accounting stuff, and you came in and John said to you, 'That tube top looks cheap. You ought to stop wearing them, Clara.' And you said, 'I'll never wear another one in my life.' Okay? It's me."

MALLARD WAS SITTING across Levy's ornate desk, with Malone beside him and the tech leaning forward, two agents behind them. Lucas was standing beside the desk, flatfooted, hands in his pockets, watching. He heard the beeping, faintly, like the beeping made by an ATM.

Then BANG.

The phone exploded, and bits and pieces of Levy's face, skull, and brains hit Lucas like a bucket of thrown blood.

Stunned by the explosion, Lucas staggered back, unsure if he was hurt, registered Malone's voice gone shrill: "Oh, Jesus, oh, Jesus, oh, Jesus . . ."

And then Lucas, losing it, freaking out, began frantically brushing at himself, wiping himself, trying to get Levy's body tissue off his face and chest, backing away from the body, saying, "Get it off me, get it off . . ."

17

THEY HAD A PANIC MEETING AT MIDNIGHT. BY MORNING, everybody in the country would know about Levy's murder. They'd had to notify the locals, who leaked like crazy, and media calls started coming into FBI headquarters at eleven o'clock, first from the late guy at the *Post-Dispatch,* and five minutes after that by a local CNN correspondent.

"We're gonna look like utter fools," Mallard said. "We might as well be braced for it."

"The cell phone—no way we should have allowed him to use that," said Lewis, the AIC. By "we" he meant Mallard, and everyone around the table knew it.

"We looked at it," Mallard snapped. "A technician looked at it and didn't see anything. And you tell me who in the hell thought she had that kind of capability."

"I doubt that she does," Malone said. "She had to know somebody. The only way she'd know somebody is through contacts here in St. Louis. The people who ran her. John Ross?"

"So we talk to Ross, tonight," Mallard said. "Tell him to call around, find some names of people who could have done this."

"He's not gonna give us anything," Lewis groaned. "If he knows who did the phone, then that guy can probably pin all kinds of shit back on Ross. Ross might take care of the guy himself, but he's not going to give him up to us."

"People are gonna go crazy with this," Malone said. "We got to get her soon."

"Ideas," Mallard said. He looked around the table, then at Lucas. "You got *anything?*"

"Just what I'm doing. We've got most of Soulard webbed up, we're running the names through Sally. We'll get the rest of the place tomorrow and the next day. If Clara's down there, there's a good chance we'll know by tomorrow night."

"Got nothing but false alarms so far. Running around like a goddamn Chinese fire drill," said Lewis.

"Better'n sitting around jerking off with a bunch of census tables and utility bills," Lucas said. "We're actually doing something."

The agent named Brown said, "Setting off false alarms is mostly—"

"Shut up," Mallard said. To Lucas: "You need more people?"

Lucas shook his head. "I think we're all right. We've got guys who know the area, going around talking to people that they know personally. . . . I think we're good."

"We gotta get something else going," Mallard said. He sounded desperate; he *was* desperate, Lucas realized.

"And we've got to cover Dallaglio and Ross," Malone said. "She's gonna do them all. She did Levy right under our noses. She's not backing off."

"Dallaglio is going to run for it, I think," said Lasch, who was in charge of the Dallaglio watch detail. "I called him tonight after Levy, to tell him, and to tell him to tighten up. He said that he wasn't gonna sit around like a target."

"Makes sense," Lucas said. "He could take off for six weeks, a week here, a week there, see Europe—no way she'd find him."

"If he leaves, and she figures it out, she's gonna take off herself, come back and get him later," Mallard said. "We couldn't find her the first time she took off. Never even got a sniff of her. If she has another spot set up, I doubt that we'll find her there, either."

They were starting to repeat themselves. Lucas stood up: "Call me if anything moves. I'm gonna get some sleep. I've talked to my guys, and we want to get an early start tomorrow. Get people before they leave for work."

Sally asked, "What'd you do with your suit?"

"Threw it in the Dumpster at the hotel. Couldn't wear it again even if we got it clean. I'd keep smelling him," Lucas said. He held his hands to his face. "I'm smelling him anyway."

Malone shook her head. "Can't believe it. Cannot believe it."

RINKER AND POLLOCK were up at first light. Rinker got the paper off the porch. Levy dominated the front page. She read the story, and followed it through to the jump page.

"Anything good?" Pollock asked.

"No, not really. . . ." She looked back at the photo of Levy on the front, and was about to toss the paper when she noticed a smaller headline below the fold: "*Webster Groves/Woman Tortured To Death: Police.*"

And beneath that:

> *The brutally tortured body of a Webster Groves woman was found in a roadside ditch in Kirkwood yesterday by a highway crew picking up trash.*
>
> *The woman was identified as Nancy Leighton, 38, who lived at the Oakwood Apartments in Webster Groves. Police said they are following a number of leads, but have made no arrests in the murder.*
>
> *"This is the worst thing I've ever seen," said Webster Groves homicide detective Larry Kelsey. "This woman suffered a long time before she died."*

Rinker read the rest of it—no details of the torture, but plenty of hints, along with vows of revenge from the cops, who apparently had not a single clue—and then crumpled the newspaper in her hands. Nancy Leighton. An old friend, now dead; and dead because of Rinker. Somebody was sending her a message, and the message had been received.

"You all right?" Pollock asked.

"Yeah . . . just nervous about this whole thing, I guess. Not too late to back out."

"No way. I'm feeling better about it all the time," Pollock said. "Should have done it five years ago."

Rinker balled up the paper and tossed it under the sink. Nancy Leighton. No help for her now; but she had one coming, Nancy did.

RINKER AND POLLOCK had been up late the night before. Pollock had said that there was nothing in the place that she really wanted, but that turned out to be not quite right. They'd gone out twice for packaging tape, and finally had four large boxes to be shipped to Pollock's parents. Pollock knew about a private UPS pickup spot at a strip mall south on I-55, and they'd drop them on the way out of town.

At eight o'clock, everything that could be packed was packed, and all the notes that could be written to neighbors, friends, and the landlady had been written, and they'd eaten almost everything in the refrigerator for breakfast.

Pollock started crying when Rinker carried the first box out to the garage. Looked around the apartment and started weeping. Said, "Oh, shit," and went into the back and came out with a framed picture that had been hanging in the bathroom. "I'll mail it home from Memphis," she said.

"Scared?"

"Ah, God."

"You can still chicken out," Rinker said.

"Not now. I finally got up the guts," Pollock said. Still, she looked around. "Like leaving a prison cell, but it's *your* cell."

"Let me tell you about my apartment in Wichita. . . ."

THEY TOOK BOTH cars in the early light of morning, a short convoy out to the interstate, the arch popping up in their rearview mirrors. Ten miles out, they stopped at the UPS place and Pollock went in and mailed the boxes.

When she came back out, they stood beside Rinker's car and Pollock asked, "What're you going to do now?"

"I've got another place I can stay," Rinker said. "Another old friend."

"If you stay, they're going to kill you."

"Not for a while yet," she said.

"Clara, you gotta get out."

Rinker hugged her and said, "You take care of yourself, Patsy. I won't be seeing you again, I guess, but you been a good friend all my life. I'm gonna get out of here before I cry."

Pollock hung on to her for a minute, a big, ungainly woman, hard-used, and Rinker started to tear up. Then she broke away and said, "One thing . . ."

She went around to the trunk of the car, took out a sack, and handed it to Pollock. "Twenty thousand dollars. For the lawyer."

"Clara, I can't . . ."

"You shush. This isn't for you, this is for *her.* She sure as hell will take it. Tell her you were afraid to put it in the bank, and it's your life savings."

Another minute of small talk, and Rinker loaded up and was gone, leaving Pollock in the parking lot with the sack. Rinker didn't know if her friend had a chance or not. Thought she *might.*

She turned out of the parking lot and headed back toward town. She still had some gear at the apartment, which should be okay until afternoon. She looked at her watch. If Pollock drove like she did, she'd be getting to Memphis around two-thirty. Pollock's parents should have been in touch with the lawyer by now, so Pollock could get in to see her by three o'clock.

LUCAS, ANDRENO, BENDER, and Carter worked the neighborhoods in Soulard, and the area just west of Soulard, for most of the morning, humping along from one confirmed contact to the next, marking off blocks on their xeroxed city maps. They worked through lunch, getting hungry and short-tempered. Then, at four o'clock, Carter found Patsy Hill's apartment.

He called just at four, not particularly excited. "Amity Jenetti says a woman in the next block kind of looks like her, her face does. Says the woman has black hair and is generally dark, and the last picture of Hill was blond, but Jenetti says the face is right and she's tall. But then, she says she's big, you know—heavy, and Hill was skinny as a bull snake. About the right age, late thirties or early forties, and lives alone. Says the woman probably got here ten or twelve years ago."

"I don't know. Sounds better than anything we've gotten so far," Lucas said. "You got a name and address?"

"Dorothy Pollock, and the address is . . ." He had to look it up.

When Lucas got it down, he said, "Call you back in a few minutes."

He and Andreno were eating meatball sandwiches at a sidewalk place, under a green-and-white-striped awning, at a tippy metal table with a top the size of a hubcap. Lucas phoned Sally and gave her the information. Sally called back fifteen minutes later. "The woman is supposedly how old?"

"Late thirties, early forties."

"She's twenty-six, according to her Social Security

account. Her application is hinky. We can't find anybody by that name at the listed address, when she was supposedly a teenager."

"Interesting," Lucas said.

"We got a driver's license, and the age doesn't match the Social Security. It says thirty-five. Hill's supposed to be thirty-seven, but she'd take years off, right? We got Neil looking at it—he's a picture maven."

"Well, what's he say?"

Lucas heard Sally turn away from the phone and ask somebody, "Well, what do you say, Neil?"

Behind Sally, he heard another voice said, "Darn. The picture sucks, but . . . You know what?"

Sally came back. "You better get over there. An entry team'll meet you in the brewery parking lot in fifteen minutes."

"Damn," Lucas said. He hung up, wiped the phone with a napkin.

Andreno said, "Nothing, huh?"

"They think it's her," Lucas said. "We're supposed to meet an entry team in the brewery parking lot in fifteen minutes."

Andreno stopped chewing long enough to look at his watch. "So we got three minutes to eat."

"Basically."

"We're so fuckin' good."

"That's true." Lucas licked his fingers, then cleaned up

his face with the napkin. "Gotta call Carter and Bender. Carter's gonna pass a kidney stone when he hears."

Andreno stood up, bunched the remnants of his sandwich in its waxed-paper wrapper, and pitched it into a garbage can. "Fuck a bunch of sitting here being cool," he said, his voice suddenly excited. "Let's go."

THE ENTRY TEAM was as tough-looking as any Lucas had seen, big men sweating in dark blue uniforms and heavy armor. Carter and Bender had brought the woman who'd fingered the apartment, along with another woman, named Amy, who'd actually been inside. The entry team leader worked through as much as Amy knew. They learned that Hill's apartment actually consisted of the converted back rooms of a house owned by an elderly woman named Betty McCombs.

Lucas and the three ex-cops stood around and watched the team get ready. Mallard and Malone arrived a moment later, in a Dodge, and then a half-dozen other agents in two other cars.

"Two options," the team leader told Mallard, and the semicircle of faces around him. "The first is, we hit them now, hard, take them down. The downside is, we might have to take them out. If the place is empty, we put the door back together and wait for them to show. The second option is to watch the place, and catch them in the open, either coming or going. There are no cars parked outside right now, but there could be one in the garage."

Sally had been on the phone as they were talking, and now spoke up. "Carson got in touch with Pollock's employer. She called in this morning and said she was sick. She's not at work."

"Can they see the street from the back of the house, where these rooms are?" Lucas asked.

Carter said, "We cruised by. They could see the street, but not much of it. They could see it especially on the north side, the garage side. The other side, they'd be looking down a little narrow strip between the next house over."

"So if we sent Sally in with another guy, the youngest-looking guy, and we got into this old lady's house with some listening gear . . . we should be able to figure out if they're in there."

"We could do that," the team leader said. "And we could get a better layout from her."

"So let's do it," Mallard said.

WITHOUT THE PROSPECT of instant action, the intensity faded a bit, the entry team guys peeled off their armor and flopped around the place, and ten minutes later, when Sally and a youthful, blond agent named Meers left for McCombs's house, Lucas and the three St. Louis ex-cops congregated around Andreno's car.

"You guys get anything to eat?"

"Meatball sandwiches up at Dirty Bill's," Andreno said.

"Nasty, but tasty. You better stick close to the can," Carter said. Then, to Lucas: "What do you think?"

"Maybe," Lucas said. "They wouldn't be going out much in the daytime."

"What about these guys?" He nodded at the federal entry team.

"Look like pros," Lucas said. "The ones up in Minneapolis are good."

Bender nodded. "Everything I've heard about these guys is, they're good."

"So we wait," Lucas said.

THEY WAITED AN hour and a bit more, the sun still bright in the sky, but angled now, and Lucas began to worry about the problems of darkness. Then Sally came back with a layout. "The old bat, you oughta see her," she said to Mallard. "She's got a bad mouth, she apparently hates people on sight, she smells—"

"Are they there?" Mallard asked impatiently.

"I don't think so, not at the moment—but it's her. It's Hill," Sally said. Sally was wearing an olive-drab shirt, made of a crinkly cotton fabric, without epaulets but with a military cut. "Tommy set up the listening gear and it's working, and we put it right on the wall, but we didn't hear anything. They could be asleep."

"How many rooms?

"Kitchen, living room, bath, bedroom and a spare room, but it's small, more like a closet. One hallway. You come into the living room and look straight back at the kitchen, down a hall, with the main bedroom on one side of the hall, and the bath and the small room opening off the other side. Thirty feet, maybe, from the front of the living room to the back wall of the kitchen. One door in and out, with a push-out fire window on the north side, in the main bedroom. There's a window on the south side. . . ."

They worked through it, still playing the possibilities. Go in hard, and if they weren't there, wait. Or wait, ready to snap when they walked in.

"I don't want to wait," Mallard said, finally. "There're too many possible ways for things to go wrong, and we've been waiting . . . "

But as he ran down his rationale for hitting McCombs's house, a call came in for Malone, and after listening for a moment, she said, "What?" in a harsh, incredulous tone and everyone went quiet. The tone was bad news, and they waited.

Malone, more puzzled than anything, Lucas thought, after a moment looked at Mallard and said, "The Memphis police just called. A woman who says she's Patricia Hill just turned herself in on the old homicide warrant. She's with her lawyer. She says she's scared and she's willing to give up Rinker. The Memphis cops want to know what to do."

"Holy cow," Mallard said. He looked around, spotted Lucas. "You hear that?"

"Yeah," Lucas said. "I dunno. Does she say where Rinker is?"

Malone was listening again, and when Lucas asked the question, she nodded and said, "She's giving up the house. I mean, *the* house. McCombs's house."

"She says Rinker's there?"

"She says she was this morning."

"Let's go," Mallard said. "Let's hit it."

"Wait a minute," Lucas said, then louder, "WAIT A FUCKIN' MINUTE."

"What?" Mallard asked.

"What if Rinker's setting us up? She says she's gonna start taking out FBI people. What if she sent Hill down there to pull us into the house without thinking about it? What if Rinker's out there with one of those rifles?"

Mallard pulled at a lip. Then: "Goddamnit." He looked at the entry team leader. "We're gonna go in, but we're gonna get every cop in St. Louis down here first. You get set up in your vans across the street, and back behind the neighbor's, where you can see the door and windows, but don't get out yet. We'll get the cops down here and jam up every street for six blocks around. If she's waiting for us, there won't be any way out."

THE COPS CAME in a wave, running with lights but no sirens. Agents in blue nylon jackets met them on the streets, routed them out to the perimeters. Nobody in or out without the cars being checked, two cops on each car check. The screen was set two blocks out from the McCombs house. A car with a Texas license plate was found at the edge of the perimeter, and cops started going door to door, looking for the owner. Another hour slipped away.

"Ain't gonna help if she's on a suicide run," Lucas told Malone. "She could be up in an attic somewhere, the people in the house already dead, looking at the front of McCombs's house through a scope. She got a seven-millimeter mag off that peckerwood down in Tisdale. If she's any good with it, if she's got a shooting rest, she could poke a hole in a pie plate at three hundred yards."

Malone shook her head. "She won't. She's not on a suicide run. Not yet."

"You know that for sure."

"Yeah. She's not done with Dallaglio or Ross. Her brother killing himself pissed her off, but her brother's not the same as losing her fiancé and her baby. She doesn't want to die yet."

"Hope you're right. But something's hinky here."

THE HOUSE SEEMED so lifeless that they had little hope that Rinker was inside. She could be asleep, Mallard argued. They might not hear her, he said, because the bedroom didn't share a wall with anything they could reach with the sound equipment.

With the sun almost on the horizon, and long dark shadows striping across the lawns, everything was finally set and Mallard gave a go to the entry team. The team's vans moved, rolling back from their surveillance sites, and the team piled out. One man set up to watch the windows, while the others came in from the front of the house, crept under one window, reached the back door.

Lucas watched, feeling the pressure. Then the door man moved, then another guy, then the door man stepped back with a monster wedge, normally used for splitting wood, ready to swing. Two guys on the sides of the house, coordinated by radio, pitched flash-bangs through the windows, and as they went off, sounding to Lucas like distant cannon fire, the guy with the monster wedge hit the doorknob. The team was inside in a second, and in five seconds, had secured the place.

"Empty," Mallard groaned. "Okay. Get some guys out in the garage, close the door. We'll set up for surveillance."

WHEN THEY WERE SET, and nothing was moving, Mallard, Malone, Lucas, and Andreno crossed the street and walked up to the house, Lucas nervously watching the windows in the houses up and down the street. Nothing happened. Inside, the surveillance team leader said, "Nothing."

They walked through the apartment, looked in the chest of drawers, looked at the walls, checked the medicine cabinet.

"Bullshit," Lucas said. "They cleared out before Hill ever went to Memphis. There's nothing left here but junk. Nothing sentimental. She wasn't running from Rinker, 'cause if she was, when did she have time to pack up?"

"When were they here?"

Lucas was still poking around, and came up with a newspaper. "This morning's paper," he said, showing them the Levy headline. "They brought it in this morning."

"And she might be hurt," Andreno said. "Look at this." They went to the bathroom, where Andreno pointed into a wastebasket. Inside, they could see a white shirt with a thumb-sized bloodstain. "Wonder what that came from?"

"Not that much blood," Malone said. "We don't even know it's hers."

"Got a Cancún label—it's from a Cancún hotel, and it's a medium, which wouldn't fit Patsy Hill," Andreno said.

"SO WHERE IS SHE?" Mallard asked.

"Running? I don't know," Lucas said. "Maybe she's got a backup spot. But maybe we've just broken her out."

"Or maybe she's coming back," Malone said.

Lucas said, "Nah."

Mallard: "We can't take a chance. We'll set up here all night. Pull the cops out, maybe she'll come in."

"Better get a bigger net around Dallaglio and Ross," Lucas said. "Better get some smart guys with them. After Levy . . . I don't know. A car bomb?"

"Don't tell me a car bomb," Mallard groaned. He looked around. "She was here this morning. *This morning.*"

HONUS JOHNSON WAS working on a chest of drawers in American cherry. A Honus Johnson chest of drawers brought in four thousand dollars in a boutique furniture shop in Boston; they looked so much like the *old* ones.

In his woodworking, Johnson tended to use British tools, like his miniature Toolman hand planes, which were simply exquisite. In his sadistic pursuits, he preferred Craftsman tools from Sears. He rejected electrical equipment, because it lacked subtlety—though he always had a soldering iron handy. He'd really found his metier in hammers, pliers, and handsaws. He'd once cut off a man's foot with a hacksaw, to make a business point for his employer.

His personal inclinations pretty much ruled out any deep friendships. Even people who knew him well, and used his services, were likely to wince when they saw him coming, though he looked harmless enough: a pinkish, white-haired gentleman in his late forties or early fifties, with square, capable hands and a thin, oval face.

He wore khaki pants and striped long-sleeved shirts and

European-look square-toed brown shoes, and tended to suck on his teeth, as though he was perplexed. He also had a tendency to flatulence, which resulted in some of John Ross's associates referring to him as Stinky—but only very privately. He'd worked for Ross for two dozen years, a weapon much like Rinker.

RINKER SPENT THE morning on the far west edge of the metro area, at the Spirit of St. Louis Airport, looking around, wandering among the industrial and office buildings. Later that day, now dressed as the Dark Woman, she spent an enjoyable couple of hours at the Missouri Botanical Gardens. The Gardens had an environmental dome called the Climatron, an enclosed jungle that offered much in the way of concealment and ambush possibilities. She looked at it closely for a long time.

WHEN SHE ARRIVED at Johnson's house, a little after four o'clock in the afternoon, he was working in his backyard woodshop, power-planing cherry planks for the chest of drawers. Johnson really had no fear of retaliation for his past acts of cruelty, simply because he was never the principal in the act. Like his favorite chisels and saws, he was only a tool, if an exquisite one. In all the years he'd worked for Ross, there'd been no comebacks.

And he was careful: Almost nobody knew where he lived.

Rinker knew, but Johnson didn't know that she did. She'd made it her business to find out when she was still working for Ross. If she'd ever gotten on the wrong side of Ross, she'd thought years ago, she might want to take care of Ross's other major weapon before he had a chance to take care of her.

She'd had a hard time finding him. Johnson was not in the phone books, nor was he in any of the records that Ross kept in the warehouse. He was paid off the books, like Rinker was, and she saw him so rarely that there was no real possibility of following him home.

She'd looked in the county tax statements, but he wasn't there. She'd once managed to get his auto license number, but then found out that if she tracked the car through the state, she had to make a formal request for the information and that Johnson would be notified. No good. One of the girls at the warehouse once mentioned that she'd had to send some stuff to him, for Ross, but when Rinker made some careful inquiries, she found that the stuff was sent to a downtown post office box.

She'd eventually found Johnson's house purely through luck. Johnson had built elaborate teak plant benches for John Ross, for Ross's orchids, and when the benches were delivered, she'd been at Ross's house. The two guys who drove the delivery truck had an invoice that showed both the pickup and delivery addresses. She took the address back to the courthouse and looked it up in the tax and plat records—Johnson was there all right, but his house was listed under "Estate of Estelle Johnson."

SHE PARKED IN the street and walked up the driveway. From the driveway, she could hear the planer screaming inside the workshop. She went past the garage, vaulted a chain-link fence—moving fast now, slipping the silenced Beretta from under her shirt—to the open side door of the workshop. As she came up to the door she happened to glance upward, and saw a motion detector tucked in the corner, and she stopped, peeked around the door frame. Johnson was looking right at her, a silent-alarm strobe light bouncing off his protective glasses, and he was moving to his right, quickly. She stepped through the door, following the muzzle of her pistol. He froze when he saw her, his hands empty. She glanced toward the wall that he'd been moving to: A shotgun leaned against a cabinet.

What had Jaime told her, at the ranch, about the need for handguns? *"The rifle will be leaning against a tree, and that's when they will come."*

SHE SMILED, THINKING about it, and Johnson flinched. He took a step back and tried a placating smile. "Hello, Clara, I . . ."

No point in conversation. Rinker shot him in the nose, and he went down, twisting away, his face striking the edge of the saw table. He landed faceup in a pile of shavings. She looked at him for a moment, on the floor, judged him dead, but shot him again, carefully, between the eyes. The planer was so loud that she heard no hint of the shot, or of the gun's cycling action.

He was dead for sure now. The planer was still screaming, the plank beginning to buck. Rinker couldn't see a switch, so she pulled the plug, and the machine wound down like a depowered airplane engine.

She couldn't leave Johnson on the floor, or even in the workshop, she decided. The yard was fenced, but it wasn't the best neighborhood, and if somebody broke in, he might be found.

She looked around for a moment, then grabbed him by the collar and dragged him to a lowboy he'd used for hauling lumber. She pushed a stack of planks onto the floor—thought better of it, in case somebody looked in, and took a minute to stack them neatly near the wall—then loaded his body onto the lowboy and covered it with four transparent bags full of wood shavings and sawdust.

She pushed the whole load out the door, up the concrete walk to the back of the garage, then into the garage, past an E-Class Mercedes-Benz, and through a breezeway to the house. She couldn't actually get the lowboy into the house, because of a step. She left the body and the cart in the breezeway and let the muzzle of the Beretta lead her through the house. She was, she found, the only living thing in it.

The house was neatly kept, but had no more personality than a motel room—a few woodworking magazines, some reference works, a television set with an incongruous Nintendo console sitting on the floor next to it.

She checked it all out, then hauled Johnson's body into the house and rolled it down the basement stairs. She first thought to leave it there, at the foot of the stairs, but then noticed a chest-style freezer against the wall, and opened it. It was half-full of Healthy Choice microwave dinners, and bags of frozen peas and corn.

She took a bunch of the dinners and some of the corn, then managed to tug and pull the body around until she could boost it into the freezer. Johnson landed facedown, and she had to twist his legs to get him to fit inside. She slammed the lid.

With a few paper towels to wipe up the odd blood smear, she thought, everything would be as nice and tidy as Honus Johnson used to be.

And she had a new phone, a new house, and a new car.

Not bad for twenty minutes' work.

Though, she admitted to herself, moving the body had given her the willies. As did Johnson's bed. She was beat from the day, needed some sleep, but couldn't sleep with the smell of him, and his body still cooling in the freezer. She found clean sheets in a linen closet, sheets that smelled only of detergent, and crashed on the couch.

Long day coming . . .

18

THEY WOUND UP SITTING IN ONE OF THE FBI RENTAL TRUCKS, a six-seater Suburban, eating Snickers and Milky Ways, drinking Cokes and waiting for anything on the perimeter, any sign that Rinker was coming in. They got nothing except distended bladders, and strange looks in a Shell station when they repeatedly tramped through to the rest rooms. Andreno gave up at nine o'clock and took off. At ten-thirty, Mallard was willing to admit that Rinker had flown.

"We go back to the four main guys," Mallard said, in frustration. "Ross *must* be a target—she worked for him for too long. He *must* be her original connection. Dallaglio is necessary because of Dichter. If she goes after one, she'll go after the other. Giancati used her at least four or five times—one of her best customers. Ferignetti is marginal, but we can't take a chance."

"If you're gonna talk to them, I want to be there," Lucas said.

"You're invited," Mallard said. He looked out at the darkness across the brewery's parking lot. "We'll make the rounds tomorrow morning."

"Don't worry so much, Louis," Malone said. She'd gotten into a sack of Cheese Doodles, and the back of the truck was suffused with the smell of cheddar. "We'll get her. We just missed her tonight. We're closing in."

"You're sure."

"Yeah, I am," Malone said. "And I can't wait. Locking her up is gonna feel *so* good."

"It's gonna be hard taking her alive," Lucas said. "I think she'll fight."

"I'll take that," Malone said. And after a moment of silence: "I think I've got a pound of yellow cheese goop stuck to my teeth."

LUCAS LAY IN bed that night, listening to the trains going by along the waterfront. There was no good reason for it, but the sound of distant trains and distant truck traffic, trucks downshifting to climb a hill, left him feeling moody. People going places, doing things, while he was here in bed, alone, staring at the ceiling. He'd talked to Weather, and she was feeling fine, although beginning to wonder how much longer he'd be in St. Louis.

"I'd just like to see you," she said. "I'm getting a little lonesome."

"I'd like to see you, too. I'll give this a couple more days, and then if there's nothing definite happening, I'll run up for a day or two."

"Fly?"

"Yeah, I guess."

"Brave of you."

"How's the kid?"

"Strong little thing. I think he or she is gonna be a soccer player."

"Not if I have anything to do with it," Lucas said. "I've already cut down a hockey stick."

"Still thinking about an ultrasound . . ."

"C'mon . . . that's the easy way out."

"You've already got a daughter."

"Two daughters would be wonderful. A son would be excellent. I *really* don't care. I just pray that the kid's healthy."

"Maybe come up for a day or two . . . at the end of the week?"

"Over the weekend, if nothing's happening. A guy down here told me about a weird way to induce labor. I'll show it to you when I come up."

"It's too early, Lucas."

"It doesn't always induce labor. It has other uses. . . ."

*

AFTER HE RANG OFF, he wondered what Rinker was doing. She was almost certainly holed up somewhere, alone, or with a scared friend like Hill, who probably didn't want her around, and might even betray her, given the chance. That must be *really* lonely. The thought gave him no comfort, and the night went slowly, patches of sleep mixed with weary semiconsciousness.

He hoped, as he looked at the bedside clock at five in the morning, that they took Rinker clean. Either grabbed her or killed her, but ended it. That the FBI ended it. That he didn't have to. . . .

WHEN LUCAS ARRIVED at the FBI offices in the morning, still sleepy, Mallard gave him a cup of good coffee and said, "Hill gave up Rinker's car and license tag. California plates. We're running them now, and every cop in St. Louis is looking for them."

"Are you going to Memphis? To talk to Hill?"

"I thought about it, but I decided to stick here. . . . You ever hear of a lawyer named Ann Diaz? In Memphis?"

"No. Should I?"

"She's representing Hill. I got a call from the Memphis guy this morning—he talked to Hill last night, with Diaz present. Hill said that Rinker showed up on her doorstep, threatened to kill her if she thought about going to the police, and threatened to turn her in if she didn't stay straight. . . . Hill says she was so scared that she froze for a couple of days, and then ran for it."

"Did your guy ask her how she managed to pack up everything in the place?"

"Yeah. She said that Rinker went out every day—and that she pretended that she was going to work, watched until Rinker left, then ran back, threw everything in her car, and took off. She said she packed it out of the car and mailed it to her folks, and then headed down to Memphis. She says if we don't get Rinker, Rinker will kill her."

"It's bullshit, Louis."

"I think so . . . but the problem is Diaz. She's pretty well known, she's got some clout in D.C., connections with all kinds of feminist groups. She could make Hill a *cause.* And she's tough. She won't let Hill give us anything that's not scripted."

"What're you saying?"

"Hill's gonna be a dry hole."

Lucas shrugged. "That's the way things work now. Fifty years ago, you could have taken her down the basement with a couple of steel fishing poles, and beaten the shit out of her, and after she confessed, you could've hanged her on Wednesday. Now it's just a bunch of sissies whining about civil rights."

"Thanks," Mallard said. "I enjoy being mocked before lunch."

Lucas raised his coffee cup in a semiserious toast.

"Rinker was a step ahead of us, Louis. But Malone's right. It's only a half-step now. We would have found her yesterday. If she hadn't decided to book, we would have had her."

"You think she spotted us?"

"Yeah. Maybe when we were going around to the houses, or maybe she spotted the guys running in after the phone calls. But we were close."

"All right. So let's go talk to these assholes."

"I want to talk to you about that. About the approach. About tactics."

THE MEETINGS BETWEEN Mallard and Malone for the FBI on one side, and the four hoods on the other side, were like the Israelis and the Palestinians working on a deal, Lucas thought—everybody smiling and lying like motherfuckers, but still, messages were sent and received, both ways. Mallard told all four of them flatly that the FBI had tried to protect Richter and Levy, and had failed, and that they believed Rinker would be back.

"She's had a lot of time to think about her approach. I'm not sure we can stop her without your help. Or even with your help," he told them.

Giancati and Ferignetti denied having anything to do with Rinker—Ferignetti said he'd never met her, didn't know Ross except to nod to him, and said he planned to carry on with business as usual. He didn't have bodyguards because he didn't need them.

Giancati, on the other hand, was leaving for England.

"You seem to think that there's some reason she'd be after me, but I don't think so," he said. He was a round, bald man, but his fat was tough fat, the kind of fat that you'd wear yourself out hitting on. He looked like he should smell of stubby cigars, but instead smelled of vanilla. "All my business is on the up-and-up, and always has been. I mean, over the years, I suppose, I'm gonna bump into some of these supposed hoodlums in my business. . . ."

Blah blah blah, Lucas thought, listening to him. A wall of bland unresponsiveness. But the kicker was, Giancati was getting out of town with his wife, and nobody else knew, he said, and nobody would know unless the FBI called up Rinker and told her.

"If she wants me, and can find me over there, then God bless her, because half the time, I can't even find myself when I'm there."

"You go there often?" Malone asked.

"All the time. My wife's parents came from Newcastle, and my mother came from Dover and went to school in Calais. The east country is my favorite place in the world. . . ."

Blah blah blah . . .

DALLAGLIO LOOKED LIKE a book editor or an accountant—tall, thin, harried, quizzical, with a caterpillarlike mustache on his upper lip. He did not look like a man who may have contracted a dozen hits. His wife, on the other hand, was short, rounded, and loud, and looked capable of doing any amount of killing. They had three armed bodyguards in the house: One of them, a former FBI agent, had known of Mallard, and said so. Mallard asked him, "You think you can cover him?"

"Nobody will get inside of twenty feet, but if Rinker has rifles . . . what can we do? We've told Mr. Dallaglio that."

DALLAGLIO'S HOUSE WAS a neo-Baroque prairie-style gothic, Charles Addams out of Frank Lloyd Wright, with decoration chosen equally from the Renaissance and Miami Beach. He led them through the carved walnut double front doors, through a highly rugged interior to an indoor patio around a lap pool, offered them Cokes from a poolside refrigerator, and sat everybody down on plastic gliders. "I have no idea why she killed Nanny. He was a good man—looked after his family," Dallaglio said. "If he was involved in any wrongdoing, I wouldn't know about it—our relationship was strictly business."

But under the *blah-blah-blah* he was panicked, and so was his wife. His wife, Jesse, said, "We only met her because Nanny was involved in a couple of business relationships with John Ross, and she worked for John. And she was a friend of John's wife, going back a while, when they both worked at his liquor warehouse. She was like a bookkeeper, but she was really outgoing, and that's how we knew her. We were in Wichita once, after she quit working for John, and we went to her bar. It really wasn't our style, but she seemed nice. That's all we knew about her."

"Are you friends with John Ross?" Mallard asked.

"Well, yeah. Sure. We do business with him all the time. He's in trucking—we need his trucks, and we need stuff delivered on time. That's no big secret. He's a good guy. We go out with them, out to dinner, or maybe he has tickets to a concert or some shit like that, and they invite us. He was really better friends with Nanny, but we know him."

The Dallaglios and Mallard and Malone went back and forth, and when they were finished, and Mallard had hinted that any help wouldn't lead to further questions—that is, if Dallaglio had some kind of intelligence connection with the local underground, and if they found her and turned her in, there'd be no questions asked—they got up to leave. As they moved toward the door, Lucas said, "Could I talk to you guys for a minute? I mean . . . " He looked at Mallard and Malone, and grinned, as they'd agreed. ". . . without the FBI?"

"Lucas . . . ," Mallard said, as though reluctant. They'd worked it through on the way to the house. To Dallaglio: "Lucas has his own ways of working. We're not bound by anything he says."

"Just a minute to talk," Lucas said.

The Dallaglios agreed, and Mallard and Malone went outside, Mallard shaking his head. When the door closed behind them, Lucas said, "Listen: I'm just a fuckin' cop, okay? I've got no jurisdiction here, my boss just loaned me to the FBI because I got lucky once before, breaking Clara loose. If you talk to me, there's no way anybody could take it to court." He looked directly at Dallaglio. "And I'm telling you, no bullshit, I talked to a friend of Clara, and she's gonna kill your ass. She's gonna kill you, if we don't get her. And get her now. If we scare her off, she'll just go sit down in South America somewhere, and wait six months, until everybody relaxes, and then she's gonna come kill you. She knows you set her up down in Mexico, that you agreed to try to kill her—"

Dallaglio put up a finger. "That's not *true.*"

Lucas continued. "But she *knows* you did. What she knows might not be the truth, but she thinks it is. The reality of it doesn't matter, because she's gonna kill you because of it. Can't stop her, can't talk her out of it. She lost her *baby.* This is a woman who hardly had any friends that we can find, who was abused from the time she was a child, and then got turned into some kind of crazy robot killer, and you, she *knows,* killed the only man who ever loved her for herself, who was gonna marry her, and her *baby.*"

"Well, what the fuck are we supposed to do about it?" Jesse Dallaglio asked angrily. "You can't stop her—we've got all these expensive bodyguards, and you can see they're worried. I've got daughters. So you tell me, Mr. Chief, what the fuck are we supposed to do?"

"You can hide, is one thing," Lucas said. "Mr. Giancati's on her list, and he and his wife are leaving town. But if we don't get her . . . she can always wait longer than we can."

Jesse Dallaglio said, "So we can't hide forever, you're saying. Is this leading up to something, or is it all just bullshit?"

"What I'm saying is, if you know *anything,* tell me. I'm not gonna play games with you like the FBI. They want to get Clara, but they also see this as a chance to fuck up a whole bunch of you guys. That's not my problem: I got my own assholes up in Minneapolis to worry about. I just want to get Clara. That's all I want. Give me a name, somebody I can talk to. Give me an old hangout. Give me *anything.*"

Dallaglio walked away, slumped into a chair. "I'll tell you, everybody acts like I'm some hoodlum or criminal, but I'm just trying to run a chain store. Just business. But Rinker . . ." He paused, cocked his head, thought for a moment, and then said, "Let me put it this way. If somebody was a hoodlum and wanted to hire Clara to do whatever, he wouldn't hang around with her. He wouldn't want anybody to even know that they'd talked. Maybe they *wouldn't* talk, so the cops couldn't draw any lines. So that if Rinker was picked up, she couldn't say, 'Well, I met with Nanny Dichter at the Balloon Ballroom on October 31, during the Halloween dance, and we made the deal.' So she couldn't say shit about who, what, where, and when. You see what I mean?"

"Maybe," Lucas said.

"What I mean," Dallaglio said, "is that this guy might not know shit about Clara Rinker. Not really."

"Too bad for that guy," Lucas said.

Jesse Dallaglio asked, "Where is Giancati going? Back to England?"

Lucas shrugged. "He just said he was leaving."

She chewed her lip. "Maybe that's the thing to do." She looked at her husband. "You like the Old Country. We could go for a couple of months."

"But if they don't catch her," Dallaglio said, "it's like he says . . . she can wait."

"But maybe they do catch her," Jesse Dallaglio said. "I'd hate for you or me or the girls to be the last ones killed before they got her."

ON THAT NOTE, with nothing more developing, Lucas said goodbye. Outside, Mallard said, "What?"

"Not much. Treena Ross may have known Clara. Might have been a friend."

Malone said, "Huh."

"Huh, what?" Lucas asked.

"Huh, nothing. I don't see where that goes. We already knew that John Ross was a friend of Rinker's. I'm not surprised that his wife knew her, I guess."

"Well, it's what I got," Lucas said.

ROSS WAS WAITING for them behind his big desk. He had a half-dozen orchids this time, including one that smelled something like cinnamon. He wanted to talk about Levy. "I knew the guy, sure—but what's this about telephones? Clara's no electronics wizard. Where'd she think that up?"

Mallard shook his head. "We were hoping you might be able to think of something."

Ross exhaled in exasperation. "I told you, I never knew about her. I didn't know she was a killer, for Christ's sake. I'm in some tough businesses, but we don't kill people. It's easier just to buy them out. And legal."

"Sounds like you're a little worried," Lucas said, letting the amusement show.

"Yeah, well. Guns is one thing. Now I'm thinking, what if a rocket comes flying through the window? A phone bomb—that sounds like something the CIA would do."

HE WAS SURPRISED to hear that the Giancatis were thinking of running.

"Off to merry old England again, huh? Home of the fruits and the nuts." He reached out and took a peppermint candy from a crystal bowl, unwrapped it, and popped it into his mouth.

"And maybe the Dallaglios," Malone added. "They may go back to the Old Country, whatever country that is."

"You do what you gotta do," Ross said.

Eventually, Mallard and Malone got tired of being stonewalled, and after another warning, got up to leave. Lucas went into this let's-talk routine; Mallard shook his head and went out the door.

"So, what?" Ross asked.

"Like Mallard said, I'm not FBI. I'm a Minneapolis cop. I have no jurisdiction. . . ." He went through the rest of it, feeling like a third-grader reciting to a skeptical teacher.

Ross said, "I can appreciate the fact that you get off on hunting Clara, and I hope you get her, but there's not much more I can do to help. I told you that the last time. There are still some people at the warehouse who knew her, but I knew her as well as anyone. I could tell you where her old apartment used to be, I could tell you where she'd go for drinks, but you gotta remember—that was all before Wichita. This was years ago, and she only worked in the warehouse a couple, three years."

"Did your wife know her?"

"Treena? Yeah, sure. Treena worked in the warehouse along with Rinker."

"Could she tell me anything?"

Ross snorted. "She can barely remember her middle name, Mr. Davenport. She's basically a great set of tits and a terrific ass being run by a brain the size of a cashew. I can't imagine that she could give you anything useful on Clara Rinker. But you're welcome to ask her. She's around here someplace."

"If that's what you think, why did you marry her?"

"It gives me about three headaches a week, going over that. She's got these tits, and I got these hormones. . . . You know what I mean. I should've stuck with the last one."

"Number three."

"Yeah. Number one was probably the best, number two was a rebound, three was pretty good, and four was another bounce. It never made any sense. I'll think a long time about number five."

"Somebody told me that number three died tragically."

There was irony in Lucas's voice, and Ross picked it up and seemed to darken. "She was killed in a hit-and-run. I was in New Orleans at the time."

"Good for you," Lucas said, smiling.

"Fuck you," Ross said.

"If I weren't working for the FBI, I'd pull you outa your chair and kick your ass," Lucas said, still smiling. "Just so you'd know."

Ross looked at him curiously. "You really think you could take me?"

Lucas nodded. "Yeah."

Ross leaned back, finally shrugged, and said, "Maybe we could try it someday. Be kinda interesting."

Lucas nodded and they both sat, and then Lucas said, "So for now, you're just gonna sit."

"No, I'm not just sitting. I go out several times a week—we got three cars, we all go different ways, nobody gets out until we're under cover, we look at the street before we go. And I got four good boys around all the time. I got the best alarms ever made. I can get on the TV with my remote control, any TV in the house, and look at any direction out of the house, through cameras on the roof. One of the boys has a night-vision scope that he watches with. If she gets me, she gets me, but I don't think she can get in. Unless she's got a fuckin' rocket."

"How long can you wait?"

He shrugged. "I'm a patient man. More patient than Clara."

"If you're so fuckin' patient, what was all that about in Mexico? You could've just left her."

"I didn't have anything to do with anything in Mexico, of course," Ross said. "But judging from what's been in the paper, I'd say somebody made a big fuckin' mistake, to use your adjective. A big, stupid mistake."

"And she thinks it was you. Was it you?"

Ross shrugged again and smiled for the first time—an unpleasant smile that said *Yes, it was his big fuckin' mistake.* What he actually said was, "I don't know from Mexico. What happened, exactly?"

"Bullshit," Lucas said. Then: "Are you going any place public this week? Any place that isn't completely shut up?"

"If I told you that, that'd be a leak. I don't even tell my boys when I'm moving."

"Listen, if you're going out, it'd be a hell of a lot easier if you told us in advance than if we have to have the cops pull over all three cars until we figure out which one you're in—all the lights and sirens and so on. Because if you're gonna act like cheese, we'd like to be there when the mouse comes out."

Ross smiled at the image, then leaned forward, lifted a piece of paper from his desk pad, and said, "I'm going one place in public: Friday night, there's a fundraiser for the St. Louis Chamber Orchestra at the botanical gardens. I'm one of the . . . pillars . . . of the chamber orchestra. And the botanical gardens, for that matter."

"Chamber orchestra and orchids. A goddamned refined little thug, huh?"

"Fuck off," Ross said mildly, and smiled again.

LUCAS GOT UP to leave. On the way to the door, a thought struck him, and he went back. "One last thing. You knew both Nanny Dichter and Levy. Are you as well protected as those two?"

"Nanny was a tough nut, but Levy was a pussy," Ross said. "I was surprised when she got to Nanny so easy."

"That's not exactly what I was asking. What I'm asking is, are you a tougher nut than Nanny?"

The question seemed to interest him. He leaned back, put his hands behind his head, thought for a moment, then said, "Yes."

"Would you have been tougher if she'd gone after you first? Could she have ambushed you as easily as she did Dichter?"

No thought this time. "No. As soon as the federal

people started calling, even before Nanny, I had an idea of what was going to happen. I shut down everything I couldn't run by remote control. If she'd called me for a meet, or wanted me to go somewhere to make a phone call, I would have told her to go fuck herself. No. I would have suggested that we meet somewhere that *I'd* control."

"What if all the feds started running around screaming, and then nothing happened? How long before you would have relaxed? Would you do what you're doing now, indefinitely?"

The question called for more thought. Ross played with one of his ears, tugged on the lobe, and then said, "Probably not. If she'd waited six more weeks, and if she'd been careful, she would have got me."

"Huh."

"Yeah. That is kind of weird," Ross said. "I'm almost insulted."

ON THE WAY OUT, Lucas ran into Treena Ross in the hallway. She was wearing a lime-green dress and matching lime-green shoes with two-inch heels. She was carrying a dog the size of a walnut that seemed to have been bred to be frightened; it whimpered when it saw Lucas, and then Ross coming up behind. Treena said, "Oh, they're nice men, Wiener." Then to Lucas: "I don't think I've met you. Are you working with John?"

"I'm a cop," Lucas said. "Lucas Davenport. I saw you once before—you were going to play tennis."

"I *remember.* And you're working with John. That's wonderful."

"He's not working with me," Ross said. "He wants to kick my ass."

"Really? Kick your ass? Why?" She looked wide-eyed at Lucas. She was a little top-heavy, Lucas thought, but she had a beautiful oval face and green eyes that seemed to be a promise of good times. He understood what Ross had said about hormones.

"Never mind," Ross said. "Are you going somewhere?"

"Off to Sophie's." She bent one of the dog's tiny paws toward Lucas. "See? His teeny-weeny nails are all chipped. They have to be recoated."

"We were talking about Clara Rinker," Lucas said to her.

"That's awful what's she's doing," Treena Ross said. "She was always so nice when we worked together. She was very lively. She used to be a dancer."

"Do you have . . . do you remember *anything* about her that might help us run her down?" Lucas asked. "Friends, anything like that?"

"I was her friend. And so was John. And for a while, I thought I was going to race her to see who *got* John," she said, and she laughed, and took her husband's arm. "He still won't tell me if he ever slept with her."

She was teasing, but Ross snapped, "I didn't."

"Now, see? Is he lying, Mr. Lucas? Anyway . . . her friends." She pursed her lips and then said, "The only one I can think of . . ." She looked at her husband. "What was that Indian guy's name? Running Horse, or something . . ."

"Tim Runs-Like-Horse," Ross said. "I don't think she's staying with him."

"Why?" Lucas asked.

"He's dead," Ross said. "He used to drink all the time, and when he was really drunk, he'd go out in the street with his jacket and play bullfighter with cars. Some redneck ran over him with a Chevy S-10."

"Oh," said Treena, a finger going to her lips. "I didn't know about that."

"Three years ago," Ross said. "He was a good guy."

"Huh. Well, too bad," Treena said brightly. "That's the only one I can think of. Old dead Running Horse."

"Let me take you out," Ross said to Lucas.

"Goodbye, Mr. Lucas," Treena said.

RIDING BACK TO FBI headquarters, Malone asked, "How'd it go?"

Lucas shrugged. "We traded threats. His wife is taking the dog to get a manicure."

"Pedicure," Malone said. "We met her." Then, a moment later, she said, "I think Treena's running with one headlight."

"Yeah, well, Ross seems to . . . see something in her," Lucas said.

"Wonder what that might be?"

THEY RODE ALONG in silence for a bit, and then Lucas said, "I don't like the phrase *jackshit,* but that's exactly what we learned, talking to these guys."

"We found out that they might run."

"We knew that anyway," Lucas said.

"My big worry is that *Rinker* might run," Malone said, looking out the window. "We need to get her now."

"She's not going anywhere," Lucas said. "She's too pissed about her brother. She hasn't done anything about it, but she will before she leaves." He looked at Mallard. "You guys need better personal security. You need to talk to the AIC and tell him to warn all his people. Don't answer the door to any strange women. You gotta take it more seriously."

"We've had experience with this, with these kinds of threats," Mallard said. "We're taking them seriously, but you gotta look at it from her angle, too. The FBI is pretty . . . frightening. We look pretty goddamn tough to a crook."

"I don't think she's scared," Lucas said. "I don't think she gives a shit about the FBI, or how tough you are."

19

RINKER HAD A BAD NIGHT. SHE WAS COMFORTABLE enough, sleeping on couch pillows, wrapped in clean sheets, but the body in the basement freezer still gave her the creeps, and she thought several times that the basement door was creaking open. She found herself staring through the dark, looking for shapes in the living room, her hand near the Beretta on the floor beside her. Not that the gun would help with a ghost.

In the very darkest pit of the night, she sat up. She'd had something close to a dream, and in the dream came an idea. She crawled over to a lamp, groped up its stem, turned it on, then went out to the kitchen and dug up a yellow pages. She found what she was looking for under "Investigations." There were several listings for private detectives specializing in "spousal inquiries"—had to be divorce work—and two of them had women's names attached.

She left the kitchen light on, turned the lamp off, and went back to her couch pillows to think about it. Dream about it. And listen for noises from the basement.

SHE WAS OUT of the house by ten o'clock, as the Dark Woman, with dark brown eyebrows and dark brown hair. She wore a loose, green, long-sleeved cotton shirt to cover her arms, the fine blond hair and too-fair skin. She'd moved her own car into Honus Johnson's garage, and took his Mercedes.

Shc scouted Nina Bennett's address and found that it was a house with a business sign on it, and a black cat sitting in the porch window. A home office for a not-very-prosperous business, Rinker thought.

Could work, she thought. She rolled away from Bennett's and went looking for a place to meet. Someplace downtown. She found it at the Happy Dragon, a dark, upscale Chinese place that seemed to be designed for St. Louis's lunchtime assignations, with shoulder-high booths and bad sight-lines.

She stopped at Union Station, found a phone and called Bennett, who picked up on the second ring. "Bennett Legal Services."

Rinker tried to sound tentative. "I saw your ad in the phone book. Do you check on husbands? I mean, watch them?"

"We do spousal surveillance, yes. We usually require a reference from an attorney." The "usually" was not stressed; was made to sound inviting.

"Oh." Disappointment. Hesitation. "I can't hire an attorney. Not yet. I don't want a divorce, I don't want to make him angry. I just want to find out."

"Ma'am, if we're going to court . . ."

"I wouldn't want that," Rinker said quickly. "I just want to . . . know."

"Maybe you should come by. We can talk."

"Oh . . . I don't . . . Please wait a minute." Rinker clapped her hand over the mouthpiece, waited for what she thought might be a minute, then came back on. "Could you talk this afternoon? I'm very busy, I'm getting ready to fly down to Miami this evening."

"Yes, I could talk to you this afternoon," Bennett offered.

"Could you come here? Downtown?"

"Yes, I could."

"Oh, that's great. There's a place down the block, the Happy Dragon, if you could meet me there. Wait a minute, let me look at my calendar." She clapped her hand over the mouthpiece again, waited a few seconds, then said, "Three o'clock?"

"That'd be fine. The Happy Dragon at three, Mrs. . . . ?"

"Dallaglio," Rinker said. "Jesse Dallaglio."

LUCAS HAD SPENT most of the day at FBI headquarters, going through paper—all the paper that the feds had put together—looking for anything that might indicate whom Rinker might talk to, anything about the way she preferred to live. Andreno called to say that he'd stopped by John Sellos's bar and apartment, and Sellos was still missing. "He's not dead. The bartender got a call from him last night, said he sounded really worried about what was happening to the place. He told the bartender that he was still traveling and playing golf, but wouldn't say where he was."

"He called at the bar?"

"On the bar's public phone, right around nine o'clock."

"We'll see where that goes back to," Lucas said. "Though I'm not sure what he could tell us." He gave a note to Sally Epaulets, and asked her to find out where the call had come from. Twenty minutes later, she told him that it had come from a gas station near Nashville.

"Does that help?" she asked.

"No."

"Don't have to be snippy about it."

MALONE HAD BEEN in and out all afternoon. She was driving the local cops to find Rinker's car, while Mallard had disappeared entirely. When Lucas asked, Sally told him that Mallard was teleconferencing with Washington.

"All of it?"

"Just the FBI part," she said.

A FEW MINUTES LATER, an agent named Leen stopped by and said that the explosive that had killed Levy had been tagged, and the tags indicated that it was a commercial-grade explosive generally used in quarries, and most of it was sold in New England.

That rang no bells with anyone, and Lucas went back to the paper.

MALONE CAME BACK and asked, "Why are you reading all that paper again?"

"I'm trying to figure out what's going on in Rinker's head, and I can't. She's got all this carefully planned, right? The Dichter thing, then the cell phone. Is there some reason for the order that she's taking them in? Why didn't she take Ross first? Even Ross thinks he'd probably be the toughest nut to crack, but if she'd done him first, she could have gotten him."

Malone shook her head. "It is possible to plan a thing and then ride the breaks. Maybe that's what she's doing."

"I'll tell you what, though," Lucas said. "Ross ain't panicking. He's got a plan. My feeling is that she's gonna go after one of the other guys before she tries for him—I think Ferignetti may be right, that she's got no interest in him. Give him that. Giancati is taking himself out of it, maybe beyond her reach. So—I think we ought to look really hard at Paul Dallaglio."

"Dallaglio may take himself out of it, too, if he goes back to the Old Country, wherever that may be."

"Then we watch Ross, and hope she doesn't take a sabbatical and come back for them next year."

AT SIX O'CLOCK, he left the FBI building and met Andreno, Loftus, Bender, and Carter at Andy's Bar. They ate cheeseburgers and curly fries and onion rings and batter-dipped mushrooms, and Lucas said, "Guys, we almost got her, but we didn't. Does *anybody* have *any* idea of a move we could make? We gotta make some kind of move."

"I keep thinking about the car," Carter said. "If the car was on the street, locally, we'd have her by now. I know for a fact that guys are driving up and down every street in the whole metro area looking for the car, and they're coming up dry. The thing is . . . maybe she took off."

"The feds have put the make and tag number out all over the Midwest and South, and she can't have outrun that," Lucas said. "If she did, there's nothing we can do about it. But I don't think she's gone. I just don't know how to put my hands on her."

"Comes back to her friends," Andreno said. "Somebody's hiding her. Somebody's helping her. If we can put our hands on that guy . . ."

LUCAS TALKED TO Mallard on the phone at eight o'clock. "I might run home tomorrow, if you don't come up with something. Catch a plane out tomorrow afternoon, spend a couple of days at home. I'm out of ideas right now."

"Lucas, goddamnit, you're the only one who's had any ideas that actually panned out. You can't leave."

"For a day or two," Lucas said. "I could be back here in four hours, if something breaks."

BUT SOMETHING BROKE sooner than that. Mallard called back at 11 o'clock, excited, words tumbling over words. "We spotted her. The guys on Dallaglio's house are watching her right now. We're pulling people in all the way around her, tightening up on her. We're looking at her with night glasses, and we can see her watching the Dallaglio place. She's in a Volvo, they say."

"Meet you in the lobby," Lucas said.

He'd been reading, still dressed, and he slipped on his shoes and got his car keys and ran for the elevator. After a short, impatient wait, the elevator door opened and Malone was there, trying to shove a gun back into her purse.

"Gonna shoot her, huh?" Lucas asked.

Malone grunted. "I've been waiting for this."

"Weird. She's been so careful, and now she's sitting in a car on the street, watching Dallaglio. She pulled Richter out of his shell, she got weird with Levy, something we never even suspected, and now . . ." He shook his head. But it happened sometimes.

DALLAGLIO'S PLACE WAS twenty minutes out, and they all went together in one of the Suburbans, a flasher working on the front, cutting through traffic like an avalanche, a heavy-footed red-haired FBI man at the wheel, one of the Washington crew. Lucas didn't like him much, but had to admit that he knew how to run the truck.

Mallard was on the radio the full time. He'd been on it when he ran out of the hotel a minute after Lucas and Malone, stopped using it just long enough to explain that he'd been getting ready to take a shower when the call came from the field, and then got back on it, with brief breaks to pass along what he was hearing.

"I've told them to move on her whether or not we're there. As soon as they're ready, they go."

"They gonna rush her?"

"They're gonna block her, front and back, with trucks. We've got people moving up through a yard that she's parked near, but there's a dog, and they're talking to the owner about getting the dog out of there quietly before they go through. When she's blocked, there'll be a guy pointing a shotgun through her window before she has time to move. They think they can close up to fifteen feet."

They kept getting closer, and nothing had happened. The dog was hanging them up, and then Mallard reported that the dog was now locked in the basement of the nearest house, and that the tac squad was moving in, cutting through the dark yards. The red-haired agent took them off the freeway and down a couple of major streets, the tires screeching on the warm asphalt, all of them leaning into the turn, and then suddenly, on a narrow street, surrounded by woods, he slowed, and reached out and killed the flasher.

"Six blocks," he said. Twenty seconds later: "Four blocks."

Then up in front of them, a block away, they saw another suburban pull away from the curb, go down another block, and turn a corner. "That's our guys," said the redhead.

"Going down," Mallard said. He couldn't keep the stress out of his voice. "I'm about to wet my pants."

"This is a rental," the redhead said. "Try not to."

They idled along for a block, paused before the corner, drifting toward the curb. Then Mallard said, "They're doing it, they're doing it, let's GO."

The red-haired man mashed on the accelerator and the Suburban grunted away from the curb and turned the corner, and, two blocks away, they could see a car in a brilliant slash of light and trucks all around it, and men with long guns and helmets. . . .

"Got her," Mallard shouted. "We got her."

AND A HALF hour later, he said, harshly, angrily, to Lucas, "What the fuck is this about, Lucas? What the fuck is this about?"

They had Nina Bennett pressed against a six-year-old Volvo station wagon, frightened, crying, hands cuffed behind her back. And obviously not Clara Rinker.

After some preliminary shouting, the next thought was that Rinker was using Bennett as a diversion to approach Dallaglio's house, and there was a rush to get a larger squad around the house. But Dallaglio was okay, and there was no sign of Rinker, or of fleeing cars, or anything else.

Which brought up Mallard's question, "What the fuck is this about, Lucas?"

"I don't know." He looked around. "Maybe she's watching from somewhere, to see what would happen."

"She had to know that Dallaglio was protected. What would she gain?"

"I don't know."

"We don't even know it was Rinker," Malone said. "The

woman who hired her—if this even happened—didn't sound like Rinker."

"Didn't sound like Mrs. Dallaglio, either," Lucas said dryly.

"Maybe she's just pulling our chain," said the red-haired agent.

That seemed unlikely, Lucas thought, but he couldn't think of anything better.

An hour later, after taking the cuffed Nina Bennett to the Dallaglios' house to confront Jesse Dallaglio—both women agreed that they'd never met—they sent Bennett downtown for a formal statement, and pulled everybody else back into position.

"She doesn't have anything to do with it," Mallard said, meaning Bennett. "We're gonna get her statement and cut her loose."

"Got a story to tell, anyway. Private eye—you don't see many of them anymore. Not like that," Lucas said.

"She even had a bottle of booze in her car, and a little on her breath," Malone said. "And she must've smoked like a chimley. The whole car reeked."

"You said *chimley,*" Lucas observed.

"Did not. I said *chimney.*"

"Chimley," Mallard said, absently. Then: "But you know what's really strange when you think about it? She smokes, like a chimley, and she drives a Volvo station wagon. I didn't think that was allowed."

"I said *chimney,*" Malone said.

After a minute of silence, the red-haired agent said, "Did not. Said *chimley.*"

THEY'D STOPPED TEASING her about when they got back to the hotel, still frustrated from the false alarm. They parked, got out, and started walking for the main entrance, under the orange sodium-vapor lights, when somebody shot at them.

BANG!

They were spread out, walking away from the Suburban, walking in a line side-by-side, like a publicity shot for the Magnificent Seven, when the BANG! echoed off the building front and they all knew what it was and the agents went down and Lucas pivoted and realized in one half-second that the shooter had to be at the far end of the huge empty parking lot, a hundred and fifty yards north, or possibly on the roof of one of the old buildings down to the right, but there was no place else, really, and he ran toward his car, thinking *Go-go-go* and flashing on the difficulty of hitting a running deer at a hundred and fifty yards, hoping, hoping, looking north as he ran, looking for another muzzle flash, and then he was at his car and inside and fired it up and pulled out of the parking lot, catching from the corner of his eyes the confused, scrambling huddle of agents in the driveway and then he was on the street and accelerating . . .

He never saw her, he thought later.

He thought he found the place from where she'd fired the shot, a spot beside a big metal-sided building that would allow her to park right there, that would allow her to fire, and then to run back and climb inside her car in a matter of two or three seconds. She was probably moving before Lucas had reached his car, he thought.

He did the neighborhood anyway, gunning up and down the side streets. There was an entrance to a whole nest of interstates right there, and he was sure that was where she'd gone, and if she had, she'd be truly gone. He'd never know what car she was in if he went that way, so he stayed on the down streets, hoping against hope that she'd gotten cute, that she'd tried to drive away slowly, that he might see *something*.

But he did not.

AFTER TEN MINUTES, he headed back, paused by the metal building, looking over the spot he thought might have given her the shooting stance. She would have been able to rest her hand against the building, and across the parking lot, now a sea of flashing lights, they would have been perfectly illuminated and silhouetted against the hotel. . . .

"Goddamnit," he said aloud.

This was the reason for sending Bennett to watch Dallaglio. Rinker had found out where the out-of-town agents were staying, probably by calling around to the main hotels and asking for them by name.

Once she had the hotel, she'd scouted it, picked a place to shoot from. But she couldn't wait out there all day with a gun, hoping somebody would come along. By sending Bennett out to Dallaglio's, she'd known that all the big shots would be pulled out of the hotel, and once they found out that it was a false alarm, they'd all be coming back, late at night. She'd be in the dark, and they'd be walking in the bright lights of the parking lot. . . .

As he thought that, he was swept by a sudden, physical chill. He hadn't even considered the possibility anybody might have been hit. He'd just run. He turned back down toward the hotel. A cop tried to wave him off, but he shouted, *"FBI,"* and was pointed into the back lot. He got out and started around the hotel, and saw a man running toward him, a big man, flapping his arms like a goose trying to take off, and not getting there.

"She . . . ," Mallard croaked. "She . . ."

"Whoa, whoa," Lucas said, and suddenly he was frightened himself. "Whoa, Louis, what happened?"

"She . . . she shot Malone. Malone was shot."

"Ah, Jesus, how bad? How bad?" Lucas looked past him, but there was nobody on the ground, nothing. She must be on the way to the hospital.

He started past Mallard, but Mallard hooked his arm and closed his eyes and said, "She's dead."

20

MALONE HAD BEEN HIT BETWEEN THE SHOULDER BLADES, Mallard said. The ambulance had been there in three or four minutes, but she was gone by then. She'd never opened her eyes after she'd gone down, had never made a sound. They put her in the ambulance and rushed her to a critical care unit, but Mallard had been a Marine lieutenant in the last days of Vietnam and had seen people shot, had picked up people hit in the back, and knew she was gone.

"But you're not right a hundred percent of the time. Let's get over there," Lucas said harshly. He was running a little out of control, he knew, but that had happened before, and he recognized it. "Let's get a car."

His reaction pumped a gram of hope back into Mallard, and Mallard was suddenly waving his arms at the red-haired agent, and in less than a minute, they were out of the parking lot heading west. Mallard was hoping again, but shaking his head. "I don't think, I don't think," he said over and over again. "I don't think . . ."

Lucas let him ramble: Mallard was in shock.

Rinker would call him again, Lucas thought. He had to talk to somebody about that—maybe Sally Epaulets. Rinker wouldn't be calling to crow about the shooting, but she'd call to talk: to make the point that this was tit-for-tat, Malone for Gene Rinker. Lucas couldn't imagine that she'd let her guard down, but he couldn't take the chance. As Mallard continued to press against the dashboard, *leaning* toward the hospital, Lucas took out his phone and called Sally.

She answered, and asked, "Is it true? It can't be true."

"She was shot. She's bad, and Louis thinks she's dead. We'll be at the hospital in a minute."

"Oh, my God. Her parents . . ."

"Listen. Sally. Listen. Are you listening?"

She was crying, Lucas realized, and he really didn't have time for that. "Stop that shit," he snapped. "Stop crying. Shut the fuck up."

That shocked her out of it, and she said, "What?"

"Rinker's gonna call me. You've got to be ready to track her. You've got to coordinate with St. Louis and everybody else. Everybody's got to be ready to roll, as soon as you have a location. Do you understand? You're monitoring me, just like we did before."

"But what about Louis . . . ?"

Lucas glanced at Mallard, then said, "Louis is out of it for now. So you're carrying it, okay? Get this set up. She's gonna call tonight. And I gotta stay off this phone."

THEY WERE AT the hospital two minutes later, Mallard hopping out of the truck while it was still rolling into a parking space. There were two agents already there, outside the emergency room doors, but he bulled on past them through the doors and inside. Lucas followed, but stopped and looked at the agents.

"She's . . ."

"Gone," said one of the agents. "She was gone when she got here. They put her on a respirator, but there's nothing to work with, they say."

"Ah, Jesus."

"There's one of the paramedics."

A paramedic had come out of the building, a black man with a shaved head. He wore a small gold earring and had a cigarette dangling from his lip. Lucas walked over and said, "I'm . . . with the FBI guys. I understand you brought Malone in?"

"Yeah. There was nothing we could do. We couldn't help her."

"Where was she hit?"

"In the spine, right between the shoulder blades. The doc could maybe tell you better. I'm not a doctor."

"Tell me what you think," Lucas said.

The paramedic took a long drag on the cigarette, blew smoke, then said, "It looked to me like a small-caliber bullet, a .22 probably. Very small entry wound, almost like the end of a pencil. We turned her over to see if she was pumping blood out of her chest, but there were hardly any exit wounds, a couple of little cuts, like. Like shrapnel, or something. I think the bullet clipped through her spine and just exploded, like one of those . . . you know, those guys who shoot prairie dogs."

"A varmint bullet."

"Yeah. Varmint bullet. Like it hit her and exploded everything, just pulped her heart and lungs."

They stood silently for a minute or so, and then the guy said, "I'm sorry."

Lucas rubbed his nose. "Goddamnit."

"She a nice lady?"

"Ohhh . . . yeah, in a lot of ways," Lucas said, not ready for that kind of question. The paramedic looked at him oddly, and Lucas realized that he had been asking a pro-forma question and had expected a pro-forma answer. Lucas nodded his head and said, "Yeah, she was, really. A nice lady."

LUCAS WENT INSIDE and found Mallard slumped in a chair, while an uncertain doctor stood a couple of feet away, looking down at him, then at Lucas. "Are you a friend?"

"Yeah."

"We might want to keep this gentleman around for a little while—he's got a shock problem."

"All right. I'll have somebody sit with him."

Lucas sat down and looked at Mallard, who had suddenly shriveled. He wasn't saying anything, wasn't looking at anything except the tiled floor. Lucas patted him on the shoulder and said, "Just sit for a while."

Mallard nodded dumbly, and Lucas got up, found the red-haired agent, and told him to stick with Mallard.

The red-haired guy nodded and said, "I jerked the AIC out of bed. He's on his way to the scene, so that's covered."

"All right. I'm going back to the hotel."

"Wait for the call?"

"If it comes."

The agent shook his head. "Gotta get the bitch now. Before it was a sport. Now it's a war."

Lucas took a step toward the emergency room door, then turned back. "When you take Mallard out of here, use some other door. She set up this last shooting—it just occurred to me that she could be setting up outside here." He nodded toward the doors. "She knows we'll all be here."

The agent looked at the doors and then said, "I'll get some guys to make a quiet sweep."

"Do it."

*

LUCAS WENT BACK to the hotel to wait; took off his shirt, got into some jeans, tried not to think about Malone. Couldn't help thinking about her: wanted to get her back, but couldn't. Finally used the hotel phone to call Weather, and told her.

"Oh, my God, Lucas. Are you all right?"

"I'm fine. I mean, I'm fucked up, but I'm not hurt. When I left, they were talking about getting somebody to do the formal identification and sign-off, and I just cleared out of there. I couldn't stand to go look at her. Jesus, we walked out of here a couple of hours ago. We went down the elevator together, and she was sure we had Rinker in a box."

"Maybe you ought to come home."

"Can't now. I'm going to get her."

"Unless she gets you."

"She's not mad enough at me. She wouldn't have gone after Malone if Malone hadn't been the one talking about her brother, in the paper."

"You don't know that for sure. She might've gone over the edge."

"I gotta give it some more time. But I'm feeling really . . . bummed."

"But not medically bummed."

He knew what she meant. A little problem with clinical depression. "Not like that."

"Then I'd say you're pretty healthy. You should be

bummed when a friend is killed. Just wait until Rinker calls. Track her down. Get her."

"I'm going to," he said. "Sooner or later."

RINKER CALLED a half hour later. The cell phone rang, and he let it ring once more, then picked it up.

"Yes."

"I'm all done with the FBI," Rinker said. Her whiskey voice sounded blue, depressed.

"Too late for you, Clara," Lucas said. "They'll never quit now. The guy that gets you is gonna be a hero, and his career will be made for life. People are going to make you into their hobby."

"Well, good luck to them," Rinker said. "This never would have happened if they hadn't killed my brother."

"Nobody wanted your brother to die. Malone took a lot of shit after it happened. There was gonna be an inquiry."

"Yeah, right, a cop inquiry. Were they planning to raise him up, like Lazarus?"

"No, but . . ."

"So what you're saying is that a memo would get written."

"Nobody wanted him to die. Nobody deliberately pulled a trigger on him."

"Might as well have. I told you myself, he wasn't right." Lucas couldn't think of anything to say, and after a moment of silence, Rinker continued. "I'm thinking about getting out. You think they would chase me to Chile?"

"I think they'd chase you to fuckin' Mongolia. And I'll tell you what, if I were you . . . when they catch me, I wouldn't give up. I'd put a gun in my mouth. They'll pen you up for ten years in a concrete box the size of a phone booth, and then they'll stick a needle in your arm and kill you. Better to go quick."

"I don't suppose you're thinking of going home."

"No. I'll be here as long as you are."

"My problem with you is, you're lucky." Again, a moment of silence. Then: "This fiancée of yours, is she pretty good-looking?"

"Pretty good," Lucas said. "We're gonna do the whole thing, except not a Catholic wedding because she'll be a little heavy by then, and besides, she doesn't care for the Church. But we got a wild-hair Episcopalian place, which is almost like Catholic, and we're gonna tie the knot up with a priest and flower girls and the whole thing."

"That was gonna be me, a few months ago."

"If you'd just stuck with killing the Mafia assholes, you would have pissed off the FBI, but you still could have pulled a disappearing act and found a guy somewhere and still had the kid. Not now. That's all gone."

"I don't want to talk to you anymore," Rinker said. "You're being a jerk."

"A good friend of mine was killed," Lucas said. "I'm gonna get you for it. Me and my good luck."

"Yeah, don't press it," Rinker said. She laughed, abruptly, a little crazily, and said, "I'm gone. I guess you're tracking this call. Tell your friends that the next sound they hear is the telephone hitting the highway."

He heard it hit. And, in a bizarre tribute to Finnish technology, the phone neither broke nor turned off, and Lucas could hear trucks rushing by.

Wherever it was; wherever she was.

THEY DIDN'T GET HER. They came close, one of the chopper pilots said. Their tracking gear put them on her; they were only a half-mile out when she tossed the phone out the window. But that was five thousand cars, rolling along the highway, getting off and on. A lot of What ifs and If I'd justs. A highway patrol cop was vectored into the area within five minutes of the first phone ring, but had no idea what he should be looking for. Another cop spotted the phone under a guardrail, picked it up, said, "Hello?" and then turned it off.

THE NEXT MORNING, Lucas and the FBI Special Studies Group, minus Mallard, listened to the tape of the phone conversation twenty times, picking it apart word by word. When she said she was gone, did she mean *gone* as in *Gone to Paraguay?* Or did she just mean that she was gone from the conversation? Why did she throw the phone out the window? She could have used it again. Was she cutting them off? Was she done talking to anyone? Had she just been pissed off? What?

During the discussion, it seemed that Sally Epaulets—Bryce was her real last name—stepped into a coordinating role, and the rest of the FBI group accepted that, at least until Mallard or somebody else in authority showed up.

Lucas spent the morning reading through the FBI paper, reading everything, until he was sick of it. Somewhere, in that mass of names and numbers, Rinker was hiding; but he couldn't find her.

Was she gone?

ANDRENO CALLED AT ELEVEN, and they agreed to meet at Andy's for lunch. Lucas arrived a little after noon. Loftus was there, and they walked to the back and ordered cheeseburgers and Andreno said, "Jesus Christ. I couldn't believe it. I got up late and turned on the TV and that's all they were talking about. It was like when Reagan got shot or something. So bizarre. Like something in a novel."

"She called me, Clara did," Lucas said. He told them about the call, and then about the shooting itself, and they were both shaking their heads.

"Got more than one screw loose, that girl," Loftus said.

"She's toast," Andreno said. "She better stay in the States. If she goes to Bolivia, the feds'll find her, talk to one of their little helpers down there, and they'll put her in a basement with an electric outlet and connect some wires to her tits and there won't be any habeas fuckin' corpus."

Lucas asked them about the botanical gardens. "John Ross is going over there for an orchestra fundraiser."

"Probably not a good idea. Lots of trees and bushes," Loftus said. "Hedges and shit."

"It's about two minutes from here," Andreno said. "We could drive over."

Lucas nodded. "It's not like I'm doing anything else."

The gardens, Lucas thought, were pretty neat. If Minneapolis had an arboretum that close to downtown, he'd probably go once a week just to look at the flowers.

To get into the place, a visitor would park in a blacktopped parking lot, walk into a ticket desk on the bottom level of a two-story building, then climb a set of stairs and walk out the back into the gardens. That was ideal from a security point of view. Anybody coming in had to climb the stairs, or take an elevator, which made handy chokepoints.

"Or she could come over the fence. The place is huge, and there are trees all the way around," Andreno said.

"Maybe get some guys looking down the fence line?"

"If you had enough of them. It's pretty big. It's like trying to protect a farm. Or a forest."

Andreno ran into a food-service supervisor that he knew, and asked about the chamber orchestra event. The food guy pointed them at the Rose Garden, and they went that way. The Rose Garden was laid out in a square, surrounded by a hedge, with a long rectangular building at the entrance and a reflecting pool at the exit. Lucas strolled up and down between the flowers, looking for shooting lanes, and decided that as long as Ross stayed inside the garden, the hedge would protect him from any long-range rifle shots.

Unless she climbed a tree, he thought. As he stood at the garden entrance, he could see that the ground rose off to the left, and they went that way.

"Put a guy right here. Or two or three guys," Andreno said, as they walked up the higher ground. "There're so many trees that she'd have to get close or she couldn't see through them to shoot. And if she got that close, and then tried to climb, she'd be easy to spot."

They walked around for a while, looking at flowers and trees, until the humidity started to get to them. "That place over there," Andreno said, nodding at a dome-shaped building, "is like a tropical jungle. All bamboo and palm trees and shit. Neat place in the winter."

"This whole place is like a jungle. I didn't know St. Louis was so hot."

"We used to have a saying, "It's not the heat . . ."

". . . it's the humidity."

"We'd never say anything that stupid," Andreno said. "We used to say, it's not the heat, it's the assholes. Goddamn hot nights, no air-conditioning, what are you gonna do? You're gonna whack the old lady around, that's what. You get nights like this one's gonna be, there'll be people smacking people all over town."

"Maybe you oughta provide air-conditioning as a public service," Lucas suggested.

"It'd be a plan," Andreno said, seriously. "It'd stop more bullshit than a lot of other plans."

ON THE WAY back to Andy's, where Andreno had left his car, Sally called and said, "The guys on Dallaglio say that he's leaving. He's going into hiding. He says they can follow along, but he won't tell anybody where he's going until he's started."

"That's a little dumb—if we knew where he was going, we could sterilize it in advance. Did you tell him that?"

"Yes. But he said there was no point in trying, and they were safer if nobody knew. They're not leaving until the kids get home from school, they're gonna get them packed up. They're going out tonight."

"Call around. You've got the weight. Check the major airlines, see where the tickets are. If they're going to Italy or somewhere, there aren't many options."

"We're doing that—I just wanted you to know."

"Is Mallard back?"

"No. They finished the postmortem, and they're flying the body out this afternoon. There'll be a memorial service in Washington, and most of us are going."

"You're just shutting down here?"

"Won't be for a couple of days, and there'll still be a crew here. We won't need the Dallaglio crew anymore, and most of the rest of us have just been walking in circles anyway."

21

LUCAS WAS WATCHING AN ATLANTA GAME WHEN SALLY called at eight o'clock and said, "Dallaglio's about to roll. Me and Carl and Derik are heading out, if you want to ride along."

"It's either that or hang myself. I'm down to watching Atlanta."

"You got two minutes."

Lucas got a jacket, clipped a .45 onto his hip, took a half-finished beer along, hid it from a prim-looking saleslady in the elevator, and caught up with the feds in the lobby. They were already moving, out the doors, into a heat-soaked night—Lucas dropped the beer bottle into a trash can—and across the parking lot where Malone had been shot and into the Suburban.

A block away, Lucas could see a Mazda MPV van, sitting

on the street, looking into the back of the buildings where Rinker had set up with the rifle. Inside the van was a bored FBI surveillance crew, hoping against hope that she'd be back. She hadn't been, although they had netted an attractive forty-five-ish commercial real-estate agent who'd come over later for drinks with one of the surveillance guys.

"Glad I'm not in that van," Sally said, picking up on Lucas's thought. "I've done that. Down in Baltimore, working with Jack Hand?"

The red-haired agent was driving again. He nodded and said, "Onions."

"You better believe it. He ate them like apples. He said they prevented prostate cancer. His father died from it."

"Onions, or prostate?" Lucas asked.

"I almost died from the onions once," the red-haired man said.

He put them on an interstate heading west, and Lucas frowned. "Where're we going?"

Sally looked at him and then said, "Oh—we're not going to Lambert. There's another airport out west. Called, um, Spirit of St. Louis. Dallaglio's signed up for a private jet, a place called Executive Air. He's flying out of there to Newark, and then from Newark to Rome to Naples on commercial flights. First class, of course. The whole family."

"Napoli," said the nearly silent Derik. Derik had a buzz

cut and high, dry cheekbones and looked like a member of the Wehrmacht. "Roma."

Sally was looking at a map now and said to the red-haired agent, "We're on Sixty-four, right? Because if we're on Forty-four, we'll wind up down in Bumfuck, Missouri, and there's no way back."

"The language," Lucas said.

"We're on Sixty-four," the red-haired guy said. "There's a sign."

Sally checked the sign and then turned to Lucas. "Malone was, like, ten years in service before I signed up. She was appointed to mentor some of the younger women agents, and one time she told me that I should carefully use a few words. You know, nothing really nasty, none of the gynecological stuff, but the occasional fuck or shit, just to let them know that you weren't a sissy. She said getting treated ladylike or if you were expected to be ladylike, it was the end of you. She said you had to be a lady, but not ladylike."

"A point," Lucas said.

"Back then, it was," Sally said. "Ten years ago. I don't think it matters so much anymore."

"Yeah, you've pretty well taken over now," the red-haired man said.

"Better believe," Sally said. Derik said nothing, just bobbed his skinhead to some unseen music with a jerky beat. Sally got on a radio and talked to the crew with

Dallaglio. "They're just getting out to the cars," she said. "We ought to get there about the same time."

RINKER HAD AN unfamiliar weight on her shoulders, the weight of death. Not the killing of Dichter, or Levy, or Malone, or even of all of them together, but rather the killing of Honus Johnson. She'd thought about it, as she waited for Johnson to come lurching out of the basement like a frozen Frankenstein, to stand over the couch while she was half asleep . . . waited for the sound of the freezer lid opening, was sure she'd heard it a half-dozen times.

One of the few literary experiences of her young life had come with a Stephen King novel, *Carrie,* which had scared the shit out of her, as she sprawled across the bed in her apartment, alone, reading. The feeling now was the same, but even more intense: There really *was* a frozen dead man in the basement, and he really *had* been a torturer, who *would* come back from hell with a bloody machete. . . .

She analyzed it, as she'd been taught in her college psych classes back in Wichita—and she decided that her problem was not so much the dead man in the basement as the fact that she hadn't left him behind. In all her other killings, she'd almost instantly walked away from the bodies. In a couple of cases, she'd had to move them, but she'd been done with them in a few hours at most. She'd been able to escape what she'd done, put it behind her and out of mind.

This one, she was stuck with, at least for a few more days. He was riding on her shoulders as she drove west into the setting sun.

She looked a little like a fashionable female Johnny Cash, she thought—thin black long-sleeve shirt, black jeans, dark blue running shoes from which she'd carefully torn the reflective patches. In the backseat she had a black silk scarf and a black baseball cap. When she had it all on, she thought, she'd be invisible in the dark.

THEY'D BEEN IN the car for fifteen minutes when Sally took a radio call, then looked at her map. "They're ahead of us, about three miles," she said, after a minute. "Four vehicles—two of ours and two of theirs. They're staying on the speed limit, so if we can step on it a bit, we'll catch them."

They caught them a couple of miles east of the airport, rolling off the interstate and down onto a country highway. "When Dallaglio gets out of here, everything will come back to Ross, unless she's really after Ferignetti, too—but Ferignetti's so sure that she isn't, that I kind of believe him," Sally said. "So it's Ross."

"If she's really after Ross," Lucas said, as they came up behind the trailing federal Suburban.

They were all slowing down, and a quarter mile ahead,

Lucas saw another Suburban take a left turn off the highway into the airport. He could see the control tower, like a lighted diamond in the dusk, atop a black cylinder, and all around it, low brick light-industrial, warehouse, and office buildings. A boulevard led into the airport, with the tower off to the right, but nothing that Lucas could identify as a terminal until they drove past a mounted military plane, which Lucas thought might have been a Phantom, and reached a T-intersection at the end of the boulevard. The red-haired agent said, "That's the terminal," pointing at a building at the top of the T, in the headlights. All the other trucks had taken a left, following signs to Executive Air.

Two hundred yards up the road, a brilliantly lighted hangar stood off to the right, with an executive jet inside; another jet, with a fold-down stairway leading to an open door, sat on the pad outside the hangar. Derik, who'd said virtually nothing during the trip, muttered, "Looks like a TV stage, a soundstage. They oughta kill the lights."

Lucas said, "Man . . . this looks like . . . this looks bad."

The lead truck had already stopped next to the jet, and a couple of agents hopped out. Then the second car pulled up, a Lincoln, and Lucas said to Sally, urgently, "Tell them to keep Dallaglio in the car. *Keep him in the car.*"

She lifted the radio to her mouth, as they stopped at the end of the lines of vehicles and Lucas popped his door and climbed out and shouted at the agents, "Keep him in the car," and then he said to Derik, who'd scrambled across to get out with him, "Aw, shit. . . ."

The Dallaglios were all getting out: father, mother, daughters, wandering around in the brilliant light, like so many lost mice. Lucas said to Derik, "C'mon," and hurried forward. The red-haired agent was coming around the front of the truck, to go with them, and a couple of agents from the trailing truck were getting out. . . .

And for a few seconds, it was a very pretty Missouri evening, too hot and humid, but not a bad night to sit around a backyard swimming pool with friends and a few fruit-rum drinks with little brightly colored paper umbrellas—a night like that.

THEN PAUL DALLAGLIO stepped into the space between his car and the lead FBI truck, the agents coming up from behind him.

He stood there for a couple of seconds, then turned to say something to his wife, did a little dance, and fell down. An instant later, they heard the BANG, and then a ripping sound as Rinker opened up with the AR-15 and everybody went to the ground and bullets cracked through glass and metal and tires and ricocheted off the sides of the hangar and the jet.

Dallaglio, on the ground, made a humping motion and Lucas, in a tiny corner of his mind as he pushed himself behind a wheel and dug for his weapon, wondered why the hell he was making the humping move, and then realized that bullets were tearing through Dallaglio's body.

LUCAS COULD SMELL gas and oil and dirt and could hear people screaming, the girlish screams of a child, and then one of the agents was up and behind the Suburban and was banging away with what sounded like a .40, and Lucas pushed up and picked up a muzzle flash and thought that unless the agent was holding about four feet above the flash, at that distance, he'd be wasting his ammunition. He didn't think anything more about it, but simply lifted his .45 and started banging away, holding very high. Rinker was shooting from the side of a single-story warehouse or office building to their left, little sparkles of flame followed by the sounds of bullets tearing through sheet metal, and in the dark it was hard to figure the range. A hundred yards, maybe a hundred and fifty, maybe even two hundred, he thought. He held four feet high and banged away, with no hope of hitting her, hoping simply to dislodge her.

Then the bolt of the .45 banged back and open and Lucas dropped the magazine and slapped in another, his only spare, and another gust of bullets spattered across the parking area and he could hear more people screaming, but couldn't tell what they were saying. Someplace in there, he felt the tires go on the other side of the Suburban and yelled at Derik, "She's taking out the tires, so we can't chase her. She must be driving, we gotta block the road."

Derik scrambled back to the Suburban that they'd arrived in and screamed something Lucas didn't understand to the red-haired agent, who was behind another vehicle. The red-haired man looked back wildly, shouted something, then dug in his pocket, found some keys, and threw them at Derik. Derik crawled into the Suburban, and Lucas, on hands and toes, scooted over to that vehicle. Derik was lying across the front seats, and when Lucas heard the engine turn over, he climbed through the back door and said, "What are we doing?"

"Gonna back it up," Derik grunted. "Can't see shit. Hold on."

Lucas peeked over the top of the backseat. He couldn't see any more muzzle flashes from Rinker, but the agents were still pouring fire into the dark. Derik, kneeling on the passenger seat, locked the steering wheel in place with one hand, and with the other shifted the truck into reverse, then reached down and pressed on the accelerator. They started backing, fast, wobbling, and Lucas risked another peek and said, "You're doing fine, doing fine—faster, though, faster. Hold it straight. . . ."

They backed up a hundred feet, running on two flats, lurched twice into the curb, and then cut an angle with the building where they'd seen the muzzle flashes, and were out of her line of sight. Lucas shouted, "Whoa, stop!" and the Suburban lurched to a stop, and Derik shouted, "What?" but Lucas was already out of the truck. He jerked open the driver's-side door and shouted, "Let me in."

Derik pulled back and Lucas gunned the truck in a circle, climbed the far curb, onto the grass, bounced around, cut back into the street and headed back toward the entrance boulevard, the flats slap-slap-slap-slap outside the open passenger door, then Derik managed to get up and he pulled the door shut and Lucas pushed the truck up to forty and they bounced down to the exit and Lucas cut across it.

NOTHING HAPPENED.

The gunfire was dwindling, and Lucas realized that he hadn't heard the stuttering bursts from the automatic weapon.

"She's running," he said. "Where is she? There must be another way out. You hang here, I'm gonna try to get back."

"Hang on a minute, they'll freak out and shoot you if you just come running up," Derik said. He slipped a radio from his pocket and got Sally. "Davenport's coming back on the road—tell everybody he's running up the road." She acknowledged, and Derik nodded at him. "Go."

Lucas, gun in hand, ran back up the road toward the terminal, then to the left toward Executive Air. Nobody had touched the lights, and the whole place still looked like a soundstage. And more than that, they had music:

Bonnie Tyler's "Total Eclipse of the Heart" was bleeding out into the night, through speakers in the open hangar, Lucas thought, as he ran toward the island of light.

Most of the agents and the Dallaglios were still huddled behind the four vehicles of the original convoy. Three people were flat on the ground, and somebody had dragged Dallaglio's body behind one of the Suburbans. Sally and the red-haired agent were both missing, and when Lucas came up, he shouted, "Where's Sally?" and somebody shouted back, "They went after her," and pointed into the dark.

Lucas said, "Ah, man," and ran that way. As he came up to the first building, he shouted, "Sally. . . ."

She called back, "This way, this way."

He went that way and found Sally and the red-haired agent, both armed with long guns, working their way between the buildings. "Anything?"

"No. We think . . . I think . . . she ran."

"Not in a car," Lucas said. "We had the road blocked, and we didn't see anyone going out ahead of us. She must be on foot. She must have a car ditched outside somewhere."

"Dallaglio's dead," said the red-haired agent.

"No shit," Lucas said. "Anybody else?"

"Two guys wounded, leg wounds. She was taking out tires."

"Goddamnit," Lucas said.

"Maybe . . ."

"What?"

The red-haired agent laughed ruefully and said, "I was gonna say, maybe we could get dogs." He looked off into the dark and said, "Fuck me. Dogs."

SIRENS. AMBULANCES AND cop cars. They started back between the buildings toward the road, walking at first, then breaking into a trot. The two wounded agents were still on the ground, each with an agent sitting next to him. Another agent and two bodyguards sat next to Dallaglio's body, and Jesse Dallaglio sat on the ground a few feet away, making a keening cry that Lucas thought might have been romantic to read about, but in practice sounded like a broken dental drill. The girls were out of sight, and Lucas thought they were probably back in the Lincoln, where they wouldn't be able to see their father.

The first of the ambulances arrived, and the paramedics looked at Dallaglio and then went straight to the two wounded agents, who were loaded into the first ambulance and sent on their way. Another ambulance came up and they also looked at Dallaglio, and then one of the paramedics lifted Jesse Dallaglio to her feet and led her back toward the Lincoln and the girls.

Lucas had nothing to do but stand around. He wouldn't be working with the crime-scene people, except perhaps to identify the spray of .45 shells as coming from his gun. Sally was walking around, saying a few words to each of the agents, then came back to Lucas and said, "She had a machine gun."

"Probably got it from Baker," Lucas said. "He neglected to mention it. Probably an illegal conversion."

"What were we supposed to do? What could we have done?"

"Nothing. You may get some shit, but there's nothing you could have done except lock Dallaglio in his basement."

They were looking at Jesse Dallaglio, who stood next to the Lincoln, talking through the now-open back door. The paramedic was still supporting her. "Poor kids," Sally said.

Lucas was staring at the dark sky past the lighted diamond of the control tower. He didn't respond, and after a minute, Sally asked, "What?"

"Huh. Something . . . I think Clara just screwed up."

"Yeah? Tell me."

"Well," Lucas said, "think about what just happened. . . ."

RINKER HAD NEVER had any intention of driving out of the airport. She'd seen too many car chases on television, the kind where the guy never escapes from the helicopter. She'd walked in, found a spot behind a low concrete drainage wall, where she could prop the gun. She'd dug up a square of sod to use as a rest, and it worked perfectly.

When the convoy arrived, she waited patiently until Dallaglio got out in the open, then nailed him with a single shot, a round of .223 hollowpoint.

Then, flipping the selector switch, she sent the rest of the thirty-round magazine into the body and at the row of vehicles, concentrating on the tires. The agents and bodyguards scattered like dust, and when the magazine ran out, she slapped in another and fired carefully spaced bursts at each of the trucks and cars.

Halfway through, she became aware of return fire, but never heard or felt anything passing close by. Never felt threatened, as she was showing nothing but three inches of forehead and rifle. Then one of the trucks began backing away, and out of sight. Time to go. She hastily hosed the rest of the magazine into the line of trucks, then turned and ran.

She ran down the length of the airport, invulnerable in the darkness. She ran across a beanfield, down the rows of thigh-high plants, letting the rows guide her back toward her car, feeling the kind of excitement she'd felt as a kid, playing war in the fields around Tisdale. She ran almost a mile, in all, the last part of it across a golf course, and took, she thought, about seven minutes to do it.

When she got to the car, she tossed the AR-15 into the backseat and eased the car out of its parking spot and up a narrow lane through a residential area. Just before she lost sight of the airport, she stopped for a last look—there were ambulances coming in now, and she could see tiny dark figures dancing in the splash of light.

"Paulo," she said aloud. "That's another one for you."

22

SALLY AND LUCAS GOT BACK TO THE FBI CONFERENCE ROOM at midnight. "Washington's gonna call tomorrow. They'll want to pull the team," she said. "The perception is, we've screwed this to the wall. Even before Malone."

"Can you stall for a few days?" Lucas asked, as Derik wandered in, carrying a six-pack of Diet Coke in plastic bottles. "I think we can bag her."

Derik dropped them on the table and gestured, and Lucas took one. Derik said, "Sally said we're working tonight. And you think we can get her."

"Yeah . . . where's that red-haired guy?"

"He's with Patrick—they're old pals."

"Patrick's the guy who got it in both legs. Broken bones," Sally said.

"Gonna be tough," Derik said. To Lucas: "Lay it out. How do we get her?"

"OKAY," LUCAS SAID. "First: Rinker knew exactly where the Dallaglios were gonna be, and when. She *knew*—she knew exactly which jet company, and it seems to me that she knew that there wouldn't be a security sweep of the place ahead of time."

"Which means somebody is talking to her," Sally said thoughtfully.

"That's right. Somebody tipped her, and the person is close to the Dallaglios. Second: I keep thinking that there had to be a reason for the order that she killed these guys in. She took Dichter first, because he was going to be the hardest, except maybe for Ross. So she tricked him, lured him out before he really knew what was going on, when he might have thought he could still talk his way out of it. And she set him up so he felt safe, and bang! Then she took Levy, because she had another trick figured out, the cell phone. Then Dallaglio, because she had a source of information that could set him up, and she knew ahead of time—weeks ago—that she could do that. It's all very logical. We really didn't have a chance to step on any of it."

"How about Ross?" Sally asked.

"We don't even know that she's going after Ross. That's kinda my point: Ross doesn't seem to be all that worried.

He's like Ferignetti—careful, but maybe not as worried as he should be."

"Maybe he's in on it," Sally said. "Maybe this whole thing is a way to eliminate competition."

"It *feels* that way," Lucas said. "But the whole thing was touched off by Paulo Mejia's killing. How does that fit? Did the other guys go after her, and Ross try to help her out? Our problem is, we don't really have Rinker's story, or Paulo Mejia's. We don't know what they expected or felt. I mean, Mejia had a guy with him who was carrying a goddamn Mac-10. Why was that? Did they know something?"

"Maybe—"

"Wait a minute," Lucas said. "Hang on—one thing at a time. So we know something: Rinker was tipped by somebody close to the Dallaglios. So if we get with Jesse Dallaglio as soon as she can think again, she should be able to figure out exactly when they knew what timc they were leaving for the airport. Probably sometime this morning. That's the first we knew that they were moving. So somebody was tipped after that, and she should be able to point us at every single person who knew. They were all penned up inside the house."

"We should be able to get the phone records of every person in the house, and all the house phones. See where they went," Sally said. "That's good. We could have all of that in a couple of hours."

"What we'll have is a few names, and most of them we

should be able to eliminate immediately. So by tomorrow morning we should have the name of somebody who can get in touch with Rinker. Or who Rinker gets in touch with. And they won't know that we know. If Rinker calls whoever tipped her off, she won't be running, she'll talk for a while."

"We can move on her in five minutes," Sally said. "Have the choppers scattered around."

"We can do all that," Derik said.

"So we've got to talk to Jesse Dallaglio. Tonight," Lucas said. As an afterthought: "Does Ross know what happened at the airport?"

"Yes. I called the team leader out at Ross's and had him go in and tell him. They know."

"Maybe . . ." Lucas rubbed his nose, thinking. "You know what I'd do? I'd check to see if the Dallaglios used a travel agent or somebody outside the family to set up the trip. They almost had to—you can't just call up one of these jet services and drive out and go. They want to see the money, or they want a guarantee."

"You think a travel agent?"

"Well, when we first got onto Rinker, up in Minnesota, we were never able to track Rinker when she was traveling—it was like she was invisible. I wouldn't be surprised if all these Mafia guys like to keep their travel private. Maybe it's somebody Rinker knew from when she was traveling to kill people. Maybe there's a connection."

"If it is something like a travel agent, and we can figure

it out, we could maybe get Ross to book a trip," Sally said. "You know, have him be sneaky about it, tell the agent to book him out of someplace like Springfield, and then just saturate the airport before he comes in. She'd have no way to know that we were onto her."

"That could work," Lucas said.

Derik said, "At least we're being . . . whatever that word is."

Lucas said, "What word?"

"You know . . ."

"Proactive," Sally said.

"So let's proact our asses over to Dallaglio's place and talk to Jesse Dallaglio," Lucas said.

A DOCTOR WAS leaving the Dallaglios' when they arrived, a tall slender woman in what would have been a tweedy dress if it hadn't been ninety-eight degrees outside; and it still looked like tweed, even if it was some kind of light knotted cotton. Sally identified herself and said, "Did you put them asleep?"

"The children were exhausted. I gave them sleep aids, they're with their mother," the doctor said. "I left some sleep aids for Mrs. Dallaglio, but I don't know if she'll use them. She was resistant."

INSIDE THE HOUSE, one of the bodyguards, still wearing bloody pants, said, "Mrs. Dallaglio's back with the kids in the bedroom."

"We'll wait," Lucas said. And, "There are ten guns around the house now. You've probably got time to get cleaned up if you want."

The bodyguard looked down at his pants. "Gonna burn these sons of bitches," he said. He looked around. "I'm gonna do that, get cleaned up. I'll be back in ten minutes." As he was going out the door, he added, "What a night."

A SECOND BODYGUARD came padding down a hall as they stood around the living room, saw them, and said, "The kids are asleep. Jesse'll be with you in a minute."

More like five minutes, but when Jesse Dallaglio came out of the back, she'd managed to pull herself together. Her eyes were still puffy and red from crying, but the first wave of the shock had passed.

Lucas had seen it before: Women recovered faster than men from the death of a spouse. Lucas believed that both men and women expected the wife to live longer, so that women were somewhat braced for the departure of a husband, while a husband, in most police cases, was absolutely unprepared—unless, of course, he'd done the killing himself.

When that was a possibility, most homicide cops liked to take a quick, hard look at the husband, to see if he was either too pulled together or too demonstrative. Most innocent husbands simply dropped into dumb shock and stayed there for a while. It was an attitude not easily faked.

"I'm better," Dallaglio was telling Sally. "The girls are sick, and they're terrified. But they'll be okay. The doctor gave them some sleeping pills. What did you . . . ?"

"Chief Davenport had an idea that we felt we had to look into," Sally said. "Could you tell us when you decided, for sure, to go with Executive Air? And when you decided what time you'd be leaving?"

She looked from Sally to Lucas to Derik, then back to Lucas as her hand came up to her mouth. "Oh my God. How did she know we'd be there?"

Lucas nodded. "That's what we were wondering."

Dallaglio turned away from them all and stared at a wall for a moment, thinking, then back to Lucas. "Exec Air had a problem. We have a deal with them, we get a rate, but they only manage three jets and all three of them were out. Two were coming back, but they didn't know until two o'clock when they'd be in, and when they could have one of them turned around. They told Paul to call at two—and that's what he did. They told us to be there at nine o'clock, or a little after."

"So you didn't know when you'd be leaving until two o'clock."

"That's right."

"Who did you tell outside the house? Paul's friends, your friends, your daughters' friends?"

Again, Dallaglio turned away, thought, and turned back. "Paul told at least two people, the Karens. We call them the

Karens—it's Karen Slade and Karen English, they're the two assistant vice presidents at work, they're Paul's assistants. But I don't think either of them was around when Clara was here. Maybe Karen Slade, but she's a dear friend of both of us, her and her husband. It can't be Karen."

Sally was making notes. "Did you talk to anyone?"

"I called my sister, Janice, she lives down in Little Rock, but it wouldn't be her. The kids . . . we'd have to wait until tomorrow, but I don't think they called anyone. They're not really old enough to have telephone friends yet. I mean, Justy does, in a way, but it's the girl down the block and we hardly know her parents. I would be amazed if Clara Rinker knew them."

The bodyguard who'd been wearing the bloody pants came back, his hair damp, wearing a fresh shirt and pants. Jesse looked at him and said, "Sy, could you get James and check out back? We just heard a noise. . . . We were about to go look."

"We'll check," Sy said, and he walked through the room into the family room, where they heard him talking with the bodyguard named James, and a minute later, they heard a door sliding open.

Jesse Dallaglio dropped her voice. "The people we really don't know in the house are the security people. There are eight of them—four of them came out to the airport with us, for all the good it did us—and they were here all the time. Every one of them has a cell phone, and Paul told them this afternoon that we'd be making a run for the airport. Two of them were coming to Newark with us. They were going to stay with us until we got on the plane tomorrow morning."

Lucas looked at Sally, who said, "We can talk to their boss and get the cell-phone numbers without them knowing about it."

"You'll have to use some pretty harsh language with the boss, so they won't be tipped."

"We can do that," Derik said.

"Okay," Lucas said. Back to Dellaglio: "Now, who else? The Karens, your sister, the security guys. How did you make the travel arrangements? A travel agent?"

"American Express," Dallaglio said. "We have a Platinum Card, and they have one of those call-up bureaus somewhere. They knew, but how would Clara get into that? I mean, it's not like we even talk to the same person every time. It's always somebody different."

Lucas said to Sally, "Okay, here's something dumb. Check the phones here, see if they're bugged. Rinker did that thing with the cell phone, with Levy—maybe she's got a high-powered phone tech working for her."

"She does," Sally said. "We already know that." She made a note, and said, "Makes me a little nervous to be talking here."

Lucas said to Dallaglio, "Think—anybody else. Think of every phone call you made. That Paul made."

She thought for a minute, then shook her head. "We were really running around, getting ready. We were gonna be gone for maybe a month, or even more . . . I . . . you know, Paul called the *Wall Street Journal* guy, I think, the delivery guy, and canceled the paper. I think he said something about it."

"We should get the call records and go over them," Sally said. "Just to make sure."

"Gotta talk to the Karens," Lucas said. "Gotta do that tonight."

THEY TALKED TO the Karens separately, shaking them out of bed, giving them the news about Dallaglio. They both appeared to have been sleeping soundly. Lucas had worked enough homicides to believe that sound sleep came with an innocent mind. If either had killed Dallaglio, she would have been on pins and needles to know what happened—or would already know, and only masterful actresses could have played the shock on their faces when Sally gave them the news.

Both said that Dallaglio had warned them against telling anyone else about the trip. Both said that they had obeyed the order—hadn't even talked to each other about it.

When the interviews were done, Lucas said, "We need to look at Dallaglio's phone records. These two didn't have anything to do with it."

"A hasty conclusion," Sally said. They were standing under a lush, small-leaved oak tree in one of the Karens' front yard. "We don't know enough—"

"I know enough," Lucas said. "Neither one of them suspected the killing was coming. Or, if they did, they were good enough actresses that we'll never figure it out. Either way, it's time to move on."

"Derik should have the phone records by now," Sally said. She looked at her watch. "It's two A.M. You want to keep running?"

"I'm just getting under way," Lucas said, grinning at her in the dark. "Love this kind of thing, tearing around in the middle of the night. Maybe we oughta find some caffeine."

WHEN THEY GOT back to the FBI office, Derik was waiting with an unhappy surprise. "We got the phones for all the security guys. There were quite a few calls, but the numbers check out, unless Rinker's working at a Pizza Hut. There was another number we didn't expect."

He pushed a piece of paper at them. The paper was a list of numbers, and one of the numbers was circled in red. "That's an unlisted phone. It goes to John Ross. The call was made at 5:10 P.M. from Dallaglio's home office."

"Somebody called Ross?"

"Yeah. Probably Dallaglio. There's a phone call from that home office number to Dallaglio's mother's home, and that lasted twelve minutes. Then, one minute later, another call to Executive Air, which we figure was arrangements on the plane. And one minute after that, the call to Ross's, which lasted for two minutes. We think it was Dallaglio, working down a list."

Lucas nodded: That seemed likely. He tapped the Executive Air call. "I wonder if Rinker used those guys—if that's how she got around. Has anybody looked at Executive Air?"

Sally shook her head. "No. We can. But that could be quite a few people. . . ."

"So get one of your paper experts to do it—find out who works there, cross-reference them against Rinker's known work record. Check criminal backgrounds, see if there was any kind of link between Executive Air and the assholes. The Mafias, or whatever they are."

Sally nodded. "There's still the problem of Ross. That he might have set it up."

"We should talk to Mrs. Dallaglio again. See if there was any kind of competitive thing going on."

"Think she'd tell us?"

"Why not? She's not a hood—we can't hang her. She doesn't know nuthin' about nuthin'."

"Too late now," Sally said. Lucas turned to look at the wall clock. Ten after three.

"First thing tomorrow," he said.

They agreed to meet in the hotel lobby at eight o'clock. They'd had enough for the night. Derik said he had a few more things to do, that he'd be another fifteen minutes, and Lucas and Sally walked out to the stairs. On the way down, Lucas stopped, said, "Goddamnit."

"What?"

"I gotta go back. I need to talk to Derik. I'll catch a ride back with him."

"Something important? A coup?"

"Probably not. Another detail to check."

Back upstairs, he asked Derik how long it would take to get all of Ross's phone calls for the past two months, since the shooting in Mexico, both outgoing and incoming, with IDs on each phone. "We practically live in the phone company computer," he said. "I could call a guy, get them here in a half-hour."

"Call the guy. And I'll need all of Patricia Hill's calls from the same time. I'm gonna get a Coke. Maybe spend a little time here . . ."

LUCAS GOT A COKE from the canteen, and when he got back, Derik said, "We know six phones that he uses personally. We're getting lists for all six. They'll come up here. . . ." And he showed Lucas how to manipulate the mail feature on the group's main computer.

"How long?"

"He said he'd run them right away. The rumor is getting around that we're in trouble, so our guys back in Washington are doing everything they can."

"Good enough." Lucas sat down and stretched. "You can take off if you like."

"I might, if you can handle this. You could call me at the hotel if you have trouble."

"Should be okay. I get along with computers."

"You were Davenport Simulations, somebody told me."

"Used to be. Got bought out by the current management," Lucas said.

"Hope you made a shitload of money."

Lucas nodded. "I did, pretty much. Right there in the middle of the dot-com thing."

"But the company's still around, right? Doing all right?"

"Yup. I'm out of it, don't even own any stock—but from what I hear, they're doing okay."

DERIK FUSSED A BIT, then left, leaving Lucas in the quiet conference room. He checked the computer every few minutes, then found that he could sign onto his home ISP and get at his e-mail. That sucked up a half hour, deleting the fast money and pornography offers, checking a few of the Porsche aftermarket companies. Then it occurred to him to check boat companies, because the FBI computer was so quick, and he started downloading photos of shallow-water boats from Maverick, and then he got onto the Boston Whaler and Hurricane sites, went out to look at C-Dory and a few more. By the time he got back to the official mail, it was after four.

When he checked the mail, he found lists for the six phones that Ross was known to use. He took a while to figure out the formatting, then started with the longest list, which showed more than a thousand calls. On the fourth list, linked to the unlisted office phone, he got lucky. A phone call went into Ross's office at three o'clock from Los Angeles, from a BP station. There was another three o'clock call from Sacramento, then another from someplace in Wyoming, a longer one, another from Kansas, three more from St. Louis. All at three o'clock in the afternoon, all from gas stations.

Rinker was calling Ross. Lucas would bet on it. There was one good way to confirm it: He pulled the Hill list, to see if he could find a duplication, a call to Hill from the same time and place as a call to Ross.

But there were none.

He took a turn around the office. Was he on the wrong trail? The line of calls coming across the country was so good, and at exactly the right time. But then, Ross was in the trucking business, and was also in the organized-crime business. He *would* get calls from phone booths at interstate gas stations.

He walked around the room a couple of times, trying to figure a way to confirm the calls, and began to worry that he was "locking in," a problem he saw with other cops, all the time, the sure sense that something was just so, when it wasn't. Something that felt so good that it *had to be.* You could build a great logical case out of pure bullshit, and it happened too frequently.

He circled the question, and couldn't make it work. Ross and Rinker were into something he couldn't quite figure. He felt stupid, and that made him angry.

"Fuck it," he said, and he walked out of the room, down the hall, had the guard call him a cab, and ten minutes later—the cab arrived at the FBI building with unnatural celerity—walked into the hotel.

He could get three hours of sleep if he was lucky. He expected to wake up pissed off and tired, and he did. At seven-forty-five, he called Sally in her room. When she answered, with a song in her eyes—he assumed that, from her chipper voice—he snarled, "I'll be way late," and was asleep again when his head hit the pillow.

Ross & Rinker, Rinker & Ross.

Had to be.

23

LUCAS SLEPT UNTIL ONE O'CLOCK. HE'D NEVER HAD TROUBLE sleeping late, and into the afternoon, even, though he often had trouble getting to sleep at midnight. He felt decent when he got up. He took his time shaving and in the shower, lingered over a sandwich and the newspaper, and at two o'clock walked into the FBI conference room, thinking, *Rinker & Ross, Ross & Rinker.*

Sally was there, and said, "Mallard called—he's on his way back. Washington is going to pull us in a couple of days, he thinks, but we're okay if we can come up with something. Anything. They're not going to do anything public, especially after Malone went down. But it doesn't look good for the hometown kids."

"Rinker and Ross," Lucas said. "Let me tell you about the phone calls."

He told her, but pointed out so many shortcomings with the concept that she said, "I'd have believed it was Rinker if you hadn't talked me out of it."

"Still think it was," he grunted. "Feels too good."

"If it was Ross, then she's gone. She's done everybody."

"Maybe we ought to brace Ross about it, see what happens," Lucas said.

"He's a smart man. He'll tell us to go have sexual intercourse with ourselves."

"He's going to this orchestra thing at the botanical gardens this evening. I'm gonna crash the party. Take Andreno along, if he'll go. Watch him. See if we can make him nervous."

"Maybe we ought to take a few people along."

"You coming?"

"If I have time," she said. "I did bring a nice little red party dress, just in case." Then she clouded up. "I wish Malone were here. She was really good at this."

WITH SALLY, the red-haired guy, Derik, and a half-dozen others, Lucas argued the question of the phone calls from the coast, and found the group divided almost fifty-fifty, with a one-man majority in favor of the calls coming from Rinker. They all went back to the paper, looking for more ties.

One guy said, suddenly, "We ought to have a few people there tonight. You know, like a crew."

"We've got a crew escorting Ross," Sally said.

"More than that, we need more than that," the guy said, excited by an idea. "Think about this. If nothing happens to Ross, we'd be suspicious. But what if he's shot at and missed? What if he's rescued before he can be killed— by his security guys?"

"You mean . . . a faked hit?"

"Yeah . . ."

"Oh, *God.*" Somebody's head hit the table with a hollow thump, followed by a groan. Everybody was looking at the guy who suggested the fake hit, who said, "*What?*"

Then somebody started to laugh, and the laughter rippled around the room, and finally Sally said, "You got one thing right. We need more people there. We'll work it out."

LUCAS CALLED ANDRENO and asked him if he wanted to go to the botanical gardens party. "Would this be, like, a *date?*" Andreno asked.

"Of course not," Lucas said. "I'm engaged to be married."

"All right, but nothing below the waist, then."

THEY HOOKED UP for dinner, a place called Brownies, ate shrimp and salads, and Andreno wanted a blow-by-blow account of the shoot-out at Spirit of St. Louis.

"Hell of a thing," he said when Lucas finished. "I was in two shoot-outs when I was on the force, and I can't remember shit about either one of them, but there was, like, a total of four shots fired. This was like a war."

"One of the agents said something to me after Malone was shot," Lucas said. "He said something like, 'It used to be a hobby. Now it's a war.' But he thought it'd be us making the war."

The waitress came by to check the state of their drinks. They were okay, but she chatted for a minute, making serious eye contact with Andreno. When she was gone, Lucas asked, "You know her?"

"Not yet."

"I felt like a goddamn cuckoo clock or something, sitting here and you guys got this lip-lock going over the salads."

"You got relationship cooties," Andreno said. "Women can pick those up in one second—they know you're hooked up with somebody else."

Lucas nodded, looking after the waitress. "Nice-looking woman, though. I could get used to this place. St. Louis. Except it's so fuckin' hot."

Andreno shrugged. "You get a pool."

"You have a pool?"

"No. But I'm used to it. I like it, the heat. Better than six months of ice storms. I was up in Minneapolis in August once—my old lady at the time had relatives up there and she wanted to visit and they said come up for the state fair. So we went up to the state fair and I almost froze to death.

I was walking around in a golf shirt and slacks, and it was twelve degrees or something."

"Twelve is a little cooler than we'd expect in August," Lucas said.

"You know what I mean."

"I like the snow," Lucas said. "I even like blizzards. I go up north in the winter. Got a couple of sleds."

They talked about their towns until it was time to leave. As they were walking across the parking lot to the Porsche, Andreno said, "Wish I had a gun."

"Got a knife?"

"Yeah, but that wouldn't . . ."

"I wasn't thinking you could *stab* her," Lucas said. "But they got all those trees in there. I was thinking you could cut down a big stick."

"Ah. I could hit her with the *stick*."

"Right."

"Wish I had a gun."

THEY PARKED IN the lot in front of the botanical gardens and took a walk around it, looking. "She knows your Porsche, right?"

"Maybe. Probably. If she remembers it." Andreno kept looking at the houses on the other side of the street. "What're you thinking?"

"Suppose she's scouted the place, and she spotted a house with some old lady in it. She's got these silenced pistols, right? So she goes up to a house, say, a hundred and fifty yards away, two hundred yards, plugs the old lady when she answers the door, and then just sits there and waits, with that machine gun. Or the sniper rifle she used on Malone. Maybe parks her car in the back so we'll never see her when she pulls out. Ross gets here, and she nails him walking across the parking lot. Just like with Dallaglio."

Lucas considered it, then said, "Look—she had months to work this all out. One thing she always did was her planning, the way she got at people, isolated them, then killed them. She's never expected. We really didn't expect her last night, but now that she's done that . . . and Malone . . . she's got to think that we're ready for rifles."

"So maybe she won't use a rifle, but the goddamn things scare the shit out of me. Never see it coming. *Whack,* and you're dead before you know it." They walked along for a minute, and he added, "Man, that must've been something last night. I wish I could've been there, as long as I wouldn't have gotten shot. That FBI guy, they say he could lose a leg."

"That's not the word anymore," Lucas said. "The word is, he's gonna be okay."

"All right. Still, this fuckin' woman ought to be in the CIA or something. They could use her."

Lucas looked up and down the street. "I'd say we could put a squad at the far end, but then . . . it'd just scare her off, if she's coming. I'd rather have her come."

"And fuck a bunch of Rosses?"

"He knows what he's getting into. . . . And yeah, fuck him."

Andreno shook his head. "That's harsh, man." He looked down the street again. "Just like standing naked in the window."

THEY WENT UP the steps and inside, showed their IDs to a guard, went up the interior steps and out the back, past the lighted fountain. To the left, on the other side of a long, low, redbrick building, a group of waiters were setting up tables and lighting mosquito-repelling tiki torches. They turned that way, down more stairs, up a sidewalk edged with button-sized red and blue flowers.

A woman in a blue dress and matching shoes, pearls, and carefully coiffed blond hair was supervising the waiters. She saw them, said something to a waiter, then hurried over: "I'm sorry, this is a private party."

She had a perfectly sculpted nose, and it was quivering like a rat terrier's.

"We're cops," Andreno said laconically. He snapped his gum. "We're . . . making sure there's no problem tonight."

"Problem?" She looked from Andreno to Lucas. "What kind of problem?"

"A woman named Sally, from the FBI, will be here in a couple of minutes," Lucas said, looking back at the entry building. "She'll explain it all. We're making a routine security check. We hear one of the cellos could . . . do something crazy."

SHE WANTED MORE, her nose quivering even more fiercely as they put her off and wandered past a rectangular bed of red and gold chrysanthemums, past a pool, then through a hedge into the rose garden, strolling with their hands in their pockets, looking at the flowers. "Rinker'd have to be thinking about climbing a tree," Lucas said, finally, as they walked out the far side of the rose garden and stopped under a crab-apple tree. There wasn't much contour to the land, but there was some, and the higher ground was to the left, and was covered with trees. "Ross'll be okay as long as he stays in the rose garden. The feds'll have three teams covering out there. They all rented tuxes, they'll come in one at a time, and once they get out in the dark, you won't be able to see them."

"You really think something is gonna happen?"

"I think . . . I don't know. These things get a rhythm. If I were Rinker, and if I were going after Ross, I'd go after him soon. Not because I had to, but because I couldn't stand not doing it. Getting it over with. Being done."

"But if she's not going after him . . ."

"Something'll happen. Something to put a period on it. If Ross gets here and he's walking around free as a bird, slapping people on the back, happy—then I'd be inclined to think that Clara's on her way to Paris. But if he's walking around keeping his head down, and his shoulder blades pinched together . . . it'll be interesting to see."

OFF TO THE RIGHT, they could see the glass-and-steel Climatron dome, with more pools in front of it. They wandered down that way.

"Can't see much from here—too many bushes," Andreno said.

"Other side would be better," Lucas agreed. "From a shooting point of view."

They paused next to a pool. A few feet from the corner, two bronze statues, naked dancing women, hung over the water. "Look at the knockers on that one," Andreno said.

Lucas had to laugh, because the same thought had trickled through his mind. "Look at the knockers on both of them."

They walked. Ambled. Hands in their pockets.

"Rinker's not gonna be here," Andreno said after a minute or two. "A: She doesn't know about it. B: He's too protected."

"She fooled us on Levy, she fooled us on Malone, she fooled us on Dallaglio—she shouldn't have been able to do any of those things. We knew she was smart, but she was a lot smarter than we were ready for," Lucas said. "She doesn't miss anything."

Andreno looked past him. "There's Sally. And Jesus, there's Mallard—he looks like he was hit by a truck."

"Man, I just . . . I think if somebody killed Weather, my fuckin' head would explode," Lucas said. "Let's go talk to him."

"What is it that the feds kept saying? *Showtime.*"

MALLARD WAS PHYSICALLY shaky, brutally unhappy. "I'm here for today and tomorrow. The funeral is day after tomorrow."

"Are you up to speed on what we're doing?" Lucas asked.

"Yes. Sally . . . sort of turned out to be an executive. I hadn't seen that before."

Lucas grinned at him, a small wan smile. "Everybody else did. There wasn't even any discussion—she just took it over."

"Good for her," Mallard said. He was wearing a tuxedo, as were the other agents that Lucas could see, and a few men who weren't agents. He and Andreno were wearing sport coats and slacks and loafers. Lucas felt like a radish at a convention of tulips. "You think she'll show up?"

"I can't figure it," Lucas said. "I'm getting the feeling, from what we've seen so far, that she started planning her moves right after she was shot down in Mexico. She's had a couple of months to think about them, and to have her show up and start blazing away—that's out of character."

"That's what she did last night," Mallard said.

"But we didn't see it coming last night," Lucas said. "The thing about last night—we could only see it later—is that she had a source of information that could feed her the Dallaglios in a hurry, somebody who could actually call her, or who she could call. I actually thought running was a great idea, from the Dallaglios' point of view. Once he was out of sight, she was out of luck. But . . . she knew where and when he was going. Exactly."

"Sally told me about the phone idea, the calls to Ross."

"And here she comes," Lucas said. Sally was wandering toward them, wearing a tight, deep burgundy dress that started low and ended low—below the collarbones and down to the ankles, slits on the sides. She was carrying a small black purse that Lucas decided must hold her pistol, because she couldn't have gotten a pencil under the dress without it showing. As she came up, Lucas said, "Nice purse."

She smiled at him. "Didn't think I could clean up, did you?"

"I thought you might," he said. "We've been talking about Ross, and what the hell's going on here."

"If she comes in, I think we'll get her. We've got teams moving all through the place."

Lucas looked away, staring at a pink rose, trying to work through it. They looked at him, waiting, and finally he said, "I can't nail it down. Can't figure what she'll do next. I've been stymied before, because I didn't know what I needed to know. But I've never felt stupid. She's got me feeling like a moron."

"We'll see," Mallard said. He patted Lucas on the shoulder and said, with a wan smile, "Dumbass."

MORE PEOPLE WERE arriving, men in tuxedos, women in party dresses. A small pop orchestra set up in front of the brick building that acted as a backstop for the party; a dozen long-haired men and women who started off with an even more orchestrated version of Air Supply's "Making Love Out of Nothing at All," as if the original weren't bad enough.

Lucas started away after the first few bars, and Sally said, after him, "Don't like music?"

"Anytime they start by playing Air Supply, there's a risk they'll move on to the Hooters," Lucas said.

Sally said, "My. You listen to rock 'n' roll?"

"It's not rock 'n' roll. It's rock. It's the music I grew up with. Just like you."

She looked at him, doing a readjustment, and said, "I guess you always think that people older than you listen to, like, Big Band or something. Jazz."

"Jesus, Sally, the first music I can remember was the Stones. Mick Jagger was probably in high school when I was born."

"Yeah, but . . ." She looked past him. "The Rosses."

Lucas moved away more quickly, far out to the edge of the rose garden, watching the Rosses as he moved. John Ross was wearing a European-style notchless tux, black on black. Treena was wearing a cream-colored dress with puffs along the edges that managed to look both expensive and tacky, like a Versace knockoff for 7-Eleven. Ross shook hands with a few people, and seemed to be accepted. If they knew he was a hood, they at least appreciated his support for the performing arts.

Lucas was watching when he saw movement on the roof of the building behind the orchestra. A head. Then a head and a man, with a radio: the red-haired guy, with another man. Lucas lifted a hand to them, and the red-haired guy mimed a rifle. Good.

Andreno came over with a plastic plate full of finger food. "Better get over to the table. The best stuff goes fast. The pâté is recommended, with them little round yellow crackers."

"Give me one of yours," Lucas said. He tried a little yellow cracker and the pâté, which *was* recommended. But he didn't have much of an appetite. The night seemed to be getting warmer rather than cooler, and a large number of good-looking middle-aged women were showing ingenious displays of skin. Lucas and Andreno began to move with them, clockwise, around the rose garden, like migrating geese. The Rosses were on the far side of the clock, and they kept it that way, although Ross caught Lucas's eye once and shook his head, a shallow, dour smile locked on his face.

The clockwork continued, around and around the rose

garden, as slow as a minute hand, people clumping and talking, but always seeming, after a few minutes, to move. More people showed up, and as the crowd got denser, there was more of the high-pitched feminine laughter that seemed to accompany a crowd of tuxedos and party dresses, rich people and wanna-bes preening themselves—Lucas checking the women, anybody close to the height and build of Rinker. There were several of them, but none was her.

At eight-thirty, the party was near its peak, the promenade continuing. At the heart of the clock face, Lucas realized after a while, were the principals of the orchestra: the conductor, the president, a couple of violinists, all with shaggy longish hair and cultivated manners, a kind of gardened drollness that led to heavy lids and rolled eyes.

Then Andreno said, "I think I'm in love."

Lucas looked and said, "Jesus Christ, she's fourteen."

"But she thinks like forty. You want some purple fish eggs?"

"This party is too good for you."

"That's possible. Did I ever tell you about the time the Prince of England came here, and I was supposed to be security, and I was wearing this tux, but my Jockey shorts kept riding up in my ass crack and were strangling my balls. . . ."

Lucas listened with mild amusement, and then realized . . .

"Where's Ross?"

Andreno stopped in midsentence, looked around, and said, "Three minutes ago, he was under that crab-apple tree." They both looked toward the top of the garden, the end away from the brick building. There were two men standing under the tree, talking, but neither was Ross. Treena Ross was also gone. "Maybe in the can."

"Not unless they're peeing in the bushes," Lucas said. They were both moving, passed Sally and Mallard. As they went by, Lucas said, "Ross is gone. You see him?"

They both looked and fell in with Lucas and Andreno, and Sally said, "Shit. He was right there." The four of them continued to the top of the garden, to the two men under the crab apple. Lucas asked, "Have either of you seen John Ross and his wife? It's pretty urgent."

One of them said, "Yes, I think they went to look at the orchids in the Climatron. Treena had a flier of some kind, a special orchid display."

They all looked that way, and saw Treena Ross stepping through the door into the Climatron, with John Ross a step behind. Lucas shouted at them, "ROSS: WAIT."

But Ross was gone, the door was closing, and Lucas started running, as hard as he could, down the sidewalk, running hard, Andreno falling behind, Sally a couple of steps behind Andreno, handicapped by heels, Mallard behind that, Sally shouting into a radio, something unintelligible, and then as Lucas came up to the door, he saw three flashes, muzzle flashes, and heard faint screaming and he shouted, "She got him, she's inside, spread out, block the place . . ." And he was through the door.

The Climatron was literally a jungle, bamboo and palms and ficuses and probably a fuckin' cockatoo, he thought. Once inside, Treena Ross's screams were shrill and close by, but he couldn't see her. He was on a pebbled sidewalk, and he drew his .45 and ran down the sidewalk, following a curve around to the right and then back toward the center. As he came around the curve, he saw Treena Ross backed against a low wall of bamboo, a body at her feet, her cream dress blotched with blood.

She saw Lucas coming and screamed, "She went that way, she went that way, she's in the trees. She's in the trees, she shot John, call an ambulance."

Andreno was right behind him and had a telephone out and was calling an ambulance, and Lucas said, "Stay here with Treena," but Andreno caught his arm and said, "We gotta get out of here, man, we gotta get outside. She'll kill you in here, you'll never see her, but we can pen her up inside."

Lucas looked around and then knelt next to John Ross and rolled him. He was dead, three shots to the back of his head at close range, massive exit wounds on his face and forehead. "Let's go," he said to Andreno. "You don't have a gun, get Mrs. Ross out of here." And he ran back to the door and outside and started shouting, "Seal the building, seal the building, spread out and seal the building . . ."

Mallard and Sally and Derik were already moving, Derik going right with Lucas and Mallard and Sally going left, two more tuxedoed men running through the crowd, more guns coming. Rinker had had time to get out if she was set up for a fast escape, Lucas thought, but not a lot more time than that. If she'd slowed down, if she'd frozen . . .

They ran around the building, past another exit, and Lucas shouted over his shoulder to Derik, "Block this, block this . . ." and Derik pulled up and Lucas continued around. There was another exit on the back, and as he came up on it, he saw Sally coming from the other direction.

"What?" he shouted.

"We maybe got her inside, didn't see anybody running."

"Get more people, get everybody here. Ross is shot, Ross is dead . . ."

And Sally was on the radio, and everybody Lucas could see was running, and they tightened the choke hold on the Climatron.

And then an agent shouted, "Window! We've got a broken window."

Lucas's heart sank, but he ran that way, to the far back side of the dome, where it sat above the landscape, on a concrete retaining wall. Above the concrete wall, one of a band of windows appeared to have been broken out.

"Goddamnit." Lucas looked around. "Somebody give me a step."

One of the agents holstered his gun and made a step with his interlinked fingers, and boosted Lucas up the wall. Lucas did a push-up onto the top, then reached down to the window. A woman-sized hole had been knocked in the glass from the inside. She'd cut herself doing it, he thought. There was a smear of blood on the glass.

"I think she's out," he shouted down. "She's bleeding. We need to block this place, just in case she's inside, and then spread out in the park, see if we can push her. She's close. . . . Let's go, let's go. . . ."

Sally had them organized in fifteen seconds, and they began moving in a wide band, behind the Climatron, spreading through the dark, jogging, looking for anything in front of them. Lucas stayed back, looking at the jungle inside the dome. He didn't want to punch out any more glass, and he eventually dropped back down the wall and ran around to the front.

Treena Ross was sitting on the ground, Andreno beside her. "Stay with her," Lucas said, and he went inside the dome. The door moved again, behind him, and Derik was there, with his pistol. "We can't do this, Lucas. We need a team with armor. If she's in here, she'll kill at least one of us, and maybe both of us."

Lucas thought about it, ten seconds, fifteen seconds. So curious that Rinker'd let herself be trapped in here, if she had . . . but then, she hadn't expected a massive number of cops.

"Come on," Lucas said. He started into the dome.

"Goddamnit," Derik said.

"I gotcha covered," Lucas said. He hurried down the path, through the jungle—saw a pistol lying on the path near a fake cliff and waterfall, called "Gun" and went on, trying to get his bearings. He finally clambered through a hump of bamboo toward the back glass, where Rinker had broken out. Derik followed, scuttling this way and that, his weapon pointed in the air, looking for movement in the trees. Lucas squatted next to the broken window, and as Derik came up, he said, "You don't have a flashlight?"

"I've got one of those things for your car keys . . . to see the lock."

"Gimme."

Lucas shined the tiny light on the window, at the bloodstain, and then handed the light back to Derik and said "Come on," and stuck his pistol in his holster.

"What . . ."

"She's not here. But I want you to pretend that she is. I want you to go out and get Andreno, and tell him to step inside to talk to me, tell him we're hunting her down, that she's maybe cornered in the basement, but get him in here. You stay with Mrs. Ross. Okay?"

"Okay, but—"

"Don't ask questions. And when you're talking to Andreno, you gotta be really excited. Get him in here."

"You think—"

"Don't ask questions."

DERIK WENT OUT, while Lucas waited just inside the door. A moment later, Andreno hurried through. Lucas caught his arm. "Is the ambulance coming?"

"Yeah. I can hear it."

"I want you to get out there and scoop up Treena Ross and carry her toward it. But you gotta separate her from her purse, and if she says something, turn around to me and yell, 'Bring her purse,' and then keep going. Okay?"

"What are . . ."

"Tell you in a couple of minutes. Just get her, and run her out to the rose garden or out to the exit. Tell the paramedics that she's in shock. But you gotta separate her from her purse, just for a minute. And we gotta do it while people are still running around like chickens. Come on: Go."

Andreno nodded, and turned and ran out the door. Lucas stepped out with him, and heard the sirens, saw the cluster of faces around the crab-apple tree. Hell of a fundraiser, he thought. They ought to get a nice chunk for this one. Lots of publicity, for sure.

Treena Ross was still on the ground. Andreno scooped her up, stepping on her purse as he did it, straightened up, and started running toward the exit a hundred yards away. Lucas heard Treena say, "My purse, my purse . . ."

Andreno staggered with her weight, half turned, and called, "Somebody bring her purse."

Lucas picked it up and, as Andreno continued to run, opened the purse and found the cell phone inside. He turned it on, punched through the menu, found the phone number, and scribbled it in the palm of his hand. Then he turned it off, dropped it back in the purse, and ran after Andreno. He caught them halfway to the exit, heard Treena saying, "I can walk, I can walk." Lucas dropped the purse in her arms, and Andreno, puffing, put her down and said, "You're sure. You gotta have the paramedic check you. . . ."

A group of women had ventured their way from the crab apple, and Andreno called, "Could some of you take care of Treena Ross? Get her to an ambulance."

"My husband," Treena called. "My husband."

The helping women closed around her, and Lucas and Andreno headed back to the Climatron. "What the fuck was that about? About goddamned killed me, carrying her. She's no lightweight."

"C'mon." Lucas led him at a run back to the dome, found Mallard and Sally together, both talking into phones. Lucas waved them off, and they both rang off and Mallard said, "We have more St. Louis cops coming."

"She's not in there." Then he thought again. "But let

them come in and tear the place apart. What we really need, though . . ." He turned to Sally and said, urgently, "Can you get those choppers? Now?"

"Fifteen minutes," she said. "They can be turning by the time we get up to Lambert."

"Then let's go."

"Tell me what's happening," Mallard said. He wasn't moving fast enough.

Lucas said, "I don't have a lot of time to explain this, because we've got to get up in the air. But the big surprise tonight was, Rinker was here, all right, but *way before* we were. Tonight, maybe, or late this afternoon, more likely. Remember those phone calls coming across country, at three o'clock? They were to Treena Ross, whose marriage was going down the tubes. Treena had to be worried about that, because one ex-wife already died in a hit-and-run. She might have known too much about Ross's operation just to walk away. He might not *let* her walk away, any more than he let Rinker walk away."

"So who . . . ?" Mallard started. Then: "*Treena Ross* killed him?"

"That's right," Lucas said. "She got a gun from Rinker, and carried it in, or Rinker left it for her in a bush or something, inside the dome. Then Rinker came here a while ago, knocked out that window, and left some blood behind. When you do a DNA on the blood, it'll be the same as on that shirt, I promise you—that's why we found the bloody shirt at Patsy Hill's place, with the Mexican label in it. And we found a gun inside the dome, Derik and me, and I promise you, it'll be the same gun that killed Dichter, and it's the gun that killed Ross. So Treena Ross has a perfect alibi—absolutely unbeatable—and Ross is dead, and we never saw it coming because we were waiting for Rinker to show up. So was Ross. Everybody was . . . but they'd had it set up for long time."

"And the call that Dallaglio made to Ross, before the airport ambush . . ."

"Yeah. Either he actually talked to Treena, leaving a message, or he talked to Ross, and Ross told Treena . . . and Treena tipped Rinker. Treena probably even knew that they used Executive Air when they were going out of town, so Rinker could have scouted the place way ahead of time."

"Jesus. And you think they'll talk now. Treena and Rinker."

"Bet on it—and I got the number of the cell phone in Treena's purse. I'll bet you anything that the phone was stolen and that Rinker'll be calling to make sure everything is okay, or Treena will call her. If we're in the choppers . . ."

"Go," Mallard said. "Let's go."

As they ran toward the exit, and Sally started working her phone to call the choppers, she asked, "How'd you know?"

"Ross was shot in the back of the head—if you know the situation inside the Climatron, that's not right, unless he walked in backwards. But the main thing was the blood on the window," Lucas said.

"What about it?"

"It was bone-dry."

"Dry."

"It'd been there for a while—a hell of a lot longer than five minutes. Rinker hasn't been here for two hours."

24

AS SALLY SAID, THE RUN TO LAMBERT WITH FLASHERS, and an occasional burst of siren for the recalcitrant, took a little more than fifteen minutes, plus another two or three to make it down the frontage road to the helicopter facility. They had three choppers, none of them turning a blade yet. Mallard climbed out of the lead truck and ran inside the chopper hut, and they could hear him screaming. Nine men, pilots, copilots and technicians, hurried out the side, heading toward their aircraft, pulling on helmets. "Two people per chopper," Mallard yelled. "Who wants to go with who?"

Sally said, "I'll ride with Lucas. He's lucky."

"Go, go . . ."

They were airborne over St. Louis twenty-five minutes after they left the botanical gardens, and spread themselves, under instructions from Mallard, along I-64. Mallard himself hovered over downtown with Andreno, while Lucas and Sally waited west of Forest Park, where they could see the lights of the inner belt, Highway 170, and the third chopper waited out beyond the outer belt, way west.

"We're good east-west, but if she goes north-south, it'll take a while to get there," Lucas shouted at Sally.

"Not long," Sally said, shaking her head. "And if she's along the main stem, here, we'll be on her in a minute. One of us will—" Her phone rang, and she put it to her ear, listened, shouted a few words, clicked it off, and said, "Treena's phone is listed to some guy from a place called Crestwood. The phone doesn't answer, just an answering machine, and the cops are on the way. If the place has been broken into, we're good."

"We're good," Lucas said. "Believe it."

The technician riding behind the pilots was looking at a computer screen that seemed to combine a local map and a radio receiver. He spoke occasionally into a radio.

And that's the way it was for thirty minutes. Sitting up in the sky, watching the cars below, not talking much because of the noise. Sally said once, "It's pretty, when you can see everything from the Missouri back to the arch."

"Where's the Missouri?"

"The line out there to the north, and over to the west, you can see the curve—looks like it really should have come into the Mississippi way to the south, but made this big jog at the last minute."

"Makes a peninsula out of St. Louis, almost."

"Yeah . . . You seem pretty calm for a guy who's famous for hating airplanes."

Lucas said, "Helicopters don't bother me, for some reason. None of it has anything to do with logic, it's . . ."

Then the phone rang and the computer screen lit up, and the technician started talking fast to the pilots and the chopper dove for speed and took off east, Lucas shouting, "What? What?"

"Somebody's talking cell phone to cell phone. Mrs. Ross's phone is downtown, but the second one is just east of us, it's moving, we've got the cell, I'm tuning her in, I'm tuning her . . . Got her."

"Where is she?"

"She's moving, she's moving. . . ." Then he was talking to the pilots on a mouthpiece, and the pilots were talking back, and the chopper made a big cut left, coming around, coming around, dropping, heading back west, slowing . . .

"We got some cops coming in. . . . See that group of cars, that group right there? She's in there, I think, four or five cars, the cops are a mile out, we got her, we got her . . ."

RINKER WAS IN the Benz, had been talking with Treena Ross, who was weeping, grieving for her late husband, when she heard the chopper. Rinker had lived in bad parts of St. Louis long enough, in her younger years, to know what it was: a kind of strange flapping sound, as if somebody were beating his chest with open palms. She said, "Cops!" and hung up and rolled along for a moment, despair creeping into her heart, hoping that Treena knew enough to get rid of the phone, thinking quickly of *Davenport* . . . and then she saw the lights of a shopping center up ahead, a thin glimmer, just a possibility, of hope, and she suddenly floored the accelerator and cut through traffic and let it run out, the car gaining momentum at a ferocious rate toward the gaping mouth of what Rinker hoped was a parking ramp. Had to be a parking ramp, or a tunnel, or something; she said, aloud, "Parking ramp, please God, parking ramp."

She was no more than a minute away. . . .

LUCAS SAW HER take off, moving through traffic like a broken-field runner, shouted, "She's onto us. Get on top of her, get on top of her."

A pilot gave him a thumbs-up and took the chopper into a screaming dive, but they gained ground only slowly and then actually seemed to lose some, and Lucas realized that Rinker must be pushing the black car into the hundreds, like a black comet surging along the street as though to catch the dead-white light of its high beams.

The tech was talking into his microphone, describing the car, describing the action, giving updates on the map as they finally started closing. Then they saw the tunnel, or whatever it was, up ahead, and Lucas said, "She's heading for that tunnel thing."

"Parking structure," the copilot shouted. "It's the parking structure for the shopping center."

"Get us down, get us down, right in the mouth of it, she's gonna beat us there, get me out and then get back up and look for her running."

And to Sally, as they dropped: "Annie, get your gun."

RINKER SAW THE chopper at the last minute, right above her, almost ahead of her, at the entrance to the tunnel, but she squirted past it, jammed on the brakes, was thrown into the steering wheel, got the speed down enough that she could cut right into a parking bay and saw, at the far end, three people walking along with shopping bags, one of them a man, jingling his car keys. She went that way, laying on the gas again.

The family had seen her coming and knew she was moving too fast and instinctively flattened themselves against a minivan and she jammed the brakes again and hopped out and started toward them and then something hit her in the butt. Something like a baseball bat, and she went down.

LUCAS WAS OUT and running into the tunnel, saw the Benz cut right and ran harder, Sally dropping behind, came around a pillar into a parking bay and saw the Benz down at the end and Rinker climbing out. Without thinking, he tracked her with the .45 and fired a single shot and amazed himself when she went down, rolled, and then she was crawling and back up and she was standing next to three civilians, two adults and what seemed to be a child, a ten-year-old girl, maybe, and Rinker was screaming at him, "Go the other way. Run the other way."

Lucas shouted, "Give it up, give it up."

Rinker shouted back, "Run the other way, Davenport, run back down the tunnel or I swear to God I'll kill these people, I'll kill all three of them right in front of your eyes."

Lucas slowed, still moving up, and shouted, "Clara, you're hurt, give it up, Clara . . ."

And Sally closed up and shouted, "Rinker . . ."

Then, horrified, they saw Rinker point a pistol at the head of the largest of the adults and pull the trigger, the man twisting and bouncing off a car, going down, as the shot echoed through the parking garage, and Rinker pointed the gun at the woman, and she screamed, "Mom goes next, Davenport, and then the kid. Mom goes next, run now or I'll pop her."

She pointed the gun at the mother, who lifted her arms to her face and shrank away, screaming herself; she backed up and tripped over her fallen husband and half fell, and Rinker screamed, "Here she goes. . . ."

Lucas shouted, "We're going," and he grabbed Sally's arm and Rinker screamed, "Run, or I'll kill her, I'll kill her, run out the tunnel, run . . ."

They ran.

WHEN SHE'D SHOT the man, he'd dropped his keys and Rinker pointed the gun at the mother and said, "Where's the car, where's the fuckin' car?" And the woman pointed at the Dodge minivan and Rinker dragged her leg to it, her leg wasn't working, but she hopped and dragged and popped the door on the van, and screamed. "Get in, get in or I'll kill you. Get in."

The mother and kid got in and Rinker screamed at them to lie in the footwell on the passenger side and they crawled into it and she cranked the engine and eased out of the parking slot and accelerated away, then slowed, took a corner, took another, and was on the street, driving out.

A helicopter hung overhead, but it stayed behind her, and then another one came in, and then she was on the next street and she saw a man behind her, running, and realized that it was Davenport and accelerated, turned a corner, accelerated again, two blocks, turned again, and again, Davenport long gone now, said to the woman in the footwell, her voice like a chain saw, as ugly and vicious as she could make it, "You stay on the fuckin' floor or I'll blow your motherfuckin' brains out. You stay there, you hear? I'm gonna stop, and I'll be right outside the car."

The woman whimpered as she pulled the car off the street. She probably wasn't more than ten blocks from the shopping center, but Davenport had seen the van, she thought, and she had to get out of it.

There was a bar off to the left, and a man was walking out, toward a lonely orange pickup truck that appeared to have been hand-painted. She pulled in beside it, said, "You stay down, hear? Or I'll fuckin' kill you."

She pulled herself out of the truck, felt her feet mushing as though she were wading in pudding, realized that one shoe was full of blood, that her butt was wet with it, and dragged her leg around the back of the truck to the driver's-side door, where the man was just getting in.

She came up, and he said, a little startled, "Hello," and she pointed the gun at him and said, "Get in."

"Oh, hell . . . Yes."

He got in, and she said, "Crawl across. Make it fuckin' snappy."

He crawled across, and she said, "Drop the keys on the driver's seat." He did, and she shot him in the head, and he fell back dead against the window.

She shouted at the minivan, "I told you to fuckin' stay down," and fired another silenced shot through the van's window, shattering glass but hitting nothing else, and as the mother cried out, Rinker crawled into the truck, fired it up, backed it out, and started away.

Three blocks out, watching the mirrors, she hadn't seen

any sign of Davenport. She took a corner and stayed on back streets, driving a checkerboard pattern away from the shopping center. Once, down a larger street, she saw the lights of a squad car flashing back toward the shopping center, and she crawled on. She thought about trying to make it back to Honus Johnson's, but then realized that they had the Benz, and they'd be over there. She had to do something. . . . A wave of nausea crawled through her on the front edge of a bigger wave of pain, and she thought, *I'm shot. Jesus, I'm shot.*

She didn't remember hearing a shot, but she remembered falling down, and then seeing Davenport. . . .

A stop sign came up and she stepped on the brakes a little too firmly, and the dead man beside her slumped forward into the footwell. Another wave of nausea. She realized that even if she wanted to go to Johnson's, she wouldn't make it.

Had to find a place. Had to *think* . . .

LUCAS RAN UNTIL the van turned out of sight, then ran some more, pulling his phone from his pocket as he ran, called Sally to tell her about the van, but Sally didn't answer the phone, and he ran some more and called Mallard, who did answer, and told him about the van and he heard the choppers lifting higher and then one moved over him and hit him with the spotlight, and he waved it off and it held him for another ten seconds as he waved frantically, and then it drifted away. . . .

Nothing was working. He never saw the van after it turned, and finally a cop car caught up with him and he flagged it down and the cop had no idea that anything was going on, but got on his radio, and nobody he called knew what was going on, but Lucas got a lift back to the shopping center, where an ambulance was screaming out of sight and Sally, covered with blood, said, "The guy in the garage was shot in the ear and was squirting blood and I, and I, and I . . ."

"Okay, okay," Lucas said. "She's in a Dodge van, a dark van, maybe dark blue. . . ."

Mallard came up and said, "A woman in a van . . . There's a woman in a van at a bar who said her husband was shot."

"Let's go," Lucas said. "That's her. . . ."

And they went roaring off in two more cop cars, a night for roaring off, Lucas thought, and on the way, Sally said, "You hit Rinker hard. I saw her go down and there's blood all over the place, she's gonna bleed to death if she doesn't get to a hospital."

"What color was the blood?"

"What?"

"What color was the blood? Dark or bright red, or was there any green stuff in it?"

"Just . . . purple. Why?"

"Real bright red is lungs, but I don't think I hit her that high. Green is guts. If it's nothing but purple, it may just be meat. If it's just meat, she could stay out. If I hit her anyplace in the body cavity, though, she'll need a hospital. I'm shooting Speer Lawman JHPs."

At the bar, the mother had collapsed, and the young girl seemed to be drifting toward a trance state.

Lucas said, "We gotta get these people to a hospital," and the bartender said, "Ambulance on the way," and Sally told the woman, "Your husband's not dead. He's on the way to the hospital, but he's not hurt bad, he was only shot in the ear, and he's gonna be okay."

The woman shook her head and curled into a tighter ball.

Lucas stepped away and looked down the street and said, "We're losing her. We had her. We're losing her right now."

25

MALLARD PULLED TOGETHER ALL THE LOCAL POLICE FORCES and had them do a grid search, starting around the shopping center, checking parked cars, any car that looked unusual or out-of-the-way; looking for blood.

The ID came back on the Benz, and they went for Honus Johnson's house, and pounced on it with a full entry crew, but there was nobody home—nobody alive. They eventually found Johnson in the freezer and the California car in the garage, and they got Rinker's clothes and her guns, but no money, no passport, no paper.

Mallard, frenzied, crazy, said, "I'm not sure where we're at. It all comes down to how hard you hit her."

"I can't tell you that," Lucas said. "I knocked her

down and she got right back up. I might have hit her in her left leg, because she was dragging a leg, but I'm not sure."

"Lot of blood," Sally said again. "Lot of blood."

THEY WENT AFTER Treena Ross, but when Rinker shouted "Cops!" she hadn't immediately dumped the phone. She'd used it to call her attorney, and her attorney had come down to the hospital, where Mallard's agents had picked her up. When Mallard, Lucas, and Sally showed up at the hospital, the attorney said to Mallard, "Is it true that you were eavesdropping on conversations between my client and myself?"

They had been, of course. They'd stayed on the phone from the time Rinker's call came in through the call to the attorney. Mallard had nodded and said, "Yes."

"That's a violation of—"

"Bullshit. I have a law degree, sir, and it wasn't a violation of anything. If your client doesn't wish to tell us what really happened inside that dome tonight, we'll see that's she's charged with premeditated murder and we'll recommend that the state seek the death penalty. So what do you want to do?"

"Charge her," the attorney said, "or we walk now. Either way, she says nothing."

"Then we'll charge her."

"That's certainly your privilege."

They smiled at each other, nodded, and Mallard said, "I'll go make the call."

LATER THAT NIGHT, he said to Lucas, "I don't think we'll get Treena. We were focused on Rinker and we didn't process her right. We didn't keep her under control."

"What happened?"

"Well, we got the phone, and she says the phone was her husband's, she was carrying it because he was wearing a tux and didn't have a place for it. And we took tape samples from her hands and arms looking for nitrites, and didn't find any. I think she used a plastic bag or a piece of cloth to cover her hand and sleeve when she fired the gun. She was wandering around in the hospital before we put a hold on her; she was in the ladies' room, and she might have flushed it. She had nitrites on her face, but she says that Rinker fired the pistol right past her, so they would be there. Smeared prints on the gun grip, clear ones on the barrel, and at least one of the good ones belongs to Rinker."

"Well-thought-out."

"For a long time," Mallard agreed. "For weeks. And they pulled it off. If we take her to trial, they'll have Rinker's gun, they'll have Rinker's blood on the glass, they'll have our whole investigation and chase with Rinker, and Ross'll say the phone calls went to her husband. All we've got is that last phone call, and Rinker called her, unfortunately, and I listened to the tape. All double-talk. I mean, it sounds good to me, but it won't be enough. It especially won't be enough when they get Ross's character into it, and they show that the third wife was killed in an unsolved hit-and-run."

Lucas was convinced. "So Treena's out of it."

He nodded. "Yes. And she knows it."

"If she had any little thing about Rinker, maybe we could deal with her . . . especially since we're not going to get her anyway."

Mallard shook his head. "She's not gonna deal. The whole thing was . . . I feel like a moron. That's what I feel like, Lucas. As soon as we clean up here, I'm going to Malone's funeral, and then I'm going home for a while, and just sit and think."

"What about Rinker?"

"Fuck her. I hope she dies of blood poisoning."

RINKER GOT ON I-44 and headed southwest, drove for fifteen minutes before the pain dragged her off the highway. Feeling faint, she took an exit at random, spotted a hotel, turned into its parking lot, and parked the truck. She pressed the dead man into the footwell, found an Army blanket behind the seat, and threw it over him. Then, moving ever so slowly, she did a survey of her assets.

She had money, ID, two passports, both good, a black wig, and a hole in her butt that continued to bleed. She also had a small toolbox, a battered leather briefcase, and a brown sack with a grease spot that might have contained a lunch. She had a day-old newspaper.

When the dead man rolled off the passenger seat, he'd exposed a copy of the *Post-Dispatch.* The news section looked unread, and Rinker had heard that unread newspaper pages were virtually sterile. She pulled out the middle section, ripped then, unbuckled her slacks, touched the wound a few times, wasn't sure she should be pleased or frightened that she couldn't feel much other than the basic pain, then, in the light of the truck's overhead lamp, made eight-inch-square pads of newsprint and pressed them onto the wound.

Digging into the toolbox for a roll of duct tape, she wrapped her leg and thigh with half the roll of tape, an awkward, unprofessional mess, but it held.

She felt sleepy, and that worried her. Even with the pain in her butt starting to come on, she felt sleepy. Struggled to stay up. Dug into the briefcase and found a cell phone. Everybody had a cell phone.

She took the man's wallet out and looked at his ID and the cards inside, a couple of notes, no pictures. She checked his left hand: no wedding band. Single, she thought. Maybe nobody to come looking right away.

Fought the sleep, kept coming back to the cell phone. Finally, she decided she had no choice: one more risk to run.

She dialed, got an interrupt, and wound up talking to

an operator before she got it right. Then she dialed again, and heard it ring, and then a man's voice said, *"Sí?"*

She switched to Spanish: "This is Cassie McLain. May I speak to Papa?"

They talked for less than a minute, and then Rinker hung up, and after a few moments, as she reconstructed it later, she passed out. She woke again later, terribly thirsty, but there was no water in the truck, and when she moved a wave of pain tore at her.

That goddamn Davenport. He'd shot her in the back while she was running away. He'd had no call to do that, she wasn't even looking at him. . . .

She passed out again, and only woke when a bright light hit her in the eyes. A man said, in Spanish, "Are you alive?"

"Yes."

"I have a car."

He'd had to lift her out of the truck and place her in the front seat of his Cadillac. The front seat was covered with plastic garbage bags so she wouldn't make a mess. When he'd transferred her, she'd passed out again, just for a moment, and when she came to, he was wiping his hands on paper towels. "Still alive?"

"Yes." But very weak now. "Where are we going?"

"Carbondale, Illinois. Maybe two hours, I've never been there."

"What time is it?"

"Five o'clock. . . . The sun is just coming up."

And she passed out again.

Some time later, the man backed into a one-car garage in Carbondale, woke Rinker, who was only fuzzily aware of it, and carried her into a house and put her facedown on a firm bed. A man's voice said, "I'm going to give you a shot."

THE FEDS WOULDN'T have found the orange pickup for a week if the hotel hadn't been feuding with a pancake house. The pancake house's parking lot was too small, so people parked in the hotel lot, and the hotel people got pissed and required guests to put parking tickets behind the windshields of their cars. If a car sat too long without a ticket, it was towed.

The orange truck didn't have a ticket, and the hotel security guard had seen it parked in the lot when he came in that morning, so in the middle of the afternoon he finally checked. . . .

LUCAS WENT OUT with Mallard and they looked at the dead man in the footwell, and at the blood-soaked front seat, and talked to the cop who'd decided that it might be related. "Whoever was driving was shot in the butt, in the left cheek, and it wasn't the dead guy, and I saw your bolo this morning and thought I'd better have my guys give you a call."

"Done good," Lucas said. He looked around. "The question is, where'd she go from here?"

"No blood on the ground," the cop said. The local crime-scene crew had taped off the area and were going over it, looking for anything relevant. "She probably didn't walk, because she was really pumping it. The seat is soaked with blood."

"Somebody else, then? She grabbed another car?" Mallard asked.

Lucas shook his head. "No. She got help. Why would she grab another car? This one was good enough, and grabbing another car would just be another problem, with no predictable outcome, especially if she's wounded."

"So she's hiding."

"Got more friends than we thought," Lucas said. "Your report said she didn't have any, and now we know of two who were willing to risk their lives on her."

"Yeah, well . . . I'll write a memo."

THEY WALKED AROUND, watching the crime-scene people for a while, but Mallard's attention was drifting and finally he asked, "You getting out of town?"

Lucas nodded. "I have no more ideas. I mean, I do, but none are relevant at the moment."

"Coming to Malone's funeral?"

"Nope. Wouldn't help her, and would bum me out worse than I already am. I liked her."

"So'd I," Mallard said. He slapped Lucas on the back. "Let's go."

WHEN RINKER WOKE UP, she was lying facedown on a white sheet. Her legs were spread a bit, as were her arms. And her cheek was wet. Drool, she realized. She tried to move but found her arms and legs restrained. Near panic, she pulled her head up and saw a piece of paper a few inches from her eyes. It said, in large block letters, "Call out."

"Hey," she called, her voice weak. "Hey!"

And a woman's voice from somewhere else said, "Coming . . . ," and a second later, a brown-faced woman with a red dot in the middle of her forehead squatted up beside the bed, her face a few inches from Rinker's.

"You're taped down so you couldn't roll over and pull the saline out," the woman said. "We didn't have anything better. Let me get the tape." There was a stripping-tape sound, and one hand came free, then her left foot, then her right foot and her right hand. She started to turn, saw the saline bottle on a hook over her head, and the woman put a hand on her shoulder. "Don't move too much," she said. "You're all taped up and you've had some analgesics, but it's going to hurt. Do you have to urinate?"

Rinker thought about it and shook her head. "No, but I could use a drink of water. How long have I been here?"

"You got here this morning. This is the afternoon, about four o'clock. My husband is a doctor at the university, and this is our house."

"How bad?"

The woman smiled sympathetically. "It's never good, but the wound was confined to your buttock." She enunciated *buttock* perfectly, with a bit of a British accent, and Rinker nearly smiled: It reminded her of a favorite *Monty Python.* "So it will hurt, and even when you are healed, you might not be able to run as fast or climb as quickly as you once did. And of course there is cosmetic damage, there will be a scar . . . but you are in no danger. Now."

"Thank you very much," Rinker said. The woman nodded but said nothing more, and after a minute Rinker asked, "So what do I do? Just lie here with my butt in the air until it heals?"

"You'll have to, uh, lie there for a while, certainly. We have been told to purchase a television set and some video games if you wish to have them."

"A TV would be good," Rinker said. "I don't need the games. Can I prop myself up?"

"You can, but I promise you, it's better to lie flat," the woman said. Then she said, "My name is Rayla. My husband is Geoffrey. He will be back soon, and we'll go to Best Buy for the television."

"Could I get water?"

"Oh, my goodness, yes, I forgot," Rayla said, jumping

up. "Would you like juice? We have papaya, mango . . . Would you like a fish sandwich?"

"Do you have an Internet connection?"

"Yes, we do."

GEOFFREY WAS A charming man, but she could never quite figure out how old he was: something between twenty-five and forty-five, she thought. He had a smooth brown oval face and a soft manner that fit well with a doctor, but not so well as an accomplice to major crime. They never talked about crime, though he knew who she was, and called her "Clara" rather than Cassie. He said that the costs of her care had been "fully funded."

He brought in a television with a DVD player, and for three days she watched TV and thought about things. On the fourth day, she made her first trip away from the bedpan, to the toilet, where she learned how hard it was for a woman to pee while sitting on one buttock and holding the other one carefully clear. Everything got squished together.

On the sixth day, she started a rehab program that featured five colors of rubber tubing that Geoffrey brought home from the hospital. She had to stretch against the rubber tubes, and could barely move the thinnest size. After a week, when she was feeling stronger and the thinnest tube wasn't stiff enough, he moved her to the next size, and again, he could barely move her leg. . . .

As she waited to heal, and practiced walking, she watched TV and roamed the Internet and thought about things some more.

She thought about Paulo and the baby. The recovery process was quicker, easier than the recovery in Mexico, but the smells and the pain brought Paulo back, and the baby . . .

She thought about those bad years, the years she'd always tried to blank out, when her brother and her stepfather were abusing her. Abusing her and comparing notes on how well she'd done.

She'd run away, and she'd tried dancing nude, and she'd been raped by a fat man and she'd killed that man with a T-ball bat, and then she'd been picked up by John Ross, who'd taught her to kill for money, and she'd saved her money and had bought a bar and had been successful and had gone to college to try to understand herself. . . .

She'd learned about herself in school. She might have avoided all this, if the killing hadn't been so easy and profitable. She never thought about the dead people, she only thought about the money. It had seemed like her *right* to kill, after all that had happened to her.

Then Davenport.

She'd feared the federal people, in a theoretical way, like you fear dying in a plane accident. Ross and his friends had heard rumors that there was a file on her, but that the file was almost empty.

Then Davenport had come along, and somehow had screwed everything. She'd lost her bar, lost a friend, almost lost her life. She'd been driven to Mexico and the disaster that followed. Nothing theoretical about Davenport.

She didn't cry about it. She might have, but she didn't.

She set her jaw, and she thought about Davenport.

She *knew something* about him. One solid fact.

She'd have to heal before she did anything. But she had time—five and a half weeks, to be exact. A Saturday in October.

Davenport was the devil, and had to be dealt with.

26

THE BRIDE WAS BLUSHING IN WHITE AND BIG AS A HOUSE, and finally said she had to go off to the bathroom to get the goddamn leg strap right. Sloan, Lucas's oldest friend on the police force, leered at her and said, "So you show a little leg. You're among friends."

She said, "Don't hold your breath, pervert-boy," and went off into the back, shouting over her shoulder, "And don't start without me."

Lucas, waiting at the back of the church, pulled at the collar of his dress shirt, plucked at his tie. Del had been in the—What'd he call it? The nave? The main part of the church—drinking what Lucas hoped was a cream soda. Now he came up and asked, "Nervous?"

"Of course I'm fuckin' nervous, what'd you think?" Lucas snapped. Then, quickly, "Sorry. I'm not sure this is gonna work out. I thought about it all night. I was one inch from canceling the whole thing." He looked at his watch and said, "One minute. Where's that fuckin' Marcy?"

Sloan said, "She just went down to the can," and Lucas said to Del, "I met this guy down in St. Louis who told me about this time he had to wear a tux and it kept dragging his Jockey shorts up the crack of his ass, and I swear to God, right now . . ."

Rose Marie Roux, the chief of police, went by and said, "I think I'm more nervous than you are."

Lucas grinned at her, a tight grin. "If I was losing my job next week, I'd be nervous too. What if something happens and queers the deal with the state?"

"One big lawsuit, that's what would happen."

Del prompted him, "The guy's shorts kept dragging up his ass. . . ."

Lucas tried to pick it up, and said, "Yeah, and he said . . ."

Swanson, an old homicide dick, came by and said, "This is the most fucked-up wedding I've ever been to, and my wife's family is a bunch of Polacks."

"Thank God your wife isn't," Sloan said.

"Where in the fuck is the bride?" Lucas snarled.

Tom Black, a semicloseted gay homicide detective, came out of the nave and said, "Look at the women in there. They're having a great time. They're gonna be breaking out in fistfights."

"If you couldn't get laid at this wedding, you couldn't

get laid," Del said. Then he glanced sideways at Rose Marie and said, "No offense."

"No problem," the chief said, taking a drag on a fresh Marlboro. "Cuts both ways."

"Where's that fuckin' Sherrill?" Lucas barked. "Christ . . . what?"

"Your earpiece is hanging down your neck," Sloan said.

"Thing is covered with somebody else's ear wax," Lucas said, looking at the earpiece. He plugged it in, and saw Marcy Sherrill coming.

"Where in the hell . . . ?"

"Gun wasn't working out. I thought I'd hold it like this, like a little black clutch purse," she said, holding her revolver in both hands.

"Like you're gonna need that," Lucas said. Then he turned, and shouted into the nave. "All right, people, we're gonna do this. Everybody sit tight, unless you're part of the porch group."

Then, to the people gathered around him: "Everybody ready, porch people? Porch people? Let's do it. Reverend, lead the way."

Del put down the bottle of what Lucas hoped was cream soda, adjusted his choir robe, picked up a cigar box, which everybody agreed looked a lot like a Bible—the prayer books had been locked up by some mistake—and led the way through the church's double doors. Marcy, all in bridal white, her revolver clutched like a purse, put her arm through Lucas's arm, pulled it tight, and said, "I always dreamed of this day," and Lucas said, "Enjoy it while it lasts. Man, you look like fuckin' Moby Dick."

"You look a little like Shamu the killer whale, yourself," she said. "I think it's the black and white that does it."

THE TROUBLE IN St. Louis seemed almost like a dream. Treena Ross had been indicted for her husband's murder, and the local cops had chased down every story of an injured woman that they could find. Three days after Ross went down, Lucas returned to the Twin Cities, and the whole episode drifted off into the past, another complicated memory, mostly bad.

Weather had been happy to get him back. The wedding planning had been completed, the invitations ordered, and the house had taken a big step toward completion. Getting through daily life pushed aside any speculation about Clara Rinker, though Lucas was careful not to pattern himself.

Clara, he thought, would come, sooner or later. He'd half expected her to call, as she had after their last collision, but she hadn't. The silence intensified his apprehension.

RINKER SAT BEHIND the wheel of the red Jeep Cherokee and looked across the valley at the front of the church, a half-mile away. A beautiful view, she thought, in the brilliant sunlight, with the pale blue skies: the white, New England–style village church sitting on the edge of the valley, surrounded by maple trees in blazing orange fall foliage, with strips of yellow aspen above and below the clutch of maple around the church.

A place to get married, she thought. They'd been in there for a while. She looked at her watch. Forty minutes, now. What were they doing? Maybe they'd written long vows or something.

As she was thinking that, the church doors popped open and a man stepped out into the sunshine, and then two more, a woman in white . . .

"Go," she grunted. She pulled the Cherokee out of the notch in the trees and turned down the narrow black-topped street. There was another notch a hundred and fifty yards out from the front of the church, but on a busier street. She wouldn't have been able to wait. As it was, she was taking a risk. She'd wrapped the rifle in a blanket, and she'd simply pull over to the side of the road as if she were having a problem, and then she'd walk back into the line of bushes and take her shot and drop the rifle and go.

HER BACKUP CAR was a half-mile away. She'd be in the second car and traveling in a few seconds more than one minute after she fired the shot. She'd timed it. She'd done *all* her research. She'd monitored the *Star-Tribune* on the Net, had found Davenport's wedding announcement, along with a couple of pieces in the local gossip columns. She'd confirmed it with the church, and then had scouted the church. And above the church, she found a sniper's nest, as though it had been created for that specific purpose.

The only little piece of dissonance was that she thought she remembered Davenport saying that the wedding would be in an Episcopalian church, and this one was a Lutheran. But maybe she misremembered. Besides, it had all been confirmed.

Now it was all coming together. The shooting point was just up ahead, a stand of oaks next to the guardrail over the valley. She jerked the car to the curb, hopped out, grabbed the blanket, and carried it past a bush to the steel barrier that overlooked the creek at the bottom of the slope. She could still be seen from the road, but again, she'd have to be unlucky. . . .

She was moving fast now, looking at the penguins on the porch step, the guys in black and white, standing stiffly beside the woman in white at the center, and the priest.

She lifted the rifle and slipped the safety and pulled down on the porch.

RINKER NEVER FELT death coming for her.

She never felt pain, never saw a shining light leading her away.

Death came without a whisper, and she was gone.

27

MARCY REACHED UP AND TAPPED HER EARPIECE AND LUCAS looked at her, irritated, and said, "It's not . . ." and then other radio people began shouting a weird mishmash of language. Everybody with an earpiece looked up at the valley wall into the notch and saw a green coat and then heard the shot, a hard, sharp *WHAP.*

Then silence, and then a lone man's voice in the earpiece, harsh but steady: "She's down. Rinker's down."

LUCAS COULD HARDLY believe it. He gaped at the hole in the trees, the sniper's nest so carefully cultivated, and saw people running toward it, people with guns. Then Black began yelling something, and they all ran for their cars—or waddled, in the case of Lucas, Sherrill, and Del, who were wrapped in body armor.

Sloan drove Lucas's Tahoe, and Lucas, in the backseat, pulled off his jacket and shirt and struggled out of the armor. Marcy was saying, "Goddamnit, undo me, undo me."

Her dress was held on in the back with Velcro, and Lucas pulled it down and helped her out of the armor straps. Underneath it, she was wearing a T-shirt and shorts—anything more had made her look too big. She said, "Throw me my stuff," and Lucas tossed a pair of jeans and a long-sleeved shirt to her, and pulled his own shirt back on.

Marcy said to Sloan, "Don't look," but Sloan looked anyway and said, "Hell, you've got underpants, they're no different than a swimming suit," and she said, "Yes, they are. They're intimate, and you looked, for which I will get you," and Sloan said, "Yeah, but if I didn't look, you'd be insulted."

"Shut up, everybody," Lucas grated. Marcy was about to come back with something snappy, but looked at his eyes and shut up and finished dressing, and Sloan drove.

THEY HAD TO go almost a half-mile to cross the valley and the creek, then a half-mile back, to cover the hundred and forty-eight yards between the best shooting spot and the church's porch, where the wedding party had posed. Lucas was churning, both excited and sick, a strange dread that had settled over him when he first walked out on the church steps.

When they arrived at the road above the creek, a half-dozen St. Paul cops were clustered along the barrier, with two Minneapolis cops, including an Iowa kid who'd become the department's designated hitter. He was carrying a rifle over his shoulder, a personally modified Remington 7mm Magnum. He was a gun freak, the Iowa boy. Lucas might have worried about that peculiar interest if he wasn't a little bit that way himself.

They climbed out of the Tahoe, still tucking and buttoning, and Lucas walked toward the form of the redheaded woman on the ground, a small body in a Patagonia jacket and jeans, now absolutely still, a purple stain on the jacket between the shoulder blades. She looked very small and very quiet, he thought, like a poisoned chipmunk. The Iowa kid said, "I had to take her. She was moving too fast. If I'd waited one more second, she would have shot one of you guys."

"Okay," Lucas said. He squatted next to Rinker's face and took a good look.

"That's her," he said. He stood up. "That's her."

MORE PEOPLE WERE arriving, to take a look. Black stuck out his hand, but Lucas pretended not to see it and moved away. Rose Marie clutched his upper arm, then let go. Del said, "Goddamn. *Goddamn.*"

A FEW MINUTES after the shooting, Lucas's cell phone rang, and he plucked it out of his pocket and heard Mallard's voice: "She didn't show, did she?"

"Yeah, she did," Lucas said, looking back at the growing cluster around the body. "She's dead."

A long silence at the other end. Then Mallard, his voice hushed, asked, "You aren't joking?"

"No. She showed, right in the slot. We had no time to take her. Our sniper nailed her from up on the ridge. Single shot, center-of-mass, looks like it clipped her spine and heart."

More silence, then: "Oh, fuck." Silence, then: "Are you okay?"

"I'm fine. She never got a shot off."

"That's not what I meant."

"Yeah, yeah. Listen, let me get back to you. We're still standing here, we got stuff . . ."

LUCAS WAS WATCHING the crime-scene team when Marcy came up. Marcy liked to fight, but never looked happy around a body. She was shaking her head, but then she looked up, a questioning look crossing her face, and then she said, "Jesus, Lucas—you're all teared up. Are you okay?"

"Ah, it's just the fuckin' allergies or something," he said. He wiped his eyes with the heels of his hands. "Man. Clara Rinker, huh? Clara Rinker."

28

RINKER WAS BURIED IN ST. LOUIS. TREENA ROSS, WHO WAS out on bail and who would probably never go to trial, took charge of the funeral. "No way she's gonna be buried in Flyspeck, or whatever it's called," she told Lucas in a phone call. "She hated that place. We'll bury her here, and the people from the warehouse can come and say goodbye."

Lucas was of two minds about going, but finally, on the morning of the funeral, flew into Lambert and was picked up by Andreno, who insisted on carrying Lucas's bag out to the car and said, "This is the most amazing thing I ever heard of, Davenport. I couldn't believe it when you called."

THE FUNERAL WAS done from a funeral home chapel, with Treena Ross's Unitarian minister presiding. Mallard was walking across the parking lot when they pulled in, and he waited for them.

"End of a part of my life," Mallard said. "I looked for her for ten years. This will be the first time I've ever seen her, when I knew it was her. I didn't know, that time in Wichita."

He and Andreno stepped toward the chapel, but Lucas hung back. "I'll wait for you guys here. I don't want to see her, and I don't want to hear what the minister says."

"You're just gonna stand here?" Andreno asked.

"I'll go to the cemetery," Lucas said.

"I gotta go in," Mallard said. He sounded glum. "So I can see for myself."

"You okay?" Andreno asked.

"Yeah. But different. I keep thinking it was worth the trade, Malone for all the people who won't be killed. Who might not be killed. But I don't feel that way."

"Malone was Malone—all those other anonymous people are just police reports," Lucas said.

LUCAS WAITED IN Andreno's car with the windows down. October, and still too warm in St. Louis—but then, it was warm in St. Paul, too. Almost seventy, the day before. Twenty people came to see Rinker buried, and Lucas suspected that there were St. Louis FBI agents somewhere out on the edges, making movies. He didn't care about that. He just wanted to get it done.

When Mallard and Andreno finally came out of the funeral home chapel, Andreno said, "Wasn't bad." They all three rode to the cemetery together, and Mallard asked Lucas, "Why'd you come?"

"I kind of liked her," Lucas said. "All the time I've been a cop, I've divided assholes into two groups: people who were assholes because they wanted to be—people who made themselves into assholes—and people who were made that way by life. Rinker never had a chance. But she kept trying."

"You sound like National Public Radio," Mallard said. They fell into the short line of cars going to the cemetery.

"Fuck a bunch of public radio," Lucas said. "Rinker was twisted and tortured by people a hell of a lot worse than she ever was, and nobody did anything about it. And she was probably getting out of it when we came along. I think if she'd never come to Minneapolis, she'd probably be out of it now."

Andreno shook his head. "Ross never would have let her get out. If she'd tried to get out, he'd have had her killed the first chance he got."

THEY RODE ALONG for a while, then Mallard said, "You're really bummed out, Lucas."

"I bum myself out. I keep thinking that for everything that was bad in the woman, there were all these good things. And one of the good things was, she was a romantic. She believed in love and marriage and babies and working hard and standing on your own. You know why we got her? Because she could never have seen that somebody would be cynical enough to fake his own wedding for the sole purpose of setting her up to be killed."

"You didn't exactly . . ."

"Yes, I did. I thought that if she showed, there was maybe a two percent chance of taking her alive. I set her up to be killed, and she was."

More silence, then Mallard said, "Good. Fuck her. She killed Malone."

"And that's your last word on it."

"It is. Fuck her."

"You're a hard man," Andreno said, and he wasn't smiling.

AT THE GRAVESIDE, the mourners dropped dirt on the coffin, while Lucas, Mallard, and Andreno hung back. Treena Ross cried, wiping her nose with a big white hanky. She was still crying when the service ended, and people began to drift away. She walked past Lucas and Mallard as they headed to their car, and she called, "Hey, FBI."

They looked at her and she said, "I was never that stupid, you know?"

Lucas nodded, and couldn't suppress an acknowledging smile. "We know."

WHEN EVERYBODY ELSE was gone, Lucas and Andreno dropped handfuls of dirt on Rinker's coffin at the bottom of the grave. Mallard watched. He hadn't had much to say after Lucas's pronouncements on Rinker. And when Lucas and Andreno came away from the grave site, he said, "I'll leave you here. I've got a ride downtown."

"Okay."

They shook hands and Mallard said, "You done good, Lucas. You ever need a job . . ."

"I'll call," Lucas said.

Andreno dropped him back at the airport and said, "Well. I'm probably not as bummed out as you are, because I never knew her. But I'm gonna have a hard time getting back to the fuckin' golf course."

"You ever do any undercover work?" Lucas asked.

Andreno's eyebrows went up. "From time to time. I make a real good traveling salesman, for some reason."

"You know about my new job. You could be getting a call."

Andreno nodded and said, "Lucas, I'd owe you more than I could tell you."

BACK IN ST. PAUL that night, Weather asked if he were feeling better. He'd been shuffling around with his hands in his pockets, hangdog and moody. She'd been playing something light on the piano, maybe Chopin, and he'd been watching the tag end of a meaningless football game.

"I'm okay, really," he said.

"Okay for the real wedding?"

"Sure. Two weeks. I'm up for it—and the house. The house is looking good, if we could just get the goddamn parquet guys to put in the trim."

"Calm down."

"Yeah." He took a deep breath and exhaled, looked up at her perched on the arm of the couch. "I wouldn't want to do this again. Run into another Rinker."

"I don't think there could be another Rinker," Weather said. She bounced and smiled and said, "Ouch."

"What?"

"The kid just kicked me."

Lucas put a hand on her belly. "Matt, or maybe Sam. New Testament or Old. Emilie spelled with an i-e, like the French do, or Annie, with an i-e, like the English."

"But never Clara."

"Never Clara," Lucas said. "Clara's gone."

An extract from John Sandford's compelling new Lucas Davenport novel, *Naked Prey*

1

THURSDAY NIGHT, PITCH BLACK, BLOWING SNOW. HEAVY clouds, no moon behind them.

The Buick disappeared into the garage and the door started down. The big man, rolling down the highway in a battered Cherokee, killed his lights, pulled into the driveway and took the shotgun off the car seat. The snow crunched underfoot as he stepped out; the snow was coming down in pellets, rather than flakes, and they stung as they slapped his warm face.

He loped up the driveway, fully exposed for a moment, and stopped just at the corner of the garage, in a shadow beneath the security light.

Jane Warr opened the side door and stepped through, her back turned to him as she pulled the door closed behind her.

He said, "Jane."

She jumped, her hand at her throat, choking down a scream as she pivoted, and shrank against the door. Taking in the muzzle of the shotgun, and the large man with the beard and the stocking cap, she screeched: "What? Who're you? Get away . . ." A jumble of panic words.

He stayed with her, tracking her with the shotgun, and he said, slowly, as if speaking to a child, "Jane, this is a shotgun. If you scream, I will blow your heart out."

She looked, and it was a shotgun, all right, a twelve-gauge pump, and it was pointing at her heart. She made herself be still, thought of Deon in the house. If Deon looked out and saw them . . . Deon would take care of himself. "What do you want?"

"Joe Kelly."

They stood for two or three seconds, the snow pellets peppering the garage, the big man's beard going white with it. Then, "Joe's not here." A hint of assertion in her voice—this didn't involve her, this shotgun.

"Bullshit," the big man said. He twitched the muzzle to the left, toward the house. "We're going inside to talk to him, and he's gonna pay me some money. I don't want to hurt you or anybody else, but I'm gonna talk to Joe. If I have to hurt the whole bunch of you, I will."

He sounded familiar, she thought. Maybe one of the guys from Missouri, from Kansas City? "Are you one of the Kansas City people? Because we're not . . ."

"Shut up," the big man said. "Get your ass up the steps and into the house. Keep your mouth shut."

She did what he told her. This was not the first time she'd been present when an unfriendly man flashed a gun—not even the second or third time—but she was worried. On the other hand, he said he was looking for Joe. When he found out Joe wasn't here, he'd go. Maybe.

"Joe's not here," she said, as she went up the steps.

"Quiet!" The man's voice dropped. "One thing I learned down in Kansas City—I'll share this with you—is that when trouble starts, you pull the trigger. Don't figure anything out, just pull the trigger. If Joe or Deon try anything on me, you can kiss your butt good-bye."

"All right," she said. Her voice had dropped with his. Now she was on the stranger's side. She'd be okay, she told herself, as long as Deon didn't do anything. But there was something too weird about this guy. *I'll share this with you?*—she'd never heard a serious asshole say anything like that.

They went up the stairs onto a back porch, then through the porch into a mudroom, then through another door into the kitchen. None of the doors was locked. Broderick was a small town, and it doesn't take long to pick up small-town habits. As they clunked into the kitchen, which smelled like microwave popcorn and week-old carrot peels, Deon Cash called from the living room, "Hey," and they heard his feet hit the floor and a second later he stepped into the kitchen, scowling about something, a thin, five-foot-ten-inch black man in an Indian-print fleece pullover and jeans, with a can of Budweiser in one hand.

He saw Warr, the big man behind her, and then, an instant later, registered the shotgun. By that time, the big man had shifted the barrel of the shotgun and it was pointing at Cash's head. "Don't even think about moving."

"Easy," Cash said. He put the can of Budweiser on a kitchen counter, freeing his hands.

"Call Joe."

Cash looked puzzled for a second, then said, "Joe ain't here."

"Call him," the big man said. He'd thought about this, about all the calling.

Cash shrugged. "HEY JOE," he shouted.

Nothing. After a long moment, the man with the shotgun said, "Goddamnit, where is he?"

"He went away last month. He ain't been back. We don't know where he is," Warr said. "Told you he wasn't here."

"Go stand next to Deon." Warr stepped over next to Cash, and the big man dipped his left hand into his parka pocket and pulled out a clump of chain. Handcuffs. He tossed them on the floor and looked at Warr. "Put them on Deon. Deon, turn around."

"Aw, man . . ."

"It's up to you," the big man said. "I don't want to hurt

you two, but I will. We're gonna wait for him if it takes all night."

"He ain't *here,*" Warr said in exasperation. "He ain't coming back."

"Cuffs," the big man said. "I know what it sounds like when cuffs lock up."

"Aw man . . ."

"C'mon." The shotgun moved to Cash's head, and Warr bent over and picked up one set of cuffs and the big man said, "Turn around so I can see it," and Warr clicked the cuffs in place, pinning Cash's hands behind him.

The big man dipped his hand into his pocket again and came up with a roll of strapping tape. "Tape his feet together."

"Man, you startin' to piss me off," Cash said. Even with his hands cuffed, he managed to look stupidly fierce.

"Better'n being dead. Sit down and stick your feet out so she can tape you up."

Still grumbling, Cash sat down and Warr crouched beside him and said, "I'm pretty scared," and Cash said, "We gonna be all right. The masked man can go look at Joe's stuff, see he ain't here."

The big man made her take eight tight winds of tape around Cash's ankles. Then he ordered Warr to take off her parka and cuff her own hands. She got one cuff, but fumbled with the other, and the man with the shotgun told her to turn and back toward him, and when she did, clicked the second cuff in place. He then ordered both of them to lie on their stomachs, and with the shotgun pointed at them, he checked Cash's cuffs and then Warr's, just to make sure. When he was satisfied, he pulled on a pair of cotton gloves, knelt beside Warr and taped her ankles, then moved over to Cash and put the rest of the roll of tape around his.

When he was done, Cash said, "So go look. Joe ain't here."

"I believe you," the big man said, standing up. They looked so helpless that he almost backed out. He steadied himself. "I know where Joe is."

After a moment's silence, Cash asked, "Where is he?"

"In a hole in the ground, a couple miles south of Terrebonne. Don't think I could find it myself, anymore," the big man said. "I just asked you about him so you'd think that . . ." He shrugged. "That you had a chance."

Another moment's silence, and then Warr said, "Aw, God, Deon. Listen to his voice."

Cash put the pieces together, then said, loud, croaking, but not yet screaming, "We didn't do nothin', man. We didn't do *nothin'.*"

"I *know* what you did," the big man said.

"Don't hurt us," Warr said. She flopped against the vinyl, tried to get over on her back. "Please don't hurt us. I'll tell the cops whatever you want."

"We *get* a trial," Cash said. He twisted around, the better to see the man's face, and to test the tape on his legs. "We innocent until we proved guilty."

"Innocent." The big man spat it out.

"We didn't do nothin'," Cash screamed at him.

"I know what you did." The crust on his wounds had broken, and the big man began kicking Cash in the back, in the kidneys, in the butt and the back of his head, and Cash rolled around the narrow kitchen floor trying to escape, screaming, the big man wailing like a man dying of a knife wound, like a man watching the blood running out of his neck, and he kicked and booted Cash in the back, and when Cash flopped over, in the face; Cash's nose broke with the sound of a saltine cracker being stepped on and he sputtered blood out over the floor. Across the kitchen, Warr struggled against the tape and the handcuffs and half-rolled under the kitchen table and got tangled up in the chairs, and their wooden legs clunked and pounded and clattered on the floor as she tried to inchworm through them, Cash screaming all the while, sputtering blood.

Cash finally stopped rolling, exhausted, blood pouring out of his nose, smearing in arcs across the vinyl floor. The big man backed away from him, wiped his mouth on his sleeve, then took a utility knife out of his pocket and stalked across the room to Warr, grabbed the tape around her ankles, and pulled her out from under the table. Warr cried, "Jesus, don't cut me!"

He didn't. He began slicing though her clothing, pulling

it away in rags. She began to cry as he cut the clothing away. The big man closed his mind to it, finished, leaving her nude on the floor, except for the rags under the tape on her ankles, and began cutting the clothing off Cash.

"What're you doing, man? What're you doing?" Cash began flopping again, rolling. Finally, frustrated with Cash's struggles, the big man backed away and again kicked him in the face. Cash moaned, and the big man rolled him onto his stomach and knelt between his shoulder blades and patiently sliced at Cash's shirt and jeans until he was as naked as Warr.

"What're you doing?" Warr asked. Now there was a note of curiosity in her voice, showing through the fear.

"Public relations."

"Fuckin' kill ya," Cash groaned, still bubbling blood from his broken nose. "Fuckin' cut ya fuckin' head off . . ."

The big man ignored him. He closed the knife, caught Cash by the ankles, and dragged him toward the door. Cash, nearly exhausted from flopping on the floor, began flopping again, but it did no good. He was dragged flopping through the mudroom, leaving a trail of blood, onto the porch, and then down the steps to the lawn, his head banging on the steps as they went down. "Mother, mother," Cash said. "God . . . mother."

There wasn't much snow on the ground—hadn't been much snow all winter—but Cash's head cut a groove in the inch or so that there was, spotted with more blood.

When they got to the Jeep, the big man popped open the back, lifted Cash by the neck and hips, and threw him inside.

Back in the house, he picked up Warr and carried her out to the truck like a sack of flour and tossed her on top of Cash and slammed the lid.

Before leaving, he carefully scanned the house for anything that he might have touched that would carry a fingerprint. Finding nothing, he picked up the shotgun and went back outside.

"WHERE'RE WE GOING?" Warr shouted at him. "I'm freezing."

The big man paid no attention. A quarter-mile north of town, he began looking for the West Ditch Road, a dirt track that led off to the east. He almost missed it in the snow, stopped, backed up on the dark roadway, and turned down the track. He passed an old farmhouse that he'd thought abandoned, but now, as he went by, he saw a single light glowing in a first-floor window, but no other sign of life. Too late to change plans now, he thought; besides, with this night . . .

The wind had picked up, ripping the snow off the ground. He'd be far enough from the farmhouse that he couldn't be seen. He kept moving, the light in the farmhouse window fading away behind him. In the dark, in the snow, there were no distinctive landmarks at all.

He concentrated on the track and the odometer. Four-tenths of a mile after he turned off Highway 36, he slowed, looking out the left-side window. At first, he saw nothing but snow. After a hundred feet or so, the tree loomed, and he pulled over, then carefully backed, pulled forward, and backed again until he was parked across the road.

"What?" Cash groaned, from the back. "What?"

The big man went around to the back of the truck, opened it, grabbed the thick wad of tape around Cash's legs, and pulled him off the truck as if he were unloading lumber. Cash's shoulders hit the frozen earth with a meaty impact. The big man got him by the tape and dragged him past the first tree into what had been, from the car, in the dark, an invisible grove of trees.

One of the trees, a pin oak, loomed at the very edge of the illumination thrown by the car's headlights. Ropes were slung over a heavy branch fifteen feet above the ground. The big man, staggering under Cash's weight, dropped him by one of the ropes, then went back for Warr. When he got her to the hanging tree, struggling and kicking against him, he dropped her beside Cash.

"Can't do this, man," Cash screamed. "This is *murder.*" The storm around them quieted for a moment, but the snow pellets still whipped through the trees, stinging like so many BBs.

"Please help me," Warr called to Cash. "Please, please . . ."

"Murder?" The big man shouted back at Cash, raising

his voice above the wind. He broke away from them, toward a tree branch that was sticking up out of the snow, ripped it off the frozen ground and staggered back to Cash. *"Murder?"* He began beating Cash with the long stick, ripping strips of skin off Cash's back and legs, as the black man thrashed on the ground, gophering through the snow, trying to get away. "Murder, you fuckin' animal, murder . . ."

He stopped after a while, too tired to continue, threw the stick back into the trees. "Murder," he said to Cash. "I'll show you murder."

The big man led one of the ropes over to Cash, tied a single loop around his neck, tight, with strong knots. He did the same with the second rope, around Warr's neck. She was now shivering violently in the cold.

When he was done, the big man stood back, looked at the two of them, said, "God damn your immortal souls," and began hauling on the rope tied to Cash. Cash stopped screaming as the rope bit into his neck. He was heavy, and the big man had to struggle against his weight, and against the raw friction of the rope over the tree limb. Finally, unable to get him in the air, the big man lifted him and pulled the rope at the same time, and Cash's feet cleared the ground by a meager six inches. He didn't struggle. He simply hung. The big man tied the lower end of the rope around the tree trunk, and tested it for weight. It held.

Warr pleaded, but the big man couldn't hear her—later

couldn't remember anything she said, except that there were a lot of whispered *Pleases.* Didn't do her any good. Didn't do her any good when she fought him, either, though it might have given her a brief thirty seconds of satisfaction.

He couldn't get her high enough to get her feet off the ground, and as he struggled to do it, a space opened between the bottom of his coat sleeve and the glove on his right hand. The space, the warm flesh, bumped against her face, and quick as a cat, she sank her teeth into his arm, biting ferociously, twisting her head against his arm. He let go of the rope and she fell, holding on with her teeth, pulling him down, and he hammered at the side of her head until she let go.

She was groaning when he boosted her back up, and she ground out, "We're not the only ones."

That stopped him for a moment: "What?"

"They'll be coming for you, you cocksucker." She spat at him, from three inches away, and hit him in the face. He flinched, grabbed her around the waist and boosted her higher, his gloves slippery with blood, and then he had her high enough and he stepped away, holding tight to the rope, and she swung free and her groaning stopped. He managed to pull her up another four inches, then tied the rope off on the trunk.

He watched them for a few minutes, swinging in the snow, in the dim light, their heads bent, their bodies violently elongated like martyrs in an El Greco painting . . .

Then he turned and left them.

They may have been dead then, or it might have taken a few minutes. He didn't care, and it didn't matter. He rolled slowly, carefully, out of the side road, down through Broderick and on south. He was miles away before he became aware of the pain in his wrist, and the blood flowing down his sleeve toward his elbow. When he turned his arm over in the dim light of the car, he found that she'd bitten a chunk of flesh out of his wrist, a lemon-wedge that was still bleeding profusely.

If a cop stopped him and saw it . . .

He pulled over in the dark, wrapped his wrist with a pad of paper towels and a length of duct tape, stepped out of the truck, washed his hand and arm in snow, tossed the bloody jacket in the back of the truck and dug out a lighter coat from the bag in back.

Get home, he thought. Burn the coat, dump the truck.

Get home.